More Praise

"A fast, sharply plotted book."
—*Daily Mail* (London)

"An excellent read . . . Davis's distinctive, focused narrative makes for compulsive reading. Her characterizations are sharp and intelligent but are also drawn with humor and sensitivity."
—*The Irish Independent* (U.K.)

"Tough, competitive, sexy, and funny, Kat turns being alone into the adventure that it should be, but all too rarely is in contemporary fiction."
—*The Times* (London)

"Stylish drama and romance."
—*The Daily Mirror* (London)

"A refreshingly good young novelist writing extraordinarily well outside the box most publishers would select for her."
—*i-D Magazine* (U.K.)

Anna Davis is a journalist and the 2001 recipient of the Arts Council of England's Clarissa Award for prose writer under the age of thirty-five. She lives in London with her husband and works part-time as a literary agent.

CHEET

Anna Davis

A PLUME BOOK

PLUME
Published by the Penguin Group
Penguin Putnam Inc., 375 Hudson Street, New York, New York 10014, U.S.A.
Penguin Books Ltd, 80 Strand, London WC2R 0RL, England
Penguin Books Australia Ltd, 250 Camberwell Road,
Camberwell, Victoria 3124, Australia
Penguin Books Canada Ltd, 10 Alcorn Avenue, Toronto, Ontario, Canada M4V 3B2
Penguin Books (N.Z.) Ltd, Cnr Rosedale and Airborne Roads,
Albany, Auckland 1310, New Zealand

Penguin Books Ltd, Registered Offices: Harmondsworth, Middlesex, England

First published by Plume, a member of Penguin Putnam Inc.
Previously published in Great Britain by Hodder and Stoughton,
in slightly different form.

First American Printing, June 2003
10 9 8 7 6 5 4 3 2

Ⓟ REGISTERED TRADEMARK—MARCA REGISTRADA

LIBRARY OF CONGRESS CATALOGING-IN-PUBLICATION DATA

Davis, Anna, 1971–
  Cheet / Anna Davis.
    p. cm.
  ISBN 0-452-28429-5
    1. Taxicab drivers—Fiction. 2. London (England)—Fiction. 3. Women—
England—Fiction. 4. Truthfulness and falsehood—Fiction. I. Title.

PR6054.A89156 C48 2003   2002192451
823'.92—dc21

Printed in the United States of America
Set in New Caledonia

PUBLISHER'S NOTE
This is a work of fiction. Names, characters, places, and incidents are either the products of the author's imagination or are used fictitiously, and any resemblance to actual
persons, living or dead, business establishments, events, or locales is entirely coinci-
dental.

This one's for the girls:

Helen Payne, Cathy Tabakin, Kate Barclay, Sarah Maber, and Daniels Bernardelle

It's also for Simon, who's not a girl

ACKNOWLEDGMENTS

Thanks to Jan and Ed Sadlier, Wendy Wright, and Philomena French for invaluable information on London taxis and what it's like to drive them.

Thanks also to Stephi Symons for helping me with my medical research.

PART I

~

STAR-SHAPED LIFE

1

NIGHT is my favorite time of day. I come alive and I hit the roads. It's 4:34 A.M. and I'm passing Westminster and skirting alongside the river with the window all the way down, letting that cool air wash over my face, drumming my fingers on the steering wheel in time to the rhythm in my head. Don't know what the song is—maybe it's just my heart. There are two guys in the back of the cab and one of them keeps catching my eye in the mirror, all twinkly. It's bugging me. Next time I'm going to snarl at him. The other man has fallen asleep. His bald head's lolling back and his mouth is gaping open—reminds me of golf courses; hole in one. He's dribbling down his neck. So attractive.

"Do you always drive at night?" It's Twinkle. Well, it would hardly be his mate, would it?

"Yep."

"Isn't it dangerous? I mean—for a girl, all on your own? Do you get much trouble?"

He's twinkling again. I'm not looking in my mirror—don't want to encourage him with unnecessary eye contact—but I can tell by his voice. His voice is sort of smiley.

"Nothing I can't handle." This shuts him up. Perhaps he's got the message. He leans back against the seat.

For a moment it's just me and the traffic lights, but then he's off again:

"Can't be good for the social life."

What does he think I am, a bloody hairdresser? Maybe he'd

like me to ask him where he's going on holiday this year. Perhaps that would make him happy.

"So are you married or what?" he tries.

"Or what."

"I was married." He's leaning forward again. He's up close to the glass and Perspex screen that separates us, and there's a change of mood. He's about to turn my cab into a confessional. It happens frequently. One of the seldom recognized hazards of being a woman cabby. "Big nose, looked a bit like a horse—but in a nice way. Good bones."

I grunt something inaudible out of politeness. The Pisshead is snoring loudly and I'm a little concerned that he might choke on his own tongue.

"She left me three years ago. Christmas. We were due to fly off to Hawaii together on Christmas Eve but when I got back from work she'd gone . . ." There's no stopping him now. He's in full flow. "She'd found out about my girlfriend."

Say ten Hail Marys and twenty Our Fathers. "So did you take the girlfriend to Hawaii instead?"

"She left me too. She'd found out about my wife."

"Serves you right." Amateur . . .

"I gave the tickets to the couple next door. They had a great time."

We've been rumbling down the King's Road and now we're turning left down Lots Road past all those auction houses and glamorized junk shops.

"Right down to the end, mate?"

"Yes, please. There's a bit of private road. I'll show you where you can pull in."

I fail to understand why anyone with enough cash to live in Chelsea Harbour would choose to do so. It's half empty even at the best of times. I think you'd need to be a waterfront obsessive to like this soulless place—with your own speedboat and a plan to retire to Florida some day.

Twinkle directs me into a side street only yards from the harbor where a variety of four-wheelers, BMWs and Lotuses are parked. I pull up and show him the meter: £15.40. He looks as though he might be about to start having a go at me for taking a slow route (which I didn't) but then seems to change his mind. I hear him mutter, "Oh, whatever." He speaks into Pisshead's ear and shakes him softly.

"Henry. Henry, it's wakey-wakey time."

My father's name. Henry doesn't respond.

Twinkle takes a twenty from his wallet and tries to push it into Henry's lifeless hand. "Henry," he tries again, a little louder into the ear. "Look, mate, here's twenty. I'm getting out here."

"No way." I'm pressing my foot down on the brake to put the central lock on just as Twinkle tries his door. "He's not staying in my cab. You're taking him with you."

"Oh, come on, love." His face wears a beseeching look. He clearly doesn't want Henry messing up his nice riverside apartment. "He lives in Crystal Palace. Look, what if I pay you thirty quid up front? Will that do it? He won't be any trouble."

I'm not having any of this. "He gets out here. I like my fares conscious."

He tries a feeble laugh, all out of twinkles now. "He's not unconscious. He's just asleep."

"So wake him up, then."

"Henry!" Twinkle shakes him harder this time, virtually bellows in the poor sod's ear. "Henry, you bloody old soak!"

Finally Henry's head jerks upright and his mouth clanks shut like a drawbridge. His eyelids flicker open, revealing bloodshot whites and dilated pupils. His skin is deathly gray. I see it happen a fraction of a second before the event actually takes place, but sadly not fast enough to do anything about it. His chin suddenly juts forward out of the folds of neck in which it nestled, the drawbridge clatters down again, and with a sound that hovers between a belch and a moan, a torrent of the foulest imaginable pink vomit comes gushing forth, slooshing onto the floor and the seating, hitting the glass and Perspex screen (a screen for which I am once again heartily grateful) and splattering over the shoulder, arm and leg of Henry's former friend, Twinkle, who yells, "Jesus fucking Christ!"

This is really all I need.

Henry gives a relieved sigh and settles back to sleep.

Golden rule number one—always stay put; don't get out of your cab. But the smell is asphyxiating and we're out fast, Twinkle and me. His face registers surprise when he sees how tall I am— half a head above him. He's rubbing his face and cursing under his breath. His suit is pebble-dashed with puke.

"Well?" I say.

"Look, I'm sorry." He reaches into his jacket pocket for his wallet. "I had no idea he was that far gone. He's had a rough time. His wife has just left him for another man—she went round with a van today and cleared out the house. She took everything worth taking . . . Look, how much do you want?"

My anger is subsiding. It's all too pathetic for words. "Another twenty'll do it. And remove the poor sap from my cab."

He hands me the notes. I stand and watch, hands on hips, as he takes a deep breath and opens the passenger door. Henry lolls sideways almost knocking him over. Henry is a big man and Twinkle looks out of condition. Twinkle puts his hands under Henry's arms and pulls. For a moment Henry doesn't move but then Twinkle gives a great heave—putting all he has into the effort—and Henry sort of slides out. His legs bump down onto the tarmac and the bulk of him is clearly so great that Twinkle's knees buckle and give way and he stumbles and falls backward onto the road. He goes down hard on his back and Henry comes down on top of him, still sleeping peacefully.

"Fuck, fuck, fuck!"

I want to get out of here. Now.

"I need some help," groans Twinkle, trying to wriggle out from under Henry's dead weight. He sees the expression on my face. "Please. *Please.*"

I contemplate stepping over them without another word, getting into my cab and driving off. The Conrad hotel leaves a hose out the back for cabbies in this situation. I'll nip round there, pull my rubber mats out the back and give the whole thing a good slooshing. I'll be off the road for an hour tops, then it's straight back to work.

But Jesus . . . that smell.

Twinkle's on his feet trying to brush the crap off his suit. Henry's still lying on the road. "What's your name?"

"Kathryn."

"Well, Katrin, I have to get my friend inside, and I can't do it on my own."

I don't want to look at him. "Listen, mate, this is really beyond the call of duty, know what I mean?"

"I'll pay you another twenty quid if you'll give me a hand."

I really don't need this . . . but he looks so desperate . . . "Make it forty and you're on."

"All right, Katrin. Forty it is. Jesus, talk about daylight robbery!"

"The name's Kathryn." I'm leaning into the stinking cab and pulling my leather money bag out from under the seat, strapping it around my waist.

I have Henry's right arm over my shoulder and Twinkle's got the left. I'm grabbing onto Henry's right wrist with my left hand. My right arm is around his waist to support him. I don't know if "waist" is actually the right word for it—he doesn't really have one, it's all blubber. He weighs a ton. We're dragging him up the sloping path to this fancy apartment block. His Italian leather shoes are scraping along the concrete. His head is hanging forward. I'm praying he's not going to puke again. We removed his jacket (my idea) as it's covered in vomit, but even with the jacket gone he still reeks to high heaven. Twinkle is puffing and blowing and sweating. He's well out of shape.

We get to the top of the path and there are big glass double doors.

"The security guard'll come and lend us a hand," says Twinkle, but this proves optimistic. There's no sign of any security guard in the white marble foyer. He probably took one look at us staggering up the path and hid. I don't blame him. We hang around for a minute or two—or rather Henry hangs, we just stand there bearing our load. When there's still no sign of this elusive security guard I decide we should press on. Twinkle's sweating more and more and I'm worried he's going to drop his side of Henry if we have to wait about much longer.

Balancing on my left foot, I kick at one of the doors with my right so it swings open. Then I barge sideways with my right shoulder to keep the door propped open so we can get through. Should have warned Twinkle I was going to do that—he almost falls over.

"You've got quite a set of muscles on you, Katerina." Twinkle sounds impressed.

"Yeah, well, I work out. You should try it." He *should* try it. He's a pathetic specimen. And as for Henry, well . . . "Where now?" I ask as we pass the front desk. Henry's shoes are leaving a greasy trail over the white alabaster floor. It's like we're carrying an enormous gray slug between us. Smells like it too.

"Seventh floor."

"You've got to be kidding!"

"Don't worry—there's a lift," says Twinkle, and nods at a steel lift door that's semiconcealed by a pillar and a huge rubber plant. We shuffle on, making some kind of pantomime progress till we reach the door and press the call button.

Getting Harry into the lift is like a scene from *Laurel and Hardy*—the one where they're trying to get a piano up a flight of steps. There's a lot of shunting and swearing and the door keeps closing on Henry's legs, which are sticking out behind us. I tell Twinkle to let go of his side for a minute—leaving Henry's whole gigantic weight resting on me—and pull the legs in. Then I have to tell him to press the button for the seventh floor. Can't this guy think of anything for himself?

As the lift starts to move, Twinkle is busy marveling at my physique. "You must be the fittest woman I've ever seen!"

"You can't have seen many women, then."

With sickening predictability we grind to a halt somewhere between the fourth and fifth floors. I'm seriously praying now—just can't bear the *thought* of being stuck here with these cretins and this appalling stench. Twinkle punches the "7" button a couple of times, muttering to himself. Then a voice comes from nowhere:

"Janice, please . . . take me home, Janice. Take me home, my love."

It's the slug, talking in his sleep. But it's like he's said some magic abracadabra, open-sesame kind of word because suddenly the lift is moving again and we're arriving at the seventh floor.

"Janice is his wife," says Twinkle, and adds, "The bitch."

The door slides open and we're out into the corridor, inch by inch, step by step. The passageway is carpeted in deep blue and the walls and ceiling are painted the same color. Soft synthetic Muzak is being piped from an unknown source. There are five doors painted in white with brass numbers. A shiver goes through me. The place gives me the creeps—all this weird wealthy anonymity: I have the sense that all the floors and the corridors must be exactly the same as each other. The thought comes into my head that I will never escape this building—I'll be zooming up and down in the lift and the door will keep sliding open onto this corridor. A whole labyrinth of identical floors and passageways leading into each other and me running and running and screaming . . .

I guess, technically speaking, it's a form of claustrophobia. I've always felt like this—I call it my mazophobia. I could never work in an office block. Coping with my secondary school with its endless identical classrooms and twisting dark stairways was more than a bit tricky. I avoid large department stores and tube stations. Hospitals are pretty much impossible, and as for prisons . . . well, let's just hope I'm never required to walk into one.

We've come to a halt outside one of the white doors. I have to support Henry while Twinkle rummages in his pockets for keys. This is unfortunate because I've broken out in a sweat and I'm just getting to the point where my mazophobic panic is becoming overwhelming.

"Hurry up," I say, grimacing, and mercifully Twinkle finds his keys and opens the door.

While he's still groping about for the light switch, I've already single-handedly dragged Henry through an open door and dumped him on the king-size bed inside.

"Not in there——" Twinkle begins, but when he sees the expression on my face he shrugs resignedly and says, "Oh, well, I suppose it won't hurt me to take the spare room tonight." He unlaces Henry's shoes and eases them off, dropping them on the floor. Then he goes and shouts in Henry's ear: "If you spew on my rug I'll fucking kill you."

I wander into the living room. It's pretty flashy—big picture window looking out over the harbor and a glass door leading onto a balcony with wooden garden furniture and a couple of bay trees. There's a very fine cream carpet and a Chesterfield and armchair in russet velvet. The bookshelves and cupboards are all made of glass and steel. Clearly a man of considerable means, our Twinkle.

I hear a zipping noise and then the sound of something soft falling to the floor. Shit—Twinkle is undressing.

"Something to drink?" he calls from the bedroom. "Whatever you want I've got it."

I doubt it, mate. "Can't. I'm driving."

"You could have just the one, couldn't you?" comes his voice again. "You certainly deserve one."

I'm heading for the front door but I hear footsteps behind me. Bare feet on the carpet.

"Katerina?"

"That's *Kathryn*."

"But you're too exotic for a plain name like Kathryn. All that curly black hair—those big eyes . . . you should be Italian or Spanish or something."

I turn around, thoroughly knackered and pissed off, hoping I'm not going to have to hit Twinkle and bracing myself for the unappealing sight of the bits 'n' pieces, but in fact he's wearing a baggy black T-shirt and a pair of old jeans.

"Listen, Twinkle, it's a quarter to six and I've got a cab full of puke. I'd best be getting on."

"Craig." He holds out a hand to shake mine. "Craig Summer." He delves in a pocket and hands me the promised forty quid.

"Sure you don't want a drink?" he asks. "It'll give you some-thing to do while I clean your cab." He's sitting down, putting on a pair of old trainers.

"You what?"

He gets up and opens a cupboard. "I bet you're a Scotch girl, aren't you? I have a bottle of very good Laphroaig here."

"You're going to clean my cab?"

"Of course. If Henry was in any fit state I'd make him do it, but as it is I suppose the task falls to me."

"There's really no—"

"I insist. Ice?"

"No, thanks. I'll take it neat." I sit down on the Chesterfield and he hands me the glass of whiskey. It's a good single malt—I can smell that lovely peat before I even raise it to my lips. I'm revising my opinion of Twinkle as he clatters around his kitchen. I'm not sure this act of kindness is quite fit for inclusion in the "chivalry" category, but it would certainly qualify for "gentlemanly behavior." I like a bit of gentlemanly behavior—let's face it, it's quite a rarity.

He emerges with a couple of buckets, a mop and an old cloth. He asks for my keys and I hesitate before deciding to trust him. After all, he's trusting me to be alone in his flat. "I can get all the hot water I need from the toilet in the foyer," he explains. "Back in a bit." And off he toddles with his cleaning equipment, a right lit-tle Mrs. Mop.

Fifteen minutes have passed and I'm still alone in Twinkle's flat. Alone except for Henry, that is. But he's hardly the liveliest com-pany—just the distant sound of snoring, the odd moan and the oc-casional, "Why, Janice, *why*?"

I've been nosing about, looking at the books on the glass shelves: Lots of crime fiction. Twinkle likes his Chandler, his Ell-roy, Patricia Cornwell, Ian Rankin, even Agatha Christie. He has one of those kitsch seventies ornaments they call "love meters"; two glass bulbs linked by a twisting glass tube. You put your hands over the bottom bulb and the red liquid inside rises up into the top part and eventually starts bubbling frantically. If it bubbles a lot it's supposed to mean you're passionate. We had one at home when I was a kid—till I broke it and got into trouble with my father.

There's a "Good Luck" card with a message inside that says: "Not that you need it. Show those bastards what you're made of, Love Marianne xxx." Twinkle's woman? Or perhaps the wife who left him. There's nothing else womanish around this place. In fact, there's very little of anything that looks personal. Only an old Philips wireless in one of the glass cupboards. It seems to be intended as an ornament but it's not exactly what you'd call ornamental—not one of those brightly colored retro fifties radios that are so trendy, but a big black box all battered and scratched with a couple of knobs missing.

I'm bored of browsing now and I slump down on the couch. I'm starting to think about Richard, and I'm feeling sheepish and apologetic. I didn't mean to give him such a hard time yesterday, it's just that I was in a foul mood and I hadn't had enough sleep. Usually I love being around Dotty. She's a cute kid, but I never seem to get any time alone with Richard these days. I didn't want to sound like I hate children but I know it sort of came out that way. I certainly didn't mean to send him off on that whole "Dotty and I come as one package. You can't have one of us without the other" kick. Jesus, if you've heard it once you've heard it a hundred times! I look at my watch: It's nearly half past six. Dotty'll be awake now and she'll have got Richard up. I could call . . .

I delve in my inside jacket pocket. Good—the green phone is in there. I take it out and press "1" to call up Richard's number. It starts ringing.

"Hello." He sounds sleepy.

"Hi. I hope I didn't wake you up."

"No, I've been up for half an hour." Shit, he hates me.

"Richard, I'm really sorry about yesterday."

"Yeah, Kitty, I know." He's still pissed off with me.

"I love being around Dotty, she's one of the sweetest kids I've ever met—"

"Look, it's all right. I probably made too big a deal out of it."
Even worse—he's angry but he's going to pretend he *isn't* angry so
we can't actually talk about it and sort it out. He's a wanker sometimes.

"Richard, I'm just finishing off. How about I drive over?"

"Oh, Kitty, look, how many times do I have to tell you—I can't
have you coming over first thing in the morning. Dotty gets all
overexcited and refuses to go to the nursery."

He's being deliberately obstructive. There's nothing I'd like
more at this moment than to drive up to Crouch End and curl up
with him in his bed or sit drinking coffee at his big friendly kitchen
table surrounded by Dotty's finger paintings and seed collages.
But I mustn't beg.

"What if I waited until you've dropped her off at the nursery
and then came round?"

He sighs. I imagine him closing his eyes and rubbing tiredly at
his forehead, every inch the care-worn single parent struggling to
cope with the world's unreasonable demands.

"I've got work to do. I can't drop everything and take the day
off just like that. You of all people should understand."

"Oh, *please*, Richard. I really want to see you." Damn—didn't
mean to do that.

"No, Kitty. If you want to see more of me you should think hard
about what I said last week."

Ah, so *that's* what I'm being punished for. It has nothing to do
with yesterday after all. It's about his rant last bloody week! Funny
how suddenly I'm not bothered at all about going over there.

"Sorry, Richard. I know it's hard for you to take time off. I'll go
home and get some sleep. See you Friday?"

"Yeah, sure. Whatever."

"Bye." I end the call.

Twinkle's been ages now. My cab must be gleaming by this time.
Richard's got me riled and I'm restless, itching to get on the move.
Where will I go? Home? Its emptiness doesn't appeal. Who could

I visit at this early hour? Maybe I should drive to Amy's place. No, that's not a good plan. I really can't be doing with Amy first thing in the morning. Way too strident.

I delve in my inside jacket pocket. Other than the green phone I'm only carrying the red phone. Jonny. Not sure this is a good idea but I press "1" to call up his number.

It rings for a long time and I'm about to give up when there's a click and then the dial tone sounds its hollow buzz in my ear. The bastard has picked up the receiver and then slammed it down! I redial. This time it's busy. He's taken it off the hook. Well, I suppose that's no surprise. I can picture the carnage; Jonny lying on his scuzzy couch or maybe stretched out on the floor fully clothed, comatose, stinking. He'd be surrounded by take-out cartons, empty lager cans and full ashtrays. Breakfast TV would be blaring away, unheard, unwatched. Would he be alone? The ringing of his phone would be like some pesky insect buzzing at his face, teasing him. He'd have to kill it. Well, fuck him! I didn't want to see him anyway. He can just lie there and fester for all I care.

I don't know if it's down to the rather nice Laphroaig or what but somehow I've dozed off, the red phone still in my hand. And then I'm waking up with a start from a horrible dream in which someone is driving off in my cab. It's nasty waking up in this strange place and it takes me a few seconds to work out where I am: Looking out on early morning in Chelsea Harbour—gulls squawking, the cozy rich coming out onto their balconies while back in their new kitchens the percolators are plop-plopping. What time is it? How long have I been here and what the hell is going on?

The dream. Oh, God, a paranoid thought has popped up in my head and I can't get rid of it. Maybe I've been *had* . . . Maybe Twinkle *has* nicked my cab. He could be miles away by now . . . What if this flat isn't actually his at all? He's a scammer who finds a wealthy loser drinking in a bar—in this case Henry—buys him drinks, asks where he lives and if he lives alone, gets him totally plastered and then has some unsuspecting cabby drive them both back to the loser's place in order to rob the cabby . . . Or perhaps

Henry's in on the scam too! It was fake puke, and now I'm meant to go chasing downstairs after my cab only to find it gone and when I get back up here again Henry's also vanished and there's just some old lady screaming at me to get out of her flat and denying knowledge of any of it.

I try to shake the paranoia but it's not going away. Twinkle's been way too long cleaning up my cab. I get up and make for the bedroom.

"Henry." I shake him none too gently. "Henry!"

He groans and makes a feeble attempt to fend me off.

"Henry, wake up. Wake up, you git!" I try a light slap to his face.

"*Janice . . .*" He doesn't even open his eyes, though a tear oozes out of the right one.

This is useless. I can't waste any more time. Panicking, I blunder for the front door. I run down the passage, the coins in the money bag around my waist jingling, my feet making no sound in the soft blue carpet, and hit the lift button.

Come on . . . Come on . . .

A full minute passes. The lift seems to be stuck on the third floor. The Muzak is unbearable—John Lennon's "Imagine" being played by what sounds like electronic pan pipes. I punch the button frantically a few times to no effect. Another whole minute goes by. I can't bear being in this corridor.

I spot the emergency exit and take the stairs. *Seven floors'* worth of stairs. I'm dizzy by the time I hit the ground and I'm so scared about losing my cab that my heart is pounding in my throat. My mazophobia is giving me jelly knees. I burst through the heavy fire door into the foyer and sprint to the glass doors, almost bowling over a skinny, perplexed security guard.

The cool morning air smacks my face as I emerge, blinking and gasping. I take a second or two to calm down. There, in front of me, making his way up the path, is Twinkle. He's looking tired and grubby and he's carrying his mop and buckets.

"Katerina," he says. "I was just coming up to fetch you. Why so red in the face?"

Down in the street is my lovely old Fairway cab, clean and happy, surrounded by a puddle of mucky water.

Sometimes I am a first-class twat.

The September sun is up and shining feebly by the time I arrive at my flat in Fontenoy Road, Balham, and I'm almost tearful with exhaustion after my long night. I don't like being seen in this state. I gather up all my shit from the cab—my phones, my cash. I've made over £200—pretty damn good for a Tuesday. I stagger out into the street and up the steps to grapple for the door key. I'm so weak I could shrivel up in the daylight like a vampire. I must go and hide myself inside.

I'm tripping over boxes as I enter the flat, sliding on loose sheets of newspaper used for packing and knocking over precarious stacks of books. The real estate agents would be horrified if they could see the condition of this "charming Victorian conversion with original features" now. I moved in almost a month ago but I've hardly unpacked a thing.

I had been living in a rented dump in Peckham Rye, but when the nice neighbors downstairs moved out and were replaced by a bunch of crazy Nigerians who played throbbing reggae all day when I was trying to sleep and kept accidentally setting the place on fire—well, I decided the time had come for me to take the plunge and buy a place of my own. This was a divergence from The Plan but that couldn't be helped. The Plan was to drive the cab for as many hours as I could physically cope with and live as cheaply as possible so as to save up enough dosh to hock everything and take off abroad—maybe open a beach bar somewhere hot—basically to leave this stinking country and go far away . . .

Balham is "going up" and I had to practically scrape the real estate agents off my shoes. My mortgage is hefty but it's not just the purchase of my flat that has pushed The Plan onto the back burner. Certain people are making heavy demands on my time and money, and I'm having to spend more and more cash on the now and spend more time out of the cab than in it.

I'm lunging to pull down the blinds and shield this chaos that's pretending to be a living room from the daylight. I own an embarrassment of crap, but what I don't possess is useful stuff like furniture. I have a bed, a wardrobe and an old armchair on its last legs. That's the lot. Once the blinds are firmly down, I blunder through the open doorway into the darkened bedroom. I undress, dropping my clothes in a heap on the floor, and slide under my duvet.

Although I'm knackered it takes a while to relax. My neck is full of tension and doesn't want to let go of it. I've got that thing where you're so tired it's actually an effort to close your eyes. The lids keep popping open. The episode at Twinkle's flat is running through my head as though it's on a loop. I'm forever wandering around that living room, staring at the old wireless. I'm seeing the moment when Henry vomits again and again. I'm lost in that maze of blue corridors with a Muzak version of Sting's "Every Breath You Take" flooding my ears.

The next thing I know I hear the sound of my own voice shouting *"No!"* and I'm squirming in the bed, trapped in the duvet and bathed in sweat. In the fold of time that lies between sleeping and waking I can still see the color—it's there behind my eyes, that color that I cannot articulate in my waking hours and that frightens me so much in my sleep. Seconds later I'm fully awake and my eyes are open and the color is gone. But I know it was there. It's happened again.

The bed is drenched with my sweat. I strain to see my watch in the dark and manage to make out that it's still only 10:50 A.M. I've had nowhere near enough sleep and the sleep I've managed has done nothing but terrify me.

I drag myself to the kitchen for a mug of water (I haven't unpacked the glasses yet). Leaning on the sink and gulping down mug after mug of tap water I try to calm my nerves and tell myself it's safe to go back to sleep—the color has never appeared more than once in a day. But my attempts at self-soothing don't work. I'm too frightened to get back in that sweat-soaked bed and close my eyes again. I wish I was at Stef's place—he'd give me one of his amazing massages and pummel and squeeze every drop of fear out of me. But Stef's in Spain until tomorrow doing God knows what and I'm stuck here on my own.

I lay down my mug and go to sit in my armchair. I have to call someone. But who? Stef's in Spain, Richard's angry with me, Jonny's comatose, Amy'll be running around being efficient and hyper . . . That only leaves Joel. Sweet Joel. My latest acquisition.

The blue phone is conveniently lying on the floor next to the armchair. I press "1."

"Joel. Hi, it's Kat. Can I come over? I'm lonely."

2

I'M lying on my side in Joel's bed and he is curled around me in spoons, his head nuzzling into the back of my neck, his breath warm against my shoulder. His knees are tucked into the back of my knees, one arm is draped over my waist, and his shrunken, sleeping cock rests against my bum. He is such an innocent, such a child. No, I take back "child" as uncomfortably close to the truth. Joel is only eighteen; an age difference of twelve years. Am I some horrible exploitative old hag?

I don't feel like an old hag, lying here with this beautiful young man, snug in his single bed, smelling the sweet scent of his skin, comforted by the rhythmic heat of his breath; soothed—if I'm honest—by the pressure of that soft stupid penis. Here in his little boy's bed in the cute flat paid for by his father and decorated with regency stripe and chintzy frill by his mother, I feel just a little bit beautiful myself. I feel sleek, muscular, catlike. That's what he calls me. Kat.

We met in the gym of the East Dulwich leisure center. I used to go there to work out when I lived in my tatty Peckham Rye flat. It's a poky gym with no air-conditioning and you could guarantee that at least two of the machines would be labeled "awaiting repair—we apologize for any inconvenience" on any one visit. But it was cheap, and at least it wasn't crowded.

I'd start with twenty minutes on the treadmill: beginning on incline five at seven miles per hour, and then gradually decreasing the incline and accelerating the speed until I hit nine miles per hour on incline zero. There were two treadmills next to each other and occasionally some cocky geezer would try to outrun me. The girls never even attempted it. My rival would be peering over at my display to see how fast I was going and he'd match me step for step and then try to exceed my speed. But nobody had the staying power. Ten minutes in they'd be sweating and floundering. After fifteen minutes—just as I'm really hitting my stride—they'd be slowing down, giving me evil looks as they ground to a halt and skulked off to the changing rooms. I'm not proud of wanting to outdo these men, but they were such wankers they deserved it. It was a pride thing. They couldn't stand the idea that a girl could run faster and harder than them.

I was even more competitive with the weights. Still am in fact, though I've changed to a different gym now that I've moved to Balham. I can't quite resist sitting down at a machine where some macho hero has just been puffing and straining for the last half hour or so—moving the key to increase the weight by just a few extra kilos and then lifting it effortlessly. I'm the same with the free weights. Just as some slick guy in his Lycra bodysuit with his special leather grip-gloves reaches for a couple of really heavy irons, I grab the next size up. You should see the boggly eyes of those blokes. You should see the anger in the tightening corners of their mouths and in their clenched fists. Boy, do they hate being outclassed by a woman! It's my competitive streak that's made me end up so muscle-bound.

I would have a sleep in the mornings after work and then I'd get up and go to the gym. I used to go every day—not like now when it's difficult enough finding the time to get there three or four times a week. I'd do the bike, the treadmill, the Stairmaster, the rowing machine, stretching and sit-ups, some free weights and the weight machines. I'd spend about two hours over there. It got so that I was the fittest person I knew.

You don't talk to people in the gym. It isn't done. You might nod and grunt at one or two of the more sociable ones, but on the whole you do your best not to catch anybody's eye. It's silently understood that you need your peace of mind to concentrate properly. It's different in the evenings when the place fills up with squeaky secretaries and overweight couples in matching tracksuits, but in the daytime the gym is the domain of the serious gym fanatics, the unemployed and the students. And it's the gym meisters that set the tone.

So every day I would recognize people and they would recognize me and we wouldn't speak to each other: The good-looking skinny guy who works out hard but clearly has such a fast metabolism that he can't put on weight for love nor money; the slicked-back dude in the shiny Lycra cycling shorts with the mobile phone tucked into his belt who spends all his time posing and does very little; the stocky Japanese man with the intensely meditative stare and loud grunt; the fat redhead with the huge arse and the folds of stomach so lined and wrinkled they resemble the pages of an atlas (can you *believe* she wears a cropped sports vest?); the tattooed builder type with the serious sweat problem; the sickeningly pretty Dutch girl with the all-year-round tan—and Shelley.

I was on one of the exercise bikes on a March afternoon, puffing my way through my fifteen-minute stint (all I could stand on the bike without getting bored to death). The only other people in the gym were the Japanese, the fat redhead, the good-looking skinny guy and one unknown. The double doors opened and in strode this—well, this smooth, toned, muscular black body, not too big, a fit person rather than a powerhouse. Flatteringly cut orange Nike top, black track shorts and Nike Air trainers. Head shaved—a beautifully shaped head. Full lips, wide angry nostrils, pronounced eyebrows. Piercings: three sleepers down the left ear, one in the lower lip, one in the right eyebrow, a stud in the nose. And the eyes . . . Wow, those eyes, dark brown and glittering. The brown of the shiniest richest chestnut you ever polished and hid as a child.

I kept pedaling but my gaze followed this new arrival striding across the room with *such* presence and starting a well-practiced stretching routine on the floor mats. This was a person you couldn't just pass in the street—you'd have to turn back to check

what you'd seen. For this was a person of absolutely indeterminate
sex. The face was feminine but boyish, the buttocks pert and sassy
but somehow not decidedly female—were those well-developed
pectorals or tiny flat tits? The shoulders were broad but the neck
delicate, the calves full but the ankles not particularly slender. The
shorts were loose around the crotch, too loose to make anything
out. I tried to spot the shape of an Adam's apple or a shaving
shadow and at moments I thought I saw both but seconds later decided it was just the light. I was transfixed.

The person's routine focused mainly on the weights. He or she
would sit at a machine for half an hour at a stretch, lifting some serious kilos. In between lifting the person would stare straight
ahead into space—but not vacantly. The concentration was fero-
cious. It was as though they were staring at the back of their own
eyeballs and the gaze stopped right there. The sheer *attitude*. If
you reached out to touch this person, there'd be a fizzle and you'd
be leaping back, nursing your burned finger.

I remember how, driving the cab that night, my thoughts returned over and over to the stranger in the gym. Man or woman,
who could tell? Anything was possible. I wondered if I would see
this person again.

A couple of days later he or she reappeared. I was alone in the
gym but for the tattooed builder with the sweat problem, so it was
a relief to have something attractive to look at as I ran and
pumped and lifted.

I'm not sure when I invented the nickname Shelley, but it
seemed to fit. I remained totally undecided as to whether this person was male or female, and I'm sure my own workouts were suffering from my level of distraction as I tried to puzzle it out.
Shelley seemed to be the right sort of name: Pretty, fey, with a hint
of vulnerability—for yes, I did think I sensed a vulnerability beneath all that front. I invented all manner of histories for Shelley.
I longed to know this person, and yet I realized that the truth
could only be a disappointment after all the fantasy.

Then the unexpected happened. Shelley spoke to me. We were
in the room adjoining the gym that is sometimes closed off for ex-

ercise classes. The gym was crowded and we'd both escaped into
the next room for some peace. The room has two mirrored walls
and Shelley was sitting on a chair lifting free weights, gazing at his
or her reflection with that amazing concentrated glare. A panther
staring at prey. I was on the floor doing some stretches. I lay on my
back, arms out. My left leg was straight out in front of me and my
right drawn up, bent at the knee. Slowly I closed my eyes, brought
my right hand up to my right knee and then twisted at the waist
and the small of the back to bring the right leg across the left,
pushing the knee with my hand to make it touch the floor while I
turned my head in the other direction. It's a yoga twist. Pulls all
your muscles taut from your neck and shoulders all the way down
your back and into your thigh. You're twisting your body like you
would wring out a cloth, squeezing out every last drop of water.

"What kind of move is that?"

I concluded the twist and opened my eyes. Shelley was standing above me, hands on hips, looking puzzled, curious.

"It's a yoga stretch. It's really good."

"Will you show me?"

As casually as possible, I scraped myself off the mat and into a
crouch. Shelley lay down in front of me. What followed was one of
the most sensual experiences of my life. Shelley's arms were out as
mine had been. I put my hands down and touched the inside of
the arms where the skin is soft, encouraging Shelley to stretch
them further, feeling the muscles in the elbows go taut. With
hands that were tense, almost shaking, I slowly eased Shelley's left
calf and lower thigh to straighten the knee joint. Shelley let out a
kind of groan that I hope signified pleasure rather than pain. I
glanced down at Shelley's face and those brown chestnut eyes
were gazing up at me expectantly. Shelley drew the right leg up and
I placed my right hand squarely on the knee, smooth and warm.

Shelley twisted and I pushed the right knee down hard against
the mat. At the same time I placed my left hand on Shelley's right
shoulder and pressed to try to make it touch the floor and give the
full stretch. Shelley was deliciously supple.

"Breathe into the twist," I said.

A smile spread across Shelley's face as the stretch went right through his back, side and shoulders and his eyes closed. "Oh, *yes*."

Oh yes, indeed! Shelley was a boy all right. I could see the Adam's apple now. I could make out the soft down around the jaw bone (you could hardly call it stubble). I wasn't looking where I wanted to look. In any case the angle of the twist hid it.

He held the stretch for about two minutes, and we went on to do the other side. And then it was over. Shelley jumped up and returned to his free weights as though the interruption had never taken place. One second my hands were flat against his skin, the next they were touching mat.

"Thanks," was all he said as he got up, and he gave me a curt nod. Then he was deep in his own world again.

After the workout I went to the Ladies' toilets to change. The Women's changing room was out of order—for over six months they'd supposedly been putting down a new floor and the usual sign was hanging on the door. "Awaiting repair—we apologize for any inconvenience." As I pulled off my shorts, standing on one foot on the cold tiles, wobbling and gripping the edge of a cracked sink to steady myself, the door flew open and in strode Shelley, making straight for one of the cubicles. He didn't bother closing the door—just unzipped and stood there with his back to me, pissing. That *attitude*.

"Hey!"

Still urinating, he turned his head to look at me. I was wearing only my T-shirt and a pair of black knickers—hardly the picture of authority. He looked as though he was going to laugh.

"What the hell is wrong with the Men's, then?" I tried, struggling to sound intimidating.

He finished and zipped up. He turned to me and shrugged. "It's all the way down the corridor. I guess."

A girl is vulnerable when she pisses in front of someone. But a man pissing in front of a woman like this? As far as I'm concerned it's an act of aggression.

"You should show some respect," I said.

He flushed and came out of the cubicle toward me.

"I'm sorry," he said softly. He was standing too close to me. I could feel his breath on my face.

And then he did it. He leaned forward and kissed me. His lips were gentle and warm except for the cold metal of the lip ring, becoming more firm as he put his hands on my shoulders to draw me closer. I let myself be drawn in. I brought my hands up around his waist. I pulled him toward me, wanting to feel his erection against me. His mouth was minty from the gum he'd been chewing. The backs of his teeth were even and smooth. His tongue stroked mine like you'd pet a cat.

We left the gym together. He waited while I put my trousers and shoes on and stuffed my gear into my little rucksack. He didn't say anything while he waited. We'd done no more than kiss.

He broke his charismatic silence and began chattering as we walked down Lordship Lane past the Cheese Block, le Chardon, Apollo Videos, Starburger and the Lord Palmerston pub.

"I've been training to be a dancer since I was four," he said.

"Then you shouldn't be working out with heavy weights. You'll overdevelop some of your muscles and tighten your hamstrings."

"I know what I'm doing. I have an audition tomorrow for *Saturday Night Fever*, the musical. Not the lead of course, but they need two extra male dancers. One's having his tonsils out and the other has AIDS."

"Your lucky day."

"Something like that." He was young. Very young. I hadn't realized until now.

"My name's Joel," he said.

"Can I call you Shelley?"

"*What?*"

"I'm Kathryn. Kathryn Cheet."

We arrived at his front door. He lived directly above a vegetable shop and next door to a dentist on North Cross Road, East Dulwich. I climbed the narrow stairs ahead of him while he went through his junk mail.

His flat was all ribbons and bows, stenciled cherubs and net curtains. I sat on a heavily floral couch and gazed around me at the unexpected decor.

"It's my mother," he said. "She does a class."

"This is your parents' place then?"

"It's just temporary. When I start earning proper money I'm going to get my own flat. Primrose Hill, or maybe Belsize Park . . . My dad owns lots of flats and houses round here." Then he took my hand and led me through to the bedroom.

He wasn't great at sex—the pure mechanics of it. His cock was small and it took a lot of sucking for him to get a hard-on. When we finally got down to it the whole thing was over in about three minutes. But there was something intoxicating about him. The taste of him; that perfect balance of salt and sugar in his sweat. The beauty of his body, the ambiguity. Those lips. Afterward I felt refreshed rather than sated, but the feeling was a good one. I felt protective of him as we lay cozily beneath the buttercup duvet. I had my arm around him and he lay sleeping on my shoulder, breathing through his mouth, a thin line of dribble playing down onto my skin. He was eighteen. At this moment he seemed younger.

We lay like that for maybe two hours, while my brain slowly whirred back to life. I began to fret. What had I got myself into here? As if I didn't have enough on my plate with the others: Jonny had phoned to threaten suicide while I was driving the previous night, Stef had got himself into another stupid scam with his dodgy flatmates, Richard wanted me to meet his parents, I had the distinct feeling that Amy was seeing someone else and I hadn't earned anywhere near enough money that week. What was I doing having substandard sex with some teenager I'd picked up in the gym when life was already so complicated?

But then Joel opened his eyes and looked up at me with an expression closer to pure adoration than anything I'd ever seen, and all my frets, questions and chiding evaporated. Would anyone be able to resist this sweet, beautiful boy? I knew right then that the shape of my life was set to evolve from a four-cornered square into a five-pointed star. I didn't have a choice in the matter.

* * *

"Kat?" He's awake, wide awake, and I haven't slept at all. Not even for a minute. "Kat, are you sleeping?"

"No." How could I possibly sleep? How could I even close my eyes when I'm so afraid of the color I might see . . .

"Are you OK?"

"Yeah, sure."

"Tea?"

"That'd be great."

He wriggles out from behind me and goes off to fill the kettle. He makes the world's most awful tea but he likes to look after me and I like to indulge him. It is this love of indulging him that is the hook. I'm half addicted to it.

I hear him setting two mugs on the side and the kettle starts to hiss. Then he comes back and puts on boxer shorts and a T-shirt. That's the end of Bed then. And we haven't even had sex. Not that sex has ever been a key feature of my relationship with Joel. We weren't even what you'd call "hot" at the beginning. Now, six months in, we're positively refrigerated. No, that's not fair—that suggests a coldness, while in fact there's a lot of warmth between us. And a lot of touchy-feely stuff. Just not much actual shagging.

He's back in the kitchen stirring the tea. I hear the tinkling of the spoon. "I've decided to train to be a hairstylist," comes his voice.

"What about your dancing?"

There's a sigh and he reappears to search about for coasters so the mugs won't make marks on Mummy's nice white bedside table. "I've been thinking about it for a while. And now I've decided."

"But you love your dancing."

He sets the two mugs down on the coasters and perches on the edge of the bed. "Yes I do, but I've never gotten through a single audition. Don't look like that—I wouldn't have to give up *altogether*, would I?"

He has a point but I'm distressed. He's talking about abandoning his big ambition.

"There's this salon in Brixton—" he begins, and suddenly I see it all. He's down at the Electric Avenue market with his mother, carrying her bags while she sniffs at melons and points out the sign hanging in some tatty Afro-Caribbean barbershop saying that a junior is needed to sweep up hair on a Saturday.

"This is your mother's idea, isn't it?"

"I do have a mind of my own, you know!" he snaps, slamming his mug down so that tea slops over the side.

It's a good thing that I've moved away from the area now and changed gyms. I need to keep a healthy distance from this boy. I'm in danger of trying to become his mother myself.

"So this really has nothing to do with your mother?"

"No!"

"I'm sorry, Joel. I just—well, you know what I think."

"That's all right," he said, still a bit sniffy about it. And then he begins to tell me about this new salon called Shaman (how very Brixton!), owned by Gino, a former hairdressing world champion who's landed some government grant to start up his own business by cooking up a crazy plan for a Brixton Hair Festival and a "unique training program for the local unemployed." Joel is apparently to be one of five new apprentices and he'll also go to college and end up with a certificate. He's full of Gino this and Gino that. Gino took Joel out to the pub last night and told him at some length what a great stylist he's going to turn him into (which must have been a barrel of laughs for both of them as Joel doesn't drink and hates pubs).

Well, if this genuinely has nothing to do with his mother, then maybe it's a good thing. Anything that might set him on his feet and get him out of his parents' pockets has to be a good thing in the end. So I soften up and tell him how great this is and what a fantastic opportunity it could be for him and I'm so eager to please him that I even drink the whole cup of his disgusting tarmac tea. And finally he's so happy with me and so full of his plans for his new life that he slithers out of his shorts and T-shirt and back under the buttercup duvet and we actually make love for the first time in almost a month and its actually *good*—by anyone's standards.

But when we're done and we're lying there together all spent and spoony and he's doing what he does best—cuddling me close and falling asleep—my mind starts racing again and I can't put the brakes on. And I'm thinking about Jonny and how he slammed the phone down on me earlier, and I'm angry with him and I'm worrying about him. And I suddenly have this horrible feeling that I've left the red phone—*Jonny's* phone—in the Chelsea Harbour apartment of Craig "Twinkle" Summer.

3

IT's four o'clock and I'm sitting in the cab, parked outside Joel's place, all showered and groomed and ready to go. I'm using the pink phone to dial the number of the red phone.

"This is Kathryn. I can't take your call right now. Please leave a message."

Shit—it's switched off. I hate speaking to my own answer service but I don't have a choice.

"Hello, Mr. Summer. This is Kathryn Cheet, the taxi driver. I'm hoping you'll pick up this message and that you have this phone somewhere safe. I'd like to arrange to come and collect it some time. If you can, would you please call me on 07946 441359? I guess if I don't hear from you I'll just have to drive over to your flat some time on the off chance that you're in . . . Anyway, please do call me. Many thanks."

No sooner do I end the call than the phone rings, making me jump. Twinkle calling back already?

"Kathy, it's me. Where *are* you?"

It's Amy. I'm racking my brains trying to work out where I'm supposed to be. I'm gripping the phone to my ear with my shoulder and delving about in the glove compartment for my diary at the same time as saying to Amy, "I'm at home with Mother. We've just been shopping." I'm still trying to extract the diary from glove compartment jungle and find the place when she launches into one:

"That's bloody typical. You're supposed to be shopping with *me*. You promised. That woman is a menace."

"Sorry. She's old and helpless, what can I say?" I have hold of the diary and I'm trying to find the place.

"Save it, Kathy. Just get yourself over here. Pronto." The line goes dead.

I finally find the right page. "Wednesday—3:00 Amy's. Shopping. 7:00 dinner with Cheryl and Greta. Night off."

Nightmare! And multifaceted nightmare at that. First, Amy will want to go to a supermarket, probably Sainsbury's. So I'll be pushing a cart around sweating and panicking with my mazophobia while she badgers me with questions: "What do you think— chorizo or prosciutto? Can I use mascarpone for a cheesecake?" Second, I've just had a plate of oven chips and mini chicken kievs with Joel so I'm not remotely hungry and would rather not eat anything for the rest of the day, particularly stodgy dinner-party cuisine. Third, I can't *stand* Cheryl. Fourth, I've been taking too many nights off lately and I can't afford any more for at least a week. Fifth, I wanted to go and see Jonny.

Fantastic.

I put the key in the ignition and set off for Islington. The traffic is bad and it's starting to rain. People try to flag me down even though I don't have my light on. A man bangs on my window with the flat of his hand when I stop at a junction and yells something incomprehensible but no doubt offensive.

I shrug at him. "I'm not working, mate." He gives me the finger. I turn away.

The big question: Is Amy worth all the stress? I'm starting to think she isn't. And yet I've been seeing her for almost two years now. Only Jonny and Richard have been around for longer. Jonny is manageable (strange but true). He doesn't have the same level of expectation. He doesn't interrogate me like Amy does. And Richard isn't contradictory and flaky like Amy.

Amy thinks she wants to *be* with me, live with me, adopt kids with me, grow old with me. She thinks there are only two obstacles to this, both created by me. The first obstacle is that I haven't "come out" as a lesbian. I keep telling Amy that my sexuality isn't as simple as that. I respond to the person, not the gender, and actually she's the only woman I've ever slept with. What I can't tell her is that I like fucking men and continue to do so on a daily basis. She won't have any of my flannel—she's determined that over time I will come to understand myself better and discover my true sexual identity. She's waiting for this to happen.

The second obstacle is my mother. In order to keep Amy out of my private life I had to tell her that I live with my aging and infirm mother, who wouldn't even be able to cope with the idea that her precious daughter is not a virgin, let alone that she may be a lesbian. This story stops Amy from expecting to come over to my flat and provides any number of ready-made excuses for not spending more time with her. But it may ultimately have been a mistake: Amy has built up an intricate picture of my psychology which attributes almost all my problems and character defects to my mother. She blames my mother for my elusiveness, my reluctance to come out—which she calls my "sexual cowardice"—for my bad dreams, my "emotional coldness" . . . and the list goes on. Listening to Amy's rants about my manipulative, selfish, devious, sadistic mother, I almost start believing in her myself. Amy thinks my mother dominates my life and is waiting for Mummy to die so she can take over the job herself.

But it's rather convenient for Amy to decide that all obstacles to our blissful union are on my side. Amy is full of psychobabble—it's her version of being full of shit. She might think she knows everything there is to know about everyone but she doesn't know her own mind: She is no more capable of holding down a monogamous relationship than a traffic warden is capable of parking on a double yellow. Monogamy is not in her nature. She thinks I don't know about all her little flings, her one-night stands, her flirtations. But I sniff them out. I can see it in her eyes when she's done the dirty on me. She's a terrible liar. Amy might complain about not having enough time with me, not going over to my flat, et cetera, but in reality it suits her just fine.

As for my real mother—she died when I was fifteen.

❊   ❊   ❊

It's nearly five by the time I arrive at Cafford Square. I'm surprised to see there's a parking space almost outside Amy's and it's only as I'm pulling up and the wind shivers through the old chestnut tree sending ripe chestnuts showering down and bouncing off my bonnet and windscreen that I realize why the space has been left vacant. In Peckham or Balham the kids would long since have thrashed all the chestnuts out of the tree with big sticks but I guess there aren't many kids around here—they've all been sent away to boarding school or are simply too well brought up for that kind of base activity. Where are the little yobs when you need them?

I lock the cab, ducking and dodging to avoid another hail of chestnuts. Then I run up the steps to the three-floored white-fronted Georgian terraced house in which Amy lives, and beat the heavy brass knocker three times. Needless to say this is not Amy's house. She's doing well to afford a room here. It is owned by her landlady, Willa Finkleman, the food writer and restaurant critic. Willa is loaded. She doesn't really need to have a lodger but she's lonely. I think she misses her ex-husband, the publisher Sam Finkleman, who left her for a younger woman. She likes to make a fuss about having to share her space with other people but it's all for show. Amy works with Willa at *Up West* magazine. Willa contributes a food column and Amy writes a column called "Muff Matters."

The door is opened by Willa, who peers at me through the spectacles hanging from a chain around her neck before admitting to recognizing me. This is an affectation—there is nothing wrong with Willa's eyesight. It's probably better than mine. I tried her glasses on once and the lenses are plain.

"Tush tush, Kathy," says Willa, wagging a finger. "You've got yourself in madam's bad books today. I don't envy you." She blocks the doorway, all sixteen-odd stone of her in her tentlike Hampstead Bazaar caftan.

"Yeah, well, are you going to let me in or what?"

She deigns to step aside.

"Amy went off to Sainsbury's half an hour ago," she calls as I'm heading down the parquet toward the kitchen. "She said to tell you she couldn't wait any longer."

I'm clearly in trouble but I can't help feeling relieved that I've skipped the supermarket experience.

I slip off my jacket and sit down at the enormous green table in the kitchen. "Any chance of a cuppa?"

"*Bien sur*. What kind would you like? Mango, nettle, mint . . ."

"Normal, please," I get in before she can reel off any more.

She fills her designer kettle from the water filter jug and sets it to boil. Then she starts wittering about some restaurant she went to last night with Janet Street-Porter. Chez something or other. I actually quite like Willa but I'm not in the mood today. I gaze around at the kitchen, my favorite room in Willa's house. It's a huge room, the best-equipped kitchen I've ever seen. She had it specially designed—big table in one corner, dressers along the back loaded with her collection of antique china (God help you if you use any of it). Then she's got her Aga and the extra oven and a load of dark green stained wood units. Shiny steel pans hang from rows of hooks on the ceiling . . . All in all it's like something off the telly. Which is handy since that's exactly what it will become when filming of *Willa Entertains* begins next month. Amy's none too pleased about that.

Willa puts a mug in front of me and pulls up a chair. "Actually, I'm glad I've got you on your own, Kathy. I was hoping I'd have a chance for a quiet word."

"Oh yeah?" I'm edgy. What's she going to say—that I leave towels on the floor, that I park my cab in the wrong place, that she doesn't like all this girl-on-girl stuff going on under her roof?

"It's about Amy." Her face is motherly, concerned. Is she going to tell me that Amy has been sleeping with someone else? If that's the case I'm not sure I want to know. I gulp my tea nervously and burn my tongue. "She's—how can I put it—she's going into the Agony trade."

I'm relieved. What is the old bint going on about?

"She's doing really well at *Up West*. The column's become

something of a cult feature and I happen to know there's a lot of interest in Amy. But for some ridiculous reason she's decided to become an *Agony Aunt* of all things—for *two* cheap rags!"

They'd have to be very cheap rags to be cheaper than *Up West*, which, after all, is nothing more than a freebie sub–*Time Out* that gets shoved at you outside tube stations in central London . . . I don't say this, though. "Come on, Willa. You know Amy—she's probably only doing it for a laugh."

She sighs, exasperated at having to deal with a person as dense as me. "Kathy, one shouldn't organize one's career around *laughs*."

"Is it really so awful to be an Agony Aunt?"

She shrugs, plays with her pearls. "She says she's going to use pseudonyms, so I suppose people won't realize it's her, but still . . . She shouldn't be wasting her energy on this. She could have had a broadsheet column by now if she'd only let me help her." She suddenly grabs my hand across the table, gripping it in hers so tightly that her big diamond ring digs into my fingers. "Would you talk to her, Kathy? She might listen to you."

"I don't know, Willa . . . I mean, what would I say?"

"Just tell her not to do this. Tell her to accept my help."

At that moment the front door opens and Willa releases her grip on my hand. Amy's voice calls out, "Willa, are you here? Any sign of Kathy yet?"

She's all flushed with the rushing around and the weight of the shopping bags—her cheeks are radiant, her green eyes sparkle, though there are dark shadows under them (what has she been up to?). Bedroom eyes. She's had her hair cut—it's shorter than before and a bit spiky. It looks good, emphasizes her cheekbones. She has lovely cheekbones.

"So you did decide to turn up," she says grumpily. But she fails to hide her pleasure at seeing me sitting here. I see it peeping out.

"Course."

"Are you going to give me a hand, then?" She bends to put down the bags she's carrying and I'm treated to a great view of her bum, round and appley in her jeans. Her bum is one of her best features.

I follow her out to the hall where the shopping bags are stacked. "Jesus, how much stuff have you got?"

She catches me at the foot of the stairs, puts her arms around my neck and kisses me deep. Her mouth tastes of chocolate cookies. She must have opened a packet on the way home. She breaks off to tell me, "We're having grilled goat cheese and roast shallots with a roquette salad to start with, followed by *osso buco alla Milanese* and then *petits pots aux chocolat.*"

I feel faint with exhaustion just thinking about it. I imagine the hordes of calories storming through me like an army on the march. "Sounds yummy."

"Does, doesn't it. I hope to God Greta eats veal. I forgot to check."

"Amy." I catch both her hands in mine. "Look, I don't think I can stay late tonight. I have to work."

"What?" The cheeks are flushing again but this time it's anger.

"I've had a lot of expense lately. I can't afford to take the night off."

"But you promised!"

"I know, but . . ."

"Oh, forget it. Just forget it." She turns and grabs a couple of shopping bags in tight fists.

"Amy . . ."

"I don't want to hear it."

We're sitting around the table in Willa's dining room, which is all muslin and creamy colors and bits of gold stenciling. We've just finished our starters and Willa is smoking a cigarette in the face of Cheryl's obvious but unspoken disapproval. Cheryl is coughing and waving the smoke away from her, even though she's right across the other side of the table. Cheryl has a voice like a fog horn and says "sh" instead of "s" and she's just moved seamlessly from a lengthy tirade about the state of the tube system to a wildly attractive monologue on the state of her own fallopian tubes to the more general issue of lesbians and artificial insemination. Amy likes Cheryl because she's a radically political animal in an age of apathetic namby-pambies, and because she isn't afraid to speak her mind. I dislike Cheryl because she's a big ugly dyke with a shaved head and an enormous nose who rants and won't listen to anybody else's opinions. She should have been a cabdriver.

Every now and again Cheryl says, "Don't we, Greta?" or "Isn't it, Greta?" or "Haven't we, Greta?" And Greta smiles and nods and peers at us through her steel-rimmed glasses. Greta is tiny and has a shrunken pointy face. She rarely speaks. Occasionally I find myself inadvertently imagining them in bed together—Greta pinned to the bed peering up through her spectacles while Cheryl goes grunting and snuffling all over her like a pig sniffing out truffles. It's enough to put you off your feed.

"It's almost impossible to get AID through the NHS unless there's actually something physically wrong with you," Cheryl is saying. "The only way is to go private and even then you're subjected to interrogations and accusations. And private medicine is fundamentally against my principles."

Willa is suppressing a yawn. Greta is nodding and peering. I'm getting riled. Amy comes in with the steaming pan of *ossi buchi* nestling in tomato sauce. Amy looks great in her new gray pinstripe trousers and the angora sweater.

"Smells divine," says Willa.

"The secret is the fresh lemon zest," says Amy and starts dishing up. "Get the risotto, would you, darling?"

I stumble off to the kitchen, slightly surprised and alarmed by the "darling." It's tempting to stay out there for a while but I grit my teeth and return with the saucepan of fragrant saffron rice. I so need a drink but I have to drive later—it's killing me to have to remain sober in this company.

No sooner are we all digging in than Cheryl starts up again. "I was just talking about the difficulty of getting AID on the NHS as a lesbian," she tells Amy.

I'm fed up with this. "Well, why *should* you get AID on the health service when there's thousands of women who physically can't conceive queuing up on the waiting list? If you really want a baby, why don't you just stop being so bloody squeamish about men and go out and get yourself laid!"

There's an awkward silence. Amy glares at me. Willa quietly says, "This is really delicious, Amy."

"Well, I'm not surprised to hear that from you," says Cheryl. "Just what exactly is it about lesbianism that you find so threatening, Kathy? Don't you think it's about time you got to grips with who you really are?"

Greta nods her tiny head and smiles a shriveled smile.

Amy decides to defend me. "Go easy, Cheryl. Kathy won't decide to define herself as gay just because we tell her she should. She needs time . . ."

I'm really pissed off now. "Can we please stop talking about my sex life!"

Willa tries to come to my rescue, pouring me a glass of wine that I shouldn't drink and saying, "I went to the most sensational new restaurant last night with Janet Street-Porter. I really must tell you all about it."

Cheryl is scraping the bone marrow out of the middle of her osso buco and licking it off the edge of her knife. The sight of this is utterly nauseating. I can't eat another mouthful.

The main course is over and Cheryl has gone out to give Amy a hand with the dessert. Greta is actually speaking. Her voice is thin and squeaky. "Did Amy tell you—Cheryl and I are getting married next May?"

"Well, that's just dandy," I say, wondering if there's any way for them to accomplish this in the full legal sense. "Congratulations."

"You're both invited, of course," says Greta. "And you, Willa, if you'd like to come."

"Excuse me," I say. "I'd better check on Amy."

God, what a must for my diary! I'm out in the hall making for the kitchen, thinking I shouldn't have drunk the wine that Willa poured me. And as I reach the doorway I see something I'd rather not.

Amy is standing with her back to me at one of the kitchen work surfaces, on which is placed a tray bearing the five *petits pots*, and Cheryl is standing next to her. Amy's left hand rests on the surface and Cheryl's right hand is covering it. Cheryl is staring into Amy's eyes. Cheryl is holding her left hand against Amy's cheek—just holding it there and gazing at Amy. There is an intimacy about them. A tenderness.

For a moment I am frozen. Then I start walking noisily into the room. They show no shock, no surprise at being interrupted in this way. They don't leap apart. Cheryl doesn't even remove her hand from Amy's cheek. But there is a subtle adjustment in the mood. Subtle but definite. Cheryl turns to smile at me.

"You're a lucky girl, Kathy," she says. "To have someone like Amy. Now you just pull yourself together and start treating her properly." And she finally drops the hand, picks up the tray with a smile and walks out past me, heading for the dining room.

"What—" I start, when we're alone. But I'm interrupted by a sudden trilling from the pink phone, which is lying forgotten on the kitchen table. Before I can get it Amy lunges for it.

"Hello?" she says into it, looking at me with an expression that strikes me as being slightly guilty. "Oh, really? . . . Well, actually this isn't *Katerina* but I'm sure she'll be delighted." She thrusts the phone at me aggressively and stands with her hands on her hips while I take the call.

"Katerina?" It's Twinkle of course. His voice is ridiculously jolly.

"Hello, Mr. Summer." Why did he have to call *now*, of all times? "Do you have my phone? When can I come and collect it?"

"Call me Craig. Please. As it happens I'm using it to talk to you now. I'm so sorry about last night. Would you let me make it up to you?"

I turn my back on Amy. "Well, Mr. Summer, could I call over to your flat tomorrow morning sometime to pick it up? Would that work?"

"Ah, tomorrow morning . . . well, the morning's a little difficult. I was thinking perhaps we could have dinner tomorrow evening. As it happens I have a table booked at Club Gascon. Have you been?"

He's doing my head in. "Look, Mr. Summer, I'm kind of busy at the moment. If it's all the same to you I'd rather just come by and pick the phone up some time—"

"But it *isn't* all the same to me," he butts in. I can just imagine his eyes twinkling. I'm back in that apartment hearing the muffled *thlunk* of his trousers dropping to the floor. "I'd like to buy you dinner. Is that really so terrible?"

Amy steps round in front of me, taps me on the shoulder, mouths "Who the hell—" I turn away from her again. She taps a second time.

"It's not that," I say, trying to ignore her. "It's just—ow!" Amy grabs a handful of my hair and yanks. I try to bat her off me. "All right, all right. Tomorrow evening. What time?"

"Eight o'clock. Do you know where it is?"

"Yeah, yeah." Amy is bearing down on me again. "'Bye." I end the call.

"Who was that?" She tries to snatch the phone.

"Just a fare," I begin.

"Precisely," she snaps. "Affair!"

"His mate was sick in my cab. I had to help carry him out. I left my other mobile in his flat."

"What *other mobile*?" snarls Amy. "And since when did you start carrying your customers around? Cheryl's right. You need to get to grips with who you are! I'm sick of being played for a fool."

"Amy, there's nothing going on. I'm telling you the truth." I can hear the whine in my voice—so defensive, so guilty-sounding. I rally, remembering that *I* am not the guilty one here. "More to the point, what the hell was going on just now with you and Cheryl?"

"Oh, grow up! We're old friends. She's getting married." But she can't look me in the eye. "We'd better get back to the others," she says more quietly. "We'll talk about this later."

"But I have to work . . ." I say to her retreating back. She's already halfway down the hallway.

4

PESKY drizzle. It should either rain properly or not at all. It's 2:30 P.M. and I've just come out to give the cab a cleaning out only to discover a blood-filled syringe lying on the backseat. Not for the first time. That couple I picked up at King's Cross and drove to Brixton at the end of the night. I knew it—they were quiet, too quiet. They had an unhealthy look to them and they were dazed and saucer-eyed. I don't know when they could have done it, though. Whenever I glanced at them in the mirror they were just sitting there nice as pie with their hands folded in their laps. They looked back at me with vacant stares.

Without touching the syringe I slam the door shut and lay down the garbage bag and cloth that I'm carrying. I'm swearing under my breath as I climb the stairs to my flat and face the mess of unpacked boxes.

I have a pair of work gloves that I bought especially for occasions like this. The kind that garbagemen wear: Thick rubber with a cotton lining. But where the hell are they? Can't be in that box—that's kitchen stuff and I wouldn't put *these* gloves anywhere near my plates and cups. Those boxes over in the corner are books and CDs. Those two there—Jesus, what *are* those two? This is an absolute bloody nightmare. I'm stumbling about among the balled-up sheets of newspaper, tripping over black garbage bags filled with cushions and pillows, randomly delving in boxes and finding nothing. I hear a crunch as I roughly handle some objects wrapped in newspaper and realize I've broken one of my lead crystal wineglasses. I can't deal with that now. I just put the paper-wrapped broken glass back in the box.

I woke, an hour ago, from my first decent day's sleep in ages—no dreams, no trilling phones, no workmen drilling in the road—only to have my head invaded from all directions by worries. I fretted about Jonny—I called round to his place on my way home this morning and he wasn't there. I rang the bell repeatedly for a full five minutes in case he was asleep but there was no answer. He must be on a bender, which is bad news. Then I worried about Amy—Amy and Cheryl. I should have taken the night off and stayed there, talked to her, sorted it out. But no, I was more bothered about losing money than I was about losing her. And to tell the truth, I was after an excuse to get away. Frenetic, that's what Amy was last night. Too bloody frenetic for me. She wouldn't really be sleeping with that *dog*, would she?

It's so dark in here, is it really any wonder I can't find anything? I blunder to the window and open the blind. Light floods in, illuminating the mess. I bought this flat to create a safe haven, a secure and private place where I can just be myself, the calm at the center of the storm. But look at it! And what did I expect—that the boxes would unpack themselves? What am I, the sorcerer's bloody apprentice expecting to sit back and watch while books jump onto shelves and cutlery hops into drawers? I squat down next to a knackered old suitcase and undo the straps. There's a chance . . . Eureka! Here they are. Now I just have to find an old box or something to put the syringe in. It isn't enough to wrap it in newspaper. Can't have the garbagemen getting spiked, now, can I?

I'm on my way out with the gloves, some newspaper and an empty cornflakes box from the kitchen when I spot the envelope lying on the doormat. I know before I even pick it up who it's from. Dad always uses those long cream-colored envelopes. He orders them in bulk from a stationery catalogue. Ever the thrifty one, my dad. I turn it over in my hands, tempted suddenly to put on the gloves. It's been forwarded from my old flat. I wish I could chuck it away unopened, but I'm too curious.

Dear Kathryn,

Forgive my intrusion but I thought you should know that I'm
holding a memorial service for your mother at the church on
October 13th at noon. I'm sure you're aware that it's coming up
to the fifteenth anniversary and I feel badly that we didn't have
a proper funeral at the time. People are still angry with me
about it—Roy and Gina in particular. They think I deprived
them of the opportunity to grieve properly. I couldn't face
people. It was all too awful. But I realize now that that was a
terrible mistake: My need for privacy was interpreted as guilt.
There are people in the town who still cross the road rather
than talk to me.

   I've had dilemmas about it. Some might say, what's the
point of raking it all up again and upsetting everyone afresh,
but I want to show them I have nothing to hide. I want to show
the whole town. And I want to show *you*, Kathryn. I hope very
much that you will come. I'd like to see you.

   I trust you're keeping well.

Dad

I can see him sitting at his desk in his slippers and his gray
pullover, scribbling away with his scratchy old fountain pen, paus-
ing to change his cartridge, fiddling about with blotting paper, ad-
justing his half-moon spectacles, letting the pen hover in the air
while he rummages around in his head for the right words, the
right tone—respectful, apologetic, aloof. I can smell the stale old
carpet—tobacco and dust and time. My head thuds to the ticking of the carriage clock. *For Henry Cheet, with all our thanks
for twenty-seven years at Roger Sterton Comprehensive, Saffron
Walden. Teacher and Headmaster. We will miss your wisdom.*

"So are you going, then?" Winnie lays the letter down on the
stained tabletop and lights a cigarette.
   "You're joking, aren't you?"
   She inhales and goes off on a session of rasping coughs.

"State of you, Win. You want to take it easy with the cigs."

She settles down. Scowls at me, her bushy eyebrows almost meeting in the middle. "Why not?"

Big Kev comes over with a coffee for me and a tea for Winnie.

"Why not what?" I'm reaching in my jeans pocket for some change, slapping it down on the table for Kev to scoop up. Whoever's the last in buys the drinks and somehow Winnie always gets here first.

"You know. Your dad. This could be a chance for bridge-building, fence-mending . . ."

"Give it a rest, Win." I have to stop her before she goes into one of her self-help spiels. She was reading one of her pop psychology books when I arrived ten minutes ago. *Soul Dancing* it's called. The author's face is emblazoned across the cover—immaculate side-parting and perfect white smile. Easy to see what he spends his royalties on—his dentist must be even richer than he is. I hate those kind of books. They're full of quick-fix sound bites and nifty catchphrases and the message is always the same.

"Why not, Kath? He's facing up to what happened, isn't he? I think you owe him a chance."

"I owe him nothing." God, why won't she shut up about this? I wish I hadn't shown her the letter now.

"OK, so you don't owe him anything, but what harm would it do to go along there?"

"Shut it, Win." I snatch the letter back and stuff it in my jacket pocket.

Winnie shrugs and puts out her cigarette. "Suit yourself. You asked my opinion and I've given it. Seems to me you knew what I'd say. Seems to me you wouldn't have asked if you didn't want to hear me say it. 'S logic, innit?"

She starts coughing again. Steve Ambley's on the next table studying the form and eating fish and chips with Rog Hackenham and some bald geezer I don't know. He leans over and shouts, "Pack it in, Winnie. You're putting us off our food."

Winnie's too busy coughing to say anything back. I snarl at Ambley. "You're a one to talk, Steve. Looking at that big ugly gob of yours is enough to turn anyone's stomach. You wanna get yourself a face mask or a nice bit of plastic surgery."

Steve gives me the finger and Rog and the bald guy laugh.

"Bloody cabbies. I bloody hate them." I turn back to Winnie.

"Don't bother with them," says Winnie, when she gets her breath back, and calls out, "Kev, could you bring me another cuppa, love?"

"Seriously, Win, you should cut down on the cigs. You sound rough."

Winnie waves a dismissive hand, revealing two bright yellow stains on her fingers. "Nah, this is a flu thing. I caught it off the kids, didn't I. Sandra and Tommy had it last week and Lindy was hacking away for all she was worth today."

"Kids, eh? Sooner you than me." I slurp my coffee. Hits the spot.

She smiles and the whole of her huge face softens up like a big sugary doughnut. "Just you wait a year or two, Kathryn. When your clock starts ticking you'll be dropping rugrats like there's no tomorrow."

I shudder. "Oh yeah? And who's going to be the doting daddy, then? Jonny? Stef? Joel? Not exactly what you'd call ideal, are they?"

"Well, there's always Richard, isn't there?" she says, avoiding looking me in the eye. She's a bit of a Richard fan.

"Hardly! His ex-wife made him get a vasectomy after Dotty was born."

"Oh. Shame. Still, he could get it reversed . . . ?"

She's got a lot invested in the family lark. She'd love it if I made the same decisions she has. Truth is she has a crap life—nothing in those self-help books will genuinely convince her otherwise, not deep down in her heart—and she doesn't want to think there may be another path, another route to happiness. Winnie's forty-one and she's been married to a limp waster called Paul for nearly twenty years. He's managed to father three kids with her but hasn't managed much else in almost a decade. He used to drive a cab but the Public Carriage Office took his badge off him when he developed diabetes. Now he keeps house and watches daytime TV and that's about all he's good for. He's not even particularly good at that by all accounts.

Winnie got into cabbing a while after Paul got out of it. I met her at KPM Knowledge School, where we paired up as call-over partners, learning Blue Book runs together, calling them out to each other. We were both good. I got my badge in two and a half years, she got hers in three. The average is three and a half to four years. And contrary to what idiots like Steve Ambley might say, we did not get our green badges on our backs. There's some drivers out there—mostly the old boys but some of the young ones too— who just can't stand the idea of women driving cabs. I reckon we have to work even harder to get the license than they do. After all, how many men have to put up with being yelled at to get back in the kitchen and have some more babies when they're tootling around on their scooters trying to learn routes.

Winnie and I meet up in the Crocodile Cafe in Pimlico. She drives nights like I do. She puts Sandra, Tommy and Lindy to bed in the evening and then she gets in her cab and goes. She drives all night and arrives home in time to cook breakfast for the kids and take them to school. Then she goes to bed and sleeps into the afternoon. Money's a struggle—she makes good fares but Paul is spendy and brings in nothing himself. And the kids are growing so fast . . . She says she and Paul are happy, that they love each other. But I figure it's easy to pretend you get on with someone when you barely see them. They pass each other on the way to and from the bathroom first thing in the morning and chat over the tea table with the kids around in the early evening, but then she's off to work and he's off to bed. I don't like to ask Winnie about her sex life because I don't suppose she has one.

"Anyway, you're looking a bit swish tonight," she says, seeing I don't want to discuss the tricky subject of Richard's vasectomy any further. "You cabbing in that getup?"

"No, not tonight." Under my jacket I'm wearing a little black number, cut low across the chest; short, strappy and slinky. I have a silver chain around my neck that belonged to my mother. I'm wearing high heels—my new "fuck-me" shoes. I have to kick them off when I'm driving. "Believe it or not," I say to Winnie, "I'm having dinner at Club Gascon with a fare."

"Good God, you're not starting up *another* relationship, are you?"

Winnie is the only person who knows about my star-shaped life. She's a mate and she's solid and I had to tell somebody. In fact, she's fascinated by it—always asking for the latest gossip, getting me to tell her every last detail. She thinks I'm a dysfunctional who won't face up to the really important things in life, but she loves my stories. Vicarious pleasure, that's what it is.

"No way! There's not enough hours in the day. No, this geezer has one of my phones, and he refused to give it back unless I agreed to have dinner with him."

She smiles knowingly, which irritates me.

"Cut it out. This bloke is short and dumpy and he annoys the fuck out of me."

"So why are you dressed up like that?" She looks me up and down.

I wag my finger at her. "You're letting your imagination run away with you, Win. You'd quite fancy a swanky evening out with a bloke yourself, now, wouldn't you?"

She holds up her left hand, waggles her fingers, showing me her wedding ring. "Nice try, Kath, but the dress tells all."

"Yeah, yeah, Winnie, I know. But listen, the reason I'm dressed up is because of where I'm going *after* dinner."

"Where's that then?"

"Never you mind." It's no big secret but it's nice to keep her guessing. A healthy dose of suspense is the perfect revenge for her insinuations.

Stef is back from Spain. He'll be loaded down with gifts and goodies and I'm dying to see him. I've missed him so much over the three weeks he's been away. I didn't realize he was so important to me. Tonight I plan to show him just how important he is . . .

Big Kev's frying up something that stinks like putrid dog and I'm bothered the smell will stick to my clothes. I grab my keys and my wallet, lay a couple of quid down on the table.

"I'd better be off, Win," I say. "Can't keep Club Gascon waiting, now, can I? Drive safe."

"Oh, Kathryn, I nearly forgot—" she says, and I know what's coming—Winnie's wisdom, her statement for the day. She thinks for a moment, knitting her fingers together. Then she prepares to pronounce.

"If life were a form of bed cover . . ." she begins, "Mine would be a candlewick bedspread and yours would be a patchwork quilt."

"Why's that, then, Win?"

"Mine's the candlewick bedspread because it's knackered and frayed, but it's also reliable."

"So why am I the patchwork?"

"Well, your life is cleverly stitched and intricately composed. Each patch has its own involved pattern which is entirely self-contained and seemingly unrelated to any other patch."

"Seemingly?"

She smiles and folds her arms. "That's right. Seemingly. Because beneath all the individual patches there's a carefully planned underlying design. 'S logic, innit."

Getting out of the cab on West Smithfield, just beside the cavernous old meat market, I tread on a loose cracked paving stone, which tilts and clunks. I wobble and my foot turns sideways, hard. I'm falling off my heel and my right ankle twists. I feel the stiletto ripping off my fuck-me shoe. The rain is heavy and I'm standing in a puddle, balancing on my left foot and holding on to a lamppost while I lift my right to survey the damage. The heel has almost completely torn off. It hangs by a few silver threads of adhesive. Sighing, I rip it off completely and put it in my handbag. Those shoes cost me a hundred and thirty quid! I hobble on into Club Gascon, lurching like a drunk.

Club Gascon is low-key swanky. Not like one of those enormous flashy loud joints where they pack you in like cattle, serve you a carnival of confused food stacked up in towers and boot you out precisely two hours later. This place has one square room, spacious but not cavernous, all done out in deep purple, dark wood and mellow alabaster. Everything's discreet and subtle, nothing brash or tacky. And it's proper French—none of your pseudo bullshit. This place has a real identity. I admire Twinkle for selecting it.

A smooth, dark waiter speaks to me in a lovely French accent and takes my coat, then leads me over to where Twinkle is already seated at a corner table. He stands to greet me, notices my shoe and does his best to pretend he hasn't seen it.

"Katerina," he says with a smile, and leans forward to kiss me on the cheek. I don't offer the cheek, however. Instead I extend a hand to shake his. Disconsolate, he plays along.

"What a beautiful necklace," he tries.

"Thanks." I can hear the stiffness in my voice. We sit. The waiter arrives with a bottle of champagne—Bollinger. This is too much. I'd realized the man wants to bed me but hadn't figured he was *that* desperate.

"Just the one glass for me. I'm driving."

I see the disappointment cloud his face. He tries to conceal it. The waiter pours and for a moment we're both transfixed by the glittering gold liquid and the gentle fizzing. He holds his glass out to clink mine. I comply.

"How's Henry?" I begin.

He looks confused, then remembers. "Oh, him. He's fine. Miserable of course, but basically fine. He'll get over it."

"Good." What am I doing here? Why did I go along with this? Even Twinkle isn't looking so sure of what he's up to anymore. He seems a bit tongue-tied and keeps fiddling with his cuffs.

We are eating tiny ducks' hearts on skewers. It's a little like eating very high class sausages on sticks. I am calling the man I inwardly think of as Twinkle Mr. Summer. He is insisting I call him Craig. He has found his tongue now and is firing questions at me relentlessly, giving away little about himself. This makes me uneasy.

"How did you get into cabbing, then? I've never come across a woman cabby as young as you. Isn't it rather an odd career choice?"

"I inherited the cab. Simple as that. My mother died when I was fifteen and I went to live with a neighbor. Maeve. She was a cabby. Drove down from Saffron Walden to London every morning and cabbed all day."

"What about your father?"

"Maeve taught me to drive as soon as I was old enough. I saved up for a used, clapped-out Fiesta. When I left school I came down to London and did crappy office jobs. I hated it. Filing and typing and making coffee for total knobs. I was desperate to get out of working for other people and be my own boss. Used to talk about cabbing with Maeve. She was funny about it—loved it herself but she wanted something else for me. Wanted me to go to university—be a teacher or something. Said cabbing was no real life. Then when I was twenty-four Maeve died suddenly. She had a heart attack in the shower . . ."

I haven't talked about Maeve for quite a while and it makes me feel emotional, almost weepy. I remember how unlike herself she looked in the coffin—ridiculously composed. Maeve was restless in life. Wouldn't sit still even for a moment—said she had to do quite enough sitting when she was in the cab. And there she was in her best blouse with her hands folded across her chest. They'd twisted her mouth into a slight smile, which lent a fake sense of grace to the scene. Her skin was strangely shiny. Like they'd shrink-wrapped her. A far cry from how she must have looked when they found her spread-eagled across the bathroom floor, the pink shower curtain half dragged off its rail and shrouding her, the water still running.

"She left me the cab and that sort of made my mind up for me. I went down to the Public Carriage Office and enrolled in the Knowledge. Took me two and a half years and it's as difficult as any university degree. Got the cab overhauled and reregistered in my name and there you have it. Been driving nearly three years now."

He pops the last duck heart into his mouth and chews. "If the course is that tricky, how come so many thick wankers are out there driving cabs?"

This is all so tedious. People have a weird thing about cabbing. Any minute now he's going to ask me if I think *he* could do it. "Listen, mate, there are wankers in every job. Less than twenty percent of the people who start studying for the Knowledge actually end up getting their green badges. You have to learn everything that lies in a six-mile radius around Charing Cross. There's over four hundred routes in the Blue Book, plus places' of interest—*thousands* of them, which can be pretty much anything from strip joints to churches—plus suburban routes . . . They can ask you about anything they like up at the Carriage Office, and you've got to know it. The examiners sit in these poky little rooms off this long corridor. The corridor of fear, the cabbies call it, and with good reason too."

"So do you reckon *I* could do it, then?"

Does he honestly think he's the first person to ask me this? "If you want to let yourself in for three to five years of utter hell—yes. If you want to dream about maps of London every night and wake up on the morning of one of your Carriage Office Appearances panicking because you can't remember whether you take the A404 when you're going from Paddington to Wembley, or whether it's one-way round Whetstone High Road—then yes, you can do the Knowledge. It's an obsession, Craig. It has to be or you'll never get through it."

"Wow! And can you remember it all now?"

"Nah, course not. You remember what you need to know. The rest is spam."

He's raising one eyebrow. "And does all that spam leave you time for a life, Katerina?"

"Oh yes. I have time for five lives."

He chuckles. I snigger. The waiter brings the next course. "Grilled foie gras with grapes on slate," the menu said. That's exactly what it is. Foie gras served up on a piece of slate.

❊   ❊   ❊

We're on to a casserole of wild cêpes and I'm developing a theory about Craig Twinkle Summer. The guy's obviously loaded: The flat in Chelsea Harbour, the fact that the waiters at this pricey restaurant know him by name, the suit he's wearing—Gucci if I'm not mistaken; the chunky gold ring on the little finger of his left hand; the Rolex on his wrist . . .

A man with money like that—regardless of the fact that he's not exactly model material—can have virtually any woman he wants. So why the hell does he bother to coax me—a *cabby*, for God's sake, who clearly doesn't even fancy him, into going on a date?

"You're a very bored man, aren't you, Craig?" I say, noticing that he's topped up my glass again. "You're sick of all those pretty little blonde girls from Surrey, those accomplished older women in PR who know about wine and speak fluent French. You didn't care that your wife found out about your girlfriend and your girlfriend found out about your wife. You didn't care because you were bored to death of both of them."

His mouth is tightening. The twinkle in his eye is more of a glitter at this moment.

"You meet someone like me and you think, she's different. She's a bit of rough and she's a loner and she'd punch your lights out if you crossed her. You liked that. It amused you. That's why we're here, isn't it? That's why you held my phone to ransom."

I've got to him. He looks down at the mess of mushrooms on his dinner plate and stays silent for a few seconds. Then his face comes up again and he speaks.

"We're here because you have eyes that are the color of the first bluebells of spring, because your hair is soft and thick and the sight of it makes me want to bury my face in it and breathe its scent. We're here because after you left my flat that night I couldn't get you out of my head and I wanted to see you again. And because when I found your phone lying on my couch I thought it was a sign. I thought I was meant to have a chance with you."

He reaches into his inside jacket pocket and pulls out my

phone. He lays it on the table. "I'm sorry you feel I forced you to come here against your will. That was never my intention."

His eyes are full of hurt and sadness. I hadn't meant to do this to him. What did I *do*?

I try to reverse. "Listen, Twink—Craig—I didn't mean anything by what I said, OK? I was just pissing about. Playing a game. We were having a laugh, weren't we? *Weren't* we?"

He's getting out his wallet. Counting three fifties onto the table. "That should be enough to cover the bill . . ."

"Can't you take a joke?" I'm genuinely stricken now.

He freezes, wallet still open. He holds my gaze and gives a little sigh. He looks as though he might actually cry.

"Ha! Gotcha!" he says suddenly. He's twinkling ferociously and showing me a set of uneven gappy teeth in his monkey grin.

"You . . . bastard." But I'm smiling with him.

5

I'M back in the cab, on my way to Stef's place. I'm in a good mood and I'm tapping the steering wheel and singing along with the radio—Tammy Wynette wailing "Stand by Your Man." Classic number from the Queen of Tragedy who smiled through her tears and cried through her smiles.

I have to acknowledge that I enjoyed the meal with Twinkle. The man has a kind of style—taking me to a classy restaurant, wining and dining me, pulling that joke that neatly undercut me just when I was getting overly cocky. And he gave very little away: I have no idea what he does for a living, whether he has kids, what his interests or hobbies are, or pretty much anything else. We talked about me the whole time. He asked me questions and I answered them. Any question I asked him was twisted around and turned back at me. Yep, he's a clever one, and that's rare. He was perfectly courteous too—holding up my jacket for me to slip into, taking my arm in the street so that I could keep my balance in spite of my heelless shoe, and not making a big deal out of his own chivalry like most men would. And to my great relief he didn't try it on—he didn't ask me to come back to his place or attempt to stick his tongue down my throat in the street. I always expect that men who buy you dinner will want something in return, but not him. I reckon he just thought an evening with me might amuse him. He didn't even ask to see me again. Which suits me just fine.

The rain has stopped by the time I drive past Liverpool Street Station but the sky has that thick, impenetrable look to it. You can't see the stars or the moon. The air is stale and everything is close and claustrophobic. It's like someone's stuck the whole of London in a Tupperware box and then put the lid on. I turn into Brick Lane, where Stef lives. Spitalfields, where the City meets the East End, only now they call it Banglatown in recognition of its large Bangladeshi community. They put banners up in the street to celebrate the change of name, and then in Spring '99 that fascist nutter came and nail-bombed it. Stef's flat is down the other end of the street from where the bomb went off. He and his flatmates barely heard it but they were evacuated for thirty-six hours all the same. When the police came round to turf them out, Stef's flatmate Jimmy was terrified they'd discover all the VCRs he had stacked up in his bedroom and arrest him, but they had bigger things to worry about.

I pull up outside Stef's place and park. I hate leaving the cab out here. This area may have become trendy as the hip young artists and filmmakers came trailing in after Gilbert and George and moved into those big old houses with the shutters in the cobbled side streets—Fournier Street and Fashion Street—but here on Brick Lane you're still on the front line. This place is rife with nutters screaming into the night, whores hanging out on street corners, scum staggering out of the curry houses to scuffle in the gutters. Stef's flat got burgled last summer by two men who crawled along the rooftops of the whole street, crowbaring the skylights open and sliding in. Nothing has actually happened to my cab when I've left it here, but it's surely only a matter of time.

A couple of squirts of breath freshener and I'm out on the pavement locking the cab and breathing in the heady potpourri of Balti, Masala, Korma and Dansak that permanently hangs in the air. A waiter is coming out of one of the curry houses to harangue me, menu in hand, but I wave him away and head toward the door of 134A, the flat immediately above Le Taj, Brick Lane's self-consciously hip, purple-and-gold-clad curry brasserie. I ring the bell.

"Hello?" It's Stef's voice in the intercom.

"It's me."

"K! Honey . . ."

The buzzer goes and I push the door open and climb the stairs.

I'm in his arms and we're leaning against the wall, kissing. His eyes stay open while we kiss. I breathe in his scent that I love so much—the scent of his skin, his neck, his hair. It's hard to explain the smell—it's a bit like the smell when you open a new bottle of ink. I've missed it. I reach up to ruffle his floppy blond mop and we come apart as he bats me off. He hates it when I mess with his hair.

"K—you look . . ."

"Yeah, I know. You should see what I've got on underneath." I take his hand to lead him up the stairs to the second floor where his bedroom is but he pulls away.

"Cheeky! Turning up here at—what is it—ten forty-five when dinner's nearly ruined and trying to get me in the sack straight off?"

Oh, God. He's cooked. I can smell it now, wafting from the kitchen. Smells like . . . it smells like roast chicken. *Jesus*. He's all dimply and pleased with himself. And this is *my* fault. I'm wishing now that I hadn't given him a hard time about not cooking for me just before he went away.

"Babe, it's been three weeks. *Three weeks* with no sex. I've been climbing walls. I've been doing . . . unspeakable things."

"I bet you have." His dimples are deepening. He blows hair out of his eyes. "But I've been slaving away over a hot stove for hours. Come on." And he's off to the kitchen, leaving me to follow. I genuinely don't think I could manage a single mouthful.

There are a whole load of boxes stacked in a tower in the hallway. They are about the size of shoe boxes and they are all identical.

"What's all this stuff?" I ask.

"Oh, you know. Jimmy and Eddie. Nothing to do with me," he calls from the kitchen.

"Yeah, but what's inside?" I'm peering at the stack.

"Furbies. Those interactive cuddly toys. You can teach them to speak and all that shit. Old stock. Three hundred of them."

Old stock, my arse. But I'm saying nothing. It's not my business. Not unless Stef is involved.

"Drink?" He holds out a glass of red wine as I come into the kitchen. "That is if you haven't had enough already."

"What makes you think I've been drinking?"

He gives me a look. It's his "knowing" look, but it's cute. Stef is unbelievably cute in that ex-public-schoolboy way of his. It's even cute that he talks in that fake "street" accent. Ridiculous but cute. Jimmy does the same thing but it isn't attractive in him. Obsessed with gangsters, the pair of them. Too much Martin Scorsese at too impressionable an age. Eddie, on the other hand, doesn't need to put on an accent. He's the real thing and is consequently more subtle. I worry about Eddie—the effect he's having on Stef.

I sit down at the wobbly table while Stef dons his apron like a proper little hausfrau, pours boiling water onto some green beans in a pan and switches the heat on. Then he joins me at the table.

"How was Spain?" I ask. "Love the tan."

"Yeah, not bad is it?" He shows me a deep brown arm covered in pretty golden hairs. "What do you reckon to the wine?"

I take a sip. "It's OK."

"Only OK?"

I sip again. What does he want from me? I don't know much about wine. "It's good. Fruity."

He grins and pushes the bottle across the table toward me. He seems to want me to read the label so I do. "Jose Maria Marquez, 1996, Rioja."

"How much would you pay for this?" he asks.

I'm tiring of this game. "Oh, Stef, I don't know. Six quid? Seven?"

His smile gets bigger. "Excellent," he says. "This wine retails at £5.99 in the airports and ferry terminals. £6.99 inland."

"So?"

Stef pushes another open bottle across the table, a bottle without a label. He reaches for a second glass and pours me some. "Now taste this one."

I try the second wine. I can't taste the difference. "If I didn't know any better I'd think you'd just spent three weeks on a wine-tasting course."

He's becoming impatient with me. "So what do you think of this one?"

"Sorry to disappoint you, but it tastes the same to me."

"Excellent!" he says, clearly delighted. "*Respect*. This one's just a Spanish table wine. Retails at £2.50 in the shops, £1.50 in the airports and ferry terminals."

"Well, I'm glad you're so happy that I can't taste the difference between good and bad wine, Steven." I call him Steven on purpose to annoy him. It's his real name. Steven Moore became Stefan Muchowski a couple of years ago for no good reason. He just wants a romantic alias, I guess. I didn't know he used a fake name until I saw the real one in his passport when he was packing to go to Spain. Twattish of him, I know, but Stef is *so* endearing. Beneath all the bravado he's just a sweetie.

"Not at all, K, not at all. You're cool." He puts the two bottles next to each other. "They're actually both the same stuff."

"But you said—"

"I know what I said. Fact is, Jose Maria Marquez Rioja 1996 is worth six to seven quid a bottle, and that's just what people are going to pay for this Spanish table wine worth a maximum of two pound fifty which happens to carry the Marquez label."

"Stef, are you saying—"

"It's all in the label, K. That's how people choose wine—by the label. They have no idea whether the wine inside is any good." He's excited. His beans are boiling over and he hasn't even noticed. "Did you know that at least a quarter of the wine we buy in the shops is slightly corked? Well, did you?"

"No, I didn't."

"But people don't know what to expect from the taste. They know fuck all about wine and so they drink it anyway. They believe the *label*."

Now I understand what this trip to Spain was all about, why he had to fix it up at such short notice. I thought it was funny that he hadn't mentioned this "best mate" in Madrid before.

"Just how big is this racket, Stef? What exactly have you got yourself into?"

I'm sitting in Stef's kitchen trying to eat chicken. He's given me a huge portion—a leg and some breast. He's given me seven roast potatoes—*seven*. He's given me a whole stack of green beans, so many they threaten to topple off the side of the plate. And he's smothered the lot in a thick pool of gravy. He's telling me that the secret to the taste is the tarragon garlic butter he smothered all over the chicken's breast before he put it in the oven. I'm smiling outwardly while trying to blot out thoughts of the food I have already eaten; ducks' hearts, foie gras (on slate), casserole of wild cêpes, cappuccino of black pudding and lobster bisque, scallops in a cream sauce, blackberries and red currants in champagne jelly. Tiny portions but somehow they've added up to a mountain in my stomach. I'm slicing away the smallest sliver of chicken and bracing myself to put it in my mouth—it isn't just the fact of more food, it's the idea of dealing with another whole set of flavors—as Stef refills my glass with cheap Spanish table wine masquerading as Jose Maria Marquez 1996 Rioja and tells me how he is the architect of this highly illegal scheme. It was his "baby," and he is the connection between the man with the labels, the man with the lorry, the man with the cheap table wine and all the rest of them. And he thinks he isn't taking any risks himself—his bunch of mad Spaniards are the foot soldiers out front while he lounges around in his Brick Lane flat with a roast chicken, three hundred dodgy Furbies and a cabby girlfriend five years his senior whose once-admired physique is about to disappear beneath a vat of gravy and a ton of nouvelle cuisine.

All the while Stef is telling me about the wine scam I am watching his face: the light in his pale blue eyes, the shadows beneath them from lack of sleep—all that partying, those long coked-up nights that become days and then nights again; the pretty blond lashes that give him the innocent look of a child. I'm watching the movements of his sensual mouth, the dimples appearing and disappearing deep in his cheeks. And I'm thinking, how can I just sit back and let this magical boy ruin his life? For Stef is magical. He has a special something. How can I explain it? He's good in bed, of course, but that goes without saying. And he has amazing hands—a way of touching you that is quite out of the ordinary. He's a great listener, too—he remembers everything I tell him and he doesn't judge me. He knows instinctively when something is wrong. Like now.

"K, what's up? You've hardly touched your food."

I'm trying to force down another mouthful of potato. I've made almost no impact on the roasted landscape on my plate except to remold it—pushing it around and shaping it into the smallest possible pile.

"I'm worried about you, Stef."

"Worried? Why?"

"I think you're getting in over your head with this one. I don't want to see you end up in prison."

"Yeah, K, nice one. I'll just stay home like a good boy and cook chicken, shall I?" His dimples have vanished. He drops his fork with a clatter on his empty plate and gets up to dump it in the sink.

"Stef, think about this rationally. If the Spanish guys get caught, they'll pin it on you. They'll be out to save their own skins, won't they? Stands to reason."

"Well, I'll just have to make sure they don't get caught then, won't I." Stef reaches for a packet of cigarettes at the end of the table. "Is that really all you're going to eat after all the time I spent cooking?"

"Sorry." I lay my cutlery down. "I guess I've lost my appetite."

We're interrupted by the noisy arrival of Jimmy and Eddie, who come crashing up the stairs in a flurry of laughter and boozed-up banter, kissing me on both cheeks with beery breath, slapping high five with Stef and diving on the remains of the chickens. Within minutes Eddie's skinning up and giving me sneaky sidelong smiles that show his gold tooth, while Jimmy is demanding the full story of the wine scam from Stef, and drawling:

"You're the man, Stef. You're the *man*."

An hour later they're well into the spliffs, someone's opened a bottle of whiskey and the cards have come out. I usually like poker but not tonight.

"Sorry, K," says Stef, with a half shrug. "First night back and all that. Can't let the boys down, now, can I?"

"Don't worry about it. I'm crashing. See you later."

He pinches my bum as I squeeze past him and winks at me before turning to his cards. "You're a doll, K," he says.

Yeah, right.

The color. All around me, pushing in on me, blinding me. I'm spinning, reaching and groping into empty space, trying to find the place where the color ends and the world begins but there is no end—no beginning. I can't breathe—the color is filling the air, using up the oxygen. What *is* it? Not solid or liquid or gas, just color. A color that isn't in the spectrum, a color that I cannot describe.

I feel myself lurch and my back goes into spasm. My eyes spring open and I know I'm awake but still there is only the color, waiting for me behind the darkness. Where the fuck am I?

"K? K, it's all right. You're safe. It's Stef, yeah? Stef."

The lamp goes on and the color disappears. I see Stef's room: The old hat stand in the corner, the stereo system with its massive black speakers, the desk and computer, the unpacked rucksack, the mess of underpants, dirty shirts and empty condom packets on the floor. Stef's arms go around me and he pulls my head to rest on his chest. The golden chest hairs tickle my nostrils. He smells of smoke but behind the smoke is that heady scent of fresh ink. I am drenched in sweat and my heart is pounding.

"Relax, babe. You're here with me. It's OK."

I try to find my voice. "It was that dream again, Stef. The one I told you about. The color."

"I know." He strokes my head with his magic fingers.

We lie together like this for a long time. He soothes and strokes and gradually my heart slows to normal. I begin to unwind.

"I've got a present for you," he says, just as I'm drifting off.

"A present?"

He wriggles out and goes scrambling over the floorboards to the rucksack. Undoes the straps and delves inside, pulling out crumpled T-shirts and socks, and then, finally, a plastic bag, which he hands over.

I feel a childish excitement as I reach into the bag. What has he got for me?

It's a doll, a plastic flamenco gypsy doll, in a swirling red and gold dress. Castanets in her hand, comb in her hair.

I feel tears coming. "You remembered . . ."

"Of course I did." He's grinning and his floppy hair is hanging in his eyes.

I'd forgotten that I told him about the foreign dolls I collected as a child. I had a glass-fronted cabinet in my room crammed with them. French, German, Italian, Belgian, Yugoslavian . . . you name it. Plastic smiling faces and national costume. I don't know what's happened to my doll collection—whether my father's thrown them out or whether they're still there in my old room, along with all my other childhood toys.

I open the clear plastic box and take out the doll. She's standing on a little wooden plinth, and she's wearing red high-heeled shoes. I lift her skirts like I always used to when I got new dolls to see if she's wearing knickers. She has little white bikini briefs.

"Thank you." I turn to kiss him.

"Pleasure. Now you lie down and relax. I picked up some lovely almond oil in Spain and I'm going to give you the massage of your life."

6

Friday morning. Good gym session. It's no wonder I was having nightmares after all that food! I nearly started the day by driving over to Jonny's and I got within sight of the Elephant before deciding that was the *last* thing I needed this morning and rerouting to Balham. It was the right decision, even if I did have to tell some obnoxious twat to get off the treadmill—he'd been on there for a full forty minutes in spite of a sign on the wall right in front of his face saying you should only be on the cardiovascular machines for twenty maximum. He pretended not to know what "cardiovascular" meant but I wasn't having any of it.

As I pounded the belt and the incline eased down to zero, I let my thoughts settle on Stef—his silky back, his coat hanger shoulders, his cheeky face. That little fucker is going to wake up one morning and find himself in a heap of shit that no amount of boyish charm is going to get him out of. And I don't want to be around to watch. Much as I love him.

I love them all. That's the trouble. Stef's hunger for life and magic hands, Joel's sweet mouth and touching helplessness, Amy's crazy cocktail of neediness and unpredictability, Richard's soothing solidity and selflessness, Jonny's . . . well, Jonny's tragedy, I guess. That's why I've got a toothbrush in six different bathrooms around London. That's why I've got five mobile phones, bags under my eyes and a gigantic overdraft. That's why I wake up every morning in a state of total confusion and disorientation. I never know where I am but I know I'm not home.

I nip back to the flat to shower and change. I can't think straight in that place with all the bloody boxes everywhere. Bagels. Proper bagels baked in a proper bagel oven from the twenty-four-hour bakery near Stef's place. I picked them up on the way home and now I stick them under the grill and smother them in cream cheese. Check the phones for messages:

Pink phone—Amy: "Kathy, we've got to talk. What is the *matter* with you? Call me."

Blue phone—Joel: "Hey, Kat. Started my new job today. Not bad except for this girl with head lice. *Minging*. When you coming over?"

Yellow phone—Stef: "Sugar pie, honey bunch."

Red phone—Jonny: Nothing.

Green phone—Richard: "Hi, Kitty. I've got someone here who wants to speak to you . . ."

Dotty: "Kits, are you coming to see us? Bye."

I'm sitting with Richard and Dotty in the Big Top of Zippo's Circus, waiting for the show to begin. It's the circus's first day in Finsbury Park and it's filling up with people. We have ringside seats—the best. A clown is spinning plastic plates on sticks in the gangway and Dotty wants one. Instead she is given an ice cream in a plastic tub.

"Spoon, Daddy. I want a spoon."

"Magic word, Dotty?" prompts Richard.

"Abracadabra," says Dotty, without hesitating.

We giggle and she preens. She knows exactly what she's doing, that one.

I put my hands in my pockets. There's a piece of paper in the right one. I pull it out to see what it is. It's that letter from my father.

A large woman with three kids is trying to get past us and we have to stand up and step out into the aisle to let her by. I hold Dotty's ice cream for her. Richard looks across at me and catches my eye. I feel heat in my cheeks. I'm blushing even though I'm not a blusher. He smiles and I blush even more.

"Kits, can I have a hat?"

She's got brown eyes. Like her father's but bigger. She's got his nose, too—turns up at the end just a little. Her dark curls must come from her mother. Actually her hair's a bit like mine. Jesus, all these people must think she's *mine*.

We sit down again. There isn't enough space for my knees and I have to sit sideways. Dotty is swinging her legs. She's got mud on her favorite patent leather shoes.

"Sit nicely, Dotty," says Richard.

Sit *nicely*. What planet does he come from? She's bored, waiting for the show to start. She wants acrobats and horses and ringmasters. So do I.

"What have you been up to, then?" asks Richard.

"Nothing!"

He flinches and I realize too late that he was only making conversation.

"Just, you know, driving. Working."

"Oh. Right."

"Hat, Daddy!"

Thank God Dotty's here. Talk about stress—you'd need a hacksaw to cut through the tension between us. Dotty's sitting in the middle so he can't whisper to me. He can't pester me about our little discussion last week that's clearly still gnawing away at him. He's rubbing his forehead, pressing his temples as though he has a headache in just the place where his sandy hair is beginning to recede.

The man with the Zippo's hats and sticks that glow in the dark is now standing in front of us and we can't ignore him any longer.

"Do you mind if I . . . ?" I ask Richard, reaching into my jacket for my wallet.

He waves acquiescence, and Dotty claps her hands together in excitement. I pay the man and relinquish the goods to her sticky, grabbing fingers. I don't remember ever going to the circus with my parents. I don't suppose my father would have approved of circuses. Too much like fun—no stale, fusty school hall odor, no hymns, no sermon.

"What?"

Richard's saying something to me but I didn't quite catch it. "I said Jemima called me yesterday."

This time he gets my attention. Jemima is Dotty's mother. "What did she want?"

"Just to know how Dotty is." But he looks uncertain.

"She hasn't been bothered about how Dotty is before, has she?"

He looks down at his little girl. She's waving her stick around and giggling. "No," he says. "No, she hasn't. I can't help thinking she's up to something."

"You don't suppose she wants to take her, do you?"

He shakes his head, but there's a vagueness in his response. He puts a finger to his lips to indicate that we should watch what we say in front of the little one. Jemima has been living in Paris with another man for three of Dotty's nearly four years and hasn't seen her in all that time, or indeed expressed any desire to see her. I glimpse the fear in Richard's face—a certain tightness in his mouth, an edginess in the way he's rubbing at his forehead. This fear has probably been lurking somewhere inside him ever since she left. Now it's bubbling up. He seems suddenly small, huddling inside his overcoat, nestling up close to his daughter and hunching over in that way he often does, all lousy posture and worry. I reach over and stroke his warm cheek. He smiles at me.

The drum rolls, the band strikes up a cheerful friendly number and as the ringmaster strides out—clad in a black and white Pierrot costume complete with a shining silver tear pasted onto his cheek—a searchlight flashes around the faces of the audience, illuminating them, moonlike, for just a second, and I jolt and panic. There is a familiar face over on the other side of the ring. It's half hidden among the crowd but distinctive, nonetheless. It isn't, is it? . . . The light was on that face for barely an eye blink—I must be mistaken. And yet I'm left feeling uneasy as a girl in a spangly yellow costume comes dancing into the ring and shimmies up a rope made from silk scarves, swinging around and turning upside down, her gleaming white smile never once slipping.

It's still light and we're heading across the grass to the car through the heavy odor of hot dogs. Richard has his arm around me and Dotty is chirping and chattering. Her favorite was the performing dog—no, it was the tightrope walkers—no, the clowns throwing water over each other. I'm trying to conceal my disappointment that there were no lions, elephants or chimps. I suppose I should be glad that circuses don't go in for all that cruel caging and drug- ging of wild beasts anymore but selfishly I would have liked a bit more danger in this show; the crack of the whip, the glimpse of sharp teeth and cavernous insides. Dotty's final verdict on the best bit is that it was when her daddy got dragged out of the audience and made to participate in a clowning sketch, along with three other daddies. Her daddy was the real star of the show. Isn't he always?

His arm tightens around my waist in a loving sort of squeeze. I squeeze him back.

"Do you fancy Chinese, then?" he's saying.

"McDonald's, McDonald's!" squeaks Dotty, flashing her bril- liant smile. The girl is learning fast.

And, Christ, there she is again! She's only a little way ahead of us. She's wearing her fake Dalmatian jacket and her Paul Smith jeans. If she turned her head, she'd see me, cozying along with a strange man and a small child, playing at mummies and daddies.

"Fuck!" I stop dead in my tracks.

"Kitty, what's wrong?"

My mind is blank. My worlds are colliding.

"Kitty?"

And who is the girl? Who is Amy linking arms with? They're getting further ahead, approaching the line of trees. They seem to be laughing together. Short hair and a denim jacket—is it Cheryl? No, doesn't look like Cheryl. Shit, I shouldn't be staring. What if she turns around . . .

"Kitty, what is the matter with you?" He's grabbing both my shoulders, staring earnestly into my panic-stricken face. Dotty is skipping in rings around us, casting spells.

Say something. Anything. "Keys. I've lost my car keys. I think they must have fallen out of my pocket in the tent."

"I'll go back and take a look," he says, all chivalry. "You stay here with Dotty."

"No. It's all right. I'll go." And I'm off, running back to the Big Top. Undiscovered.

This has never happened before. I don't like it.

We've put Dotty to bed and I'm drinking tea in Richard's kitchen at his lovely old table while he unloads the dishwasher. I can feel the Big Mac lying like a lump of granite in my stomach. I'm thinking about Finsbury Park. I shouldn't go there with Richard again. Or with Amy.

"Really took me back," Richard is saying, as he clatters the plates. "That smell of straw and dung. The candy floss, the plastic seats. Only it's on a different scale now. Circuses used to be enormous, the tightrope walkers were *way* up there in the heavens. It felt really small in there, don't you think? I'd love to see it through Dotty's eyes, to experience what she experienced tonight. I'd love to be a child again, wouldn't you?"

"God no!" The trouble with Finsbury Park is that it lies roughly halfway between Islington and Crouch End, a sort of no-man's-land in the middle of Amy and Richard.

"Were you unhappy, then, as a child?"

"Isn't everybody? You can't mean to tell me you were blissfully and continuously happy from the day you popped out till the moment you blew out your eighteen candles."

"You know what I mean."

Come to think of it, there are a whole load of no-man's-lands scattered around London. I might easily brush past Jonny while walking out of London Bridge tube station with Stef. I could be strolling along the towpath of Grand Union Canal one Sunday morning with Amy when Stef shoots by on his bike. And why should the danger be restricted to their immediate localities? Joel might be wandering aimlessly out of a Covent Garden dance studio when Amy nips into a neighboring bar for a gin and tonic, Richard and Dotty stop off in the Neal's Yard Dairy for organic cheese, Stef emerges from Belgo's full of Belgian beer and venison sausages, only to collide with a drunken Jonny who takes a random swing at him and then passes out on the pavement.

I hear the chair scrape on the quarry-tiled floor and he's sitting down next to me. He takes my hand and holds it in his.

"Kitty, you're miles away. You have been all day."

"I'm sorry." I try to smile. His hand is warm. "I did enjoy it, you know. The circus."

"Will you stay tonight?"

I disengage my hand, reach for my mug. The tea is cold.

"I'd like you to stay."

"What about what you said before?"

"Never mind that. I want you to stay." His eyes are sad. He's gazing out of the window with a wistful yearning look.

"I can't. I have to work tonight. I can't afford not to."

He lets my hand go and returns to the dishwasher with a sigh.

"Don't be angry with me."

"I'm *not*, for Christ's sake!" He bangs a cupboard door.

"I'm not ready for that kind of commitment, Richard. I'd love to say I am, but I'm not. I know it wouldn't work if I moved in. It's too soon . . . it wouldn't be fair on you. Or Dotty for that matter."

"Hey, look at this." He's twirling a long wooden spoon like a majorette's baton. Then he gets his fingers all mangled and drops it. He bends to pick it up and his face is serious. "Don't worry, Kitty. We don't have to have this conversation again. I've got the message, all right? I don't like it but I've got my head around it now. No more pressure."

This is quite a turnaround from the other day when he told me he didn't want me spending any more nights with him unless I agreed to move in. He said it was like when you're really hungry and someone keeps offering you crumbs instead of the whole cake. I replied that you can't have your cake and eat it too, which was supposed to make him laugh but didn't.

"Listen, I'd better be going." I'm getting to my feet yet lingering on. This kitchen is probably my favorite room in the world.

And then he's up close to me and I feel his hot breath on my neck. I'm lying down on my back on my favorite table and unbuttoning my combats, and he's climbing on top of me, getting his cock out. That's the other thing about Richard. He's got a big cock and he knows how to use it.

7

THE red phone. Jonny.

"Katy?"

"Jonny, where've you been? You've been missing for days and fucking days."

"Don't start on me. My head hurts."

"Look, I'm driving, all right? I'll call you later. Don't bloody disappear again." It's true. I'm on my way down Wood Lane and there are two sozzled BBC office girls in the back of my cab.

"Come over, Katy. Come see me."

It's only 9:30 and I still have a whole night of serious earning in front of me. What's more, I can smell Richard on my skin. This boy really picks his moments.

"Katy?"

"I can't, Jonny. Look, I'll call you in a bit, OK? I'm driving."

"You've got to come. *Please* come." That awful wheedling tone. Like a five-year-old who wants his mummy.

In the back of the car one of the girls is telling the other one that a sighting of Jeremy Paxman is really not so rare—nor yet a sighting of French and Saunders, and that she'll soon tire of star-spotting in the TV Centre bar, dropping in incidentally that she once saw Michael Caine strolling down a corridor.

"Katy, I'm getting one of my headaches. The bad ones."

"I said I'll call you later, Jonny. I'm in the middle of a job."

I switch the phone off. We're now on the Westway, possibly my least favorite road in London. Back when I was earning my license, I used to have nightmares about gray ribbons twisting in and out of each other, ribbons with no beginning and no end. At the heart of those dreams was the Westway. Until I began dreaming of the color, those were my worst ever nightmares.

"I told him I wasn't having any of it," one of the girls in the back is saying. "Not while he's still with *her*. I mean, what the bloody hell does he think I am?"

"So what did you do then?" asks the other.

"Shagged him, didn't I."

They break into spluttering wet giggles. The girl who did the shagging loses control and almost slips off the seat onto the floor, which makes them both laugh all the more. The other one has mascara streaked across her pale left cheek. She stops giggling very suddenly and beneath the merriment her eyes are sad. She reminds me of the Pierrot ringmaster at Zippo's.

"I'm not sleeping with him again, though. He's a right bastard thinking he can have it all ways."

She catches my eye in the driving mirror, and I look away, embarrassed. Stop listening and bury myself in my own messy love life.

Jonny.

He appeared in my cab one windy November night, three years ago. I was driving past King's Cross when I saw this long dark streak being buffeted along by the wind, coat flapping, face buried in collar, arm stuck out straight like a broom handle once he'd spotted the orange light. I pulled over and he asked me to drive him to Elephant. It was late—maybe 4 A.M., maybe later. I was living in Peckham, and Elephant was on my way home. I told him to hop in.

He didn't try to talk to me. Just sat and gazed out the window. Suited me. I was turning a lot of things over in my mind at the time. Until I saw his face illuminated for a second by a street light. Until I saw the scars.

His face was a mess of them. Jagged lines across his right cheek, a bunching of the skin by his right eye, which was all but closed. Skin grafts. He wore his black hair longish and shaggy, flopping forward—perhaps to conceal the worst of the damage. His left side was clearer.

Poor bastard, I thought. I wonder what happened to him.

I remember him catching me looking. His face was angry. I guessed the accident or whatever was recent. He hadn't grown used to being stared at.

And suddenly I plunged. One second I was gazing at those tortured red eyes in my rearview mirror and the next I was somewhere else. At school, in the hall, surrounded by screaming girls, pressed up against my classmates, fighting for a clear view of the boys on the stage. Jostling for position, trying to get as close as I could to the gorgeous singer.

It couldn't be—could it?

They called themselves The Capones. Four of them, like The Beatles. Drums, two guitars and bass. The singer also played lead guitar—an electric-blue Fender Stratocaster copy. He was the driving force, the real talent. They did covers, mostly: Duran Duran's "Planet Earth," The Police's "Roxanne," The Undertones' "Teenage Kicks." But they had a few of their own songs too. "Chocker Later," "Maddy," "Please Mrs. Sinclair," and my favorite: a doleful love song called "Weeping Willow." They made a demo on somebody's four-track and sold copies to the school kids. I listened to it until the tape wore out, then bought another.

Sixth-form boys are always glamorous in the eyes of first-year girls. They have the bodies of fully grown men and are thrillingly out of reach—but these boys were more than that. Mobs of girls followed them around at lunchtime, giggling and blushing if they gave us a smile. We'd sneak into the forbidden sixth-form common room to leave love letters in their lockers. We'd hang around by the goalmouths if they played football, we'd wish all manner of horrible painful deaths on their girlfriends. These boys were heroes and the biggest hero was the singer.

It was him. Jonny Jordan, the front man of The Capones, the boy I'd longed and screamed for fifteen years earlier, and for whom I had never even existed. He was here in the back of my cab, his once clear skin maimed and scarred almost beyond recognition. Almost . . .

I felt tears coming. It was all I could do to keep control of the wheel, but somehow I did. We were crossing Blackfriars Bridge and London was spread out to either side of us, twinkling and magical, casting glittering reflections in the water.

"It's beautiful, isn't it?" My voice was emotional and unsteady.

"What?"

"The bridge. The river. These are the moments when I love my job."

"Not a patch on Brooklyn Bridge," came his voice—harder than it once was. Brittle. "The way Manhattan looks in the dark. Makes your heart go *bang*."

"I've never been to New York."

"I lived there for a while," he said.

"Did you like it?"

He gave a kind of sneer. "I should never have come back."

All I could see in my mind was the boy, Jonny, playing that electric-blue guitar. He wanted the world—he could have opened his mouth and swallowed it whole. Now it was more as though the world had eaten him—or had a good chew, sucked away all the sweetness and then spat out the bones and the gristle. He leaned his head back against the seat. I glimpsed his neck, a tuft of chest hair at the V of his T-shirt. The scarring went all the way down the neck. God, was his whole body in that state?

We drove on in silence down London Road and out past the lurid pink Elephant and Castle shopping center.

"Where exactly do you want?" I asked him.

"Appleton Street."

I took the New Kent Road. The wind had upturned rubbish bins and refuse was blowing across the road, making it look even more wrecked than usual. I hate this pocket of London; it stinks of misery. I turned into Appleton Street; all squat fifties council blocks, poky staircase, outside walkways and boarded-up windows.

"This it?"

"Yep."

"Where shall I stop?"

"Anywhere. Here." He sniffed.

I pulled up behind a knackered white transit van, my arms heavy with melancholy. Fact was, I didn't want him to leave, to disappear again. I wanted to ask him about his scars, about his music, his life. I wanted to tell him about my soured teenage years, about my mother . . . But I knew I couldn't. There was something impenetrable about him. His battered face warned against attempts at intimacy. Trying to get close to him would be like nestling up to sandpaper. I would have to find another way.

"Scuse me." He was knocking on the Perspex half of the screen, holding out a tenner and a fiver. "Is there any particular reason why we're just sitting here?"

"Sorry. Got things on my mind." I took the fifteen quid. I could sense him waiting for me to unlock the doors but I didn't want to. Another few seconds passed.

"What's your problem? Are you going to let me out or what?"

I twisted around to look at him—at his red rage-filled eyes, his barbed-wire skin. "I was wondering," I began, and trailed off.

"What?"

And what exactly *was* I wondering? "I was wondering . . . if you'd like a blow job."

"If I'd *what*?"

Shit. Why did I *say* that? I twisted back to the front and released the door lock.

But he didn't move. "Are you a whore? Is this some weird way of soliciting?"

"I'm not a whore. I just . . . . I find you attractive."

He made a noise, not quite a laugh, not quite a snort. "You're sick or something."

This was enough, even for me. My face was hot with humiliation. "All right, so I'm sick. Please get out of my cab."

He fell silent. I could sense him looking at me.

"I said get out of my cab!"

I heard the door open but I didn't turn around. Then it

slammed. Sounds of his shoes on the pavement, walking away. I started the engine.

A knock on the window to my left. He was there, bending down, staring at me. He raised his eyebrows, quizzically. "Were you serious?"

"I don't know."

"Do you want to come in for a coffee?"

"Yes."

Kilburn. Or probably Hampstead if you asked the opinion of a real estate agent. I drop the girls off outside a tall Victorian terraced house in Dynham Road. There's a party going on inside—three guys are making their way up the front path carrying Threshers bags. The girls don't have a bottle—well, I guess they've had enough already. I watch them flounce in as I fumble for the red phone. There's a woman in a trouser suit on the step air-kissing everyone. If I'm not mistaken she doesn't look too pleased to see the girls.

I check the messages on the red phone. Jonny has called twice; once to beg me to come over, once to tell me to fuck off.

I can't afford not to work tonight, but I can't just ignore him. Not when he's in this state. I start the engine. Maybe I can do one more fare on the way down.

Jonny rode a motorbike. That was his big mistake. All the other drivers were in cars—except for the lorry driver, of course. They were armor-plated, cased in, while Jonny was exposed, vulnerable. I don't know the full details—could never get him to tell me. I'm not sure he could if he wanted to. He says he remembers nothing. I know it happened on the M4 with everything moving at high speed. I know there were a number of vehicles involved and Jonny on his bike caught in the middle of it. I know something caught fire.

Jonny was a mess. Burns, shattered glass embedded in his skin, broken bones, the works. He didn't recover consciousness before being rushed into surgery, and after they wheeled him out again he lay senseless and motionless for way too long. Everyone prepared themselves for the worst. But then the amazing thing happened—he opened his eyes and he knew his name, the names of everyone around him, his age, his shoe size. He could tell you how many fingers were being held up, he could recite the Lord's Prayer. He was still Jonny Jordan.

It was only once he was back at his mother's house convalescing that the more subtle damage was revealed. Jonny would sleep most of the day and when he woke up he would sit silent in his darkened room for hours on end, doing nothing. His two guitars stayed untouched, clipped into their cases at the back of the wardrobe. The cause of the depression seemed obvious. Wouldn't you be depressed too if someone took away your face and gave you a patchwork quilt in its place? But there was more. Jonny flew into rages, yelling obscenities at his poor old mum, hurling his crutches at her. He suffered from headaches so severe that he would thrash around in his bed wailing and shouting and beating his head with his fists. A distressed Mrs. Jordan sought help. Jonny was sent for scans.

They gave him Paramax for the headaches, a strong cocktail of paracetamol and codeine. They asked him if he'd suffered any blackouts. He said no and they seemed pleased. He ended up in the office of a clinical psychologist who specialized in head injuries. She talked to him about establishing a routine—about getting up at eight o'clock every day and taking a morning stroll. She said he should take things slowly, one step at a time on the road back to his past life. He hated the smugness of the woman with her neat little hands and her tidy silk scarves but the sessions began to help. He moved back into his old flat in Elephant. He ate steamed vegetables and swam at the local leisure center. He took out his guitar—not the Gibson he now used for performing and recording in place of the blue Capones Strat copy—but the old acoustic that he bought with his saved-up pocket money when he was a kid. And he started practicing again. This was a big hurdle to get over—he'd been afraid he would no longer be able to play. He was rusty but that was all. The psychologist said she was proud of him.

For a while he ignored the phone calls. He wasn't ready to re-join the music world. But then they started slackening off and he realized he would have to get back in the studio if he wanted to save his career. For Jonny was a professional musician. The Capones were long gone, as was the jazz-funk band he'd played with in New York, but over the last few years he'd been making a decent living as a session guitarist. He had the skill and the con-tacts. He did mostly studio work but touring was what he liked best—being up there in front of a crowd, backing some angel-voiced teenager in hot pants. Snorting coke and copping off with a groupie afterward. Jonny was proper rock 'n' roll.

The morning he was due to start he woke up with that back-to-school feeling and he knew something was wrong. They treated him like a hero when he arrived at the studio but whenever he left a room he could tell they were talking about him. The backup singers were whispering to each other and he felt the paranoia building even though those two had always gossiped in corners. After a morning spent hanging around smoking cigarettes and drinking coffee, they were finally ready for him and he put on the headphones and plugged in.

Where the hell did this shaking come from? He could hardly hold the plectrum let alone hit the right strings. And all the sweat? It dripped off his face onto the golden wood of the Gibson. He'd never even sweated like this onstage let alone in the studio. Tony said not to worry and that he should take a fifteen-minute break, get some fresh air. It was understandable given the circumstances.

The break made no difference. If anything the shaking was worse. He looked up and caught his reflection in the glass wall of the sound booth—the mess of scars and the terror lying behind them. This frightened animal wasn't him. Then he focused on Tony—saw the pity in Tony's eyes. And he stepped out of the booth, handed his guitar to Tony, and left.

❖   ❖   ❖

I drop off the old geezer with the crutches and the shopping bag at Liverpool Street Station. £6.60, no tip. That brings my earnings tonight to a grand total of £57.80. No wonder I'm not saving any money. Then I switch the orange light off and call Jonny.

"Jonny?"

"Katy, *when* are you coming over?" In a voice like he's dying.

"I'll be there in twenty minutes. Maybe less."

Why do I let myself get manipulated like this?

The Elephant and Castle shopping center is red these days. They painted it for Comic Relief last year. The big red nose of South London. Typically they only bothered doing one coat and now the pink is starting to show through. That indestructible unearthly pink lying underneath.

I turn into Appleton Street and pull up in the space in which I parked that first night with Jonny. The same dirty white transit van is still there, in front of me. I'm not sure that it ever moves. Scanning the brown brick walls of Jonny's building, I count seven floors up and three windows in. His light is on. I feel queasy, nervous. I'm not sure if I'm dying to see him or if I never want to see him again. The line between the two extremes seems ridiculously thin and fragile.

Get my money bag out from under the seat, lock the cab and bury the keys in my pocket. Feel the crunch of paper—the letter from my dad. I walk up the path and take the stairs two at a time, ignoring the lift. I could do with the exercise.

When I met Jonny he was latticed with scars and reeling with hurt and anger for what he'd lost. He was the opposite of constructive, making everything as difficult for himself as he could. When his psychologist suggested that perhaps he would be happier if he gave up on the music and tried something new—a job or a college course, he screamed:

But I don't want to be happy!

When she mentioned that he could carry on playing the guitar as a hobby, he walked out of her office and never went back.

❀   ❀   ❀

Jonny stands in the doorway looking at me. Just looking. Red-eyed, greasy-haired, unhealthy. I can smell the cigarettes, the whiskey.

"How's your head?"

"Bad," he says, and immediately begins clutching it, as though to prove the point.

"You going to let me in, then, now you've fucked up a night's work?"

He turns and walks into the flat. I step inside, close the door behind me.

The TV is flickering away in the corner with the sound turned down. Looks like he's tidied up for my visit—the usual debris of take-out packaging, empty cans and overturned ashtrays is gone. The coffee table is bare except for the whiskey bottle (half empty), a glass with a healthy two fingers' worth in it, an ashtray (half full) and his packet of Marlboros. His old acoustic guitar is lying on the couch and he's been scrawling something on a piece of paper.

He's standing by the window with his back to me, looking down at the street.

"What's up?" I ask him.

"You *know* what's up. My head."

I notice a second whiskey glass on the edge of the mantelpiece, next to the pile of unopened mail. So it wasn't me he tidied up for.

"Who's been here?"

"Jason Greaves."

Jason Greaves—the rhythm guitarist with the cheeky grin from The Capones . . . But he couldn't have seen Jonny in years! I almost exclaim aloud but manage to stop myself. The thing is, I've never told Jonny that I remember him from before. He has a difficult relationship with the past. I sensed it that very first night—I knew it wouldn't be a good idea to dabble. So instead I say: "Who's Jason Greaves?"

"Oh, he's this guitarist I used to know. Played with him in a band at school."

"Yeah?" I move the guitar to one side, take off my jacket and money bag and sink down on the chocolate-brown couch.

"He lives in Cornwall now. Got a wife and a kid. Works for the *National Trust.*" Jonny speaks these words as though they are another language entirely—as though he doesn't understand what they mean—and I suppose in a way he doesn't. He stays where he is at the window.

I pick up the glass with the whiskey in it and take a sip. "Was it good to see him?"

"We had a jam," says Jonny, gesturing at the guitar. "Tried to remember the songs we used to play when we were kids. He doesn't really play anymore. Only messing about, you know."

"Oh, right. Same as you, then."

He gives me a look.

"So did he stay long?"

"No."

"Do you think you'll see him again?"

"No."

He leaves his place at the window and moves the guitar off the couch entirely. Sits down next to me, and then lies, head in my lap. His head is heavy, like the rest of him. I take the hint and start to stroke his temples. He moans with pleasure.

"I've missed you, Katy."

"I've missed you too." I'm acutely aware of Richard's smell on me. I don't suppose Jonny will notice but I wish I'd had a shower all the same. Amy would have smelled it the minute I walked through the door. Amy . . . who the hell was she with at Zippo's?

Jonny sits up and pulls my face to his, kisses me slowly, deeply. The couch has turned to liquid and I'm sinking down and down. There is only his mouth. My eyes are closed and when I open them I become dizzy and have to shut them again. I reach up to stroke his face, touch the cobbled surface of his cheek.

He breaks off. Clutches again at his head, wincing.

"Have you taken any pills?"

"They're shit."

"Yes, but have you taken any?"

He staggers off through the open door into the kitchen. I sit alone for a moment, take another sip of whiskey. I hear him run-

ning water into a glass. The cupboard door creaks and there is a
rattle of pills in a bottle. A moment later he calls me:

"Katy . . ."

"What?"

"Nothing."

Being with Jonny is like being with an animal with its leg
caught in a gin trap—dragging the trap along behind it.

I reach for the piece of paper he's scrawled on. It's an old gas
bill. I look more closely.

> *You are sailing*
> *While I am trailing*
> *Through the water*
>
> *Weeping willow sees you sail*
> *I look on behind the veil*
> *Of leaves.*
> *As you leave.*

A tear falls on the paper. I drop it on the floor and give in to the
memories, the emotion, but no further tears follow. They've all dried
up. I'm thinking of my mother's car parked on that cliff top in Kent,
the engine still running, and of my mother slumped over the wheel,
and of the rubber hose leading from the exhaust pipe into the car.
She was wearing her new Monsoon dress, her birthday dress.

"What's up?" Jonny is standing in the doorway with the glass of
water in his hand.

"Just PMS." I know this will shut him up. "Shall we go to bed?"

"It's early yet." He glances at his watch.

"Please."

He sits down beside me, drains the glass of water and reaches
for the whiskey bottle. "Have another drink."

"I'd rather go to bed."

The trill of the red phone is sudden and shrill—too clear and pre-
cise for this muzzy-fuzzy mood that Jonny and I have drifted into.

"Who the . . ." he's saying and his arm is shooting out to my jacket which is lying at the end of the couch, even as I snap, "Leave it."

"Just leave it," I say again as he extracts the phone from my pocket and presses to take the call.

Someone is speaking but I can't hear who it is. His face darkens. He darts me a look from his angry red eyes. "Wait a second," he says and thrusts the phone hard at my chest. I try to grab it but don't get a proper hold and it drops to the floor. I scramble down for it and Jonny steps on my hand, crunching my fingers. He picks up the phone and switches it off, still pinning me to the floor with his foot.

"Jonny—" My hand is in agony.

"Who the fuck is Craig?" He finally moves off my hand and I pull back, nursing it, huddling on the floor. He's standing over me, glaring at me. "I said who the *fuck* is Craig?"

"He's just some guy I had in my cab."

"Yeah, I bet you *had* him in your cab."

"For God's sake, Jonny. He's nobody."

He's over by the window again, his back to me. I think he doesn't want to look at me. Looking at me would make him more angry.

"If he's nobody, what's he ringing you for?" He's trying to calm his voice but the anger shows through the veneer like the lurid pink showing through the red on the Elephant and Castle shopping center.

"I don't know!" The tears are coming back. I'm feeling too weak for this.

"You're lying, Katy."

"I'm not lying. I don't know why he's ringing me. I haven't done anything." I'm getting to my feet, reaching for my jacket. I want to get out of here.

"So why does he have your phone number?"

"His friend was sick in my cab. I had to help carry him into Craig's flat. I left my phone there. I had to meet him for dinner to get the phone back."

"What is this shit? You had to *meet him for dinner?*"

"Yes, but nothing happened, Jonny. I swear to you that nothing happened!"

"You lying whore!"

A thousand fireworks explode deep in the socket of my left eye and the pain is so intense that I don't feel it. I go down flailing and bash the back of my head on the edge of the coffee table before I hit the floor. I might be completely out for a few seconds or minutes because then I seem to be waking up and I can't open my left eye. I can smell musty old carpet and somewhere above me Jonny is nursing his fist and crying and saying, "I'm sorry, Katy, I'm so sorry, I don't know what came over me, I'm sorry." My legs are splayed open and my arms flung out. In my head I'm stooping over a rock pool on a beach, peering at one of those dead starfish you find washed up after a storm. And Jonny's crouching down beside me and cradling my head, saying, "Oh, shit. Oh, shit, what have I done to you? I love you, Katy." Paper crackles under one of my feet and for a moment I think it's my father's letter but actually it's that old gas bill with the song lyrics on it.

Weeping willow sees you sail
I look on behind the veil
Of leaves.
As you leave.

PART II

DREAMING OF A COLOR

8

Pink phone—Amy: "You're not sexy when you sulk . . . Oh, *come on*, Kathy. Call me. Come over. Or has your mother grounded you?"

Blue phone—Joel: "Kat, I'm ringing from the salon. Can you hear the dryers? It's apprentice night tomorrow. Why don't you come by at six and I'll do your hair? I'm dead good at it, honest. I wanna see ya. Bye."

Yellow phone—Stef: "Hi, K, hope the trip to Scotland's been fun. Are you back now? I've got lots to tell you. Oh yeah, I don't suppose you know anyone who wants a few cheap Furbies, do you? Our buyer only took two hundred in the end. They're not dodgy or anything. Giz a bell, innit."

Green phone—Richard: "Kitty, it's me. Is the flu any better? Dotty wants to come to your flat and nurse you. So do I. Where exactly *is* your flat? I'm beginning to think you're married or something . . . Seriously, though, it would be nice to see where you live. Anyway, I'm waffling. Speak soon. Get better."

Red phone—Jonny: "Katy, I love you. For the thousandth time I'm *so so sorry*. It'll never happen again, I promise. Look, I'm going to get my act together, OK? It's not *me*. I'm not like that. *Katy* . . .

Winnie is reading the *London Taxi Times*. Another whine about the licensing of mini-cabs, no doubt. I walk over to her table and she looks up and says, "Jesus, what happened to you? And get us another cuppa."

The bruise is a mottled mixture of lurid yellows and murky greens. If she thinks it looks bad now, she should have seen it a week ago.

I take off my jacket and hang it on the back of the chair. Through the window I see the sky starting to lighten, becoming indigo around the edges of the heavy black rain clouds. October rain, cold and dreary. I've made almost £300, which is phenomenal for a Sunday night, and I'm knackered. After over a week of not working I've had to go all out. Now I need a fry-up. The table wobbles as I sit down. Winnie lights up and drags heavily on her cigarette as she leans forward to peer at my eye. She squints and her pallid face wrinkles like a scrunched-up bedsheet.

"That's it, Win. You have a good old gawp. Get it over with." I cast about for Big Kev through the crowded room. The air in the caf is thick with smoke and steam. "Full English and a coffee over here, please, Kev. Ta."

Rog Hackenham is advancing across the room, proudly bearing what looks like a cheap pink polyester blouse in his huge hands. "Girls, you're just the ladies I've been looking for. What say you to this quality merchandise, then? All genuine designer labels, one for fifteen quid or two for twenty."

"Leave it out, Rog," says Winnie.

"Go on, treat yourselves," he persists. "Look at the finish on them collars. Proper lace innit. I've got some other colors out in the cab."

"Forget it, Roger. I'd never buy anything from a man with such a shocking comb-over." And as I turn to face him, he notices the bruise. His smile slips slightly and then fixes itself back into place as he gives us a silent nod and turns to head for the table near the door where Janet Whatsname is sitting with Fat Richard.

Winnie sits back and shakes her head. Her all-knowing manner irritates me. "It was Jonny, wasn't it?" she says. "Has he hit you before or is this a new trick to add to his charming repertoire?"

"What are you on about?" I'm staring at old coffee rings on the Formica tabletop, playing with the sachets of sugar in the china bowl.

"What do *you* think?" There is anger in Winnie's voice. "He did this to you. And you've been hiding away, waiting for the bruise to start fading."

"Actually it was a fare." I burst a sachet by mistake and spill sugar into the puddle of Winnie's spilt tea. "This bloke tried to rob me. He didn't manage it though and he came away with worse than this."

"So why've you been hiding, then?"

"Who says I've been hiding? Just because I haven't been in *this* dump for a while . . . don't you ever get sick of coming in here?"

Winnie sighs and focuses her attention on her cigarette, staring so intently at it that she goes cross-eyed. "Well, it's your life," she pronounces, primly.

"Win, it *wasn't Johnny*." I've raised my voice without meaning to and I'm suddenly aware of just how many people in this room are looking at me. Rog Hackenham with his tatty merchandise glancing back over his shoulder every now and then, Frank Wilson hovering over his *Daily Mail*, some bald geezer whom I don't even know whispering to Orhan Ataman. I seem to be the resident entertainment—perhaps I should take a hat round.

Mercifully, the pink phone trills out from my pocket. I haven't called Amy since the night of that awful dinner party but now I'm glad of the diversion.

"Scuse me," I say to Winnie's accusing face, and turn away from her as I press to accept the call. "Amy, hi."

"Katerina?"

Oh, God. Him.

"Kathryn, is that you?"

"Hello, Craig."

"How are you? I . . . is this an OK time to call? Only last time—"

"Yes, yes, it's fine." I sense Winnie is trying to eavesdrop and twist further away.

"Well, I . . . are you sure?"

"*Yes*. What do you want?" I realize I'm grinding my teeth and try to stop doing it.

"I was wondering . . . Look, I was thinking about what you said when we went to dinner you know, about working out, getting fit . . ."

"What about it?"

Big Kev brings my coffee over and I nod my thanks to him without looking at Winnie.

"I've been mulling it over, and I think you're right. I'm sadly out of shape. Pathetically unhealthy."

"Is this actually going anywhere, Craig?"

There's a pause as he tries to work out why I'm being hostile, and then he ploughs on. "Well, yes. The thing is, I was wondering if you'd mind giving me some advice—"

"Join a gym."

"Um . . . I was hoping for something a bit more *specific*. I thought maybe we could meet up somewhere—say, for dinner—and I could ask you for some recommendations. What about the Sugar Club tomorrow evening at eight?"

He's so transparent that I smile in spite of myself. "Craig, you're never going to lose weight if you keep going to all these flash restaurants."

"No, I suppose you're right. We could always give the desserts a miss . . ."

I take a sip of my coffee and catch Winnie's eye by mistake. She looks so smug it makes me want to give her a slap. I return my attention to the floundering man on the phone. "Listen, Twinkle, I'm a bit busy at the moment, all right?"

"Just a drink then? It won't take long," he protests. "I only want a few names of some good health clubs."

"Try the Yellow Pages." I switch off the phone and return it to my pocket.

"Is that the man you were having dinner with the other day?"

Winnie stubs out her cig. "He's a bit keen, isn't he? All this wining and dining . . ."

"Would you shut up, please? It's just some bloke who's pestering me. Look, if you really want to know, it's down to him that I got *this*." I point at the bruise.

"What? That guy on the phone did it?"

That's foxed her good and proper. She's all round eyes and open mouth. Like a goldfish except for the bushy eyebrows.

The other drivers have lost interest now and I feel myself relax a little. I pause to take a sip of my coffee and decide to take pity on Win. What's the point in lying, after all? To her, of all people. "No, Win, it was Jonny that did it, like you said. I was round at his place and this Craig geezer rang up. Jonny was pissed, you know how it is. And he got the wrong end of the stick."

"And he hit you. I bet you didn't even hit him back, did you?"

"I couldn't. I was on the floor, down for the count."

She reaches over to stroke my face but I flinch away from her. I don't want her sympathy.

"What are you going to do?" she asks softly.

I shrug. "He's never hit me before. He says it won't happen again. Maybe it was a one-off . . ."

"For Christ's sake, dump him, Kathryn. He'll do it again, whatever he says. These things are habit-forming."

She lights up another cig and sits back in her seat, suddenly distant and fragile. I notice her hands shake. She starts coughing and gulps at her tea. She looks the way people look when they're talking from personal experience.

"Maybe you're right," I say.

"I *know* I'm right. He's all bitter and twisted about his accident and he's taking it out on you, petal. He's probably even enjoying the guilt. Makes a change from anger, doesn't it? He'll hit you harder next time just so he can feel as guilty as he does now. 'S logic, innit?"

I see what she's saying, but ironically it makes me feel sorry for Jonny. What a terrible life he has. I'm the only good thing left in it.

"All right, Win, you've had your say. Let's change the subject now, shall we? Let's have one of your wisdoms."

That's finally done the trick. Winnie looks pleased and starts peering into the bottom of her teacup for inspiration. "Got it," she says, with a lopsided grin.

"Let's hear it then."

She concentrates and her eyes become tiny, buried beneath those huge fuzzy eyebrows. Kev brings my breakfast over on a chipped white plate—I swear the Crocodile's plates have a regulation chip—and my stomach growls at the overpowering smell of it. Fat is trickling off the two fried eggs and sitting in pools around the sausages. The bacon lies in a shriveled curl at the side. I haven't been to the gym in a week . . .

"If life was a form of gambling," Win begins, stopping briefly to get the pronouncement exactly right, "then my life would be a trip to the local bingo and yours would be Russian roulette."

"But Winnie," I say, with a smile. "Life *is* a form of gambling."

There's this machine in the gym called The Pyramid Challenge. It's a stepper machine. You hold on to two long handles and tread two big pedals. While you trudge you stare at a little screen like a video game, which shows two men in athletics strip running up the side of a pyramid. The graphics are primitive—the machine is far from new—but they're effective. The faster you go, the faster your man goes. The other runner is the pacemaker. Up they run, up and up, while stylized clouds and an occasional cartoon plane slide across a flat blue sky. As you climb, more of the landscape comes into view: Pyramids, a pool with a camel drinking at it, a couple of palm trees. It amuses me to think of the designers coming up with the idea. *What can we do to make our new stepper machine something out of the ordinary? Of course—Valley of the Kings!*

You'd think, wouldn't you, that a machine called The Pyramid Challenge would actually *be* a challenge. You'd think it would have an objective—that if you ran hard enough for long enough your little man would finally get to the top of the pyramid—that he'd turn to face you with a big smile on his face—that you'd see right the way across the valley. But no. However long you go on, the man just keeps climbing and climbing . . . It's a loop, of course. It's a con. But still you keep on.

This morning I've been treading The Pyramid Challenge for almost sixteen minutes, level twelve (the thing has gears like a bike), and the sweat is dripping off my chin and trickling down my neck. Puts me in mind of the fat running off my fried eggs earlier this morning. I like to think it's that fat sweating out of me now. My sweat is a weird peachy color because of all the foundation and cover stick I have on the bruise around my eye. The effect of this cover-up attempt is unconvincing but I have to try. Fortunately there are only two other people in the gym to stare at me: A weedy little guy with red hair who's struggling with weights far beyond his capacity on the machines and a housewifey woman who's reading a Marian Keyes novel while she cycles slowly on one of the bikes. They both stare at me as I walk in but I nail them with a warning glare and they don't look again.

The unconquerability of The Pyramid Challenge is bugging me this morning, and I'm treading it so fast I'm working myself into a frenzy, even though I know it's pointless to think I can ever get to the top. I guess I must look aggressive—my face red and screwed up tight, the sinews in my neck and arms standing out from the muscle, my feet pumping those pedals like I'm part of the machine. My bruise could be a sign of danger rather than weakness—one-eyed war paint. But if you had seen me splayed out on that stinking carpet—if you saw me easing myself free of Jonny's cradling arms and crawling across the floor like a mangy old dog that can't run anymore, dragging myself into the darkened bedroom where I would curl on my good side between Jonny's grubby sheets and lie staring at the peeling paintwork until sleep came—well, you'd have seen a rather different woman, wouldn't you.

Waking at 4 A.M. with that shattering color all around and through me, I was glad the pain in my face was there to distract me and pull me out of the nightmare. I got out of bed and stumbled into the living room to find my shoes and my jacket. Jonny was lying on the couch, fully clothed, one arm flung across his face, snoring. The whiskey bottle sat empty on the coffee table beside him. I had to pull my jacket out from under his feet and he stirred in his sleep, moaned wordlessly. Made me think of a sleeping tiger I saw at London Zoo when I was a kid.

Now I'm pumping the pedals so hard that the machine is creaking and wobbling. How dare he do that to me! I don't have to take that sort of shit from anyone, least of all that hulking, whiskey-soaked, yellow-fingered, smoke-stinking mess of a man who was once pretty boy Jonny Jordan. Never in my life have I hidden away like I did last week—putting sunglasses on just to go down the road to buy bread and milk, shying away from the gaze of old women at the bus stop. I tried telling myself that this was a great opportunity to start putting the flat straight but I couldn't even bring myself to do that. Instead I kept the blinds closed and sat among the boxes in the half-light watching endless TV and sleeping fifteen hours a day. The phones kept ringing and most of the time I ignored them. Eventually I returned a few calls and made a few excuses. But I ignored Jonny. By the end of the week I was sick of my own company and the cheesy quiz shows and soaps that were filling my days. And I'd started thinking about my mother's last weeks—the way she'd drifted listlessly about the house in her dressing gown, cigarettes in one hand, glass of something strong-smelling in the other . . .

The bruise turned from vehement red to papal purple and then to this ugly swamp color. And last night I got back in my cab. Imagine the embarrassment, though—the shame of having a fare tap me on the shoulder when she got out in Highgate and hand me a card with the address of a women's refuge on it. I tried to give it back but she wouldn't take it, just smiled knowingly and slammed the door.

How dare he do this to me! How *dare* he!

"Excuse me, is everything all right?"

My feet slow on the pedals as I turn my head to see Jem, the

track-suited duty manager, gazing up at me with a concerned look
in his eyes.

"What?"

He blushes. "Well, it's just that . . ."

I grind to a halt, noticing the faces of the ginger wimp and the
housewifey woman with the Marian Keyes book, along with a little Japanese girl who must have come in since I've been on the
stepper. They're all staring at me.

I realize with horror that I have been swearing and cursing
aloud.

Jem is still struggling to find a tactful way of speaking to me
about this. I spot the pulsing vein in his forehead and see that he
is nervous of me. Perhaps he thinks I am violent; out of control.
He doesn't know that *I* am not the violent one.

I climb down off the stepper. "Sorry, Jem. Bad week, I guess."

"Sure." He looks relieved. I see his body relax. "What happened to your eye?"

"Oh, you know. Sport," I say, inadequately, and reach for my
towel. The towel is white but orange patches appear on it after
I've rubbed it across my face.

Shaman is all retro seventies yellow tiling and kitsch leopardskin.
They have a row of seats with those old-fashioned bowl-head dryers that have long been ripped out of all but the most blue-rinsy
old ladyish of hairdressers—but here they have them with irony
so it's OK. I'm peering down the rows of seated customers and
excited-looking apprentices with their tight jeans, bleached tou-
sled mop cuts and acne, searching for Joel.

"Are you here for apprentice night?" the blue-bobbed girl at
the front desk asks.

"Not exactly." I've already made up my mind *not* to let Joel
loose on my curly mess of hair, much as I need a cut. I'd never forgive him if he ballsed it up.

"Do you want to make an appointment?" The girl has a red
Hindu spot on her forehead, though I doubt it has anything to do

with religion in her case. It's like one of those stickers they put on the spines of library books. I'm tempted to reach out and see if it peels off.

"I'm looking for Joel Marsh."

She seems momentarily confused. "Joel? Oh, he's gone."

"Are you sure?" I peer again at the rows of aspiring stylists. This is a big place full of apprentices—it would be easy for her to make a mistake.

"Just a second," she says and reaches for her phone; punches in a number and says into the receiver, "Gino, would you mind coming out for a second? Lady here looking for Joel. Ta." She glances back at me as she replaces the receiver. "Take a seat." She indicates one of the brown leather seats with the ironic bowl dryers. They remind me of space helmets.

I sit for a couple of minutes waiting for Gino, wondering what's going on. Then a man clad in black Paul Smith jeans and shirt comes over. He has gelled dark hair, a nose ring and hair on the backs of his hands. He's very pale with a widow's peak—makes me think of Dracula. I stand up to speak to him.

"Gino?"

"That's right," he says, twisting a ring on the middle finger of his right hand. "And you are . . ." He trails off, confused. "You're *not* Joel's mother, are you?"

Is he stupid? Has he not noticed that Joel is black? Not half-caste but one hundred percent *black*? "Were you expecting Joel's mother?"

"Well, she did say on the phone earlier that she might . . ." He glares angrily at the receptionist as though she has got him out of his office under false pretenses. "Look, who are you if you're not Joel's mother?"

"A friend." Gino is half a head smaller than me and weedy. I don't like him.

"I'm not going to be drawn in to justifying myself to all and sundry." He flaps his hands dismissively. "If the boy has a complaint to make he can put it in writing and send it to my solicitor, but he's wasting his time."

"Complaint? What are you talking about?"

He's angry. His nasty little face is hot and pink. He points a finger at me. "Listen, lady, I am a respectable businessman, an ex-world-champion stylist! I will not have my reputation dragged through the mud by every little blackmailing hustler that walks through these doors, do you hear me? The boy is a liar and a thief and that is the end of the matter. Good day to you." He turns to the receptionist. "No more calls, Judy."

I half expect to find Joel's entire family round at his flat having a council of war but there's no answer when I ring the doorbell. I hang around for a few minutes before finally giving up and walking back to the cab. I'm parked up outside the Lord Palmerston pub on the corner and as I search my pocket for keys I glance in the window and catch sight of—

Yes, it's him. Joel. In the pub. *Joel in the pub?*

"What's going on?" I pick up his empty glass and sniff it. Smells of aniseed. "What are you drinking?"

He has his elbows on the table and his chin in his hands. He's staring into space. "Pernod," he says without looking at me.

"But you don't drink."

"I do today. Would you get me another?"

"*Pernod!*"

"With black currant, please. Please, Kat."

Reluctantly I do as he says. I get a pint of Stella for myself and some prawn cocktail crisps for us to share. As the barman pulls my pint I look back over my shoulder at Joel. He's still staring at nothing.

"What's going on, Joel?" I ask again as I sit down. "I went to find you at Shaman. I met Gino."

"What did he say?" The pernod and black is making a stain at the corners of his mouth. It makes me think of drinking Ribena as a kid. I wonder how many he's had.

"Not a lot. He seemed . . . scared," I say, only realizing this as I say it. "He thought I was your mother."

This raises a brief chuckle then he falls silent again.

"He called you a liar," I say, "And a thief. And a blackmailing hustler. What did you do, Joel?"

"I did fuck all!" he blurts. "It's *him* that did it. Gino!"

"Did *what*?"

He drains the glass and smacks it down on the table. Munches a couple of crisps. Crumbs fly out of his mouth when he continues. "Yesterday. He called me into his office at the end of the day, didn't he. Said he thought we should have a little chat. He was sitting behind his desk. I could only see the top half of him. He said I was doing really well. He could see I had talent. He said he'd singled me out—he would see to it that I got a permanent job at the end of the course. But he said there was something I could do for him in return."

"Joel—you don't have to tell me if . . ."

He turns frightened eyes on me. "When he stood up, he had his dick out. He had his dick out, Kat. He told me to kneel down . . ."

"Jesus, that *fucker* . . . No wonder he's scared!"

"I didn't do what he wanted, Kat. I tried being polite. Told him I wasn't into men. And do you know what he said? He said I was full of shit, that he knew a queer when he saw one and he's never made a mistake yet. Told me I should do myself a favor and give it a try."

"But you said no."

"You're dead right I said no! I mean, what's the guy thinking of—trying to say he knows me better than I know myself! So then he tells me I can forget about the job—that he wants me out. He *screams* at me to get out. Like as if it was *me* that had done something to *him*."

I reach an arm around him, pull him close to me. "And you went over to your mother's place."

He nods against my chest.

"And now she's on the warpath and you're hiding in here."

"Yeah." He looks up and notices my bruise for the first time. "What happened to you?"

"Oh, nothing. Bit of trouble with a fare. Joel, what are you going to do?"

He shrugs.

"You can't let your mother fight your battles forever. You've got to learn to stick up for yourself."

He's angry with me now. His eyes have taken on that concentrated fierceness that I know so well from when I first saw him in the gym. "Well, what do you suggest I do, Kat? Write a letter to the guy's solicitor like he says? Who's gonna believe me over him, eh? Unemployed black youth, innit. Ex-dancer who can't even get a part as a disco dancer in *Saturday Night Fever.* Yeah, I fucked that up too. Good for fuck all, that's me. Good for a cheap blow job."

He gets up and makes for the door, bashing into a chair as he goes, pushing rather than pulling the door and tripping up on the step. I'm just getting up to follow him when I change my mind—decide to let him go, give him a chance to calm down.

I wonder, though . . . Joel seemed more bothered by what Gino said about his sexuality than by what he actually *did*.

9

IT's dead tonight, even for a Monday, and so *so* wet. A sudden
rain shower can send people scurrying for cabs, but if it's been
pissing down all day they just don't go out at all. By 12:30 A.M.
I've still only taken seventy quid. This is never going to compen-
sate for my week of no work. What was I thinking of—hiding in
the flat like that! I pick up a blind man with a guide dog at Totten-
ham Court Road and he asks me to drive him to Mile End. I didn't
realize he was blind at first and almost refused to take him—I
don't let animals in the cab. Allergic to fur, you see, but you can't
refuse to take blind people with guide dogs, can you? And at least
he won't comment on my bruised eye.

The cab fills with the stench of wet dog. The dog keeps shaking
the rain out of its fur, making the stink worse. I consider asking the
blind man if he could command it to stop doing that but think better of it. The blind man is about my age. Poor sod.

"It amazes me how you manage in this city," I say. "I can hardly
cope with it myself. Can't imagine trying to get around without my
sight."

He sighs. I see the boredom creep across his face, followed by
frustration. "It's my life," he says. "I've never known it any other
way."

Immediately I regret speaking out. It must be as dull for him as
it is when people ask me about being a woman cabdriver. I shut up
and drive, sneaking the odd look at him in my mirror.

I drop the blind man off, and watch him wander up to his front door and put his key straight in the lock. There is no moment of fumbling. Then I drive off past the odd assortment of open green spaces, ugly high-rises and occasional brief stretch of elegant Victorian terraces that are the Second World War's legacy for this part of the city. It's late and I'm tired of watching the windshield wipers scrape and squeak back and forth. This fare puts me not far from Stef's.

There are lots of prostitutes hanging about, clientless, in the vicinity of Brick Lane. Seems the rain has caused problems for them too. We have something in common. The curry houses are mostly still open, though empty, and waiters stand in doorways touting for trade. The air is heavy with rain and Balti.

I'm just getting out of the cab to wander over to 134A when I spot a familiar blond head at a table in the window of Shameer, Stef's preferred curry house. He's sitting with Jimmy and they're leaning toward each other, talking intently through a cloud of cigarette smoke. I switch direction and head into the restaurant. They don't notice me crossing the heavily patterned carpet until I come up behind Stef and slap my hands down on his shoulders, at which point he jerks round, panicked.

"Jesus, K, what the hell are you trying to do to me?"

"Where's my kiss, then, Stef? Where's my, 'K, I've missed you so much, how was Scotland?'"

The muscles in his face relax and the usual dimply smile appears, devilish under the glow of the dim red lighting, "K, I've missed you so much, how was Scotland?" he recites, mock stiffly, and slaps me lightly on the bum. I muss his hair and pull up a chair.

"Ciao, K," says Jimmy, lazily, and I give him a nod.

There is an awkward silence and they exchange glances. I realize I have interrupted something. The waiter appears at my side to clear away the boys' curry wreckage and scrape spilled rice off the table with a small plastic tool. Then he hands me a menu. By the time I've ordered lamb buna with plain rice and a Heineken, Stef and Jimmy have concealed all trace of their awkward secretiveness and are ready to be social.

"Hey, Stef, show her the thing," says Jimmy.

"What thing? Oh, that thing." Stef reaches into a bag at his side and produces a Furbie. He holds it up close to his face and clearly enunciates, "I love you." Immediately the grotesque thing starts fluttering its eyelids, squeaking and gurgling. "It's telling me it wants to give me a kiss," explains Stef.

"Oh, *please.*"

"No, really." Jimmy lights a cig. "They learn language. You can have conversations with them."

"Christ, I hate those things."

"Patience," instructs Stef, and puts the Furbie, still chattering, on the table. Then he reaches into the bag again and pulls out another Furbie, places it opposite the first.

"Stef—"

"Shh. Listen." Stef holds a finger to his lips. Furbie number one repeats its request for a kiss to Furbie two. Furbie two says something back.

"She says she loves him," translates Stef.

Furbie one speaks again.

"They're talking to each other. Isn't it cute!" Stef squeezes my hand. "Hey, K, what's happened to your eye?"

"About as cute as two alarm clocks beeping at each other."

The waiter brings my Heineken and I take a long cold gulp.

"Your eye, K?"

"Disagreement with a Scottish barmaid," I mutter.

Stef bursts out laughing. "You fucking nutter!" He shakes his head at Jimmy and jerks a thumb at me. "What is she like?"

A phone trills out. For just a second I think it's one of mine, but mine don't play "The Entertainer"! I hate phone tunes. They're as bad as "on hold" jingles and lift Muzak. Instant aural lobotomy. I'm screwing up my face in disgust as Jimmy slaps a Motorola to his ear. "Yes?" His blank expression changes, warms up. "Hey, wass 'appenin, man? Yeah? . . . *Tomorrow?* What time?"

I watch Stef's face click into alertness. On the table the Furbies are flapping their stubby wings at each other and fluttering their eyelashes.

"Sure. Yeah. Laters." Jimmy ends the call and stuffs the Motorola back in his pocket. Something about this makes me uneasy.

"Tomorrow?" repeats Stef.

"Yeah. Half twelve," says Jimmy.

"Ah, *man*. I have to be out at half twelve," says Stef. "Why didn't you let me speak to him?"

Jimmy waves a dismissive hand. "Chill. I'll be in. I can deal with it."

Stef nods, sips his beer.

Deal with what? I want to ask. But I know better than to pry with Jimmy here.

My lamb buna arrives. In fact it's not lamb at all. They've given me chicken but I can't be bothered to complain.

The Furbies look as if they're about to try to mate.

"Have you managed to flog the rest yet?" I ask.

"Nah," says Jimmy. "Trouble is they're the old model. Nobody wants the old ones anymore. Everybody wants the baby ones—Tweenies or Dweenies or something."

"We were conned," adds Stef.

"Oh, really. What a surprise." I try to keep the sarcasm out of my voice but it breaks through. The Furbies are going totally apeshit now.

"Here they go," says Stef. "That's what happens if you leave them together for too long. They freak out."

When I first saw Stef he was being chased along the South Bank by two men, both of whom were at least twice his size. I was parked up, bending down behind the cab to check my left rear tire, which I thought might be flat. And I looked up to see this scraggy figure with flailing arms, a bright red face and mad eyes coming at me full pelt, yelling,

"They're gonna kill me. They're gonna *kill* me!"

I didn't spot the men for a few seconds. It was a Sunday afternoon and JTQ were playing the *Starsky and Hutch* theme on an outdoor stage in front of the Festival Hall. Hordes of people were milling about and grooving to the music. But then I saw the two

hammerheads pushing their way through the crowd, saw the look
in their piggy eyes, heard their boots thundering down the steps
and onto the pavement.

Little Blondie had halted next to me. He was bent double,
panting and coughing. Looked like he'd been running so hard he
was about to throw up or something. "Please . . ." he managed, but
that was all he could manage.

I opened the door of the cab. "Get in."

The stupid fucker was laughing and giving the finger to the
hammerheads as we pulled away.

"Where are we going?" I asked him once we'd made some distance from his pursuers.

"Maida Vale."

The whole way there he was calling people on his mobile. I
tried to eavesdrop but there was so much banter I couldn't make
any sense of it. I wanted to ask him why the men had been chasing him, but he seemed to be keeping to himself and was kept
busy by his phone calls.

When we got near he told me to take a couple of rights and a
left, and we pulled up in front of an elegant 1920s apartment
block. I checked the meter.

"Right, that'll be ten sixty."

I saw the look of panic cross his face and I had the doors locked
a second before he could grope for the handle. Should have
known he'd be a bilker but I was intrigued by the situation and I
hadn't wanted the hammerheads to get him. I don't expect this so
much when I drive in the day, so maybe I'm not as wary as I am at
night. Bilking is much more a night thing.

"So this is how you thank me for saving your miserable skin!"

"Sorry, it's not what you think. I didn't plan this." At least he
had the decency to look embarrassed.

I twisted round to face him. "How much have you got on you?"

"Well . . ." He groped about in his jeans pockets. Then he gave
me a helpless smile, and let his blond hair flop forward over his
eyes.

"So are we driving to a cash point or what?"

"Haven't got my card on me. It's in the flat . . . If you'll just let me go and get it . . ."

When exactly did the little crud think I was born? "Well, now, we have a small problem here. Just how were you planning to pay me, I wonder?"

He was squirming. "Look, the trouble is I had to leave all my money behind when I ran from those guys."

By now I was more amused than angry but I wasn't about to let him see that. "Listen, Blondie, by the time I've finished with you, you're going to wish I'd left you to those meatheads."

"Look, how can we . . . er . . . how can I settle this? What if I make a call? Get someone to bring some money over?"

"You think I've got all day to sit around here with you?"

"No, I . . . er . . . I fully appreciate that your time must be precious." He was scratching his head frantically and peering out of the window, clearly wishing he was out there in the street rather than stuck in this cab with me. "You see," he continued, "I am a purveyor of quality merchandise for cabdrivers such as yourself. In fact I was happily and innocently purveying this merchandise when those two large gentlemen took offense and decided they wanted to slaughter me . . ."

"What exactly were you *purveying*, then?"

"Beaded seat covers. I've got some more in the flat. Don't suppose you'd take one instead of . . . no, I see that you wouldn't."

All the time he was talking, I was hearing the occasional vowel tone that didn't fit with his dodgy salesman persona. I was noticing something in the cut of his jaw, the look of his mouth, his chin. This "cheeky cockney chappy" was pure blue-blooded public school rich boy, I was ninety-nine percent sure of it.

"What about payment of a more intimate kind?" he giggled nervously.

"All right."

"You *what*?" He looked utterly terrified.

The flat was his mother's, I later found out. She'd moved to Suffolk with her new husband but she was letting him stay there rent free until the sale went through. There was a photo of his mother and the new husband on the living-room mantelpiece. She looked a bit like *my* mother. In the Crocodile, a few days later, Steve Ambley told me a story he'd heard about Fred Zeffy. Fred still drives a bit but he's mainly a market trader these days, does better at that than cabbing. He'd been mosying along the South Bank when some stupid little bleeder had tried to flog him a beaded seat cover. Trouble was, Fred recognized said seat cover as one of a job lot he'd had nicked when his lockup was done over earlier in the week. And it wasn't only the seat covers that were nicked. He reckoned he'd lost a couple of grands' worth of stuff in the burglary. Fred drove over to his cab shelter to get some assistance but when he got back with his mates, the little runt was gone. All that was left were a few seat covers stashed in a skip.

Stef sticks an arm out of bed to reach for his bottle of Jack Daniel's, finding it easily even though we're lying in pitch dark. He takes a swig then passes it to me. Fire water. It warms me up, loosens my tongue.

"What was all that stuff with the mobile earlier, Stef? What's going on?"

"You don't want to know."

I wish we had the light on so I could see his eyes. "Yes, I do."

"Can't I keep a few secrets to myself? You have enough of them."

"I don't! It's just my natural mystique."

"Yeah, yeah, K."

"Oh, go on, Stef, tell me. Is it something to do with all that Rioja business?"

"Er . . . yeah, that's right."

I don't even need to see his eyes now. "You're lying." I pass the Jack Daniel's back to him and he swallows some more. "Tell me, Stef."

I hear him sigh. "All right, then. I'll trade you a secret for a secret."

"OK . . . You first."

He passes the JD over again and clears his throat, procrastinates. "It's another bit of business," he says, finally. "Lucrative. Minimum effort for maximum profit."

"What do you have to do?"

There's a silence. The room is so dark I can't make anything out, even now my eyes have had a chance to adjust. I feel as though my pupils are so dilated they're opening up my entire eye sockets. The darkness has weight to it and color—it's purple.

"A man comes over and brings some money. We hold it for a week. Then he comes back and takes it away again. We get a cut."

"What man? How much money?"

"Varies. Tomorrow it's going to be over a million, I think. Next time it could be more."

"And how much will you get?"

"Ten thousand, to split between the three of us."

Everything spins. I need to be able to see something so I can anchor my vision but still the dark shrouds all. I drink another mouthful of the Jack Daniel's and break out coughing. "Jesus fucking Christ, Stef! What the hell is it all about?"

"Shh. Keep it down. I don't know, all right?"

I'm groping for the lamp switch but I can't find it. I can't control the volume of my voice. "Stef, you should stay out of this . . . This has to be heavy shit! Why does someone need to pay you ten thousand to hold money, eh? Why can't they hold it themselves? Who *are* these people?"

"I don't know. Eddie knows them."

"Stef, you utter *twat*!"

There's a creak on the floorboards outside the door. Stef puts a hand on my arm and I clam up immediately.

"Hello?" calls Stef.

"Steven, put a sock in it and leave your domestic till the morning," comes a familiar voice. "Some of us are trying to sleep."

"Yeah, Eddie. Sorry, mate." The floor creaks again as Eddie walks away.

I wait for almost a whole minute. "Do you think he heard?"

There's a click and light floods the room. Stef has switched on the lamp at his side of the bed. I see the anxiety in his face as he turns to me and whispers, "What are you trying to do to me, eh, K? No, I don't *think he heard*. We'd know if he had."

"Stef, I'm sorry, really I am. The last thing I want to do is land you in the shit with Eddie but—"

"Hey." He holds up a hand to stop me from saying more. I notice hundreds of little strands of his hair sticking up with static like a wispy gold crown. His expression softens and he reaches over, strokes my tit. "K, you have to understand that this is what I do. And I know what I'm doing. If you're going to act like this I just won't tell you anything. It's as simple as that. You wanted to know so I told you. OK?"

I hesitate. I want to ask more but I know I've blown it. "OK."

"Right," he says, and the smile is back. "Now *your* secret."

"Oh, Stef . . ."

He kisses me and I breathe in that delicious inky scent. "K, what's been making you sad lately? Something's going on. I saw it in your face last time you came over and its still there today."

"I don't know what you're on about."

"Yes, you do." His eyes are up close to mine. The palest blue.

"Give me some more of that Jack Daniel's."

He lets me drink again and then takes back the bottle.

"It's my mother."

"Your mother?"

"Yes. It's coming up to the anniversary of her death. I feel haunted."

"What, like she's a ghost or something?" He looks confused.

"No, no. Nothing like that. It's just a bad time of year for me. That's all. There's no big secret."

He reaches over to touch my face, holds his hand there.

Sleep is dangerous for me. I can't trust my own head anymore. I'm back on the road by 5:30 A.M., my sweaty palms sliding on the wheel, my throat dry and sore, my eyes so wild I'm scared by my own reflection in the window. Often the dream sends me flying over to Stef's for a soothing massage, but this morning I creep out of bed and fly away from him. Maybe I don't want to disturb him after keeping him up so late sharing secrets, or maybe it's just that I want to be alone, on the road. The color rips through my head like I imagine ECT would, jangling my nerves, frying my senses. I swear I could smell burning when I wrenched free of my dream.

My light isn't on but I find myself pulling over for a waif with an outstretched arm just before Tower Bridge. I see the damage in her smudged eyes as the window slides down.

"Will you take me to Pimlico?"

I hear the weariness in her voice.

I nod. She eases herself in and I pull away.

She's dressed for clubbing—teeny-weeny hot pants and cropped top. She's either a clubber or a prostitute. She's very young. She cowers in the corner of the seat and snivels on her arm. Someone has upset her. Either that or her drugs have given her a downer.

I wouldn't have stopped for just anyone, not when I'm still shaking from my dream. But I sensed something in her as I was about to drive by. I sensed her desperation.

At night people are raw, exposed. You see what lies behind the office suit, the carefully arranged smile, the polished veneer. You get a glimpse of people's stories—the real stories. A glimpse is enough. I drop the girl off at one of the big white Georgian houses on Bessborough Street—a whore, I think. How else does a girl like her afford to live somewhere like that?—and wait while she finds her key and lets herself in. Then I drive to the Crocodile.

"Fog's coming down," I say to Winnie by way of a greeting as I drape my jacket over the back of a chair and sit down.

"Hello, Kathryn." She's oddly hesitant, peering over my shoulder. Makes me turn and look behind but of course nobody's there.

"How's the cough?"

"Oh, much better, thanks." She's still glancing around.

"Is something wrong, Win?"

"Wrong?" Now she's even more startled. "Course not. Should there be?"

"Two poached eggs on two rounds of white toast, a coffee and another tea for Winnie, please, Kev," I call out. It's quiet in the cafe and Big Kev is wiping tables in the far corner with an ancient gray cloth.

Winnie sips her tea. I notice there's an extra mug on the table, half filled with coffee. I'm about to gesture to Kev to come and take it away when I catch Winnie's eye. She looks down.

"Win—"

To our right the toilet door opens.

"Kathryn—how delightful! What's happened to your eye?"

"What are you doing here?"

Craig Summer straightening his olive green tie, pulling down the bottom of his black suit jacket to make it hang property, checking that he's zipped up his fly, letting the toilet door swing shut behind him, smiling like Christmas when he sees me sitting there. Twinkling.

He steps over to our table, sits down in the empty seat next to Winnie, reaches for his coffee. "Well, funnily enough—"

"Don't try to tell me this is a coincidence!" I look at Winnie, who is blushing furiously. "What's going on, you old witch?"

She opens her mouth to answer but Twinkle butts in first. "You're quite right of course, Katerina—it isn't a coincidence. Not entirely a coincidence, anyway. I just happened to be in the area, and—"

"You *happened to be in the area* . . . at six o'clock in the bloody morning! Are you stalking me? Is that it?"

"Don't be ridiculous," he says, and calls out to Kev. "Could I have another coffee, please?"

I decide to ignore him. "Winnie?"

She says nothing. Looks pissed off at being called an old witch.

I turn back to Twinkle. "But how did you know to find me here?"

"You told me over dinner at Club Gascon. You said most days you stop off in a cabbies' café called the Crocodile in Pimlico. I was on my way home, noticed the cafe—distinctive name, the Crocodile—and called in on the off-chance."

"'S logic, innit," concludes Winnie, with a nod.

"I was worried about you, Katerina. I so enjoyed our dinner that evening. But when I called you the next night—"

"All right, all right." My head is aching, traces of the color still lurking there. "Kev, forget about the breakfast, will you?"

"Eh?" comes a grunt from the rear of the café.

I get to my feet, reach for my jacket. "Cancel the breakfast, Kev. I'm not hungry anymore."

"Where are you going?" Winnie is perplexed.

"I need some air."

"But he's waited over an hour for you!"

"Did I ask him to?"

As I'm passing through the door I hear Twinkle saying, "Let her go, Winnie." This infuriates me more than anything else.

I leave the cab parked and walk down to the Thames, shivering but enjoying the cold. There's something about the river that helps me breathe more easily and I so badly need to breathe. The sky—a foggy predawn mauve—is beginning to blend with the color of my nightmare, mixing like paint, merging into a background I can cope with.

After I've been walking for a few minutes I hear a puffing sound behind me. I turn and see Twinkle thundering down the pavement, then grinding to a halt, panting.

"Can't you take a hint? Couldn't you tell that I wanted to be on my own?"

He tries to catch his breath but can't.

"What is it with you, Craig?"

Still puffing, he delves in his pocket and produces something jangly, which he holds out.

My car keys.

"Oh, shit." I can feel myself blushing. I take the keys. "Thanks. But you can't blame me for thinking . . ."

"I know," he says, finally getting his breath back. He's all shaggy and ragged, lolling about like a dog. He looks sad.

I'm softening. "Look, I'm just heading down to the embankment for a little walk. Do you want to walk with me?"

"That'd be nice."

We wander together in silence until we reach the river. We stand for a time, gazing at Westminster Bridge, at County Hall, listening to the hum and buzz of the West End waking up. The London Eye towers over everything, dwarfing Big Ben. He reaches into his coat for a cigarette and places it in his mouth but doesn't seem to have a lighter. He glances at me and I think he's about to ask for a light but when he sees the expression on my face he shrugs and puts the cigarette back in its box. We start walking again, accompanied by the tap tap of the metal on the heels of his shoes.

"How did you get that black eye?" he asks, suddenly.

"Someone hit me. A friend. He was drunk."

"Was it the man who answered your phone that night?"

"What's Winnie been saying to you?" I keep my eyes on the river.

"So it was, then. Winnie didn't say anything. I'm sorry, Kathryn. I didn't mean to get you into trouble with your boyfriend."

"He's not my boyfriend." The words come out quickly, automatically. The truth but not the whole truth.

He opens his mouth to ask something else then thinks better of it. I'm not looking at him but I know what his face is doing.

"Who's Marianne?" I ask.

I've caught him out. He stops in his tracks and I let myself look at his face. I enjoy the confusion there.

"How did you know about Marianne?"

Ha! Got him. "There's a card from her in your flat."

"Ah." He's starting to twinkle again. "Had a bit of a nose around, did you? Well, I suppose I'd have done the same if I was you."

"So who's Marianne?"

"My ex-wife."

"Your ex-wife who left you when you were supposed to be going to Hawaii."

"No. I got married again. And then got divorced again. Irreconcilable differences."

"Why do you keep the card?"

He shrugs. "I don't know."

"Does funny things to you, doesn't it? Love, I mean."

He glares at me. "I'm not in love with her anymore."

"Oh."

We pass a wino lying on a bench, sleeping. A pigeon settles on his boot, pecks at something stuck in it. The wino doesn't stir. The sky is glowing orange now, the light shimmering on the water. Cabs are shooting by with their lights on, the same color as the sunrise. Danny McKay is driving one of them, and he waves at me over his wheel.

"Do you get nightmares?" I ask Twinkle.

He frowns. "Not often. Sometimes I dream about serial killers."

"Serial killers?"

"It's not what you'd think. It's always different but it's always a version of the same thing: I'm the one that's after *them*. I have to chase them, catch them, wrestle them to the floor and hold them down to wait for the police. I'm lying on top of some knife-wielding nutter who's struggling for all he's worth. I'm holding him down. Trying to keep him there. When I wake up I'm weak from the exertion."

"Jesus . . ."

He mutters something I can't quite hear. I think it was, "Inner demons." He reaches for his cigarettes again, and this time he finds a lighter. "Sorry. I'm trying to kick but the mornings are hardest."

I resist the impulse to start lecturing him on his health and fitness and tell him about my dream instead. "I dream about a color. A color that isn't like any color on the spectrum. It fills my head and it scares the living daylights out of me."

He raises one eyebrow and blows out smoke. "What's it like, then, this color?"

"It's like a pink, but it's not. Or maybe more of a green . . . Sometimes I think it's an off-blue."

We pass the Tattershall Castle, that pub pretending to be a

moored ship. On the South bank lights are flickering on in the big concrete complex that makes up the Festival Hall.

"Maybe it's more like the gray of the Festival Hall . . ." I ponder.

"You're nuts," Twinkle says. "How can you have a color that doesn't exist? All color arises from the spectrum. It must exist somewhere. It's a question of working out exactly what it comprises."

"It *isn't* in the spectrum! It's the color of the inside of my head. How can you tell me the inside of my head comes from some spectrum? It's something else, that's all, and it's fucking terrifying."

I storm ahead, past murky Hungerford Bridge and Embankment tube station, leaving him behind.

"Sorry, Katerina. I didn't mean . . ."

"*Don't* call me that!"

Twinkle and I are sitting in an Italian sandwich shop–cum-café-cum-bakery near the Oxo Tower. It's a favorite haunt of his. He says they do the best croissants in town and he offered to buy me breakfast. My appetite has come back and my stomach is rumbling loudly so I don't even think of saying no. The café has only just opened and we're the first customers through the door. A mingled odor of frying bacon and bleach. We sit at a cozy corner table with a green and white checked cloth beneath the Specials board. The three blousy Italian women running the place are arranging dishes of brightly colored sandwich-filler concoctions in their glass-fronted counter. The little girl who serves us is whistling "The Star-Spangled Banner" as she takes our order. I don't think she knows she's doing it.

The croissants are good but I wouldn't call them the best in town. I lick my fingers and reach for the butter. "So, tell me, Twinkle, what exactly is it that you *do*?"

He flaps a hand dismissively. "Oh, let's not talk about that. It's too boring for words."

"But I want to know. You've asked enough about me. This is one simple, basic thing I'd like to know about *you*."

He rubs at his head, looks cagey. "I'm in business. My own. A sort of PR company. At the moment I'm working on setting up an international conference for toothpick manufacturers."

"I see."

"Yes, I told you it's boring but you had to ask." He slurps his cappuccino.

"It's not as boring as cabbing," I say through a mouthful of croissant, but while my mouth makes appropriate noises I'm actually thinking, *he's lying*. I'm certain of it. Maybe it's the box of toothpicks on the table that gives him away: How feeble a liar is this man? Couldn't he even have come up with something that's not sitting straight in front of him? Maybe it's the way that he described his company as a *sort of* PR company—are people really so vague about what they do? Or perhaps it's his general shiftiness, his reluctance to talk about himself.

"I'd like to take you out of London for a day," he's saying. "I'd like to drive you around. I bet nobody ever drives *you* around, do they?"

"It's not advisable. I'm an appalling backseat driver."

"Nonetheless I'd like to try." There's icing sugar all over his face from his *pain au chocolat*. He looks foolish and friendly but suddenly that kindly smile doesn't seem real. Why should he lie about what he does for a living if he has nothing to hide?

"Oh, go on," he says.

"I have to work. I can't afford not to."

"I won't stop you working. I can get you back anytime you like." He's holding his cappuccino cup in two hands, leaning his elbows on the table. His shirt cuffs poke out of the end of his jacket sleeves. He's wearing cufflinks. Who the hell wears cufflinks these days? Dodgy types, that's who.

"What about Friday?" he says. "Are you free?"

Friday. The thirteenth. The day of my father's fiasco of a memorial service for my poor dead mother. A thin gray man shuffling about at the entrance to the church wearing the suit he used to wear for school parents' evenings. Shaking hands, thanking people, oddly smug beneath it all. Nothing left of that laughing, dancing, gin-drinking, pill-popping, self-destructive woman but a pot of ashes in the ground.

A phone trills out—not mine. The irritating Nokia tune. Twinkle pulls a mobile from a pocket.

"Hello?" He listens and I can hear the tinny scratching of a voice at the other end. He nods, frowns, starts to clamber to his feet. "Yes. I'll be right there. Half an hour." He presses to end the call.

"Is something wrong?"

"What?" He gives me a look that says, *who are you anyway*? It's as if his brain is already out on the street.

"Craig?"

"Got to go," he manages. "Sorry." And with that he bolts for the door. I hear him call something back over his shoulder. It might have been, "I'll phone you," but then again maybe it wasn't.

The little waitress is advancing with the bill.

Thanks a bunch, Twinkle.

I'm pedaling on one of the exercise bikes, working off the croissants I consumed two hours ago, letting my thoughts slide around. The gym's good for that. Your body's busy pumping for all it's worth, while inside yourself you're taking a little trip.

Twinkle.

I keep telling him to go away. He keeps on coming back.

The secret of running five lives successfully is to be sure you always remain in control. That's not so easy with him. He's full of surprises and that's difficult to deal with. But it's also what makes him attractive. There's an edge to the man—I like a bit of edge. And he intrigues me.

Maeve used to say that if someone flags you down who's leaning against a lamppost, you should stop a few yards away—make them walk to the cab so you can be sure they can stand up. If you're in a dodgy area and you're flagged down by a girl on her own, pull up slowly and move ahead of her so you can check your mirror and make sure there's not a group of lads hiding in a shop doorway. And when someone gets into that cab, they're entering your territory. Keep it that way.

A girl I hate comes through the doors into the gym and clocks me. I stare her out. I hate her finely plucked, beautifully arched eyebrows, her blonde ponytail that swings as she walks. I hate her expensive blue tracksuit and the way her cute little arse wiggles as she crosses to the running machines. I hate the way she does her warm-up stretches—all graceful and lithe like a ballerina—and the way she tilts her chin as she puts her lemon-yellow Walkman headphones on. She begins to jog with a delicate mincing rhythm—ladylike and sexy. All of the four men doing weights are watching her and she knows it. Queen of the gym. I try to ignore her and concentrate.

It's all about instincts. If your instincts are unreliable you'll never make a cabby. You take a risk every time you let someone through that door. My instincts are good. My instincts tell me to stay away from Craig Twinkle Summer.

Queenie is speeding up and emitting light little grunting sounds as she pounds the belt. The sounds are suggestive. The boys are still watching her and I know what they're thinking.

Thing is, it would be so good to go out with Twinkle on Friday—to allow myself to be driven somewhere and entertained and wined and dined. No pressures, no problems, no memorial service. If I could only keep him under control . . . *Surely* I can manage that. After all, he's just some bloke . . .

I focus back on the bike. I've been cycling for twenty-five minutes. Time to stop. I begin to slow and watch the speedometer trickling down to zero. Then I clamber down and coolly cross the room to step up onto the treadmill next to the grunting blonde Queen. Time to kick some ass!

10

7:03 P.M. on Tuesday and I've just called in at Lost Property in the Public Carriage Office on Penton Street to see if anyone's claimed the Sony Discman I handed in to the police three months ago. Damn thing's gone. Shame—I fancied that. I stop to check the phones before heading off to do some work.

Pink phone—Amy: "Hi, Kathy, it's me on Tuesday evening. I *so* want to see you. Why don't you drive over here when you've finished your night's work? I'll leave the key under the flowerpot outside the front door. You can let yourself in and snuggle in beside me. Now, wouldn't that be just dandy?"

Blue phone—Joel: "Hey, Kat, I'm sorry it's taken me so long to get back to you but I just wanted to tell you not to worry about me. Everything's cool. I've checked my diary, and I can squeeze you in on Thursday. Two o'clock. OK?"

Yellow phone—Stef: "K, why did you run away? It's horrible to fall alseep with your woman and wake up in an empty bed. I'm well narked. Are you all right, honey?"

Green phone—Richard: "Hello, Kitty, it's me. You're not *still* in bed with flu, are you?—Dotty, not now, Daddy's on the phone—Dotty, don't do that you'll break it, you'll—oh great . . . Sorry, Kitty, I have to go, she's just broken my—"

Red phone—Jonny: "Katy, *please* come over. Don't leave me like this. I don't know what to do to make it better. Please, Katy, I'm begging you."

Waking up to an insistent pattering sound. I'm lying under a warm duvet and when I open my eyes the sun shines straight into them. The quilt smelts deliciously clean and fresh. The pattering stops.

"So, you're awake, are you?" comes a voice.

Oh yes. I'm at Amy's.

"Maybe." I peep out.

She's sitting at her computer, typing. She's wearing tight jeans and a cute brown cashmere sweater. She twists around and smiles at me, and my mind floods with memories of the sex we had when I arrived a few hours earlier. Crawling into the sweet-smelling bed where she lay on her side, facing the wall, naked. One hand up by her face, fingers gently curled. I sat for a while watching her sleep. She has the most beautiful long back. After a couple of minutes I found I had to bend and kiss it—between the shoulders, down the spine, working my way to its base. And then I kissed her in a wicked place and she woke up and pushed herself against my mouth.

When I first met Amy at the drinks reception, she was telling people she wrote for *Up West* but didn't mention it was the "Muff Matters" column. I suppose I should have guessed. What kind of journalist would seriously be interested in crowding into an airless room with a couple hundred cabbies to drink warm Chardonnay and eat crisps while some bod from the London Taxi Benevolent Association thanks everyone for their hard work this year and presents a check to the president of a kids' charity?

Come to that, I don't really know what *I* was doing there either. I'd joined in on a few kids' runs—driving underprivileged children down to Margate for the day, that kind of thing. I'd mainly done it because I'd heard that the only women involved with these cabby charities are the wives of some of the old boys. It's good to show people that there *are* women in this profession and that we play

our part—not as committee wives but as *drivers*. Not that I've
done any charity work lately. I don't exactly have the time anymore . . . But in those days I wasn't so stretched—I only had
Jonny and Richard to worry about.

I was at the reception with Winnie but after the presentation I
lost her in the crush. And it was while trying to find her that I noticed a perfect peachy bum in white Levis. The owner of the bum
was bending down to delve in a bag. She straightened and I noticed the glossy red hair (at that time worn long), the long neck,
the cute little waist. This girl didn't look like a cabby—most of
whom are either huge or tiny, rarely anything in between. She was
talking to Jenny Farrow from Knowledge Night School. I spotted
the microphone and the mini-disc recorder, and realized she was
a journalist. Jenny saw me looking over and waved, causing the
pretty journalist to turn around. I couldn't quite believe it when she
very visibly gave me the eye, her gaze moving slowly down and up.

Though I'm not totally sure if I'm now elaborating on the in-
tensity of that moment, I'd almost swear there was suddenly a
weird *pang* sensation in my cunt.

And then Jenny moved to speak to someone else—perhaps
seeing her chance to escape from the journalist. And the journalist began slicing through the mob toward me.

I panicked and started desperately searching about for Winnie,
only to catch sight of her retreating back as she headed out the
door. And as I was about to follow her I felt a hand on my shoulder and knew it was the pretty journalist.

"I'm writing a column for *Up West* magazine," she said. She
had the most flirtatious green eyes and a truly wicked smile. "And
you look as though you want to be interviewed."

"I do?" I *didn't*. I wanted to leave now—to drive over to Jonny's
or Richard's. A mere two lovers then but they kept me busy all the
same. I knew where I was with them. It was all about the insertion
of a penis into a vagina. Nice and unambiguous.

"Well, no, you don't actually." She reached out and took my
glass from me, drained the dregs of my wine, grimaced, and
placed the glass back on the table. "To be utterly truthful, you

look as though you want to know what it's like to fuck a woman. To fuck *me*."

Later, in bed, she interviewed me. When she asked me what the average cabdriver's biggest problems are, I replied, "Boredom and loneliness."

"I can help you with those," she said.

"Dear jealous from Leicester," reads Amy as she types the words. "No, you're not being silly. Why do you think there are so many corny mother-in-law jokes? It's because lots of people genuinely have this problem. Mad though it may seem to you, your boyfriend's mother may well be afraid that you are taking away her little boy. She sees you as her rival. She will certainly continue with her manipulative behavior until you do something about it."

The duvet isn't thick enough to block her out. "Do I have to listen to this?"

She continues, undaunted. "Perhaps you should spend some time getting to know your boyfriend's mother—just you and her without him there. Does she like the theater or the cinema? Does she play bingo? There must be something you can share together. A chance for you to bond. Grit your teeth and go for it. You might not enjoy her company very much but the end result could prove worthwhile."

OK, if she wants confrontation, then that's what she's going to get. I sit up, my back against the cold metal headboard. "Amy, did you go to the circus in Finsbury Park a couple of weeks ago?"

"I think I should meet your mother," Amy announces. Her face wears a determined look. She has the advantage—she is more wide awake than I am.

"Only I went to the circus with a couple of friends and I could have sworn I saw you there."

"Did you take your boyfriends to meet your mother? Is it because I'm a girl?"

"Oh, Christ. What time is it, anyway?"

"Just after ten."

"Oh, *Christ*. I've only had four hours' sleep!"

"Dear Stella," reads Amy from a scrap of pink paper. "My boyfriend and I have been together for over a year. We really love each other and have been very happy, but now I'm worried my jealousy may tear us apart. Recently his ex-girlfriend returned from a yearlong trip to India. I know they only broke up because she went away, and I'm terrified he'll dump me to get back with her. Whenever he goes out to meet his mates, I get obsessed with the idea that he's with her. I've tried talking to him about it and he insists it's me he wants. But I can tell his patience is wearing thin. He says I should trust him and I know he's right, so why do I feel so sick with worry over this? Yours, Paranoid of Doncaster."

I'm rubbing my tired eyes, vaguely thinking about all that stuff Willa was saying the other day in the kitchen.

"Dear Paranoid of Doncaster," Amy reads as she resumes her typing. "The key to unlock your fears lies in the second line of your letter. *We really love each other.* If you love your boyfriend you must learn to trust him as he says. OK, so he may have been happy with his former girlfriend, but she is a part of his past now. People change and move on—*you* are his present. But I know it's hard to just snap out of it. If you can't let this go, why don't you tell your boyfriend you'd like to meet her—invite her round for dinner or go out for a drink. You'll no doubt find she's not such a threat—maybe you'll even like her. And in the unlikely event that there's really anything to be frightened of, you'll face it head-on."

This advice is vintage Amy. Her basic philosophy is to deal with life in the most direct way possible. To confront your fears—bam—like a car crash. Well, now it's my turn.

"Amy, stop typing for a second. I want to ask you something."

She swivels around on her stool and gives me a glare. Arms folded, chin jutting out in that brazen-it-out way. "Kathy, you know that I totally adore you . . . But there's a limit to what I'm prepared to take from anyone—even you!"

"Amy, I'm not—"

"Let me finish! I've put up with a whole heap of shit from you, Kathy. I've swallowed the fact that you won't ask me over to your flat because it might upset your precious bloody bitch of a mother.

I've sat back while you diss my column and make scathing comments about my friends and their sexuality—which is *my* sexuality too, Kathy, and probably *yours*, though you don't like the label. I've listened to your accusations and insinuations about my fidelity and done my best to convince you that you are the only woman on this planet I really want . . . And all for what? For the privilege of having you come round once a week, bed me and bugger off again. Well, whoop-de-do!"

"But—"

"No, Kathy. That's enough. I'm not sleeping with Cheryl and I didn't go to any circus and now I want you to shut up and get your act together." She holds up a thumb and forefinger, leaving just a little space between them. Sunlight glints through the gap. "You are *this* close to being dumped, girl. Don't make me do it." Having delivered her missive she visibly relaxes, runs a hand through her hair and bends to click her mouse and print her agony page. "Now, how about some breakfast?" She is smiling a bright efficient smile.

I'm slumped at the big green kitchen table while Amy makes coffee and chops mangoes and strawberries. I'm playing with a red Bic, absently scrawling a mesh of spirals on a pad of Post-it notes, trying to work it all out: Amy is incredibly slick—she should have been a spin doctor. Her version of our relationship leaves out the weekend-long fling she had with that girl Linda, whom she met on a conference. Amy fessed up to that at the time—though of course she found a way of spinning it into a part of her tortured investigation into whether monogamy is about love or possession. She finally decided it was both but was also necessary for a functional relationship—but not until she'd tested out the alternative. Her version also leaves out Sarah the shaven-headed club chick who was coming out of the front door covered in love bites as I arrived unexpectedly at the end of a long night's work three months ago. Amy is more than capable of gathering up her personal chaos and molding it like clay into a form of truth that suits her purpose: *I* am the only one who can't commit. *I* am the only one whose fidelity is in doubt and I am also the only one who is unreasonably paranoid and insecure.

"Kathy, my dear. How's life in the bus lane?" Willa spills into the room in a floor-length sky-blue silk shift, propping her plain-lensed glasses up on her nose and slicing at an envelope with a vicious letter opener.

"Jammed up."

"Cigarette?" She nods at an open packet of Camels. "Oh, no, you don't do that sort of thing, do you."

She lights one herself and settles down at the table. We both watch Amy rinsing and slicing. I notice the soft blonde hairs on Amy's arms. The long white neck. That mouth. She's the only woman I've ever been attracted to and I find myself wondering if many straight women catch themselves looking at her differently from the way they look at other girls—the merely pretty, the simply cute. Amy is pure sex. The jeans are tight around that lovely arse and my eyes are drawn to it . . .

And so, I realize for the first time, are Willa's eyes.

"Kathy," she whispers—her whisper is impossibly loud—reaching over and putting a hand on mine. "Have you had a chance to talk to Madam about that little *thing* we spoke about the other day?"

I'd always thought her interest in Amy was a motherly one. How wrong could I be?

"What little thing is that?" Amy calls.

"Willa thinks you're cheapening yourself with this Agony Aunt stuff. She thinks you're far too talented to be Dear Stella." I speak the words plainly, flatly. Willa gives me a glare that says I have betrayed her and kicks my shin with a fluffy muled foot.

"Oh, honestly, Willa!" Amy plonks the knife down, exasperated, hands on hips. "We've talked this to death, haven't we? It's just a bit of fun and some extra cash. And I'm so bored of trying to find witty things to say about women tennis players and the Corrs and special new funnels that enable girls to take a pee standing up . . . I need something *else*."

I watch, satisfied, as Willa squirms. "But, Amy, you have to think about your future. Where is this Agony Aunt stuff heading, eh? How is all this crap going to get you a broadsheet column? I thought if Kathy talked to you—"

"Do you plan on dropping my rent by half, Willa?" Amy picks up the knife again and attacks a pineapple. "No, thought not. Don't suppose you want me to move out either, do you? In which case I'd better carry on as I am . . . Fruit salad, anyone?" She looks me in the eye and something passes between us. She sparkles like glass.

Amy keeps lingering by real estate agents' windows as we wander down Upper Street in the warm October sun. It's a not very subtle hint.

Islington is a place I don't understand. All the svelte young Blairites with their nice haircuts, their agnès b. and Nicole Farhi suits, barking into their mobile phones as they hail cabs. The wealthy alternative types, like Willa, shopping for dried cannellini beans and wild rice, the prim old "women who set" promenading out of their hair salons with their silly little dogs. I smell exhaust fumes, pizza and Calvin Klein in the air. It's just like any other place in London—not especially pretty, not especially green. There are bums and alkies and beggars here just like everywhere. Peckham has Georgian town houses and big open squares and so does Mile End, for Christ's sake. So why does the equally dirty and smelly *Islington* ooze money so obscenely?

"Look." Amy jabs at yet another real estate agent's window. "Cafford Square—just down from Willa. Two bedrooms, two reception rooms. *Seven hundred fifty thousand pounds!*"

"Come on." I drag her away by the arm. "Let's go and look at the antiques."

We mosy down Camden Passage, passing shopfronts crammed with horse brasses and door knockers, breathing in the rust and dust, to grind to a halt in front of a window displaying a pretty cedarwood desk.

"What do you reckon to that as something for my—" Amy begins, but—

"Kitty, it *is* you."

Richard is standing behind me. I see his reflection in the shop-window before I turn to face him—the big sloping shoulders, the receding sandy hair, the brown eyes. He looks happy to see me. I register his happiness even in the fraction of a second before I spin round. There is a small dark shape at his side. Dotty, holding his hand. She is already tugging on my jacket sleeve as I'm turning to face them both.

"Kits, Kits, look at my new shoes!" Dotty is bouncing around, doing high kicks. Bright red Dorothy shoes, in patent leather.

Richard grabs me in a Patagonia-fleece hug, my face muffled against his shoulder. As I pull stiffly away from him, I'm somehow making my mouth work to say, "Richard, wow, what a coinci-dence."

Amy is standing with her hands in her jacket pockets, looking puzzled, lost even. I'm struggling to find a way to make my worlds blend rather than crash.

Somewhere in the background Richard is talking. "So, you're over the flu, then. You look pretty well except for . . . what hap-pened to your eye?"

"Hi, I'm Amy." She's extending her hand to shake his. He hadn't noticed her until now and hesitates, startled, before taking the hand and shaking it.

"Richard, this is my friend Amy." I'm choosing my words care-fully. Amy looks put out to be explained away as my "friend," but she doesn't protest, thank God. "Amy, this is Richard and Dotty."

"Hello, Dotty." Amy bends and ruffles Dotty's hair. Dotty hates it when people do that and she shrinks away and tries to hide be-hind her father's legs, peeping shyly through the gap.

Please, God, don't let *either* of them do *anything* . . .

"So when did you get rid of the flu?" Now he's got over the sur-prise of bumping into me, Richard is hurt that I'm out and about with some friend before I've even caught up with him. He's even a little angry. I see the anger in the spots of color under his cheek-bones. The habitually soft, friendly brown eyes seem hard and oddly opaque.

"Oh, you know, a couple of days ago. I was *so ill*, Richard, you wouldn't *believe* it."

"I didn't know you were ill," says Amy, suddenly.

"Well, I don't like to make a big deal of it."

A young couple are standing a little distance off looking at antique jewelry on a stall. She is picking up rings, trying them on her engagement finger, holding out her hand for him to a admire. She is not a particularly pretty girl but she radiates happiness—they both do—and it makes them beautiful. Jealousy bites at the inside of my chest.

"Why don't we all go and get a coffee?" suggests Amy. "There's a café five minutes from here that does great banoffi pie."

I would like *so much* to hit her.

"Thanks, but we can't stop, I'm afraid." Richard is still angry but I think he's also genuine about not being able to stop. "We're on our way to pick up some photos and then I have to drop Dotty off at the nursery."

"Oh, shame." I'm trying really hard to sound sorry that they have to go but I can't manage it. "I'll give you a call, later, OK?"

"You do that." He gives me a *we need to talk* look and then mutters, "Nice meeting you . . . Amy."

"Likewise." She's losing interest, returning to her examination of the cedarwood desk.

He reaches over to kiss me goodbye—mercifully he's pissed off enough to make it a peck on the cheek.

"Bye, then." I stoop to give Dotty a smacker on the lips and she says, "Ugh, yucky wet one!" as she always does when adults kiss her, and grabs her father's hand, tries to drag him away.

He allows himself to be dragged but calls back over his shoulder, "You'll have to stop by soon to see the photos. We should have some great ones from the circus."

I glance anxiously at Amy but she's still looking at the desk. She doesn't seem to be listening anymore. Richard and Dotty are disappearing around the corner now, onto Upper Street. Next to me the young couple have found a ring. Looks like silver, though it could be platinum. A large blue sapphire. The girl's face creases up and I hear her excited giggle. Her boyfriend pulls her to him and kisses her on the forehead, then on the lips. The crabby-faced stallholder is smiling fondly, transformed.

"Eh?" What did Amy just say?

"I said, should I get the desk? I mean it's really lovely but I'm not so sure about the price. Do you think four hundred is too steep?"

I shrug. "I don't know about these things."

She catches the edge of my sleeve. "Come on. Let's go in and talk to the man."

She pushes the shop door open and a bell tinkles somewhere in the musty darkness of the interior. I'm beginning to think I've got away with it, but then she pauses, hovers in the doorway.

"Who was that guy, Richard?"

"My cousin."

"You never mentioned you had a cousin."

An old woman in a mink coat is trying to get out of the shop but Amy is blocking her way.

"Amy—" I say. She notices the old lady and steps back onto the pavement.

"It's weird that you've never talked about him."

"Have *you* got cousins?" I try.

"Yeah, four."

"Well, then. I didn't know about them either."

She's giving me a steely look. "But I don't see my cousins from one year to the next. You're obviously close, you two. I'm surprised you've never mentioned him, that's all."

"I must have mentioned him some time or other."

"No, you never have. Or the little girl. I'm sure of it." She's folding her arms, getting her stroppy look. The chin is jutting forward. "And yet you went to the circus with them recently."

"I *told* you I went to the circus. In fact—"

"You said you went with friends. You didn't say anything about a cousin."

"Well, we *are* friends, he and I. That's how I think of him. He's more of a friend than a cousin."

My face is twitchy. My reflection in the shopwindow looks shifty, guilty. She's sniffed me out. I've always thought there would be a day when I'd finally come a cropper. After all, most people can't even get away with stringing two lovers along at the same time, let alone five. I'm unbearably tired all of a sudden. I just want to lie down in the road and sleep. Instead I wait for the worst.

"Why are you so ashamed of me?" Her voice is very small.

"*What?*"

"You wouldn't have introduced me if I hadn't done it myself. You wouldn't have even told me he was your cousin."

"Amy—"

"I thought it was just your mother that I'm not allowed to meet but now I see it's your whole family!" Her volume is rising steadily. "Why are you so embarrassed of what I am—of what you are? *What is so fucking terrible about being in love with a woman, eh?*"

The stallholders and shopkeepers fall quiet. A stocky man with a mustache, sweeping the doorway of an Italian restaurant, is leaning on his broom, watching the show. The young couple are gaping openly at us—he has a protective arm around her shoulders. Even the pigeons have stopped gobbling at debris in the gutter to stand and stare with their nasty, unblinking, creepy little eyes.

"Don't worry, darling," shouts the man with the broom. "I'd give you one any day!"

"Bloody hell." Amy wipes her eyes on her sleeve and dives into the shop, to the tinkling of the bell.

I turn to follow her.

"I'd give it to both of you," the man calls as the door slowly swings shut behind me. "I'm a generous man—I've got enough for two!"

11:02 P.M. I've picked up two women from outside the Royal Opera House in Covent Garden and I'm driving them home to Muswell Hill. They're a mother and daughter—mid-fifties and thirtyish, respectively. Jewish—maybe Hasidic. Someone once told me that Hasidic women shave all their hair off and wear wigs, and now I'm peering hard into my mirror, trying to work out whether those long brown curls are real or nylon. They're all dressed up and it's the mother's birthday. She's been thanking the daughter for giving her such a wonderful treat but you can tell they haven't enjoyed themselves. There's something jaded in the way they're talking about the evening. The daughter is making the kind of noises you make when you're not really listening to what someone is saying to you. The mother keeps yawning behind her hand. The most they can say about the opera is, "It was really good, wasn't it?" And they repeat this phrase to each other at regular intervals. Maybe the opera was crap or maybe it's just that they both have other places they'd rather be, other people they'd rather be with. I finally lose interest in the hair and switch on the radio—Jazz FM.

Today has been a strain. I still can't quite believe that I emerged unscathed, undiscovered. Amy smelt a rat but it was the wrong rat. Richard was annoyed that I hadn't called him but suspected nothing, I'm sure of it. After all, why would Richard be suspicious of the idea of me being out and about in Islington with a girlfriend? I got away with it—just—but I have this feeling that time is running out on me.

Maybe it wouldn't be such a bad thing if I got caught. I am so weary of trying to be everything to all of my lovers but failing to really be *anything* to any of them. Trouble is, I'm used to a varied menu. Why should I be stuck eating pasta every night when I might instead be in the mood for roast beef or chicken curry . . .

I turn right past Highgate Woods and then right again to drop the women off outside a large house in Woodland Gardens with a Mercedes in the driveway. They've run out of conversation and are visibly relieved to have reached their destination.

On the way back to the West End I pick up a nerdy young man in an anorak carrying a laptop. When I agree to take him to Camberwell he looks so grateful that I'm worried he might try to lean in through the window and kiss me.

I'm still lost in thoughts of my predicament as we drive. If I chucked one or two of my lovers I might actually have the time and the money to do up my flat. It's cripplingly expensive having five lovers and I'm too much of a soft touch. Today, for instance, I ended up buying Amy the cedarwood desk—all four hundred quids' worth of it. Forgiveness is a pricey commodity. But if I were to dump some of my lovers, which ones would I get rid of? How would I choose?

I've driven all the way down to Camberwell while thinking about this stuff. Camberwell is one of my least favorite areas of London in spite of the fact that I know there are some quite nice bits if you only get away from the main drag. But that long tatty strip of off-licenses and bookies, bus stops and corner shops—all those depressed-looking people shuffling into gray buildings and huddling against the wind—the road goes on and on and it's always jammed up with traffic. It's enough to make you want to slit your wrists.

"Thanks for agreeing to drive me home." My fare is leaning forward in that conversational way and pushing his glasses up his nose. "You know, I flagged down four cabs before you and not a single one would take me. Even though they all had their orange lights on!"

"South of the River, innit," I've had this discussion so many times . . .

"What is wrong with going south, I'd like to know," he says, quite the little politician. "South to north is no problem. East to west or west to east the same. Why this big deal about going north to south? Taxi drivers are so prejudiced."

"Well, it's tricky getting a fare back in again, that's the trouble. But I know what you mean. Cabbies are a bunch of cunts."

It seems our nerd is a touch delicate when it comes to the "c" word. He clams up and sits back in his seat, his lips all tight and prissy.

Fine by me. Just hope I haven't done myself out of a tip.

It's 4:53 A.M. and I'm knackered. When I've dropped off three lads at Clapham Common I pause to check the phones for messages. Nothing on any of them. Nobody loves me.

There's a knock on the window and I glance up to see a fat pal-

lid face staring in. Five-day stubble and a funny look in his eyes—
disconnected, somehow. I don't like the look of him but I open the
window two inches out of courtesy.

"Charing Cross." Trace of a northern accent.

"No, mate, sorry. I'm knocking off for the night."

"But your light is on. You have to take me."

Shit. Must have forgotten to switch it off. He's smiling—nasty
yellow teeth. I don't want this man in my cab.

"Actually I don't have to take you. I didn't stop for you and I'm
not at a rank. I'm just going home."

"Please. Please drive me to Charing Cross." His smile has vanished and a look of desperation has come over him. I'm starting to
feel sorry for him. My instincts tell me he's a loon—quite genuinely mentally ill. If I don't take him, who the hell else is going
to? Though God knows if he has any money.

"I don't want to sound funny, mate, but can you pay for this?"

Clearly feeling insulted, he pulls a small wad of notes out of a
pocket and waves them at me.

"All right. Hop in." I unlock the doors. I'm too soft by half.

In he gets. He's wearing a brown overcoat that reminds me of
greengrocers and he has Jesus sandals on his feet, worn over
socks. He's smiling again, flashing the yellow gnashers.

It's another one of those long, dull drives in a more-or-less
straight line. We pass alongside Clapham North tube station. I
heard someone describe Clapham as "South Chelsea" the other
day. Londoners do talk some shit, don't they? The road snakes on
past seedy nightclubs and Irish pubs, through Stockwell and up
into Kennington.

I become aware of a flicking sound, and glancing into the mirror I see that my passenger is playing with a Zippo lighter. There
is a No Smoking sign directly in front of him.

"Hey. Can't you read?"

There's a glazed look on his face, as though he isn't in my cab at
all but is lost in empty space. He isn't lighting a cig. He's just toying
with the Zippo. The flame flicks and goes out, flicks and goes out.

"Stop doing that." Loud and clear. But still he continues. Flick and out. Flick and out. "I'm not having you do that in my cab." No sign in his eyes that he even hears me. I cross a red by mistake and horns blare all around me. Recovering my composure I turn left to take a double-back shortcut, heading down a deserted tree-lined road. Behind the trees a sprawling row of low-slung 1930s flats. Flick and out. "Pack it in. You're distracting me and that's dangerous."

Suddenly he stops flicking the flame, though his eyes still reveal no hint of his having heard me. He lets his arm fall to his side. I breathe out my relief. The sooner this journey is over, the better.

He's trying to set fire to the seat.

At the training schools they advise you not to take chances. If you've got trouble in the back on a quiet road at night, you're vulnerable—forget the fare, unlock the doors and chuck them out.

I'm turning the wheel, pulling up sharply at the curb, braking hard, unlocking the doors and twisting to face him. "Right, that's it. *Out.*"

The smile is back. Sinister. He's still holding the flame to my upholstery.

"*I said get out!*" There's a smell of melting plastic.

I could call the coppers on one of the phones but it would take too long. I could drive to a police station but I don't want to turn my back on this piece of shit. I don't know what he's going to do next.

Cabdrivers aren't supposed to carry weapons. The Carriage office can have your badge if the police catch you carrying. But there are ways around this: A big metal torch or a heavy spanner can do some serious damage.

I have a torch and a spanner in the boot. The trouble is, I would have to get out of the cab to fetch them, breaking another unwritten cabbies' rule—don't leave the cab when someone's in the back. They can have your money bag in a flash. But if I don't get a weapon, how the hell can I get him out?

My breath is coming in short shallow bursts as I grope for the door handle and my hands are shaking. He doesn't move while I get the torch from the boot. Then I'm yanking the rear door open, grabbing hold of his left arm. He stinks of booze and alleyways. He's not moving, even to try to see me off. I'm heaving and dragging and he makes no response. He has the lighter in his right hand and he's still trying to set my upholstery on fire.

I raise the torch. Am I really going to have to use it? *"Get out of my cab, you creepy fuck!"*

Then, quite suddenly, his head is coming at me, hard, like a battering ram, right at my stomach. I'm stumbling backward, trying to get my balance, and he's barging out, shoving me to one side and scurrying away down the street, disappearing between the blocks of flats.

I slouch against the cab, winded, trying to get my breath back, listening to the slap-slap of his Jesus sandals fading into the night. Above me, the moon is pallid and round.

11

JONNY makes me some soup—or rather, he pours it in a pan and heats it up. Nothing fancy—not your fresh carton of Covent Garden or Joubére—just a small tin of Heinz Mine-strone. When it's hot he pours it into a chipped mug and delves in a drawer for a spoon.

"Sorry," he says, as he brings it to me, where I'm sitting on the couch. "I'd offer you some bread and butter to go with it but I've run out."

"Doesn't matter," I say, and it doesn't.

Jonny picks up his acoustic guitar and tunes it while I slurp my soup. The guitar is covered in cigarette burns, greasy smears and the leavings of stickers that have peeled away. Battle-scarred like its owner. He plays "Wish You Were Here" by Pink Floyd, and makes it sound plaintive and nostalgic. He doesn't ask what has happened to me and I don't tell him. These are the best moments with Jonny—the times when he doesn't ask and I don't tell. He plays "Hotel California." He plays "Roxanne." He starts to play "Psycho Killer," and when I close my eyes I see that round pallid face in the moonlight. Flick and out. Flick and out.

Did I come here because Jonny's place was the closest to the police station, or was it more than that? Any of the others would offer more comfort but they would fuss and fret over me. Jonny knows better than to do that. He soothes me the best way he knows—by singing to me. I knew I would come back. I knew I would forgive him.

"Hey," he says, laying down the guitar. "I've got something to show you."

"What?"

He reaches under a couch cushion and pulls out an old brown envelope. Passes it over. "Open it."

I look up at him. He's smiling—a rare event.

"Go on. Open it."

The flap is tucked in rather than stuck down. I pull it open and feel inside. "Jonny—" A wad of cash. Tens and twenties, some old, some new. "How much is here?"

He's rubbing his hands together, chuckling. "Five hundred and forty of Her Majesty's lovely pounds."

"Where did you get it?"

The chuckle fades. "Jesus, Katy, you sound so suspicious."

"That's because I *am* suspicious." I shove the money back in the envelope. "You don't have money."

"Nice to have your vote of confidence." He snatches the envelope and stuffs it back under the couch cushion. "I *was* going to ask you if you'd fancy a week's holiday somewhere. *Was*."

"Oh, Jonny, I'm sorry. It's been a lousy night. But you've got to admit it looks a bit funny. You *never* have money."

He reaches for the can of Becks in front of him and takes a swig, eyeing me irritably. "I won it, all right? I won it at a poker game."

"Straight up? You're a dark horse, Jonny. Since when did you start playing poker? Who did you play with?"

"Never you mind, my girl. Now, you'd better start behaving yourself or I'll forget the holiday and buy myself a new guitar instead." He reaches for the old one. "Where do you fancy? Greece? Italy? The Canaries?"

"Let me think about it." Holidays are complicated for me. When you disappear for a week or two and come back with a tan and a load of mosquito bites, people realize you haven't spent the time driving a cab around London . . . "You'd better put that money somewhere safe in the meantime. Stick it in the bank or something. Somewhere it can't be got at."

"Yeah, yeah." He strums a couple of random chords.

I'm coming over all dreamy. Maybe it would be nice to go somewhere with Jonny. Perhaps we should pool our money and escape together. Get away from London and all its freaks. We could go away and never come back.

"Play me that song you wrote," I say. "Weeping Willow."

He ignores me and starts back on "Psycho Killer."

11:03 A.M. No sleep. Jonny's still out like a light as I'm leaving the flat. For hours I lay beside him, watching his eyeballs roll and jerk under the closed lids, the mouth twitch and the fingers clench and loosen. He's so busy when he sleeps. I wonder what he dreams about. I tried waking him up and suggesting we go out for break-fast together but he didn't fancy that. I told him he should get out more or he'll start going all weird and agoraphobic. He told me to fuck off and went back to sleep.

It's damp outside and the pavement is covered in tiny snails threading their silvery tracks back and forth. My cab is parked be-hind the rusty white transit van as usual. Getting in I can still smell melting plastic. I roll the window down to get some air and check the phones one by one. My tired eyes feel glutinous, jellified like a couple of slimy hard-boiled eggs.

Pink phone—Amy: "Babe, thank you *so* much for my desk. It looks stunning in my room. It's so beautiful and antiquey it's al-most a shame to put my computer on top of it. You're fab."

Green one—Richard: "Hi, Kitty. Call me please. I feel like you're avoiding me and I don't know why. Just call me."

That's all. No other messages. And in particular, nothing from Twinkle about tomorrow. It seems unlike him not to have called to make arrangements. I wonder if it has something to do with what-ever made him rush out of the café the other day . . .

I'm not in the mood to call Richard but his voice on the answer service is all quivery and strained. I'd better not leave it any longer. I press "1" and the phone dials his number. He picks up after two rings.

"Richard Meadows speaking."

"Hello, Richard. It's me."

"Oh, hi." I can hear pleasure and annoyance warring with each other in his voice. "How are you, Kitty?"

"I'm fine. I'm not avoiding you, Richard."

"That's not how it feels. You say you're in bed with flu, you won't let me come to your flat—let's face it, you won't so much as give me the *address* of your flat—and then you don't return my calls for days. I'm worrying about you and I can't get hold of you and then suddenly I run into you with some friend in Islington! What am I supposed to think, Kitty? What exactly *am* I to you?"

I can imagine him pacing back and forth in his hallway, coiling the phone cord tightly around his wrist. I hope Dotty's at nursery. I'd hate for her to hear this. I grapple around in my head for the right thing to say, the smell of burnt plastic still filling my nostrils.

"I'm sorry, Richard. The truth is that just over a week ago I was attacked in my taxi. Some nutter with a lighter who tried to burn my upholstery—"

"Oh, my God, Kitty. Why didn't you tell me?"

"It's OK. I'm all right. I came away with a black eye—you saw it yesterday, didn't you? Trouble is it sent me a bit funny. I just wanted to hide. I didn't want to see anyone. My friend Amy—she works for Victim Support. I needed to talk to her."

I hear him sigh. I think it's worked.

"Kitty, I don't know what to say. It sounds awful. Really awful. I wish you'd come here. We're together, aren't we? Don't shut me out."

"I'm sorry, honey. I know I should have come but it's hard for me. It's just the way I am." I'm wincing as I say these words. "I'm still a beginner at this. I'm still learning how to *be* in a relationship."

Another sigh. "Look, why don't you come over?"

"What, *now*? Don't you have to work?"

"I reckon I could take the day off. I got the Jeckson website finished yesterday, so I'm ahead of myself for once. I thought it was going to take much longer than that. How about it?"

He hardly ever takes a day off . . . I could smooth things over, make it all better. Something is gnawing away at me, though. I'm supposed to be somewhere else. I just can't remember where.

"Kitty?"

Joel. That's it. He asked me to come over this afternoon. I remember him sitting at the pub table drinking pernod and black, the teetotal boy drowning his sorrows. I can't let him down. "Sorry, Richard. Not today."

"Oh." So crestfallen. "What about tomorrow, then?"

I know I should say yes but I don't want to. The truth is that I want to drive into the countryside with Twinkle. "I could do Saturday . . ."

"I can't manage Saturday. I have to take Dotty to see someone."

"Sunday?"

"Whatever."

"*Please*, Richard. Sunday?"

"Like I say. Whatever."

Joel answers the door in a sharp black suit with silvery tie, white buttoned-up shirt collar, shiny shoes with metal caps, sleek mirrored sunglasses. Big cheesy grin.

"Wow, look at you!"

"Armani." He gives me a twirl.

I move toward him, stepping into the hallway, ready to kiss him or hug him or something, but he's already gamboling away up the stairs into his flat, leaving me to close the front door and follow.

Someone's been cleaning and sprucing the chintzy lounge. His mother, no doubt. The cushions have been plumped that little bit extra. Everything looks shiny, polished, even the phone. There's a smell of air freshener, sickly and flowery.

Joel's in the kitchen, poking his head through the doorway. "Cup of tea?" He's still wearing the sunglasses even though it's quite dark inside.

"Yeah, sure. Joel—"

I'm about to launch into a whole series of questions but he's filling the kettle and wouldn't hear me over the rush of the cold tap, so I give up and wait. An appointment diary lies next to the phone, open to this week. I reach over and pick it up, glance at today. It says:

Thursday, October 12th
14:00—Kat
15:00—M
18:00—H
22:00—Q

He's only scheduled me for one hour, the cheeky little runt! And who are all these other people, "M" and "H" and "Q"? Who the hell does Joel think he is, James bloody Bond?

I put the diary back in its place just before Joel appears with two mugs of his undrinkable tarmac tea, and sets them down on coasters.

"Well, things have certainly changed since I last saw you," I try.

"Aha. What do you reckon to the suit?" He's prancing up and down and preening. He's removed the sunglasses, thank God.

"You look fantastic."

I go to give him a snog, but he's off into the bedroom, calling, "Come and look."

He's opening up his knackered old MFI wardrobe and showing me a selection of ties neatly arranged on a rail inside the door. Shimmering ties; orange, green, lilac, blue.

"Are you going to tell me what's happened?"

"My new job happened." He selects the orange tie and brings it out to show me, stroking it. "Feel the quality."

"Very nice. What's your new job?"

"I'm in hospitality," he says. Then he pulls a second Armani suit out of the wardrobe. Navy blue, single-breasted. "It's the same cut as this one," he says.

"Joel—" He's reaching for one of a row of white shirts but I grab him by the shoulders, anchoring him to the spot.

"Hey, watch the suit!" Anger flashes in his eyes and I let go. Maddeningly he takes the opportunity to run away again, this time back into the kitchen.

I pause and take a few deep breaths before returning to the lounge and sitting down on the couch. A familiar smell starts wafting in, at odds with the air freshener. It's something I've never smelled in Joel's flat before.

He emerges from the kitchen smoking a cigarette, and carrying a saucer to serve as an ashtray. Or rather, he's pretending to smoke—he isn't inhaling.

"For Christ's sake, Joel!"

"What are you, my mother?" He sets the saucer down on one of his nest of tables and settles himself in a floral armchair, one leg crossed over the other, all prissy.

His comment stings but that doesn't stop me saying what I feel. "Last time I saw you you were getting pissed. Today you're smoking. I've never known you to do either of those things before. Most kids have their teenage rebellion at fourteen or fifteen, don't they? Haven't you left yours a bit late?"

"Jesus, Kat, get off my case. Look how well I'm doing and all you can do is have a go at me for smoking one little cig! Chill, girl, and check out my threads."

He's still going on about the damned suit. Just how much more admiration does he expect? I sip my tea and grimace as it coats my tongue. "So tell me about the job."

He shrugs. "Not much to tell yet. I'm still being trained up."

"Who are you working for?"

He pretends to drag on the cigarette and makes a great display of tapping ash onto the saucer. "This is the really excellent bit," he says. "Although I took all that shit working at Shaman, something good has come out of it after all."

"How d'you mean?"

"Well—" He leans forward, smiling. That gorgeous sugar smile of his that never fails to melt away my irritation. "There's this guy who comes in on my third day at Shaman, yeah? I hear him talking to the receptionist. He's one of Gino's regulars and he wants Gino to cut his hair. But she tells him that's not possible 'cause it's apprentice night. Gino has to teach. So the guy—he says, "I need my hair cut tonight. What are you going to do about it?" And the receptionist is explaining all about apprentice night, but the bloke—he catches sight of *me*, right? I'm sweeping up the hair clippings, minding my own business, like you do. And he says, "What about him? Can he do it?" She starts telling him that I've only just started at the salon and that I'm not supposed to cut yet. She says if he wants a good cut she can slot him in with Gino the next day. Or if he really needs it done now she can make sure he gets an apprentice who's been here a good few months. But he's made his mind up. He wants *me* to cut his hair."

"Why you?"

He shrugs. "So, anyway, I'm doing his hair and we get to chatting. Gino comes over now and again and talks to him and tells me one or two things about how to do the cut, but I just know that I'm doing really well and that I don't actually need Gino's advice. And when I've done all the cutting and drying I show the bloke the mirror and he really *loves* it—says I've done it better than Gino does. He says in future he's always going to request that I do his hair. He gives me his business card and he tells me if I ever need a favor or if things don't work out with Gino, I should call him."

He stubs out his cigarette. It's only half smoked but he can't finish it.

"I didn't know you were so talented."

He looks wounded. "Don't be so bloody snarky, Kat."

"I'm sorry, Joel." I reach over and put a hand on his knee, give it a squeeze. His smile returns, but it's a little sheepish now.

"You know, Kat, I ain't never going to drink that pernod shit again. It made me sick as a dog. And can you imagine what your sick looks like when you've been drinking pernod and black? Can you imagine what it *smells* like?"

"Yeah, all right." I hold up a hand to stop him but he presses on.

"I made it back to the flat but I chundered all down the front of my T-shirt and my track shorts."

"Enough already, Joel!"

"No, but the thing is, Kat—when I went to put my trousers in the washing machine, I found that bloke's card in my pocket. And I remembered what he said—about how I should give him a ring . . . So I did. And you know what? He gave me a job! I wish I'd met him months ago. When I think of all the time I've wasted on dancing and hairdressing. It was all just a load of bullocks. Now I've made it. I've got a *real* job."

"So what exactly *is* this job?"

He looks irritated that I've presumed to ask this. "Well . . . hospitality, innit."

I put my hand back on his knee. He actually flinches and then seems to make an effort to relax. I keep my hand there, hoping I can somehow steady him, calm him down. "But what do you *do*?"

"I told you, I'm being trained. Mr. Fisher's training me himself. He says I'm talented. He says I could build a real career there."

"Joel, what *is* this training? What *is* this career?"

"Look, I dunno yet, do I? I'm still learning. Mr. Fisher has faith in me. D'you know, I went into his office on my very first morning and he got a big wad out of his pocket and gave me a whole load of cash—just said, 'You look a mess, boy. Go get yourself a couple of suits.' He didn't say it in a nasty way. He was dead nice. And he's not even taking it out of my wages. Says it's an investment. He's a geezer, Mr. Fisher is."

I'm struggling to control an urge to grab hold of Joel and bash his stupid innocent head hard against the wall. Instead I keep my temper and speak to him softly. "Joel, you clearly have no idea what this man's business is or what this 'job' is going to be. Don't you think it's weird that he's so keen to have you work for him? Doesn't it strike you as just a little bit odd that he gives you all that money straight away—just to buy some new clothes?"

He gets up, hands on hips, marches off to the kitchen, returning with another freshly lit cigarette, which he wags at me in anger. "Why can't you be happy for me? Why is it so unlikely that someone should be impressed by me? Am I really that useless, Kat? Is that what you think of me—that I'm a lost cause?"

"Not at *all*, Joel. You're special. You could be a great dancer."

"Oh, stop going on about the dancing. It's cloud fucking cuckoo stuff, the dancing."

"I just don't want to see you hurt, that's all. Look what happened with Gino."

"*Forget* about Gino." He turns and disappears into the kitchen. I hear him filling the kettle again. "Gino was a mistake. But I can learn from my mistakes, Kat. I'm learning all the time."

Learning what, I wonder . . . I get out of my chair to find him leaning on the work surface, waiting for the kettle to boil. I move up behind him and put my arms around his waist, holding him close, resting my head on the back of his shoulder. I turn my face in to nuzzle the base of his neck. I kiss it. He mutters something about how I shouldn't crease up his suit jacket but he lets me hold him.

"I don't want you to be my mother, Kat," he whispers.

"I don't want that either."

I'm about to try to lead him into the bedroom when the doorbell rings.

"Shit!" He looks at his watch. "I didn't realize it was so late."

"Who are you expecting?"

"Mr. Fisher said he'd send a taxi for me at three." He wriggles out of my grasp and scurries down to the front door.

"You don't need a taxi," I call after him. "I'll drive you!"

But he's already talking to the driver on the doorstep, telling him he'll be down in two minutes.

"You're early today, aren't you?" says Winnie, looking up from her book and peering at me through a cloud of cigarette smoke as I walk into the Crocodile.

"No lunch. What about you? Shouldn't you be at home giving the kids their tea?" Apart from Winnie, there's only two blokes talking quietly together at a table near the wall. I don't know either of them.

"I had a row with Paul. Or rather—Paul had a row with me. He can get their tea for once, the lazy sod."

I sling my jacket over the back of the chair and sit down, deciding not to comment on Paul's laziness. We both know my views on Paul and if I welly in she'll only start defending him.

"Good book, this," she says, holding it up for me to see. It's called *Women Who Love Too Much*. "You should read it."

"No, thanks. No time for reading." I call out to Big Kev, "Don't suppose you do mini-kievs do you, Kev?"

Kev's big face is entirely vacant.

"No, thought not. Baked potato with chili and cheese and a coffee, please."

Kev nods and carries on tinkering with the tea urn.

Winnie's cough is back. She's hacking away for all she's worth while I stare into space, worrying about Joel. She only manages to stop coughing when she brings an asthma inhaler out of her pocket and squirts it into the back of her throat. Her face is bright red.

"I didn't know you had an inhaler."

"I don't," she says when she can speak again. "It's Tommy's."

"Well, what are you doing with Tommy's inhaler? What if he needs it?"

"He's got a spare."

I shake my head. "Winnie, there's no two ways about it, you've got to get yourself along to the doctor. Jesus, what are you thinking of!"

"Don't you start on me too," she says fiercely. And now I realize what she has been rowing with Paul about. For the first time, I find myself inclined to side with him. She's looking daggers at me, though, and I figure I'd better drop it.

"Your life, your body," I say under my breath.

"Exactly so." She sparks up another cigarette and takes a sip of tea. "So, what have you been up to?"

"Me? Oh, the usual."

"Anything in particular?"

"Well, I got attacked last night."

"You *what*?"

"Some shithead loon. Tried to set fire to my upholstery, didn't he. Nothing to worry about, though. I saw the freak off."

She knits her eyebrows together, shakes her head. "I hope you went to the police."

"Course. Not that they'll do anything."

"You should get on the radio, Kath." She points her cig at me. "It's so much safer driving with Computercabs or one of the others. Especially driving at night. The jobs are good, you know you're going to get your money at the end of the run and there's always someone on the end of the radio."

"Nah, it's not for me, Win." She's always on about me getting a radio. "The best thing about cabbing is that you work for yourself. I don't want to have to pay someone for the privilege of being told what jobs to do—may as well drive a mini-cab if you're going to do that."

She shakes her head. "You won't listen to sense, will you. Not about this—not about *anything*."

"*You* can talk."

Kev brings my potato and coffee over and I'm glad for the momentary diversion.

"So, you back with Jonny, then?" Winnie asks as I'm shoveling up mouthfuls of potato.

I nod.

"You're a fool, Kath."

"He was sweet to me last night. After my spot of trouble with the freak. He's not all bad, you know."

She stubs out her cigarette viciously, as though she wishes the ashtray was Jonny's face. Or maybe Paul's . . . "You seeing that Craig Summer again?"

"I might be."

And yes, sure enough she's beaming all over her face again. "He's very charming, Kathryn. Bet he has a few quid 'n' all. Get you out of cabbing. 'S logic, innit."

"Whoa, hold up, baby! I said I *might* be seeing him again."

She shrugs, looks at me like I'm some hopeless case. "You

could do worse, Kathryn. That's all I'm saying. Look, I know you don't want to give any of them up, but sometimes you've got to think about what's best for you. You could use some time to yourself."

"I know. You're right." God, I hate her when she goes wise on me. Now she's chuntering on, like she always does.

"If life was a drink, my life would be a cup of tea—lukewarm with too much sugar—and yours would be a bottle of champagne that someone's shaken up so the cork comes shooting out and the froth goes all over the place."

I raise one eyebrow. "Sounds a bit phallic, all that froth."

She smirks and reaches into her cigarette packet but her smile slips away when she realizes it's empty.

12

FRIDAY the 13th. Eight A.M. No visitation from the color, but I wake up alone, brooding on the memorial service and feeling like a fool. How many times must I have checked the phones last night to see if Twinkle had called? Seems like every time I dropped off a passenger I'd be reaching for the red and pink phones (Twinkle only knows the numbers of those two) and dialing in for my messages. Nothing. Nada. I even started driving especially early so I could knock off at 1 A.M. and get some beauty sleep. What an idiot.

Fighting the urge to check the phones again, I throw on my terry cloth dressing gown and stumble through the unpacked boxes and general debris to the kitchen to make some coffee.

I stand and gormlessly watch the slow drip-drip of the thick black liquid. *Fuck* him. Why am I doing this to myself? It's not as though he even *means* anything to me. But I'm left with no plans for the day—nothing to take my mind off the memorial service. I wonder if it's too late to phone Richard and tell him I'm unexpectedly free after all . . .

Wait—there's a sudden sharp buzzing sound. My doorbell. It's the first time anyone's rung it in all the time I've been living here.

The blue stair-carpet is dirty and smells of cat piss. They have four cats downstairs and when their door is open the stench is overwhelming. Sometimes, on wet days, the smell even sneaks its way up into my flat.

The buzzer goes again, head-shatteringly loud down here, as I'm fumbling with the Chubb lock on the front door. "Yeah, yeah, just a second."

Finally I get the door open.

"Katerina—you're not dressed yet!"

Craig Twinkle Summer. Large as life. Big smile on his face. Clutching a brown paper bag.

"What the fuck are *you* doing here?"

The smile slips and he looks perplexed. "Don't you remember? We have a date. I've come to pick you up." He pushes the paper bag at me. "I brought bagels."

I have the oddest sense that everything is imploding on me. Lost for words, I peer into the bag. Poppy-seed bagels. Four of them.

"What's going on, Twinkle? What kind of game are you playing?"

He's baffled. "I thought we could have a bit of breakfast before we set off. I reckon I owe you a breakfast . . ."

I stand my ground, keeping him on the step. "Are you trying to fuck with my head?"

He shakes his head vigorously. "Sorry. I thought you wanted to go out for the day. Do you want me to leave?"

Recovering my composure, I fold my arms and look levelly at him. "Craig, I'm trying to understand how you found me. I have never given you my address and I'm not in the phone book."

"Oh." He shakes his head again. Puts me in mind of how you'd shake a shoe to try to get a stone out of it—only you can't find the stone. "Are you sure?"

I nod.

His brow creases up and he looks pale, slightly ill. "Maybe Winnie gave it to me?"

I turn this over in my mind. I suppose it's just about possible. Winnie does have my address. But she'd be unlikely to remember it off the top of her head. "What are you on about—*maybe* Winnie gave you my address? Did she or didn't she?"

He tilts his head to one side, then to the other. He seems to be trying to weigh up whether to say yes or no. Then he brightens. "All right, then. Let's say she did."

"What sort of an answer is that?"

"Well, if you didn't give me the address, it *must* have been Winnie. Mustn't it?" He smiles helplessly.

"But don't you *remember*?"

"To be honest," he says, sheepishly, "no." He shuffles about on the step, glances around him at the old woman shambling down the street, at the grumpy man across the road washing his brown Metro. "Kathryn, are you going to let me in or shall I go?".

I hesitate before replying. "All right, come in. It's the only way I'm ever going to get to the bottom of this."

I'm embarrassed about the cat smell as he follows me up the stairs. I'm embarrassed at the thought of him seeing the mess inside my flat. It's like when someone barges into the bathroom and catches you naked. Worse, it's like when someone barges into the bathroom and catches you bleaching the hairs on your upper lip.

But my feelings of embarrassment in turn make me resentful and even angry. I never asked him to come here—I've never asked *anyone* to come here! How dare he take such liberties? How dare Winnie make so free and easy with my address? Particularly in view of what she knows about my life and my need for privacy. Jesus, only yesterday she sat there and preached to me about how I should keep time for myself . . . This is a violation.

As he walks in he skids on an empty garbage bag and almost trips over a box of books. I'm opening the blinds—reluctant to let the light reveal the full extent of the mess in my hovel but deciding that if I don't, one or other of us is going to fall and break something—whether it be one of my belongings or a bone. Maybe a neck.

I clear some space on the couch and gesture to it. "Sit."

He does as he's told.

I go out to the kitchen with the bagels and scrabble about in the cutlery drawer for the bread knife.

"Nice place," he calls from the lounge. "Lots of potential. Just moved in, have you?"

I say nothing, slice the bagels and stick them under the grill. I'm doing my best to stay cool and get my head together.

"What's that Peter Sellers song?" comes his voice. "Balham, gateway to the South . . ."

Something snaps and I'm ducking back into the living room, still brandishing the bread knife. "What d'you think you're doing, asking Winnie for my address? What's wrong with phoning me?"

"Sorry. I wanted to surprise you."

"I don't like surprises."

The car is parked all the way down the road. He didn't want to drive it right up to my flat because it would spoil the surprise. It's a little silver Mazda MX5 sports car, a convertible—he's hired it for the day. Lying across the passenger seat are half a dozen long-stemmed red roses.

"They don't have thorns," he says. "But then, roses don't any-more, do they. Not the ones you buy."

The car's beautiful. The roses are beautiful.

I get in, placing the roses on my lap. "Where are we going?"

He pushes a button and the top slides open. "Wait and see."

Oh God, another surprise.

He has to check his road atlas before we start. I try to peer over his shoulder but he hides the page from my view. Then he spends some time scrabbling about in the glove compartment for a CD, finally settling on Van Morrison. *Moondance*.

We're moving—at last—heading down Bedford Hill, past the two bedraggled prostitutes who always hang out there. I notice the envy in their faces as we slip by in the spangly little sports car. We stop for a red light at the junction with Balham High Road, and when it turns green he stalls. Horns blare out and he swears, crunches the gears.

"Not used to this car," he mutters. "Be all right in a minute."

God, I hate being a passenger.

Streatham, Tulse Hill, Forest Hill, Catford. The nasty gray no-man's-land of the South Circular.

"Why can't this be a proper road, like the North Circular?" he moans as we grind to a halt at yet another set of traffic lights, and then go inching forward in stops and starts. The skip lorry in front is farting exhaust fumes at us and I grope for the button to get the top over us again.

"If you'd only tell me where we're going I could find us a short cut," I try, but he isn't having any of it.

Hither Green, Eltham, Blackfen, Bexley. Bowling alleys, furniture warehouses, industrial-sized McDonald's buildings and golf courses.

The Dartford Tunnel. I keep the car fastened against the fumes and shut my eyes tightly. I love bridges but tunnels get my mazophobia going. They put me in mind of rats running through sewer systems. I don't want to think of the river rushing above us, of the stream of traffic that carries us relentlessly forward. My chest tightens and I dig my nails into my sweaty palms.

On one of my family's rare visits to London when I was a child, we went down into the Greenwich foot tunnel. My nerves began sending me warning signals as soon as the lift doors closed. Once we were down in the tunnel where buskers' guitars and children's shouts reverberated around the stone walls, I noticed a steady drip-drip coming from one tiny dark spot on the ceiling, and I began screaming and wailing, working myself up to a pitch of frenzy that only intensified when I heard my hysteria echoed back at me. I'm sure I wasn't the only *child* who's had to be carried out of the Greenwich foot tunnel by her father, but I don't suppose many *nine*-year-olds have had to be removed in such a way.

"Are you all right?" says Twinkle, noticing my shut-tight eyes, the rictal tension in my face.

"I will be."

And out again into the sunshine. I manage a smile.

South Ockenden, North Ockenden, Brentwood. Into the heartlands of suburban Essex, where I was conceived, birthed and schooled.

"What's the destination, then, Craig? Cambridgeshire? Suffolk? Norfolk? East Anglia? Just how far are we going today?"

"All the way, darling." He laughs! "All the way."

"You wish."

And we're off the M25 and onto the M11.

We pass Harlow, the concrete New Town where my mother used to take me to buy my school uniforms, and I'm wishing we were going west rather than east.

Twinkle is groping about in the glove compartment. The back of his hand and his arm brush against my legs and I realize it's the first time he's touched me today. The movement is accidental but feels strangely intimate. He produces a pack of cigarettes and switches on the car lighter. Then he notices my face.

"Oh, go on, let me. I wouldn't do it in an enclosed space but we've got the top down, after all."

Now I understand why he chose a convertible.

"I've taken your advice about getting fit," he says, lighting up. "I've bought myself a course of fencing lessons."

"Fencing!" I try not to laugh at the mental image of Twinkle—stocky body encased in dense white padding and one of those silly masks—jabbing and slicing and moving about in a faux balletic manner.

"Yeah. All that gym stuff—it's not for me. I don't fancy running endlessly on some machine but not actually getting anywhere. I like the idea of fencing—aggression coupled with precision. Strength and strategy. Right up my street."

"Just don't expect me to play at damsel in distress," I warn him.

Junction nine and we're coming off the motorway. We've been on the road for just under two hours. There is a tightness in my chest. My arms are stiff with tension and I have pins and needles in my fingers.

"I've had enough of this game, now, Twinkle. I want to know where we're going."

He glances at me, startled, maybe hearing the dread in my voice. All he says is, "Don't worry."

Great Chesterford. Little Chesterford. The B184. Cottages with thatched roofs, Volvos parked in gravel driveways; old houses painted in bright pink or lurid yellow with curious patterns scraped above their doors—squares and circles, polka dots and shells. These designs are an ancient local tradition, and I've always suspected they are the grim progenitor of ceiling artex. I haven't traveled down here in years but I could tell you the names of every shop, pub and hotel in these twee villages. I know the road so well I could tell you where the puddles form when it rains.

"We're not going to Saffron Walden, are we, Twinkle?"

He's lighting up again, tapping his ash out on the road. He says nothing.

"Craig, I need you to tell me whether we're stopping in Saffron Walden or whether we're just driving through it on our way somewhere else."

He seems to be about to speak but then—"Fuck!"—we swerve sharply and I'm thrown sideways, my seatbelt cutting into my chest. He blares his horn. A white duck is waddling across the road, oblivious of how close it just came to being turned into paté. "Jesus, I hate driving in the countryside. It's fucking animal dodgems all the way," he says, recovering himself. "Are you all right?"

"Sure. Craig—"

We're into the outskirts of the town. The Eight Bells pub flashes by on our left, apparently unchanged. My parents used to take me there on Sundays for a pub lunch and we'd sit at the big round table in the noisy family room. When I was nine or ten I was sick in their car park, just outside the main entrance. My mother held my hair out of the way and rubbed my back until I was done.

"Cook this up with Winnie, did you? Whose idea was it—yours or hers?" I rub at my aching forehead. "And to think of how I was looking forward to my day out with you . . . Did you never stop to think that this should be *my decision*?"

I'd forgotten how huge the church is—almost a cathedral. Its spire is visible for miles around.

"*Why*, Craig?"

He peers about for a parking space at the side of the road, spots one between a Toyota and a Volvo. Ten or eleven brown, black and gray-clad people are making their way up the path to the gaping doorway. I recognize podgy Mrs. Dewer from the school, leaning on a man who I assume must be her husband. There's Uncle Peter, who isn't really my uncle, walking with a stick. I don't know the young couple with the child . . . Oh, God, there he is.

I had imagined that he would arrive first so he could stand on the steps like the host of a party, to kiss cheeks and shake hands. But in fact he's only now getting out of a blue Renault parked farther up the road. His hair has turned from gray to white, and his black suit hangs loose on him. He is thinner than I've ever seen him, somehow smaller too. The combination of the suit and the white hair makes him look vaguely aristocratic, like one of those shambling, hollow old men who get in the back of my cab and ask me to drive them to the Garrick Club. I had such a clear image in my mind of how he must look, twelve years on from our last meeting, but it's all wrong.

"That's him, isn't it? With the white hair?"

I feel Twinkle's hand on my shoulder. It squeezes reassuringly.

My father puts the keys in his jacket pocket and stands next to the car, staring into space. I notice his jacket cuffs come right down over his hands, to halfway down his fingers—maybe he *has* shrunk.

"What are you going to do?" comes Craig's voice.

Dad cocks his head slightly to one side, as though he's listening to something. And then, slowly, he turns around, peering, craning his neck like some old tortoise to see who is walking up the path to the church, who is parking their cars. I see his eyes, their darkness. And then I know what he's doing.

He's looking for me.

There's a click and a swish as my seatbelt unclips. My hand is on the door handle.

Dad is still turning, searching for a black cab parked among the cars. His shoulders begin to sag—an almost imperceptible movement but a movement all the same. Then a young vicar whom I haven't seen before is appearing through the church door, bounding down the steps toward my father with perhaps an inappropriate level of spring in his step. Dad notices him—shuffles forward to shake his hand.

I see my chance and I open the door.

"Kathryn, do you want me to come with you?"

"Fuck off."

I'm out of the MX5 and running hard down the hill away from the church, away from my father, away from meddling Craig. I'm wearing my trainers and cargo pants so I'm not hampered by high heels, slippery soles or tight skirts. To begin with, my heart is thumping but then my pulse normalizes and I feel myself opening out. My breathing deepens and my legs start to fly. It's effortless. I am a machine.

Turning the corner, I almost knock over a middle-aged woman in a hat but manage to dodge her at the last moment. I hear the engine of the MX5 starting up behind me and I accelerate as I dive across the road and into the town center into lanes that cars can't enter, past gift shops and tea rooms, shoving my way through the browsing hordes.

Cutting across the market square I'm aware of being out in the open, vulnerable, and I speed up again, but there's no sign of Twinkle. He won't catch me—not here, in this place which is alien to him but more familiar to me than the layout of my own mind. I'm burning through the narrow alley that runs along the side of Boots, and emerging onto the Common—sprinting straight across the green, past a young couple larking around in the fertility maze, and hurtling on toward Thaxted Road. I'm going so fast now that I don't think I could stop, even if I wanted to. I'm barely aware of where I am or where I'm going. I only know that I'm heading out of town, my feet scuffling up the fallen leaves, smacking the puddles and pounding the pavement.

A car honks its horn at me as I'm pelting across a road and I almost go flying over the hood. Reaching the safety of the pavement, I finally manage to slow up and I make myself stop. I lean against a lamppost and breathe, trying to calm my shattered nerves. Then I realize where I am.

Maeve's house doesn't look like Maeve's house anymore. If it wasn't for the familiar oil marks on the driveway I might not even have recognized it. Someone has converted the garage where she used to keep the cab into an extension. It even has a little window with lace curtains. There's a new gate out in front—green wrought iron with curling bits and a sign: "Bluebottle Cottage." Bluebottle Cottage indeed! If Maeve were still alive she'd be disgusted—either that or she'd just laugh. There's a new front door with frosted glass where there used to be an old wooden one with peeling paint. The front lawn is well kept and someone's planted a hedge. The old apple tree is gone. I feel the urge to cry building strongly inside me—out of my control, like the urge to vomit. This place was my home—maybe the only real home I've ever had—and now I can barely recognize it.

Audley End station. I'm sitting on a bench on Platform 1, coughing and getting my breath back, staring at the track. I have just run a very fast three miles down country roads—and I guess that's a good thing, seeing as I haven't been to the gym for a couple of days. But now my throat is parched and there is no drinks stand (let alone a café) on the station where I could buy a bottle of water. I'll have to wait till I'm back in London.

I've missed the last London train by five minutes so I'll be stuck here for half an hour. There's nobody else around on this two-platform mini-station. Only the birds. When I was a child there used to be a ticket office with a grumpy old bloke working in it, but now that's all gone and this place is no better equipped than your average bus stop.

So I'm stuck here waiting, with jelly legs and a raging thirst. What a bastard Twinkle is, bringing me back here . . . And as for Winnie—well, my best friend has betrayed me.

That thin white-haired man comes into my mind—the way his eyes looked, their emptiness. It was like catching a glimpse of my father's ghost. In fact, that is exactly what it was like—after all, he's been dead to *me* for the last twelve years, fifteen if you count the years when I lived with Maeve and refused to have anything to do with him.

The church service must be in full swing now. I wonder if my father is having people back to the house afterward for tea and sandwiches—all the stuff people do when a loved one has died, but that he has left undone for fifteen years. I wonder if it was difficult to persuade the vicar to hold a memorial service in his church for a woman who took her own life.

"Kathryn!"

Oh fuck, it's Twinkle.

He's striding up the platform toward me, his hands deep in his pockets. He has a humble look about him.

"I'm sorry." He sits down beside me on the bench.

I shuffle myself sideways, edging away from him, saying nothing, just staring down at the tracks.

"I'm *really* sorry . . . I was worried when you ran away. I'm so glad you're still here."

"Quite the opposite of what I was just thinking."

He sighs, puts his head in his hands and seems to be trying to work out what to say. "I was wrong to bring you here. This should have been your decision, like you said. I've fucked up, haven't I?"

"Dead right you have."

"Would you believe me when I tell you that I did the wrong thing for the right reasons?"

"I don't know what to believe." I sneak a look at his contrite face.

"I'm an incurable fixer," he says. "And I wanted to fix your relationship with your father. I thought if I could only get you here, it would all take care of itself."

"You've got a bigger ego than I realized," I snap. "And you've paid too much attention to Winnie's self-help crap."

"Kathryn, this isn't Winnie's fault. She told me about you and your dad, but—"

"I knew it! What else has she been telling you?" I could picture them sitting in the Crocodile, heads bent low so they could whisper to each other. *Kathryn's in a mess—someone needs to sort her out . . .*

"Nothing. Like I say, it's not her fault. She warned me not to do this."

"And you thought you knew better."

"Something like that."

I get up and walk away from him, up to the far end of the platform. I know he'll come after me in a second or two, but I need a moment to get a hold of myself.

He gives me half a minute's grace, but then, sure enough, I hear him traipsing along behind me. "Kathryn," he says to my firmly turned back, "Would you listen to me for a minute? Just *one minute*? Then I promise I'll go away and leave you alone."

I turn slowly around to face him. "You have one minute."

"OK." But now he's just staring down at his feet, jingling keys in his pocket.

"Well, go on then!"

"Um . . . yeah."

I notice where his hair is thinning slightly on top. I have the strangest urge to ruffle it, but I don't.

He takes a deep breath and says, "The thing is, I fell out with my parents a few years back. They disapproved of something I'd done, and . . ."

"What? What did you do?"

"It doesn't matter."

"Yes, it does. Tell me."

He gives me an evil look. "OK. It's about my first wife."

"The one who didn't go to Hawaii with you?"

"No. *She* was my second wife."

"And Marianne—"

"Was my third."

"Jesus, they're really coming out of the woodwork now, aren't they! I thought you said you were married twice."

"I've never said that. You must have made an assumption. I've been married three times." He steadies himself. "And I've been divorced three times. That's the lot. The first one . . . Well, I married too young—should have just shacked up with her or something. We didn't know each other well enough, and once we'd got hitched and moved in together I found I didn't actually like her very much."

He pauses, reaches into his inside pocket for cigarettes. I wait for him to light up, oddly intrigued.

"I didn't know what to do. I wanted to leave her but I didn't want to hurt her. And then I met this other woman . . ."

"Here we go."

"Yep, here we go. Me and this woman, we got involved. Well, you know how it is if you're with someone you don't really love and then you meet someone you think you *might* be able to love . . ."

I give a half nod.

"But what I didn't know was that Nicola—that's the wife—she was pregnant. And for some reason the only person she chose to confide the happy news in was my *mother*, of all people."

"Ah."

"Next thing is Nicola finds out about the other woman—I'd slipped up a few times and she'd put two and two together. We had a big row and I walked out. A few days later I get this call from my mother: *What kind of a monster are you, walking out on Nicola when she's having your baby?*—and all this."

"But you hadn't known about the pregnancy . . ."

"Exactly so. If I'd known . . . well, I don't know what I'd have done if I'd known. By the time I got to speak to Nicola, she'd already had an abortion. My parents—they were strict Catholics, you see, and very straight people, the pair of them. My mother said she didn't want to have anything more to do with me, and my father backed her up."

There's a tremor in his voice. He stops to drag on his cigarette.

"So what did you do?"

"Nothing. My wife divorced me and I married the other woman."

"The one who didn't go to Hawaii? Or have you just remembered *another* wife?"

"Yes, the one who didn't go to Hawaii. I didn't hear anything further from Nicola or my parents for two years. Then I had a letter from my father telling me my mother had died. He wanted me to come to the funeral. I didn't go—didn't even answer the letter."

"I'm starting to get your drift, Twinkle."

"Two more years went by and my second marriage went down the toilet. Finally a letter came from Dad's best friend. He'd collapsed and died of a heart attack. I hadn't seen him in years but I was his only son, and he died intestate. It was so weird going back to that house after all that time—arranging his funeral, sorting through his stuff. It had been so long that I somehow couldn't connect with my emotions. It was like I'd packed away my feelings for him in a box and I couldn't remember where I'd put it. It was horrible. Regret was about the only feeling I could manage."

He trails off and we stand together in silence, looking at each other. I'm weary. He looks as weary as I feel. And then there's an announcement by a dead electronic voice. The next London service is approaching.

"Well, I guess I'll leave you to it, then," says Twinkle. "I just wanted to explain."

I shrug. "It's a sad story."

"Yeah."

He wanders away down the platform as the train eases up and grinds to a halt. There's a beeping noise to indicate the doors are about to open and the "Open" button flashes green. I press the button and find myself staring into the train, and into the eyes of a pale, mousy woman. To begin with she stares back at me placidly, but then, as the doors remain firmly shut in spite of the beeping and the green light, she looks away and starts worrying at the equivalent button on the inside. Still the doors won't open. Her mouth forms swear words. Her face is turning red with frustration. Glancing along the length of the train I realize that none of the doors have opened. The mechanism must have jammed. The train is motionless while the beeping continues. A guard has jumped out and is skittering down the platform, panicking uselessly, shouting something inaudible to the driver. People inside the train are banging on windows. I hear the crackle of speakers but no announcement is made. I turn and look back over my shoulder. Further down the platform, Twinkle has reached the gateway through to the car park.

Again I feel the urge to run—but this time not away from him.

He suggests Cambridge but Cambridge is too close. I want to get right out of this memory-laden corner of the country and make for somewhere neither of us has ever been to. So we drive on to Suffolk, and as we cut across the open flats and marshland to Southwold, I find I can breathe again.

As we drive I try to explain what my father did to my mother—how he'd coped with her depression by trying to pretend it wasn't happening. How he'd dealt with her alcoholism by pretty much confining her to the house, preferring to leave her with her gin and vodka than to risk the embarrassing consequences if people found out the truth about the headmaster's wife. How he'd told her she should stop drinking and pull herself together whenever she asked for help. How he'd turned his back while she slipped quietly into her breakdown and yelled at the family doctor to stay away and mind his own business when I phoned the surgery and got him to come over. When they found her dead in the car, how he had her quietly cremated with no proper funeral service. And when I packed my bag and moved in with Maeve, how he didn't try to stop me. I was *her* daughter, after all—I looked too much like her and my grief was embarrassing.

We drink pints in a squalid pub where the locals give us funny looks. He drinks bitter, I drink lager. We eat battered cod and chips—he likes mushy peas so I give him mine. The cod tastes of nothing and the peas are like green wallpaper paste. We move on to whiskey and I beat him at pool five times in a row. Even after losing five times he won't concede that I'm a better player than he is—he says he's not playing at his best because he's tired from the driving. Poor baby. We drink on, getting progressively louder. I don't know whether it's the booze but I'm feeling horny. At closing time it suddenly occurs to us that we don't have a place to stay and neither of us is in a fit state to drive. Fortunately this pub has pretensions of being a hotel—the landlord has three guest rooms upstairs. Jesus, what a day.

The room smells fusty, as though nobody's stayed here for a long time. Four flies are circling the light fixture, buzzing loudly. They're slow and sleepy so it's not difficult for me to kill them by trapping them in the Gideon's Bible. Twinkle goes into the en suite to pee and I listen to the trickling sound. When he returns I go in myself, leaving the door open. A second later he appears in the doorway to watch me, which is what I wanted him to do.

We make a lot of noise pushing the narrow twin beds together. Twinkle falls over and says he's hurt his ankle. He's after sympathy but I just laugh at him. My laugh takes on a nervous edge when he starts undressing in front of me. I'm apprehensive about whether I'll like the look of his body, but when he takes his shirt off, I realize it's going to be OK. His skin is smooth and clear, and there's just a fine sprinkling of hair across his chest. His stomach is bigger than I'd ideally like, but it looks firm—not flabby as I'd worried it might be. There's something very animal about his naked body. I want to touch him.

PART III

THE CROCODILE

13

SHALL I go over to Craig's or shall I go home? It's 5:17 A.M. on Tuesday, October 24th, and I'm sitting with Winnie at our usual table, trailing a fork through the mess of unwanted scrambled egg and ketchup on my plate, trying to make up my mind. If I get going now I can be there by six and we could have a couple of hours before he has to get up. Make it a surprise—he'll be all bleary and grumpy, stumbling about in his boxers, but when he sees me at the door his face will light up like Bonfire Night . . .

Winnie's chuntering on in the background while I'm debating whether or not the surprise element of this scheme is a good idea. Maybe I ought to call him first . . . That reminds me: I need a new phone—a Twinkle phone. Purple?

"*Hello*—anyone home?" Winnie knocks on my forehead like it's a door, causing me to yelp. "Kath, I know you're very busy being in love, but could you at least *pretend* to listen to me!"

"You what?"

"You heard me." She's doing her folded arms and raised eyebrows thing.

"Are you saying I'm *in love* with *Craig Summer*?"

She sighs. "How many times have you seen him over the last couple of weeks?"

I rub at my head. "That hurt, you know . . ."

"Ah, poor Diddums. How many times, Kath?"

"I don't know, do I? . . . five or six, I guess."

"And how many times have you seen Richard or Stef or Jonny?"

I can't be doing with this hassle. I should just stop telling her things. Before I can respond she goes all smug and says, "See? You're in love with Craig. 'S logic, innit. So when are you going to face up to it and dump the others?"

"Look—it's the *newness* of the thing, isn't it? Nothing more than that. Isn't it your turn to get the coffees in?"

She calls Kev over and makes the order. I'm not in such a rush to leave now. I'll be heading back to Balham for a sleep after all. Winnie's way off target but she's right about one thing, at least— I'm seeing too much of Twinkle and not enough of the others and that won't do. You've got to keep things in balance when you have a life as complicated as mine or everything tips up and turns over. And it's going to be more complicated than ever now that I have to split my time between *six* lovers.

I watch Winnie take a puff from Tommy's inhaler while we wait for Kev to bring the coffees. She has huge dark circles around her eyes, and her cheeks are so pale they're almost green. I can hardly believe she's playing so fast and loose with her health when she has three kids to think of. Maybe she's worried the doctor will find something that needs to be reported to the Public Carriage Office, and they'll take away her badge. After all, that's what they did to her husband Paul when his diabetes was diagnosed.

"Have you been to see the doctor, Win?"

"Yes, actually." She says this with a snooty air, putting me in my place.

"Oh. Good!" I try to smile and wait for her to say more but she doesn't. Instead she just gazes out of the window at the relentless rain. "Well? What did he say?"

She studies her bitten finger nails. "He wants me to see someone at the hospital. You know—a consultant. He thinks I need some tests. Next week."

"What sort of tests?"

"I don't know, do I? I'm not a bloody doctor."

"Right." I'm about to ask her another question but then I see the fear in her eyes and decide against it. There's something about her today that reminds me of someone—Maeve, toward the end. And now, as Kev brings the coffees, I see her clock my sympathy, my worry, and she draws herself up, actually sitting up straighter on her chair.

"If life was an ice cream," she begins, "then mine would be a single scoop of Wall's vanilla in a cornet and yours would be one of those knickerbocker glories, all covered in syrup with a paper parasol stuck in the top and sprinkled with hundreds and thousands."

She's losing her edge, running out of ideas. It's all been food lately. And it always says the same thing. I wonder if she even realizes that her wisdoms say as much about her attitude toward her *own* life as they do about mine.

"Kits!" Dotty is annoyed with me. I'm sitting cross-legged and motionless in front of a half-built tower of multicolored wooden bricks. I have a red block in one hand, a green in the other, and I'm staring into space.

"Sorry, Dotty." I place the red block on the top.

"No!" she shouts. "The green one comes next. The green one, Kits!"

Little fucking dictator.

We are playing a game, Dotty and me. I build the tallest tower possible while she crouches and watches me, her cute, pink face wearing an expression of pure evil. She's waiting for her moment and she's becoming impatient.

It feels right, being here with Richard and Dotty tonight. It's like I've come out of a trance, and it took Winnie's comment this morning to snap me out of it. I look at Dotty—at the love on her face. She trusts me enough to fall asleep with her head in my lap. Often she cries when I say goodbye to her, but when I tell her I'm coming back she believes me. Scary love.

"Hurry up, Kits, build it *high*!"

I wonder if I will ever have one—one of her, I mean. One of *them*.

"Here you are, darling." Richard wanders into the living room and hands me a glass of red wine. He's wearing a frilly polka-dotted apron, probably a relic from his marriage. He's cooking beef Stroganoff for dinner, and his cheeks are pink with the heat from the kitchen. "It'll be ready in a couple of minutes."

"Great." I place the green brick on the tower, and watch him bend to put a CD on. Morcheeba. It's a CD they used to play in the East Dulwich gym where I met Joel.

Richard disappears off to the kitchen again as I reach for the yellow brick—tease Dotty with it, let it hover in the air before putting it in place on top of the swaying tower. And the second I do, she strikes—*Bam*!

Kids are scary. *She's* scary. Just look at her thrashing around on the floor among the scattered building blocks. She's fucking terrifying!

"Build me a boat," she says, fixing her intense gaze on me.

"A boat?"

"Yes. Mummy built me a boat. *You* build me a boat."

"Oh. Did she?"

"Dinner's ready," calls Richard from the kitchen.

I don't say anything about it to Richard until after we've made love. We're lying in the king-size bed he used to share with his wife. He's dozing but I'm wide awake, staring up at the ceiling, debating whether or not to get dressed and go to work—at least, that's *one* of the issues I'm debating. He's lying on the left side of the bed—he always does, and I'm on the right.

"Did your wife sleep on this side of the bed?"

"Why do you ask that?" His voice is as sleepy as I might expect, but there's also an edge to it.

"I want to know. Did she?"

There's a click and the bedside light goes on. He props himself up on one elbow. "Kitty—"

"She's been here, hasn't she. Jemima's back."

He rubs at his forehead and sighs.

"When was she here, Richard?"

"A couple of days ago. Look—Kitty, do you mind if I get a glass of water? Do you want one too?"

"No thanks." I watch him get out of bed and reach for his terry cloth dressing gown. He plods off to the kitchen and I hear the tap running. I wonder if they slept together . . .

"Has something happened between you?" I ask, as he comes back in with his water.

"No." He sits down on the edge of the bed, reaches for my hand and holds it in his. "No, of *course* not. What on earth makes you think that?"

"I don't know." Jemima is a witch. She walked out on Richard and Dotty when Dotty was less than a year old. She stuck around while she was still breast-feeding, but once she'd been able to fully wean the sprog she left. Gerard was waiting in Paris. What kind of a person does that?

"Kitty, I love you. I don't want Jemima back. And she doesn't want *me* back either."

There's something he's not telling me. "She's not going back to Paris, though, is she."

"No. She's left Gerard." He sips his water. "She's renting a flat in Highgate for now."

I don't like the "*for now,*" but I let it go. What else can I do without seeming paranoid? I should be happy about this, for Dotty's sake . . . But I'm suddenly aware of the fact that this is *her* bedroom, not mine. The orange walls, the Turkish rug, the lime-green padded headboard against which I'm leaning—she must have chosen them. And this bed—this is hers too.

"Do you think she's going to stick around, then? Or will we be picking up the pieces when she abandons Dotty again?"

He lets go of my hand in order to slip off the dressing gown and slide back into bed beside me. "To tell you the truth, I don't know," he says. "Are *you* going to stick around, Kitty?"

"Sure I am." I reach across his body for the light. I'm happier in the darkness—I can't see Jemima's color scheme anymore. I nuzzle down into his arms. "Can we redecorate this room?" I ask him.

*   *   *

One A.M., and I'm dressing in the dark so as not to disturb
Richard. Whether it's the worries about Jemima, the coffee I had
after dinner or the fact that I'm not used to sleeping at this time, I
don't know—but in any case I can't sleep. So I may as well do
some driving. I'll leave him a note. He'll understand. I creep out
of the room and close the door silently on Richard's snores. Dotty's
door is half open, the way she likes it, and I look in on her as I pass
by. She always lies in the same position when she sleeps—on her
stomach, with her head turned to the left, her left arm flung over
her Kermit doll, holding him close.

Eleven-forty A.M. on Wednesday morning, and I wake up confused and disoriented, thinking I'm in Twinkle's bed. But I'm
not—I'm on my own in Balham. He is so vivid in my mind—was I
dreaming about him? As I'm clambering through the rubble in my
living room, I catch sight of my naked reflection and I'm shocked.
It is my fattest time of the month hormonally, but I still wouldn't
usually have that nasty little pot. This is *his* fault. Him and his
fancy restaurants, his endless bottles of wine and breakfasts in
bed. Gym. Gym and abstinence. Got to get this under control.

   Three hours and a heavy workout later and I'm all showered
and fresh, on my way to Joel's place. The sky is gray and solid. Yesterday's rain still hasn't relented and my cab has sprung a leak.
They're not made like normal cars; they're all bolted together and
the pieces of metal continually try to pull themselves apart. Winnie drives one of those bug-eyed new TX1s and maybe I should
think about trading in my old Fairway before it gives up on me altogether. There's water getting in behind my dashboard, seeping
down and dripping on my feet. It's not so very long ago that I supposedly had this fixed and sealed. They must have conned me. But
I love this old heap of scrap metal because it was Maeve's. Once
the cab goes, there'll be nothing left of her.

I'm about to ring the bell when I realize the door has been left on
the catch. What's he thinking of, leaving his front door open for

just anyone to walk right in? I'm worried about that boy. Closing the door, I climb the stairs two at a time.

"Joel? Joel, are you in here?"

I can smell scents that I wouldn't expect to find here. Not the usual odor of air freshener or potpourri. No, today I can smell smoke, and more specifically than that—weed. I wander into the living room. The cushions on the couch are in disarray, and a suit jacket—Armani, of course—has been dumped unceremoniously on the floor. There's an ashtray on one of the incidental tables with a number of spliff ends in it, all of them smoked down to the roach, as well as cigarette butts. One empty glass sits on a coaster next to the ashtray, and there's another on the floor beside a half-drunk bottle of Glenfiddich.

"Joel?"

Recalling that his mother has a habit of turning up unexpectedly, I stoop to pick up the ashtray, take it through to the kitchen and tip its contents into the pedal bin. Then I go back for the glasses and the whiskey bottle. I rinse out the glasses in the sink and put the bottle away in a cupboard. Returning to the lounge, I open the window to let some fresh air in. I do these things slowly, aware of a heaviness somewhere inside me. Then I wander through to the bedroom.

No Joel. The bed has been slept in, but the boy is not here. I can hear the sound of the shower, though. I'm about to go through to the bathroom when I notice the mirror that usually hangs over the sink lying on the floor. A Visa credit card in the name of J Marsh has been left on it, and there are traces of white powder, the remains of lines. I see the worry in my face reflected in the mirror as I bend over to inspect the powder more closely, lick a finger and take a dab. I know that taste.

He is soaping himself, his body visible through the smoked-glass shower door. The air is filled with steam, which makes me think he's been in there for some time. When he sees me in the doorway he calls out, "Hi, Kat," and turns his back so that I can't see him soaping his genitals. He's singing softly. It sounds like "New York, New York" but he's not a good singer so I'm not certain.

"Hello, Joel." I lean against the wall, watching him, waiting for him. A minute or two later the shower door squeaks open and he emerges, his dark skin glistening with water. He's always been in good shape but today his muscles look firmer and more well developed than ever. I take his towel from the rail and hand it to him.

"You left your front door open," I say, watching him rub at his pecs.

"So?"

"Anybody could have come in."

"I needed a shower but I knew you were coming over. Is that all right with you, *Mum*? D'you want some tea?"

"No, thanks." His fucking *attitude*.

"Please yourself." He ties the towel around his waist and wanders out to the bedroom.

I follow him through and perch on the edge of the bed while he searches in a drawer for underwear.

"Do you fancy a day out?" I say, oddly nervous and self-conscious with this changed Joel.

"Can't," he says, pulling on a pair of Calvin Klein trunks. I watch him tuck his penis away. He reaches for one of the row of white shirts on the rail. "I have to go to work."

"Oh." I'm pissed off with him now. "Why didn't you tell me that on the phone?"

"You didn't ask."

I make an effort to calm my temper. "Come and sit down with me. I want to talk to you."

"Sorry. No time." He slips the shirt on and stands in front of the long mirror to button it up.

"Joel, what's going on? Who was here with you last night?"

"A friend. Not that it's any of your business." He's taking a pair of trousers off a hanger, sitting down on the dressing-table stool to put them on. Seems like he'd rather sit anywhere than next to me on the bed.

"A friend who's got you drinking? Smoking weed? Snorting coke? It's not your style, Joel."

"Styles can change, can't they?" He has his trousers on now.

He's sitting down at the dressing table, reaching for a bottle of toner and a cotton ball. I watch him cleansing his face, paying particular attention to the forehead, the chin and the nose. There's something different about his face—what is it?

"I'm worried about you. This friend . . . is it someone from work?"

"What if it is? What's the big deal?" He tosses the cotton ball into a bin and reaches for some Clinique moisturizer.

The difference is his eyebrows. He's plucked them into slender, fine arches.

I don't know what to do. He doesn't want to touch me, he doesn't want to spend time with me . . . Not for the first time, I wonder if Joel has been going through a crisis of sexuality. Has he emerged from his crisis, then? Is this new Joel the *real* Joel?

"Joel, are you sleeping with men?" The question is out before I can stop it.

He swivels around on his stool to look at me and gives me the most sensual, most mischievous and flirtatious smile I've ever seen on his face. Then he says: "Only professionally, darling."

What is my face doing? He's enjoying this, the little toe-rag. He's loving the effect his words are having on me. He can't say this to his mother but saying it to me is the next best thing. Just look at him—primping and preening!

It's weird—I knew, really. *Hospitality*, indeed. I knew last time I saw him but I didn't want to acknowledge it: Instant employment from a man who discovered him pushing a broom around a hairdresser's floor. A man who talent-spotted that girlish face, those puppy eyes, the tight little buns, and who saw pound signs in the special bittersweet vulnerability that is his trademark. Free Armani suits, a diary full of appointments, a taxi turning up to drive Joel hither and thither. It all adds up to one obvious job.

"Joel . . ." My throat is so dry I can hardly speak.

"Yes, sweetie?" He's turned back to the mirror and is examining a tiny zit on his chin. I stand up and walk over to him, lay a hand on his shoulder.

"Joel, you shouldn't be doing this. It's bad for you—all of this is

bad for you. This man, Mr. Fisher—he doesn't *care* about you.
He's just using you—".

"Spare me the speech, Kat." Joel wriggles his shoulder free.
"Hey—" my stomach is at his eye level as he twists around. "Are
you pregnant?"

He reaches out to pat me there and I shove his hand away, my
cheeks hot with an angry blush. "Don't be stupid. I'm trying to
help you, you little runt!"

"Yeah, yeah, sure you are."

I'm struggling not to completely lose my rag with him. "I'm
getting out of here, Joel. See you around. Take care."

"You're just jealous!" he calls after me. "You don't love me—
you want to *possess* me. Well I ain't your toy, sister!"

I'm running down the stairs. This place is stifling me—the smell
of the weed, the booze, maybe a hint of sweaty sex, and beneath it
all the persistent odor of his mother's air-freshening products.

As I reach the front door I turn and look back. Joel is standing
at the top of the stairs watching me leave. Beneath all the bravado
and bluster there is sadness in his eyes. He looks utterly lost.

I'm shuffling about and shifting from foot to foot in a corridor that
smells of old trainers, reading the notices on the board about judo,
meditation, swimming lessons and pensioners' tea dance. I've
been here for almost half an hour now—drove here on impulse after leaving Joel's place. The striplight above me is flickering, making my head hurt. I hadn't intended to come here. I guess I must
be upset because of the scene at Joel's flat. Either that or I'm going soft.

"Pretty nifty, huh?" comes a male voice, and I wheel around.
The speaker turns out to be a blond guy with a mustache, who's
wandering out of the changing room, talking to a skinny bloke who
looks a bit like Nicholas Lyndhurst.

The Lyndhurst look-alike replies, "I'm not sure about it, myself. I'll give it some thought."

They're followed by a trickle of men of all ages and sizes. I'm
becoming impatient. Maybe he's not here . . .

"Hey!" It's him. It's Craig. He's coming out of a different door-way with some gray, bearded geezer. He's sweaty and red-faced—unlike the others he hasn't changed out of his white, padded fencing gear.

"Surprise," I say, feeling slightly foolish.

"This the wife?" barks the bearded man.

"Nope—got rid of her," says Craig, cheerfully. "Kathryn is my girlfriend. Kathryn, this is Andrew, my fencing teacher."

"Hi, Andrew." My voice comes out coy and shy-sounding. What is the *matter* with me?

"Very nice." Andrew looks me up and down, all sleazy, and gives Craig a wink. My coyness fizzles out instantly and I feel tension in my jaw.

"Watch it, mate. I wouldn't rate your chances if Kathryn challenged you to a duel." Twinkle slaps Andrew on the back—it's a matesy slap, but if I'm not mistaken, it's also saying "piss off now." Sure enough the "piss off" message is reinforced when Craig goes on to firmly turn his back, leaving the bearded creep to grunt a goodbye and go wandering away down the corridor.

Craig shrugs. "Sorry about that. He's a good teacher, though."

"Don't worry. It's fine."

"I'd give you a kiss, but look at the state of me." Craig wrinkles his nose. "I hate showering here—the water's freezing. But if I'd known you were coming I'd have showered and changed all the same."

"Don't worry. It's fine." I move closer. He flinches when I lean in to kiss him, but then relaxes. His mouth is warm. I put my arms around him and giggle at the feel of the thick fencing padding. "It's like snogging the Michelin Man."

"Yeah, yeah." He pulls away, smirking. "What are you doing here, anyway, Katerina?"

"I had to see you." The words come out before I can stop them. The smirk vanishes, and for a moment he looks as though he doesn't know what to do or say. Then the twinkle's back in his eyes.

"Wanted to see how my jab and thrust are coming on, did you?"

"That's the basic idea, yes. Can we go back to your place?"

He catches hold of my hand. "Why don't we go to *your* flat today?"

"But my place is such a mess."

"Doesn't matter." He gives my hand a squeeze.

"Well, I . . . OK."

14

Pink phone—**Amy:** *But no, it's not Amy (must get a new phone):* "It's Craig on Friday at one o'clock. What are you doing tonight? Call me."

Blue phone—Joel: Nothing.

Yellow phone—Stef: "Hey, K, it's me. It's Friday and it's pay day! How do you fancy going clubbing—my treat? Giz a shout."

Green phone—Richard: "Hello, Kitty. I was wondering— are you free for lunch tomorrow? Dotty's spending the day with Jemima and I thought it would be nice for us to see each other on our own for once. Let me know if you're free."

Red phone—Johnny: *No, it's not—Jesus, him again . . . (must, must get a new phone):* "Hi, it's Craig. I left a message on one of your other phones but then I thought maybe I'd picked the wrong one. Katerina, why *do* you have so many phones? Anyway, call me."

Forget it, the lot of you. Fridays are good money. I'm working. End of story.

"Kath, you didn't seriously think it would last, did you? I'm sure it was good for your ego but he's just a *kid*."

Three thirty-seven A.M. Friday night or Saturday morning, depending on how you want to spin it. It's been a hectic night and Winnie and I have both made our money and knocked off early. Now I'm giving her the evils across the table.

"That's not the point, Win."

"Well, what *is* the point, Kath?" She's in such a foul mood I'm amazed she wanted to meet up at all.

"I'm worried about him. I *care* about him."

"Sure you do. You care about all of them, don't you? That's why you're spinning them all along and cheating on the lot of them. Because you *care* so much."

"You don't understand."

"Come off it, Kathryn. You're not that deep."

Winnie's still barking at me when I leave. I actually get up and walk out while she's in mid-rant—I can do without having my head put through a blender after a hard night's work. My knackered Fairway is parked behind her spangly red TX1. I'm cursing her under my breath as I fumble for my keys in the rainy dark. Interfering old cow—she should try getting a life of her own and butting out of mine. As I get the door open I hear one of the phones ringing. It's the red one. Probably Craig again, and I'm not sure that I want to speak to him but I slide into the driving seat, slam the door and fumble for the phone in the glove compartment nonetheless.

"Hello?"

"I'm ringing about Jonny Jordan." A man's voice—gruff and edgy. Unfamiliar.

"What about him?"

"Are you his girlfriend?" He pronounces the word "girlfriend" with great scorn, turning it into an insult.

"Who wants to know?"

"Jonny's in a bit of trouble. You'll need to come and get him."

My mouth is instantly dry. "What sort of trouble? What are you talking about?"

"Trouble like if you don't come and get him now, I won't be able to save him from getting his head kicked in. *Comprendez?*"

"Let me talk to Jonny, please. Is he there with you?" My voice is wobbling.

"He's not exactly in a position to talk at the moment, darling. He's had a skinful and his head has unfortunately come into contact with somebody else's fist."

A sudden bang on my window alarms me and makes me jerk so sharply that I drop the phone on the floor. As I dive down for it I hear the man's voice: "Hello? *Hello?*" I grab the phone but when I straighten up I bash my head hard on the steering wheel. I'm wincing and clutching the back of my head as I twist round and see Winnie standing outside on the pavement, looking agitated.

"Sorry about that," I say, with difficulty, into the phone. "Look, what's going on? I'm worried."

"Just get over here pronto," says the man. "Or your boyfriend is going to end up with even more scars than he has already. You need to go to Turnpike Lane. It's the red door next to Oz's Café. Ask for George. You got that?"

"Yeah. Yeah, I think I know the place. It'll take me at least twenty minutes to drive there, maybe more if the traffic's bad."

Winnie beats on the window again. I hold up my hand and mouth at her to shut up.

"Whatever. Just get here as quick as you can." There is an odd pitch in the man's voice. A note of panic. He hangs up.

Another bang on the window and I open it up, irritated. "Pack it in, Win. I've got serious shit going on here."

"Don't you go flouncing off when I'm in the middle of talking to you, Kathryn! . . . What sort of shit?" That nosy interfering look comes over her again.

"I don't know. Some geezer just called—don't know how he even had my number. Jonny's in trouble. The guy says he's out cold. Sounds like he got wankered and then got in a fight. I'm going over to Turnpike Lane to pick him up."

Winnie shakes her head. "For Christ's sake, Kathryn, don't let yourself get sucked into his mess."

I've had enough of her judgments for one night. "What would you have me do, Win? Leave him there to get beaten into a pulp? What if it was Paul, eh? You'd be over there like a shot."

"All right," she says, slightly awkward and shuffley on the pavement outside. "We'll go together."

"No, Win, there's really no need—"

"I'm not having you going off to some bloody awful pit in Turnpiki-larnie all on your own, Kathryn. Unlock your doors, I'm getting in the back. No arguments."

Four thirty-three A.M. and we're driving past Finsbury Park station, up Seven Sisters Road and onto Green Lanes. The two of us—me and Winnie. We drive in silence past Turkish bakeries, poky hardware stores, kabob shops, seedy pubs, greengrocers with empty fruit racks and battered crates stacked outside on the pavement in the dark. We're going under a railway bridge with "Welcome to Haringey" daubed on it in white paint. The back of my head is swollen and aching where I bashed it on the steering wheel. The rain has stopped.

Turnpike Lane—a name so unlike the place. Sounds pretty, doesn't it? Sounds like somewhere you'd find thatched cottages and a babbling stream—but no, this place is a litter-strewn rough-as-fuck shit-hole. The air tastes dirty as we climb out of the cab. There's no one about except a couple of geezers in hooded tops hanging around on the street corner and an old woman asleep in a shop doorway, almost indistinguishable from the pile of bags and rubbish in which she lies curled. I lock the cab, hoping the hooded-top geezers aren't as dodgy as they look. All is silent except for the echoing beep of a distant pelican crossing and the low murmur of pigeons lined up on a window ledge high above the street.

Oz's Café is a bog-standard paint-peeling greasy spoon, with grubby net curtains in the window and the dim multicolored blink of slot machines just visible somewhere deep in its interior. We approach the battered red door to the left of the shop and I ring the buzzer. After a moment an intercom crackles. A man speaks in another language—Turkish? Kurdish?

"I'm looking for George," I say. There's a buzz and a clunk, and I push the door open, glancing at Winnie as I do so. She looks pale, tired.

"Thanks for this, Win."

She shrugs. "Come on. Let's get it over with."

The lightbulb has blown on the stinking stairs, and with the front door closed we are left to blunder up in pitch dark. I'm more frightened than I'd care to admit and I have to fight the urge to reach out for Winnie's hand. A door opens at the top of the stairs, lighting the last flight of steps for us. A big man is leaning against the door frame in silhouette.

"George? Is that you?" I call out.

"No. George is inside," says the man in a heavy Turkish accent.

I can hear Winnie puffing and wheezing as we get to the top. I hope she'll be OK—I don't suppose she's brought Tommy's inhaler with her. The man stands to one side and we squeeze past him into the flat.

The air is densely fogged with smoke, and behind the smoke I can smell sweat and alcohol. The big open-plan room is grimy, the once white walls yellowed, with lighter patches where pictures must once have hung. There's a kitchen area to our left stacked high with dirty crockery, and a thin balding man is stooping over the cooker, lighting a cigarette on one of the rings.

"George?" I ask.

He turns round to face me. A pallid face, a little like the face of the man who tried to set fire to my cab. Pale eyes and a narrow mouth. He nods. "And you are . . ."

"Kathryn. And this is my friend, Winnie."

The big man closes the door behind us and stands with his back to it, arms folded. He's wearing a T-shirt with a yellow smiley face on the front of it. His real face is not smiling.

"Where's Jonny?" I try unsuccessfully to stop my voice from shaking.

George stretches an arm out. Points.

I turn and look. A couple of tatty armchairs. A round table bedecked with full ashtrays, empty whiskey glasses and randomly strewn cards. Three dining chairs upright, the fourth lying on its side. More cards scattered across the worn red carpet. Jonny's legs sticking out from behind the table. I rush across. He is lying on the floor, unconscious. His face is badly bruised on the right side. Dried blood all around his nose, smeared on his scarred cheeks, daubed on the collar of his white shirt.

"Oh my God. Jonny—"

I'm down on the floor, kneeling, cradling his head, bending low over his face, taking a hefty whiff of stale whiskey breath. He groans softly.

"So this is the great Jonny Jordan," Winnie mutters.

I ignore her. "What happened?"

"Jonny's a bad loser," says George, tapping ash onto the carpet as he wanders toward me. "Now, Mehmet's taken Oz for a walk to cool him down but they'll be back any minute. You'd better get this twat out of here before they get back. Erdahl will give you a hand on the stairs."

I take Jonny's legs and Erdahl holds him under the arms. Winnie goes ahead to open the front door. Jonny is not light and my back is killing me as I step gingerly backward and down. George watches from the doorway, cigarette in hand. As we get to the foot of the stairs he calls out,

"When Jonny wakes up, tell him he's got to bring the money round in cash by tomorrow night."

"How much does he owe?" I ask.

"Three thousand. Be sure and tell him."

It's only after Erdahl has helped us bundle Jonny into the back and I'm behind the wheel again that I really feel the full weight of the fear and the dread. We get moving fast enough but I have to pull over near Finsbury Park for some fresh air. As I'm sitting on the hood breathing deeply and trying to empty the stress out of my head, Winnie gets out and comes over—puts her arms around me.

We remain like that for a while, my head against her chest, while Johnny stays slumped in the back. I hear the wheezing sounds in her chest. It's like a steam engine in there. Then we get back in the cab.

"Do you think I should take him to hospital?" I ask her once we're moving again.

"No, just get him home to bed. Let him sleep it off. He'll be all right."

"D'you think so?"

"Yeah."

I catch her eye in the mirror. She tries to smile but it comes out wrong. Jonny's head has lolled onto her shoulder and there's blood on her cream sweater. I wonder what she'll tell Paul.

The sky is lightening at the edges, becoming less like a solid mass as we pull up behind the rusty white transit van. It's bloody murder trying to get Jonny out of the cab, up a flight of steps and into the lift without Erdahl's help but we manage, between us. There's one of us on each side of him, propping him up. Reminds me a bit of Twinkle and me trying to get Henry up to his flat that night I met him. Winnie keeps coughing and I'm worried about her.

When we arrive at Jonny's front door she has to hold him upright against the wall while I feel about in his jacket pockets then his jeans pockets for his keys.

"Jesus, what a dump," she says once we've finally got the door open, and she sniffs the air, all snooty. We drag Jonny across the room and half lay, half drop him onto the couch. He groans and manages to say what might be, "Katy . . ." but I'm not certain.

"Want a drink?" I ask Winnie. "He always has some booze in. It's just a matter of finding it."

She shakes her head. "No thanks. I want to get home to my husband and kids if you wouldn't mind driving me back to the Crocodile."

"Don't blame you." I look down at the mess that is Jonny. "Do you think he'll be all right if we leave him on his own?"

"Course he will." But the meaning behind the words is, *who the hell cares*.

"Winnie—"

"Yeah, I know."

It's on the way back to the Crocodile that she starts having a go at me.

"You can't let this go on, Kath. It's a waste of your time and energy. And he isn't worth it."

I try to keep my temper because she has been so good to me tonight but it's tough. "You don't know him, Win."

"I don't *need* to know him. I saw enough tonight."

I fall silent and sulky, hoping she will do the same. If she would only keep her trap shut until we get back to the Crocodile I won't have to lose my rag with her. This works for a while but then she starts up again.

"It's time you sorted yourself out—and I don't just mean about Jonny. If you could only *hear* yourself when you're moaning to me at Christmas because you've got to try to eat five dinners in one afternoon. Or in February when you have to celebrate your birthday five times on five consecutive days. Or in the summer when you have to decide who to go on holiday with. It's madness, that's what it is. Ditch those losers, Kath."

I've had enough of being preached at. "Look . . . Win . . . You put everything in boxes and then you put labels on them. Jonny is more than the label you've given him. So is Joel. So is Amy. So am I!"

I keep my focus on the road but I hear a sharp intake of air.

"It's because you're my friend that I say these things to you. I want to see you happy. And don't try to tell me that you are already because I won't believe you. I want to see you fall in love, get married and have kids. Would that be such a bad thing? I want to see you get yourself a *life*."

To my immense relief we've arrived at the Crocodile. There's an empty space at the rank behind Winnie's red TX1 and I pull into it. I'm so keen to get her out of my cab that I climb out really quickly and go around to open the door for her. Her face, as she gets out onto the pavement, is more concerned than angry.

"Well, anyway, Win—thanks. Thanks for everything." I'm wishing I could recapture the intimacy of the moment in Finsbury Park when we held each other close. But the moment is long gone.

"Can he pay the three thousand?" Her face is turned away from me.

"No. He has about five hundred. Or at least, he *did* have five hundred . . ."

She sighs. "What will he do?"

"I guess I'll have to help him." I'm only realizing this as I'm saying it.

She starts walking away from me, over to her cab. "You fool," she says over her shoulder as she reaches the driver's door. "You poor bloody fool."

"Katerina!"

He is standing in the doorway in his green dressing gown, his thin hair all straggly. He must have been asleep when the security man rang up to tell him I was here, but now he looks surprisingly unsleepy. He seems slightly shocked to see me.

I'm desperate to get inside, out of this maze of corridors. "Were you expecting someone else?"

"No . . . Of course not. I just . . . I wasn't expecting *anyone*—what time is it?"

"Five to seven." *Please* let me in, Craig. I can't take this corridor, its blueness, its sameness, the Muzak version of ABBA's "Knowing Me, Knowing You." I don't say it though. Just stand here in front of him, sweating.

"Oh, Jesus." He staggers back into the flat. "Five to seven on a *Saturday* morning . . . This is . . . unnatural."

"I've been driving all night. I wanted to be with you. Can we go to bed?"

❖   ❖   ❖

What is it about Twinkle? For the second time in a week I have found myself turning my cab around and driving off to find him. This bed is so warm, this room so peaceful. Such a far cry from Jonny's flat in the Elephant. He makes me feel safe—which is silly, really, when you consider that I know so little about him. He makes me want to break my own rules, like the other day when I took him back to my rubbish-filled hovel. That was the first time I've ever slept with anyone in my own bed . . .

It's the way he listens to me, always attentive. He touches me a lot when I'm talking to him. Incidental touches, on the hand, the shoulder, the arm . . . that's usually a female trait, isn't it. Doesn't seem effeminate when he does it though. When I tell him things, it's like he can always see the next layer—the hidden something that lies beneath and beyond what I am saying to him.

We've been lying here for about three hours now. He fell asleep immediately after we made love. I've been dozing on and off, but I keep waking up. My thoughts wander to Jonny: how he looked, lying there on the floor next to the abandoned card game. And to Joel: those silly plucked eyebrows and the lost look on his face. And then I think about the three thousand pounds and Winnie calling me a fool. Is that what I am?

Craig sleeps on his back, his head turned to the side. His mouth falls open when he sleeps and he snores—not loudly, though. The sort of comforting snore that reminds you he is still here. I have a sudden urge to wake him up and tell him everything . . . and I do mean *everything*. Would he understand? Would he listen in the same way he listens to everything else, as I explain about Stef and Amy and Jonny . . . I'd like to think he's different from other people, that he'd take it in his stride.

Resisting the urge to wake him up, I clamber out of the bed and wander through into the darkened living room. The back of my head is aching and when I put my hand up to it I feel a lump there. Oh yes, it's where I bashed it against the steering wheel. I'm on my way across to the French windows to open the curtains onto the weekend but I find myself drawn to the love meter he keeps on one of the glass shelves. I put my hands around its base, watch the red liquid rising up the tube and filling the top bulb.

Gazing across at the old wireless in the glass cupboard, I remember what Twinkle told me one night last week when we came back here together after a film in the West End and dinner at the Ivy. He said that when he was fourteen he had his heart broken by a girl in his class, and in a fit of teenage angst he took a load of his mother's tranquilizers and lay down in his bed, listening to the radio. He said he's not sure if he was sleeping or hallucinating or what but the voices in the radio seemed to be threading in and out of his head, talking to *him*. Some of them told him he was going to die, and some of them told him he was going to live. Eventually he freaked out and started screaming. His father was just arriving home from work, and he came rushing upstairs. Craig felt that the radio had saved his life. He kept it as a sort of warning to himself.

I wonder if my mother had the radio on in her car when she connected herself up to the exhaust pipe and waited to die . . .

Craig said he and his father kept his little "funny turn" a secret between them. They didn't even tell Craig's mother. He says I am the first person he has told.

"Hello, honey." Craig in his dressing gown, crossing to the French windows, opening the curtains. "Are you OK? You look scared."

"Yeah, sure. You startled me, that's all." As daylight floods the room I'm suddenly self-conscious, aware of my nakedness.

15

M Y building society closes at midday on Saturdays and I arrive with only ten minutes to spare. The middle-aged payment clerk is not happy when I tell her I want to withdraw three thousand pounds. She wants to see some ID, so I show her my badge, my driving license, a gas bill and a couple of credit cards. She wants to give me a mere five hundred pounds in cash with the balance as a check, but I'm not having it. She tries to make out they don't have enough cash on the premises to help me but I know she's lying. This is an Oxford Street branch—of *course* they have the cash. I wait for her to finish her rant and demand to see the manager.

Fifteen minutes later I'm walking out of the building society with a fat envelope containing three thousand pounds in fifties in my inside jacket pocket. I hang in a shop doorway down Wardour Street to call Jonny on the red phone—looking, no doubt, very shifty—and I'm surprised when he answers, his voice pained and slow. I don't bother with chat—just tell him I have the three thousand he needs. He starts to ask me to come over but I say I'm having lunch with a friend in the West End and if he wants the money he'll have to get off his arse and come in to meet me later. He's mumbling something inaudible but I talk over him and tell him three o'clock in The Comedy, a pub on Oxendon Street near Leicester Square. He continues grumbling and whining about the state of his head but I tell him to pull himself together and hang up.

*　　*　　*

Twelve-thirty P.M. on the nose and the sun is shining through cracks in the lidlike sky. Tavistock Street, Covent Garden. I'm meeting Richard in Sofra, the restaurant in which we had our first date. His suggestion.

A smiley Turkish waitress leads me into a long room bustling with people. Polished pine floor and pot plants with big glossy leaves. Waiters scurrying, cutlery clattering—only one or two free tables. Behind one of the big plants sits Richard, dressed in a rather swish suit that I've never seen before, studying the menu.

"Kitty." He stands to kiss me. "You look great."

I don't. I'm still wearing the old black trousers and knackered Lycra top that I was wearing to drive last night. He smells of body wash and newness.

"Where's the clobber from?" I ask, as we sit down.

"Oh, this old thing?" He smiles. "It's from Jigsaw."

"Not so old by the look of things."

He returns his attention to the menu. "Shall we have some wine? Red or white?"

"I prefer white at lunchtime if that's all right with you."

"Hey, let's have champagne." He's looking cheeky, beckoning the waitress over.

I'm suddenly edgy. Why has he brought me here today? I have a horrible feeling he's going to produce a ring or something.

"What's the matter?" he asks.

"Nothing." I'm looking around at the plants, the dessert trolley, the skylights. I'm trying to work out whether this is the very table we sat at on our first date.

His face clouds, darkens. "Oh," he says. "You didn't remember, did you?"

Oh, Christ. It's a nightmare trying to keep a track of all the important dates I have to remember. It would be written in my diary but that's back in the cab and I haven't looked at my diary for days . . .

"Richard, I'm so sorry . . . What can I say?"

"Nothing." His mouth is tight. "It doesn't matter. Let's order."

But it does matter, of course.

❊   ❊   ❊

I met Richard two years ago today. At a fair on Hampstead Heath. Not a big glitzy fair—the sort of fair where there's a knackered old ghost train with moth-eaten ghouls hanging from lengths of string; a couple of spinning dipping rides so slow you had to work really hard to be scared on them; a few dodgems and a load of little stalls with lurid cotton candy, sickly toffee apples and teddy bears wrapped in polythene. Add to that the fact that it was a cold day with sudden gusts of wind and brief but intense rain showers and you have the full picture. I was there with Jane and her husband, Spencer. Jane is a girl who lived next door to me in Peckham. We had very little in common but I was going through a phase of thinking it would be good for me to have more female friends— we've lost contact since.

Jane and Spencer had brought their horrible old black and white mongrel dog along to the fair, and it was only when they passed me the dog's lead for the third or fourth time while they went on the ghost train that I realized why they'd invited me along. I was standing about, feeling cold, while the dog—as bored as me no doubt—snuffled at scraps of hot-dog bap and chip paper that lay scattered around my feet. That's when I saw her: dark curls, huge eyes, open wailing mouth, pink dungarees. The smallest of toddlers wandering alone through the forest of adult legs, ignored by everyone.

People didn't respond to my "Excuse me"s, so I had to rudely shove my way through to the child. I crouched down and reached out for her hand. She was crying hard and staring up at me with fear in her eyes.

"Hello. Are you lost? Do you know where your mummy is?" I'd had very little to do with children and I was surprised at how much she moved me. Older kids and adults generally have an ulterior motive when they cry—our tears are calculated. These streaming tears were utterly innocent.

She couldn't speak, she was crying so much. Then the dog rushed forward, trying to lick her face, and she let out a scream before I could wrench it back. That's when the man with the empty pushchair came pelting out of nowhere, red-faced and breathless.

"Hey, what do you think you're doing? You're not going anywhere with my daughter!"

I straightened up, gave another tug at the pesky dog, as the man scooped up the little girl and balanced her on his hip. She put her arms around his neck and buried her face in his chest, but then twisted around so she could peep shyly at me.

"So you're the father, are you?"

"You're damn right I am! I could have the law on you." He was so self-righteous in his anger. The prick.

"Oh yeah? For what, exactly? For trying to help a lost child? You wanna keep a closer eye on her, mister. Next time it might not be someone like me who finds her."

I turned my back on him and started to walk off, dragging the dog with me. But then I felt a tap on the shoulder. I turned and it was him, running up behind me, struggling to carry the child and drag the pushchair at the same time.

"I'm sorry. I was frightened, OK? She was in the stroller. I only looked away for a few seconds . . . I was trying to win her a teddy bear. When I looked back down . . . It's tough, you know, when there's no one to share the responsibility. You can't watch them every second of the day. It isn't physically possible . . ."

The poor git looked so exhausted suddenly. All flustered and humble. A nice man, that was clear. I gave him a smile to show there were no hard feelings. "What's her name?"

"Dorothy," he said. "I mostly call her Dotty. And I'm Richard."

There's something undeniably attractive about single fathers. But in truth it was really the gorgeous Dotty who seduced me, not her daddy.

"Well, Richard . . . Shall we go and win Dotty that teddy bear, then?"

The champagne is going warm and slightly flat. Neither of us has even finished our first glass. Halfway through my lamb guvech I remember I had the same meal on our first visit here. I mention it to Richard as a throwaway comment and he just smiles weakly. Now, incredibly weary, my appetite gone, I've laid my knife and fork down in the messy remains and I'm staring hard at a small stain on the tablecloth.

"There's something I have to tell you," Richard says, awkwardly, when he's through his last mouthful of Sofra special grill.

There's a stiffness in his voice that makes me look up at him. "What? Is something wrong?"

"I'll get the bill. We can walk and talk. I need some air anyway." A nerve in his forehead twitches. He gestures to the waitress.

"Richard, I'm so sorry I forgot about the anniversary. I've ruined everything, haven't I?"

"It's OK. Honestly, it *is* OK." He reaches across and gives my hand a squeeze. "Sure I'm a bit pissed off but there are more important things than numbers in a calendar. Let's get out of here."

Now I *know* something is wrong.

He tells me as we walk down the Strand, arm in arm in the weak autumn sunshine.

"Jemima wants us to get back together."

"I *knew* it." I pull away from him. "She got tired of her flash Frenchman. How long do you think it'll take her to tire of you again? Jesus, *I* was feeling guilty about forgetting our anniversary . . . Did you think I'd take it better if you sweetened me up with a little champagne, eh? Was that the idea?"

"Hey—hold on a second." He grabs my arm and pulls me to a halt. Then he lifts my chin to make me look at him. I'm blinking a lot to keep the tears back.

"I love you, Kitty. You're a nightmare but I love you."

"What about Jemima?"

"Screw Jemima."

He kisses me long and tender. People mutter and tut around us. We're standing in the middle of the crowded pavement getting in everyone's way but I don't care. He kisses with just the right amount of pressure, and right lip-to-tongue ratio. Jemima must miss these kisses. Maybe she lies awake at night kissing her own arm with her eyes closed so she can pretend she's snogging Richard. I hope she does. I wonder if Dotty will inherit her father's kissing skills. She's going to grow up to be a right little scorcher . . .

I've had my eyes closed but as the kiss deepens, lengthens, I open them for a sneaky peep, and I glimpse something over his shoulder—

A face I know well—right there on the other side of the street. It's only the merest glimpse through the heavy traffic. But a glimpse is enough. I wrench out of the kiss, pull away from Richard's arms—

"Joel!"

He wears an expression of—what? Anger? Incomprehension? Betrayal? I see the mouth form words but I can't hear them and I can't read the lips.

"Joel," I call again but he's not looking at me now.

He's half in, half out of a glossy blue Mercedes. He must have been getting out when he spotted me with Richard but now he's bending to say something to somebody in the back of the car.

I can hear Richard in the background somewhere, saying, "Kitty, what is it?" but I'm ignoring him, stepping off the curb, trying to get across the road. The traffic is dense, impenetrable.

"Joel, wait."

He's back inside the car and the door slams. There's a face peering out at me from the back—the other passenger.

The Mercedes is pulling away into the traffic. It's all happened so fast.

"Joel!" Finally I get my chance to run out into the road but it's too late. I'm left to watch the taillights of the car as it disappears.

"Kitty, what are you doing?"

The Mercedes is gone. Another car honks at me and I skitter back to the pavement, back to Richard.

"Sorry. I thought I saw someone I knew from years ago. Kind of took me by surprise. But I must have been mistaken."

I can hear my mouth saying these words to Richard but my mind is busy with something else. The man in the back of the Mercedes . . . I've seen him somewhere before. I've got a really bad feeling about this.

16

RICHARD and I are sitting at a corner table in Cafe Bohème on Old Compton Street, Soho, drinking Kir Royale—my treat and an apology for forgetting our anniversary. I am doing my best to engage in the conversation, which is about how Richard should go about organizing things so that Jemima has fair access to Dotty while being kept firmly at arm's length. But my brain is buzzing with other stuff: Joel—is it really over between us? What the hell would I have said to him if he had come across to talk to me when I called out to him on the Strand? And how would I have explained it all away to Richard? I shouted out without thinking, without knowing what I was doing.

My mouth is saying, "Yes, but can you really trust her with Dotty?" But my mind is working on who the man in the back of the Mercedes was. Did I drive him someplace in my cab or is it somewhere else that I've seen him? And I'm wondering whether he could be the mysterious Mr. Fisher . . .

My voice says, "She's flaky, isn't she? She could take off with Dotty—run away back to Gerard or something," while my head says, *You mustn't let things get out of control. If you lose control there is only chaos . . .*

And then all at once I'm noticing the time; 3:36 P.M., and I'm checking on my jacket which is hanging on the back of my chair, and feeling something bulky in the pocket. Jonny's three thousand pounds . . . Shit, I'd completely forgotten!

❖ ❖ ❖

As I'm skirting Leicester Square on foot, dodging the tourists on Coventry Street, I'm preparing myself for the pathetic sight of Jonny, slouched over a pub table, cig in hand, several empty pint glasses in front of him. Then I'm ducking down Oxendon Street out of the crowds, drawing up in front of The Comedy and trying to avoid being dripped on by the hanging baskets outside as I'm tugging at the door.

I'm so busy searching for that slumped figure that I don't actually see Jonny as I glance around the dim room. I'm on the verge of turning round and leaving when I hear a shout of,

"Katy . . . I'm over here, you blind old bat!"

And there he is at the big corner table—sitting with three blokes and a blonde woman. They're laughing and smoking and they look for all the world like they've known each other for years. Wearily I make my way over, trying to smile.

He gets up when I reach the table, puts a protective arm around me. His face, with its mesh of scars and the new lurid bruises resembles a checked tablecloth, but he doesn't seem to care. "Everybody, this is my girlfriend, Katy. Katy, this is everybody." He bursts out in beery laughter before sitting—almost falling—down on the bench again. Still struggling to keep the smile in place, I sit down beside him.

"He's so ignorant, isn't he?" says the blonde, leaning forward to show massive cleavage. "What he meant to say is that I'm Caroline, this here is Marvin, this is Michael and this is Sean."

"Hi." That's the most I can manage.

"Jonny was just telling us how you two are going off to live in Berlin," announces Sean, the ginger-haired skinny guy down the far end of the table.

"Oh, was he really . . ." I turn to look at Jonny. He might be blushing under the bruises but it's difficult to be sure.

"Yeah, well . . . We haven't actually decided on that for definite yet," says Jonny with a false laugh. "Have we, babe?"

"No, *babe*, we haven't." My anger is bubbling up and I'm struggling to keep it under control. "Would you like to tell me more or is this plan of ours a secret between you and your newfound friends?"

"I love live music bars," gushes Caroline. "And East Berlin is so trendy these days."

"Isn't it, though?" I coo, finding Jonny's foot under the table and grinding it hard with my heel. It's only when Marvin gives a sudden yelp that I realize I've misaimed.

"Hon, you remember when the guitarist from my old school band turned up the other day?" says Jonny, nervously.

"I'm all ears, *petal*."

"Well, Jason's still in touch with the drummer, Stuart. Turns out Stuart's living in East Berlin, running a bar. They have live music every night. Jam sessions too. Mostly British bands on tour but some local musos as well. They get really big crowds in—bit of Brit pop, bit of jazz—seems the Berliners think it's well cool. Apparently Stuart wants to open a second bar so he needs someone to help him manage the first one . . ."

"And when exactly did you find out about this bar, then?"

He looks puzzled. "You know, when Jason came over . . ."

"But you only think of telling me about it now!"

"Hey, loosen up, Katy . . . Let me get you a drink. Anyone else want a pint?"

They all do, of course. Three lagers and a bitter. Jonny gets up to go to the bar and I follow him.

I wait for him to order and then snap, "I can't believe you didn't tell me about this! This is about *my* life too—but then, I don't suppose that would occur to you, would it?"

"Katy, Katy . . ." He bends low, whispering to me. "Not so loud . . . It's not so much a plan as a *hope*, know what I mean? I haven't actually talked to Stuart yet. I didn't want to tell you until I knew for certain that I can pull it off. I didn't want to disappoint you."

"Jonny, we were talking about going on *holiday*, not immigrating to Berlin."

We watch the barman filling one pint glass and then another with Stella. I hear Caroline's high-pitched laugh back at the table and the blokes joining in.

"I'm sorry, Katy." Jonny reaches for my hand, holds it in his.

"Of course I won't do anything without checking with you first. But think about it, yeah?"

"I'm not going anywhere with you, Jonny." I wrench my hand free. "Not after last night."

Jonny sighs, leans heavily on the old dark-wood bar. "Oh Christ, Katy, I'm so sorry about that. It'll never happen again, I swear it."

"No, it sure won't."

"It's this city . . . I need to get out of here, Katy," he says, looking mournfully at me from out of his red-rimmed eyes. "This place brings out the worst in me. It's going to kill me if I stay here much longer."

"Oh, spare me the melodrama."

The barman sets the pint of bitter next to the five lagers Jonny ordered. "That'll be seventeen pounds fifty," he says, looking at Jonny over his spectacles.

"Oh, yeah right . . ." Jonny reaches into the pockets of his jeans, slaps at the breast pocket of his shirt, shrugs good-naturedly, and finally . . . turns back to me. "Er . . . Katy, you know that money you said you'd get for me . . ."

I reach into my jacket, draw out the package, pass it over to Jonny's sweaty hands, and watch as he rips open the envelope and hands a fifty across to the barman. The barman holds it up to the light, nods and then takes it over to the till.

"Thanks, Katy." Jonny ruffles my hair. "You're the best."

"Fuck off." I bat his hand away. "D'you have any idea how many nights I spent driving my cab around London to earn that three thousand pounds? Well, do you?"

He shrugs, looks down at his feet.

"Those were my savings. My ticket out of here, Jonny. And I've given it all up to save your worthless neck. I only have four hundred pounds left in my account now. That's not exactly going to get me very far, is it?"

"Hey, don't fret about the money, Katy," he begins, reaching for my hand again. "I've got it all figured out."

"Don't touch me, Jonny. Go back to your friends. Go to Berlin—go to hell."

As I walk out onto the street, I'm shaking with anger.

17

SIX-OH-THREE A.M. on Sunday and I've been driving for ten hours solid. My head is killing me where I banged it yesterday. My stomach is burning up with acid indigestion, making me catch my breath. Usually I do my best thinking while I'm driving but last night nothing useful emerged. I've been fretful—my thoughts flickering from one thing to the next.

My final job of the night takes me down to Dulwich Village. A drunk and sheepish teenage boy with a public school accent. I drop him off at one of the big old houses near the art gallery, and watch, amused, as he tiptoes across the gravel drive and starts trying to climb a drainpipe at the side of the house—unsuccessfully. he falls off twice before finally giving up and making his way around to the front door. The poor little bugger doesn't have his own key. He rings the bell and stands about, all stoopy and frightened. I wait for the father to answer the door in his pajamas—see him give his son a light cuff round the head—before I drive away.

As I'm in the area, I drive over to Joel's place. But there is no answer when I ring the bell. I guess he's out working. He's a night person now, like me. Next I try calling Winnie to see if she wants to meet at the Crocodile, but her mobile is switched off and she doesn't have an answering service. I decide to head over there anyway, on the off chance. I don't feel good about how things were left between me and Winnie yesterday morning.

❖   ❖   ❖

No Winnie at the Crocodile. I order a fry-up that I don't really want and hang out for a couple of hours with the dreadful Steve Ambley and his cronies. In fact I feel sorry for poor old Steve this morning—he got mugged a couple of nights ago as part of what seems to be a series of organized cabdriver muggings. There must be a gang, Steve reckons, because the descriptions of the assailants vary widely. In his case it was a girl on her own but sometimes it's a bloke or a couple. The scam is an old one: At the end of the run the fare starts to pay you and you get your moneybag out, but then he or she drops something on the floor—change, wallet, whatever—and says it's fallen down near your feet. You bend down to pick it up and—*bosh*—you get a knock on the head with something heavy and the fare's off with your moneybag. Steve might be an arsehole but I wouldn't wish that on anyone.

I guess I've been robbed in a more subtle way. I'm so angry with Jonny that I start shaking uncontrollably whenever he comes into my head. Four hundred pounds—that's all I have left in my escape fund. I'm not going anywhere, am I . . .

Back at the flat in Balham I'm too wired to sleep. My stomach is heavy with the fry-up and my acid indigestion is newly fired up. I thrash around in the bed for what feels like forever. Somewhere behind it all, a church bell is ringing over and over again. At some point I blunder out of bed and go rooting through my unpacked boxes for a packet of Gaviscon. I eventually find some, but not before I've made the mess in the flat considerably worse. With the indigestion under control I finally manage a few hours' kip.

Two-fifteen P.M. and I'm back on the road—human again but in need of distraction. In need of Stef.

Sunday is market day. Spitalfields, Petticoat Lane, Middlesex Street . . . Four silk ties for a tenner, three multicolored mobile phone covers for a fiver, full set of kitchen knives only three ninety-nine. Pirate videos, reggae CDs, minced-lamb samosas and baked potatoes stuffed with goat curry. Hair warps, watches, perfume, multicolored plastic aliens with big black eyes shaped like teardrops . . . The bargain hunters and tourists love it, but for me it just means the traffic is terrible and most of the backstreets are closed off. As I'm struggling to get through, turning the cab past Aldwych and looking for a way in, it occurs to me that Stef might be out flogging Furbies. I should have called to tell him I was coming over . . . .

Finally I find a way through but Brick Lane is jammed solid. The curry houses are bustling with Sunday lunch buffet punters. In addition to the traffic going to and from the markets, there seems to be something happening at the mosque. Men in smart clobber and women in brightly colored silks are getting in and out of BMWs and Mercedes parked along the street. I'm inching closer to Stef's and there's not a single parking space to be had. I'm thinking I'll have to turn off—but which way? There's a black Volvo parked in front of Stef's flat, very much like Twinkle's— same model, same color.

I'm almost parallel with Stef's place now. I'm stuck behind a van that's pulling out of a side street, trying to decide whether I should turn left, when suddenly the door of 134A opens and I can't quite believe what I'm seeing.

Craig Summer. He's wearing a gray suit, looking edgy, raking his left hand nervously through his hair as he steps out onto the pavement. Stef is on the step, framed by the doorway. They are talking to each other and Craig is nodding stiffly, glancing around as though he's worried about being seen. Now he is extending his right hand to shake Stef's—but Stef misunderstands the movement and goes to give him high five. The result is something awkward—neither a shake nor a slap.

Craig Summer and Stefan Muchowski.

Stef waits on the step while Twinkle delves in his jacket pocket, pulls out car keys, gives a brief wave and goes to unlock the Volvo, then he retreats into his flat and shuts the door.

Craig looks around again before getting into the car, and I cower behind the wheel, afraid that he will see me. But no, he doesn't. The van is still trying to get out of the side street, effectively blocking Brick Lane, but Twinkle is able to pull out in front of it. I am stuck behind. The traffic is thinning out ahead of the van, and I can see the Volvo slipping away up the street. Did he notice me? Probably not. I'm only a black cabdriver—just one of twenty-five thousand. I'm part of the London landscape.

I'm turning into the space where Twinkle's Volvo was parked. I'm parking up, braking, laying my head down heavily on the steering wheel and closing my eyes. I let myself stay like that for a few minutes, and then I get out of the cab—taste dopiaza and buna on the air as I walk slowly up to Stef's front door.

I have to ring three times before I hear feet running down the stairs inside and Stef's voice calling, "OK, OK, I'm coming." The intercom must be broken.

He looks flustered as he opens the door, but when he realizes it's me his face brightens. A lock of blond hair flops forward over his baby blue eyes.

"K! How excellent! You couldn't have called at a better time."

"Really?"

He gives me a sidelong look—noticing, no doubt, the edge in my voice, the darkness in my face. He turns to lead the way up the stairs, calling back over his shoulder, "Fancy a glass of vino? I've just opened a bottle of Rioja—*real* Rioja, I mean. Mind the Furbies at the top of the stairs."

I follow him up.

The kitchen is chaos. The table is covered in dirty plates and cutlery, empty wineglasses and stray rizzla papers. The sink is full of pans. A big pot on the stove has the remains of some sort of stew in it.

"Sorry about the mess," Stef says. "We had people over before we went clubbing. Haven't had a chance to clear up yet. Wicked night!" He comes toward me, reaching out for my hand. "What about a kiss, then?"

I catch the lovely inky whiff of his neck and am tempted but I don't want to kiss him. I pull away.

There are plastic Rentokil boxes in the corners of the room.

"State of this place . . . You've got mice now, have you?"

"Rats, actually." He gives me his cutest grin and shrugs. Then, when he sees I'm still not smiling, the grin slips and his face takes on a stricken look. "What's up, K? You haven't called for ages. Not since that morning when you ran away. What am I supposed to have done?"

I'm feeling weak. I pull out one of the dining chairs and sink down, rubbing my aching head.

"K?"

"Who was that man?" I manage.

"What man?"

God, I could hit him. "The man who just came out of your flat."

"Oh, *that* man." The grin is back but it's more nervous now. He wanders over to the stove, nibbles a bit of cold stew off a wooden spoon.

"Who is he, Stef? Don't give me any bullshit."

Stef puts the spoon down, turns to face me. Seems to be considering whether to tell me the truth, then shrugs. "Oh, what the hell . . . He's the man, isn't he? He's *the* man."

"What do you mean—*the* man?"

"The man with the money. You know. He brings it round, we look after it, he takes it away again. I don't know his name, do I? He's just the *man* . . . K, why are you looking at me like that?"

"You schmuck."

"What? I ain't no schmuck. What's your problem, K? You ask me questions, I give you the answers, and then what do I get from you? Verbal—"

"No, *I'm* the schmuck, Stef. I'm the schmuck."

I'm getting out of that stinking kitchen.

"K? K, where are you going?"

I'm running down the stairs two at a time.

"You only just got here, K . . ."

Conferences for manufacturers of toothpicks . . .

I am the schmuck.

PART IV

~

TWINKLE
TWINKLE . . .

18

O K, so how can I explain what's happening in my head? It's like my head is a big house full of rooms. Each room has something different going on in it but all of the rooms have a stick of dynamite hidden somewhere—in a cupboard, under a bed—whatever. In one of the rooms, someone has lit the dynamite. When it blows, the explosion sparks off a fire which sets off the dynamite in the room next door, and then that explosion sets off another, and so on. Everything is empty and black and burned out. That's how it feels.

What else?

Do I feel betrayed? Yes. And somehow Twinkle's betrayal of my trust is worse because of the way he forced himself into my life. I never asked him in—he just pushed and pushed.

Am I angry? Jesus, yes. Things started going wrong around the time I met Twinkle and they've been getting steadily worse ever since. Twinkle's phone call made Jonny hit me. If Jonny hadn't hit me, maybe he wouldn't have gone spinning into this self-destructive spiral and I'd still have my three thousand pounds. Twinkle has tempted Stef further down the road toward serious crime. I can almost see Stef's charm melting away in front of me. He's turning into someone else, and it's all Craig's fault.

Do I deserve this? Probably. I'm a liar and I'm a cheat—how can I expect people to be straight with me when I am so incapable of honesty myself?

But I am *not* a criminal.

It takes me a good couple of hours' worth of driving around London aimlessly—east to west to south to north—before I can believe that I have the moral high ground. Once I have established this I begin to feel better. And feeling better—feeling stronger—I turn the cab around and head straight for the center of the web. Chelsea Harbour.

My palm leaves a greasy print on the glass doors. The adrenaline is pumping as I stride past the security man at the front desk to the lift, my trainers squeaking on the alabaster floor.

"Hey!" He's out from behind the desk, skidding across the floor in his haste to chase after me.

I'm hoping to avoid having to speak to him but the lift doesn't arrive quickly enough. His peaked security cap is all skew-whiff. He is barely more than a boy. His jaw is covered with acne that is red, raw and semivolcanic where he's shaved.

"Can I help you?" he says, looking up at me. I'm a good three inches taller than him.

"No, thank you." I press the button.

The poor kid is very bad at his job. The parts of his face not already red with acne are now flushing a deep scarlet. "Sorry, miss, but if you're not a resident I'll need to call up for you."

"OK, fine." I follow him back, cursing to myself. I do not want this boy calling upstairs and telling Craig I am here. I want to arrive unannounced, catch him unawares just as he's done to me.

"Right," he says, happy to be on the other side of the desk again. "Who are you here to see?"

"Craig Summer. Flat five, seventh floor."

He picks at a spot while dialing the number. When the acne finally clears up he'll be left with terrible scars. I can hear the ringing at the other end of the line.

"Sorry," he says, replacing the receiver. "He's not here."

"Well, that won't do."

"Pardon?"

"I have to get into his flat." I don't know where I'm going with this but the lies are rolling. "I was there yesterday morning, and I left something behind. Something I need."

"Look, Miss, I'm really—"

"My insulin. I'm a diabetic. I need my insulin and I've left it in Craig Summer's apartment."

"Listen, lady, I just can't let you go up there when Mr. Summer's out." His voice is firm and jobsworthy but there is fear in his eyes and he can't leave that spot alone.

"You have to. Or I'll freak out, start having fits. I might have one right here."

"Oh, Jesus . . ." He pushes his hat straight on his head and stands about, unsure of what to do with his gangly arms, his hands. "What you're asking me to do is a sackable offense! How do I know you're not making this up?"

I change my pitch, try to sound soothing, motherly. "Look . . . What's your name?"

"Terry."

"Look, Terry, you know I was here yesterday . . . I came over really early in the morning, remember? You were on duty, *Terry* . . ."

He's squirming, pushing the cap to one side so he can scratch his head. "Maybe you could wait down here for a while—see if he comes back . . ."

I'm losing my patience. "If I don't get my insulin injection in the next fifteen minutes I will go into a coma."

He looks like he's going to cry. "But I can't leave the desk unattended . . ."

"For Christ's sake, you must have spare keys to the flats. Just give me the key and I'll go up there by myself."

"I don't know . . ."

I heave a sigh. "Terry, I could *die* while you're worrying about your job. Are you prepared to take that risk? Because I'm not."

Rod Stewart's "Sailing," the Chelsea Harbour Muzak version, is scratching at my eardrums as I step out of the lift on the seventh floor, making me feel like there's some nasty little fly crawling about inside my head. That blue corridor—blue carpet on the ceiling and walls as well as the floor—muffling all sounds except the beating of my heart in a furry emptiness.

Mazophobia—ripping through my chest. I am walking into the labyrinth. I have a strong instinct that the nameless color of my nightmares is somewhere close by. Behind one of these doors or walls; woven into the warp and weft of the blue carpet. I am teetering along, barely able to stay upright, sweating. Groping for the door of number five, trying to fit the key into the lock and dropping it on the floor. Picking it up with fingers that feel like toes and pushing it again at that difficult keyhole.

And finally it slides in. Turns smoothly.

My heart is calming down to normal now as I'm closing the door on that corridor and turning to face Twinkle's apartment. I walk straight through the lounge to the sliding glass doors and let myself out onto the balcony where I take huge, steadying lungfuls of air. Leaning on the railing, gazing out across the harbor at the boats, the sparkling water, the heavy orange of London's polluted sunset, I ask myself what the hell I'm doing here. I had wanted to confront Craig—I can't confront an empty apartment. How is this going to help?

And the answer blows in off the water and sounds itself clearly in my head:

I must find a way through the lies and the half-truths. I must search this flat for any shred of information it can give me about what Craig Summer is up to.

I gaze at the old wireless, wondering if the story he told me about it was true. There was no reason for him to make up something like that but just at the moment I'm not sure I can trust anything he's ever said to me. I pick up a few books from his shelves one by one—flicking through, shaking them as though I expect something to fall out from between the pages. I have a quick go on the love meter and the red liquid inside goes shooting up the glass tube and starts bubbling ferociously. I am very passionate today, it would seem.

That Good Luck card is still there:

"Not that you need it. Show those bastards what you're made of, Love Marianne xxx."

I look inside a cabinet. Nothing there but a bottle of whiskey. Laphroaig—three-quarters full. I remember him pouring me some of that the first time I came here. I lift it out and pull out the stopper. Take a swig, cough a bit when it goes down the wrong way, a strong peaty burning in my nose. I take another swig and re-place the stopper. Put the bottle back in the cabinet and close the door.

It's so immaculate here. The cream carpet has no stains, the russet Chesterfield looks brand new, barely sat upon. There's no clutter of newspapers or unopened bills—not so much as a single mug with coffee dregs in it. There's a phone and answering ma-chine on a side table. I press "play" and the machine tells me, "No new messages" in a halting, American voice.

There's no TV here. I hadn't thought about that before, but it's strange. Craig isn't the type to be either so empty of culture or so full of it as to have no TV. The wastepaper basket has one piece of crumpled paper in it, which on close examination proves to be a dry-cleaning receipt.

I wander into the kitchen. Smooth clear work surfaces. No crumbs, no smells. I flip open the lid of the flip-top bin, revealing one empty milk carton. I begin opening cupboards: Shining un-marked steel saucepans, white crockery, a cutlery drawer with all of the knives, forks and spoons in the right compartments. None of the cupboards have any food in them. I open the door of the fridge: a half-full packet of Lavazza Espresso, a sliced white loaf, a pot of Olivio spread and a jar of strawberry jam. That's all. I guess Craig really does like his restaurant food . . .

That only leaves the bedroom. The room in which I've slept with Craig on six or seven occasions now. Something makes me stoop and sniff one of the pillows on the big double bed. Wow—

the smell of sex. I'm carried right back to that dingy Suffolk hotel
room and I can almost feel his hand on my back, his mouth on my
neck. I straighten, shake the daydream away. I am so disappointed
in him . . .

There's a digital alarm clock on the bedside table with glowing
green numbers. When I open the wardrobe door, a mere three
shirts, three pairs of trousers and one jacket are revealed. There's
one pair of trainers on the shoe rack. The top drawer in a chest of
four contains a few pairs of boxer shorts and some socks. The second has one pair of jeans and two black T-Shirts. Where's all his
other stuff? Where's his fencing gear? The remaining drawers are
all empty. That's all there is in this room. If I didn't know better I'd
think nobody was living here. It feels more like a hotel room than
a person's own bedroom.

Jesus, that's what I thought when I first came here, isn't it. I
thought this place was a setup, and that I was the victim of a scam
operated by Craig and his mate Henry.

Henry!

Big fat Henry and his river of pink puke, dribbling on my shoes
as we scoop him off the road and drag him into the apartment. Lying unconscious on Craig's bed, crying and calling out the name of
his wife over and over again.

Big fat Henry in the back of a blue Mercedes, driving away
with my lovely Joel.

"Did you find your insulin?" asks Terry as I come rushing out of
the lift. "You look terrible."

I shove the spare keys at him, along with a fiver. "I won't tell
your boss you let me in if you don't tell Mr. Summer I was here.
Got it?"

He nods and glances pointedly down at the bottle of Laphroaig
dangling from my left hand (I figured my need is greater than
Craig's just now). I ignore the look and lunge at the glass doors,
bolt out onto the street.

        ❖   ❖   ❖

Safely enclosed in my cab, I check the blue phone to see if Joel has called. Nothing. I press "1" to dial his number, listen to the empty ringing at the other end.

Cabdriving is the perfect profession for someone like me. Nobody ever knows where you are, what you're doing or who you're with. London has always seemed like an enormous sprawling mess—somewhere you can hide five lovers from each other and still keep a secret hole to crawl into alone when you need to.

I've never believed in fate. I'm free to drive where I like and *I* am the one to decide my destination. *I* am in control, moving through this random unstructured city and creating my own order. But right now, I'm not so sure. London has shrunk from a great anonymous metropolis into a tiny village. And it feels like someone or something out there is reeling me in, pulling every disparate thread of my life together. I'm stuck on a motorway with no junctions. I can't get off.

Just as I'm about to give up on Joel, there's a click and the phone is picked up. Startled, I yelp, "Joel?"

"Who is this, please?" A woman.

Christ, it's Joel's mother. I'm cringing at the sound of her voice. I've only met her once but it was memorable. She let herself into Joel's flat and found us asleep together in his bed. That was perhaps my fastest ever exit . . . "Hi, Mrs. Marsh, it's Kat. You know . . . Joel's friend."

"Yes, I know who you are. Where is my boy?" She sounds really overwrought.

"I'm afraid I don't know, Mrs. Marsh. I haven't seen him for a couple of days. Is something wrong?"

"Don't give me that, missy. You know where he is, don't you, and you're going to tell me!" She's close to tears.

"Mrs. Marsh, I'm sorry but . . ." This is so awkward. I'm suddenly desperate to get off the phone. "Look, this is obviously a bad time to call. Maybe I should call back another time . . ."

"No—hold on please!" The mouthpiece is muffled for a moment while she speaks to someone else in the room.

"Hello? Mrs. Marsh?" Perhaps I could just hang up . . .

More muffled sounds. Distant voices. Then, finally, "This is Joel's father." A deep voice. Stern, macho.

"Hello, Mr. Marsh."

"It's Kathryn, isn't it? Listen, Kathryn, Joel's mother and I— we're worried about Joel. We've hardly seen him in weeks. His mother went in to clean his flat yesterday and found it in a complete mess. It was . . . disgusting. It's not like our boy to treat his mother or his home with such disrespect."

"Joel's always been very tidy," I mutter.

"Joel was supposed to come over to the house for dinner last night. His grandmother has just arrived from Nigeria and she hasn't seen Joel in over five years . . . but the boy didn't turn up. And he wasn't at home either. This morning he didn't come to church. His bed hasn't been slept in, Kathryn. It is clear that he hasn't been back to his flat since before his mother went in to clean."

"Oh, God . . ."

"Joel always goes to church, Kathryn. He is a good boy. We had thought . . . We assumed he was with you."

"No, I'm afraid he's not, Mr. Marsh. We've had a bit of a falling out, to tell you the truth."

There's a silence and I hear him taking a few deep breaths. "When did you last see him?"

I think of Joel's face when I saw him on the Strand yesterday. That look of betrayal as he clambered into the Mercedes. I say, "Friday. The flat was in a mess, as you say. I think he'd had a friend over—"

"What friend?" He's firing words at me so fast I can barely get my thoughts straight.

"I don't know. Someone from work, I think. We haven't been getting on well lately. It's this new job of his . . ."

"What exactly is Joel's new job, Kathryn? He clearly has money to spend but when his mother asks him what he does for a living, he will tell her nothing."

"I don't know, Mr. Marsh. He won't tell me either."

There's a pause. The receiver is muffled once again and I get the impression that Mrs. Marsh is trying to snatch it back from her husband. But then his voice is back.

"Kathryn, is our son on drugs?"

I can see my face reflected in my side window. I look old, exhausted. The street outside is quiet, dead. "No. Of course he isn't."

And now she succeeds in grabbing the phone. "Where is Joel, Kathryn? Where is he? You have to tell me, please. *Please* . . ."

"I don't—"

"You *do* know. You're *lying!*" She's sobbing uncontrollably—so much that she can hardly speak. "What do you want with my son? He's a child *half* your age . . . You've corrupted him, you've led him astray . . . *Where is he?*"

"I'm sorry," I say. "I'm sorry but I don't know where he is. I'm sorry."

I hear Mr. Marsh saying, "Give me that." And he's back on the line once more. "Kathryn, my wife is very upset as you can hear. She doesn't mean to blame you—we know this is not your fault, whatever we think of . . . Perhaps we are worrying too much, but this is not the way Joel behaves. You understand?"

"Yes."

"Can I ask you please to telephone me if you hear from Joel? My number—do you have a pen?"

"Just a second." I grip the phone to my ear with my shoulder while I search in the glove compartment for my pad of taxi receipts and a Bic. "OK, go on."

"My number at home is 8637 4111. And at work my number is 8323 4982. Thank you, Kathryn. I hope I can rely on you."

"Yes, Mr. Marsh. I'll call you as soon as I hear anything."

I press to end the call, reach for the Laphroaig and take a swig.

19

"GOOD Lord, Kathy, you look terrible."

Willa rubs at the goose pimples on her bare arms as a gust of cold wind blows in at her, billowing through the voluminous turquoise silk thing she's wearing. My gaze is fixed on the turquoise thing—not a dress, not a caftan but something in between the two. I'm so weary that I go almost cross-eyed staring at the wafting layers of fabric, the mighty cleavage they almost cover. I want Amy's arms around me. I want to lie with her, to have her stroke my head gently like my mother used to do.

"Well, come on in, then, before I freeze to death," she says—as though *I* had been the one to keep *her* standing on the step.

"Where's Amy?" I ask, as Willa settles herself on a pale pink chaise longue at the far end of the living room. The color clashes horribly with her turquoise garment. There's an empty bottle of Chilean Merlot and an open South African Pinotage on the coffee table. One glass—full—the rim smeared with lipstick.

"How should I know? I'm not her keeper." She is slurring, but the anger is clearly discernible in her voice. "Grab yourself a glass if you'd like some." She gestures vaguely at the bottle.

I wander out to the kitchen, considering whether I should leave. Amy's not here and I don't have the energy to deal with Willa and her obscure traumas. But then again I'm so awfully *tired* and it's so nice to be here in her lovely house. And that Pinotage is tempting . . . Maybe I should have just the one glass of wine with Willa and wait to see if Amy turns up.

◦   ◦   ◦

Night has thrown a blanket over us. We're through the first bottle of mellow, fruity Pinotage and on to a second. I'm sitting across from Willa in the wing-backed armchair where Amy usually sits.

"We had a row." Willa fills my glass, slopping a little onto the coffee table and not bothering to wipe it up. "Madam thinks I'm interfering in things that don't concern me."

"What sort of things."

"Oh, you know . . ." She throws her hands up in a dismissive gesture. "This Agony Aunt business."

Oh. That.

"She seems incapable of taking a long-term view. I'd always thought she was ambitious, Kathy—that she had a *hunger*. I just don't understand her."

I'm doing my best to care about this and pay attention but it's tough with all the freaky stuff that's filling my head tonight.

"Kathy, are you listening to me?"

"What? Yes, of course . . . Look, Willa, *is* this actually going to do her any harm? I mean, who's really going to care if she has a bit of fun playing around at being an Agony Aunt for a while?"

She gives me a furious glare. "*I* care, Kathy. *Me*. Who do you think got her the job at *Up West* in the first place, eh? Who do you think is trying her absolute bloody hardest to help that girl find the right strategy? But oh no, she doesn't need me, does she? Or the magazine. No, she'd rather put herself about indiscriminately . . ."

This all seems a bit much to me. "Willa—we're not exactly talking John Pilger here, are we? Amy doesn't *have* big journalistic ambitions. She writes 'Muff Matters,' for heaven's sake. She uses the magazine as a way of pulling women."

She wags a finger at me. "This is your prejudice speaking, Kathy."

I slurp some more wine. I'm thinking about Joel's parents, wondering what I should do . . .

"But anyway, Kathy—I should stop dwelling on matters over which I have no control. What is ailing *you*, my love? You look . . . tense . . . distracted."

"Maybe."

She adopts a serene, therapist-type expression and seems to be doing her best to focus on me. "You can tell Auntie Willa."

As if . . . Craig and Stef on the doorstep . . . Craig's apartment—bizarrely unlived in; everything *seeming* to be normal but when you start opening cupboards and drawers, delving behind the scenes—just a great big blank. Like him.

"Kathy? Tell me what's wrong."

"Oh . . ." I grope around for something to say to her. "My father held a memorial service for my mother recently. It's been fifteen years since she died. It upset me more than I expected. That's all, really."

"Poor you." She leans forward to top up my glass and I glimpse more than I want to see down the front of the turquoise garment. "Families are a perfect nightmare, aren't they? But . . . there's something else, isn't there? Something more."

"More? No."

"But there *is*, Kathy. You know there is."

I gulp my wine nervously. "What do you mean?"

"Oh, come on, do I have to spell it out for you?" She gets up, moves around the low oak coffee table and plonks herself down on the edge of it—very close to me. She grabs my left hand and holds on to it. "You've found out about Amy, haven't you, Kathy? Amy and Cheryl . . ."

I try to pull my hand away but she's grasping it firmly with an incredibly strong grip and looking at me with cow eyes.

"What?"

"*You know*," is all she says.

"You mean—about them sleeping together?" I try to make my voice sound casual. "Yes, of course I know. How much do *you* know?"

"So it's true! I knew it . . ." She drops my hand and stares off into space.

"Hang on a second." I'm rubbing at my baffled, exhausted forehead. "What are you telling me, Willa? I mean, are you *telling* me or *asking* me about Amy and Cheryl?"

Her eyes are filling up. "I love that girl, Kathy. You know that, don't you? I'd do anything for her—*anything*—and all she does is wound me, *stab* me . . ."

"Willa—" I reach out and lay a hand on her shoulder, trying to comfort her. God, how I wish I hadn't come here.

"I'm sorry, Kathy. What must you think of me?" She wipes away the tears with the back of her hand and gives a deep sniff. "Look, I never meant to say anything to you about my feelings. I'm all right as I am. And I *like* you, Kathy. I can cope with seeing you two together. I can be happy for you both. Genuinely happy."

"Willa, stop. Don't say any more. You've had too much to drink . . ."

I withdraw my hand from her shoulder but she grabs it again. Squeezes it even tighter than before.

"You have to *believe* me, Kathy. It's important that you believe me. I'm fond of you. I want it to work for the pair of you . . . But she's so fickle. So *fickle*—going off and sleeping with that dreadful mutt . . ."

And she's suddenly holding my hand to her giant bosom. Pressing it there.

"Willa, no—"

I'm trying to wriggle out of this but she's way stronger than she looks. Jesus, you'd think the woman was a professional arm wrestler . . . She's pulling my hand *inside* the turquoise garment.

"No!" I wrench free and spring to my feet, almost knocking the wine bottle over. "No, Willa, that's not a good idea."

"But we both love her." She's looking up at me with a dreadfully beseeching expression. "It would be the natural thing, wouldn't it? A bit of comfort, nothing more . . ."

"I can't." I'm standing over her, trying not to show my revulsion. "I'm sorry, Willa. I don't actually know if Amy's sleeping with Cheryl or anyone else. I was only guessing. All I know is I have to stay faithful to her. It isn't in my nature to be unfaithful."

"No. Of course not." She reaches for the Pinotage, swigs out of the bottle.

"I'd better go." I'm looking at my watch. It's only 9:43 P.M., but I can't remember ever feeling so tired. "I need some sleep."

"You shouldn't drive." Willa seems to have gotten control over herself again. "You've had far too much to drink. Why don't you go to bed in Amy's room? You wanted to see her and I'm sure she'll be back in a while." Then she adds, "She went out to the cinema with a couple of old university friends."

Odd that she didn't tell me that in the first place, but never mind—I don't think I want to know why. And she's right. I shouldn't be driving after all that wine.

"Thanks. I'll do that. And Willa—this is all forgotten, OK? This didn't happen."

"Thank you," she says, lower lip trembling. "You're a good girl, Kathy."

"Good night." I leave her alone with her wine and her unfulfilled lust.

Amy comes back late. Maybe one o'clock but I couldn't swear to it because I've been so deeply asleep. This bed is heaven. I hear the bang of the front door and the sound of voices as she stops to talk to Willa, who's apparently still up drinking. Amy's voice is soft and low, Willa's is loud—dipping and swooping. Then the bedroom door opens and Amy creeps in—undresses in the dark so as not to wake me. I play my part by pretending to be asleep as she gets into bed beside me. She nuzzles up and I notice her smell, musky and sweet. She's wearing a new perfume—something cheap but erotic. I put my face to her neck to breathe in the scent. And soon, without having spoken a word to each other—not even to say hello—we are making love. It is close and tender. I am passive and childlike in her arms, letting her look after me. Wanting just to be looked after.

In the morning, Amy almost succeeds in distracting me. She is at her most frivolous playful best: bringing me croissants in bed and swooping down for the crumbs that fall between the sheets. Suggesting a shopping trip to Kensington and the King's Road and lunchtime dwinkies at Harvey Nics. But I'm haunted by the voices of Joel's parents. I am stung by their hatred of me, of what I have done to their little boy. And I'm uneasy about Fat Henry. He is Craig's friend and Craig is "the man." I need to know that Joel is safe. I tell Amy I have to take my mother to a hospital appointment and leave.

Sitting outside Willa's house in the cab, I check the phones.

Blue phone—Joel: Nothing. Well, there's a shock.

Green phone—Richard: "Hi, Kitty, it's me. It's Sunday evening at . . . er . . . nineish, and I was wondering what you're up to. I'm lonely without you. See you very soon."

Yellow phone—Stef: *Four messages:* "K, it's me. What the hell's the matter? Why did you run off like that? Jesus, K, what's the big deal?"

"K, it's me again. I've been trying to work out what's going on and I *can't.* Why've you suddenly gone all self-righteous on me? You've always known about what I do. What's changed?"

"Me again. It's this one job, isn't it? You've got a problem with this one thing that we're doing. Look, K, we've got it all sussed. It's safe, yeah? No worries. No shit, honest. I want you to come over here. *Please* come over here."

"Don't fucking ignore me, K! I know what you're like. You must have got my messages by now. How could you just walk *out* on me like that. How could you do that to me!"

Red phone—Jonny: Nothing.

It's half past eleven by the time I pull up outside the flat in North Cross Road, East Dulwich. There's a fierce wind hurling tin cans, plastic bags and pizza boxes down the road, blowing so hard at old ladies who can barely manage to walk that now they are carried along by it and seem to run and skip up and down the street. When the rain starts it's horizontal. I can hardly remain upright as

I repeatedly ring the doorbell and shout through the letter box. Nothing. Returning to the cab I rip a sheet of paper from the ring-bound A5 pad I carry around and write,

> Joel,
>
> Whatever you may think of me, and however uninterested you now are in me—please call me as soon as you get this message. You won't regret it if you call me. You *might* regret it if you don't.
> Love
>
> Kat

I shove it through the letter box and head back to Balham, listening to an old Joni Mitchell tape as I drive and doing my best not to let myself think about the way my life is folding in on itself. Crumpling up. I make myself think about Amy instead—of how beautiful she was this morning.

"Big Yellow Taxi"—Joni's right; you don't know what you've got till it's gone.

Arriving at the house, climbing the blue-carpeted stairs that stink of cat piss, I hear a noise. A cough. My front door is closed as it should be but I was not mistaken—that was definitely a cough. Someone is inside my flat.

20

I T's him. It had to be, didn't it?

"How the fuck did you get in here?"

He is sitting in the battered old armchair in my living room, smoking a cigarette in the half-light.

"Ah, Katerina, here you are," he says with a welcoming smile.

I snatch the cig from his mouth, take it out to the kitchen and flick it into the pedal bin.

"Hey, I'd only just lit that!"

"This is a no smoking flat." I'm picking my way through the debris to open the blinds and let some light in. The air is full of smoke and dust. "How dare you break in! What the hell do you think you're doing?"

His mouth twitches slightly at the corners. To my delight, I realize that he is afraid of me—afraid of the physical reality of me. I'm bigger than him, and fitter. I could beat him into a pulp if I wanted to.

"Well, Kathryn, I came to ask you why you broke into *my* flat yesterday,"

Damn that wanker of a security guard. "I wanted to talk to you. You weren't there."

"Ditto." He shrugs helplessly.

I struggle to keep my cool in the face of this supreme casualness. "Craig, I want you to tell me exactly what you do for a living."

"I told you. PR."

My fists are tightly clenched. I feel my toes curling up inside my trainers but my voice remains calm. "Do you know someone called Stefan Muchowski?"

That twitch again, just at the corners of his mouth. "Stefan—who?"

"Stefan Mu-chow-ski. Do you know him? And what about Jimmy and Eddie?"

His shoulders are slumping slowly. He knows he's cornered but says nothing.

"I'll take that as a yes, shall I?"

"Kathryn—look, please will you let me have a cigarette? You let me smoke in here the other night . . ."

"No. Tell me how you know Stefan."

Twinkle's face looks pale and nervous, his skin paper thin. He takes a cotton handkerchief from his pocket and makes a big business of blowing his nose. This reminds me of my father blowing his nose at the breakfast table when I was a kid. Mum used to yell at him to go out the back when he did that but he always ignored her. Eventually he emerges from the handkerchief and says, "Stefan Muchowski is an unpleasant little toe-rag and I'd be interested to hear how *you* know him."

This description of Stef rankles but I try to keep control of my temper. "So you don't deny it?"

"Why should I deny it? What is he to you?"

"I saw you." I'm taking a few steps toward him, trying to look threatening, but as I move forward I trip over a hair dryer and a box of my mother's best silver cutlery. Twinkle's hand shoots out and grips my arm, steadying me. Now we stand only inches apart, sizing each other up. Suddenly he leans in—

"Don't you kiss me!" I wrench away and take a step back, finally losing my cool. "I *saw* you yesterday, coming out of Stef's flat. I know that he and Jimmy and Eddie have been holding money for you. A lot of money. What is it all about, Twinkle? Drugs? Something worse than drugs? Tell me."

He looks down at the floor, frowns. "I'm touched by your faith in me, Kathryn. Truly touched."

And that's when I hit him. A good open-handed slap—hard as I can manage.

He doesn't react except to put a hand to his red cheek. He seems too stunned to speak.

"Why weren't you straight with me, Twinkle?" Oh God, I'm about to cry. I'm going to dissolve in tears like any ordinary weak girlie. My vision clouds. "If you'd just told me the truth, then maybe . . . I am so *disappointed*."

He tries to give me his handkerchief but I don't want it. Instead I blunder into the kitchen to get a piece of paper towel. When I get back he's sitting down again.

"Kathryn, it would be a mistake to let some shitty little piece of low-life ruin everything . . ."

"*You're* the low-life!"

Infuriatingly he chuckles, rubs at his sore cheek. "Yeah, I guess I should try to be more like you, eh? I mean, you're always straight with people, aren't you?"

I don't like the new direction this conversation has taken. "This isn't about *me*, Craig. This is about you dragging my friend Stef into something really dodgy. This is about you leading me to believe you are one type of person when really you are something else entirely."

"That's right. I am something else entirely." In spite of what I've said to him about smoking he takes another cigarette from his packet and lights it up. Takes a deep drag and tilts his head so that he's looking at me sidelong. Then he smiles again, and this smile isn't a nervous one—it's arrogant, cocksure. And he says it. Just says it. "I'm a policeman."

I'm spooning coffee into the percolator. Coffee is the opposite of what I need—my nerves are jangling and prickling enough as it is without the addition of a caffeine injection. But I had to get out of that room and I heard my voice saying, "I'm going to make some coffee." My hand shakes as I switch on the machine.

There are weird palpitations going on in my chest and my

breathing comes fast and shallow, as though I'm on the verge of a panic attack. I used to get like this when I was a child. I'd be lying on my bed staring up at the ceiling and suddenly it would seem to be getting lower, inching its way down on top of me. And then I'd be so aware of my breathing; the in, the out, the expansion and contraction of my diaphragm. My rib cage shifting to let my chest balloon up and down, the air whistling in and out of my nose. And the breathing would seem to be the result of a huge tortuous effort, an effort I could hardly bare to make and that I couldn't sustain. The panic made it all worse. I'd be blowing out hard through my mouth, my nostrils wide and horselike. My heartbeats would accelerate, racing and fluttering . . . And then I'd start screaming and my mother would come rushing in and sit down on the edge of the bed, soothing me with her low, quiet voice and stroking my head. She would sit there for a long time, and we would breathe together.

Craig is in the room, coming up behind me. I turn around to face him and he pulls me toward him and wraps me tightly in his arms. My chin is resting on his shoulder and I'm looking at the cracked white tiles on the wall behind him—and at the drip-drip of the black liquid inside the glass coffee jug as my breathing gradually normalizes. And I can feel his hand on the back of my head, resting there, keeping me close to him. My arms hang limply at my sides.

"How can you be a policeman?" I say softly, when I'm able to speak again.

He sighs and allows me to pull away from him. "It's what I do. I'm sorry."

"What's going on, Craig?"

He leans against my washing machine. The left side of his face is bright red where I hit it. For a few seconds we're silent. There's only the hiss and crackle of the percolator. He takes out his handkerchief and blows his nose again—maybe just to buy time to think—shoves it back in his trousers. There is a weariness about him. He is exhausted at the prospect of being truthful with me.

"Look . . . I'm with the drugs squad. I'm undercover—that's why I had to lie to you. I didn't *want* to lie to you . . ."

"Yeah, sure." My voice is heavily sarcastic. It could be just another lie, of course, and yet there is a ring of truth about this . . . the unlived-in apartment . . . "So you're—what—*acting* as some big drug dealer to trip up the real ones?"

"Something like that."

"*What*," though. Tell me more."

"I can't, Kathryn. I've already said what I shouldn't say. I put my life at risk telling you any of this shit. Pour me some of that coffee, will you?"

As I pour the coffee into two mugs I realize—"Oh, God. Stef's in real shit, isn't he?"

This pisses him off. "What is that toe-rag to you?"

"What's going to happen to Stef?"

"*I* have no interest in Stefan Muchowski, Kathryn. What is he to *you*?" He reaches for his coffee.

"So it's not Stef that you're after."

"*No*. He's *nobody*. Oh, for Christ's sake!" He smacks his coffee cup down on the worktop. "Are you shagging him? Is that what this is about?"

"That's none of your business."

"So you *are* shagging him." He gives a humorless chuckle and licks coffee off the back of his hand. "I'd have thought you'd have better taste." He stares at me for a moment, his face empty of expression. "I think I'd better go." He turns and walks out of the kitchen, heading for the front door.

"Craig—"

"What?" He twists round to look at me. His hand rests on the door handle.

"Would you promise me that you won't arrest Stef?"

He sighs. "Kathryn—"

"You said he's nobody. If he's nobody, why do you need to arrest him?"

"I have no plans to arrest Stefan Muchowski."

"Would you promise me, Craig? If you care about me, then you'll leave him alone."

"That's rich, Kathryn. That's fucking rich!"

He opens the front door and passes through it. I hear his feet on the stairs.

I put the coffee cups in the sink and struggle to get my head around all of this. But then as the outer door thuds shut, a thought comes flashing through—a thought that got buried under my concern for Stef and my desire to get the truth out of Craig.

"Craig! Craig, wait!" I'm tearing through the doorway, running down the stairs two at a time, yanking open the door to the street.

He is bending to unlock his Volvo.

"What?" His voice is strained and thin.

"Who's Henry? Your friend Henry. The one who puked in my cab?"

"Henry?" His face changes. He looks . . . worried. "What does he have to do with anything?"

"There's a boy. Joel. He's eighteen. He's been working as a rent boy, and he seems to be missing."

"Henry?" he says again.

"I saw Joel on the Strand on Saturday afternoon, getting into a car. Henry was in the back. Is he an undercover copper too?"

"No . . . No, he's not."

I've never seen his eyes so free of twinkle.

"Is he a pimp, then? Shit, Craig, is he the one you're after? Is it Henry?"

He opens the door of the Volvo. His face still wears that same expression. "You say he's a rent boy, this Joel?"

"Yes."

"And you last saw him on Saturday afternoon."

"Yes."

He rubs at his head. "So he's only been gone a couple of nights."

"I guess so. But—"

"Look, he'll probably be back tonight. Is there any *real reason* for you to think something's happened to him?"

I see the look of betrayal on Joel's face at the moment he got into that Mercedes. I think about him snuggling down in the back of the car with fat Henry. "No. No real reason. Just an instinct, that's all."

Craig walks back around the car to join me on the pavement. He puts a hand on my arm, gives it a squeeze. "Your friend Joel is not in the best of company but Henry Fisher wouldn't do anything to him unless he had a *reason* to."

Mr. Fisher . . . "Are you sure?"

"Think about it, Kathryn. Professional dog breeders don't bag up their pedigree puppies and sling them in the river, do they."

I wish he hadn't said that. I close my eyes, hoping that when I open them again I'll be somewhere else. I'm still here. Craig's back in the road, getting into the car.

He starts the engine, but then leans over to open the passenger window, and calls out, "Give him till tomorrow morning. If he's not back by then, call me."

His eyes are a cold unglinting blue.

21

My mother loved dancing but my father wore her down, wore the dance out of her. When I was little she told me stories about how she used to go jiving with her boy-friend, Alan. They were such good dancers that now and again everyone else would stop dancing and just stand about watching them. Alan would spin my mother around, throw her up in the air and catch her. Together they entered competitions and won prizes. They would dance in something she called "the hop," which happened every Saturday. My father used to go to the hop too, but he wouldn't dance. My father was shy and serious and awkward on his feet. He would stand around at the side of the room, looking at my mother. He was in love with her but she didn't notice he existed, that's what she used to say. I can hear her voice now:

"He was my secret admirer. He used to see me with Alan and dream I was his."

Not that my father didn't have girlfriends—he'd always have a partner of his own at the hop. But once they got inside the dance hall he'd go skulking off to stand at the side while his partner of the night jived off across the room with some other bloke. He didn't care about the girls, though. My mother was the only one he really felt anything for, and he didn't dare speak to her because she was so beautiful and so out of his league.

My mother would go on to tell the story of how my father "saved" her from Alan, who turned out to be a cad. The story was rather vague. One night at the hop my mother caught Alan out the back snogging another girl and my father gallantly intervened and won her over. My imagination filled in the rest: My mother crying prettily while my father grabbed Alan and smacked him one in the gob—then dusted himself down and straightened his tie before taking my mother by the arm and escorting her home, stepping over the unconscious body of vile Alan en route.

When I got older—teenage—my mother changed the story, or at least put a different spin on it. My father ceased being the secret admirer who saved her from the evil two-timing Alan and became a weedy dull creep who had a crush on her, and eventually took advantage of her at a moment of weakness. She finally filled in the detail she'd previously omitted: When she caught Alan with the other girl she screamed abuse at him and slapped the girl in the face. Then she went back into the dance hall and hit the booze. As she sat at the side of the hall drinking glass after glass of Pimms, she was joined by my father. He listened to her tale of woe and indulged her while she got steadily more and more paralytic. The dance ended and she was too pissed to stand up on her own, so he had to help her get home. On the way she was sick over him, and felt so guilty about it that when he rang the next day to ask her out on a date she didn't like to say no.

I know my mother was a volatile woman. I know she must have been "difficult" in many ways; a neurotic, addictive personality, a tendency toward depression. The dancing was the flip side of the same coin—that was the way it worked with her. When the dancing stopped, the depression took hold. I know that the suicide must have been lying inside her somewhere, stored in her genes or trapped in her psychology, waiting for the chance to get out. And my father, with his coldness, his fear of embarrassment, his ideas about how a headmaster's wife should behave—he wore the dance out of her even though it was the dance that first attracted him. He dragged her suicidal tendency out of hiding and into the open.

I'm chewing all this over as I'm driving through Brixton and into Herne Hill. God knows I have plenty to think about already, and yet this stuff from my parents' past is somehow relevant—it's pressing down on me.

Some people have the ability to remain essentially intact, no matter what is going on in their lives. People and events and situations bounce off them like so many tennis balls bouncing off a wall. The wall remains solid, unaffected. I'm not saying that I think these people don't *feel* anything. I'm just saying that they are copers, survivors. My mother wasn't like that. With her it was more like when a tennis ball lands on a flower, snaps the stem, crushes the petals.

North Cross Road. I'm peering through the letter box. The note I wrote to Joel is still lying on the mat inside the door. An idea glints in my dull aching head. I walk down to the b2 general store on the corner and buy a roll of Scotch tape and some paracetamol. Back outside, I open the paracetamol and neck a couple, forcing them down my throat without water, stuffing the packet in my jacket pocket. Then I return to Joel's front door, pull up a strip of Scotch tape a few inches in length and use my teeth to break it off the roll. I crouch down low and stick the strip across the crack between the door and the frame. If anyone goes in or out through this door, the tape will be displaced. Then I straighten and return to the cab. It feels good to have done something, no matter that the thing I've done is so inconsequential.

I'm well on the way to Brick Lane, driving across Tower Bridge, trying to work out what to say to Stef. I want to tell him everything I know, to warn him against . . . what? What *do* I actually know? That "the man" is an undercover copper and he should stop holding the money? How can I explain any of this?

I put my life at risk telling you any of this shit.

Can that be true?

I can't tell Stef anything, can I. I'm under an obligation to Craig, no matter how much I might hate the idea. And how can I possibly go to see Stef, knowing what I know but saying nothing?

I take the blue phone out of the glove compartment and call

Winnie. No answer. Where the hell is she when you really need her?

Fuck you, Craig fucking Summer.

Five-oh-five P.M. and I've been driving since midday. Seemed the right thing to do to take my mind off things—to make me focus on something harmless; on simply getting people from A to B. It's been a freaky day, though. I hate daytime driving, anyway—all that traffic, the soaring stress levels of the passengers—but today is particularly weird. First some rich bint flags me down in Knightsbridge and asks me to drive her to Aquascutum on Regent Street and wait outside while she nips in to get something. She says she'll only be three minutes but fifteen later I'm still outside with the meter running. Another five and I'm starting to think I have a bilker. I'm on the verge of getting out and going in to look for her when she reappears, all smiles, with four carrier bags full of shopping. Later on, I pick up an old lady at Paddington, who screams when she gets in the back—there's a leg lying on the floor. A leg! Artificial, of course, but the poor old cow thinks it's the real thing for a moment. What kind of mad world is this? Surely you'd notice if you left your *leg* behind when you got out of a cab. And I reckon I'd see if someone walked in on two and hopped away on one. This has to be the strangest piece of lost property I've ever handed in. Instinct tells me it belongs to the Aquascutum woman because she was one crazy bitch, that's for sure—but five other people have sat in the back of that cab this afternoon and it could have been any one of them . . . And cabbies say *nights* are weird!

Now I'm taking a black guy in very tight jeans with ridiculous mirrored shades from a nightclub in Ladbroke Grove to a bar in Putney. He's talking nonstop on his mobile as I drive, and chewing gum. He chews loudly, open-mouthed, making a tcha-tcha sound. Judging from the way he's ordering the person at the other end of the phone around, he is the manager of the club or the bar or both. For some inexplicable reason he keeps calling me "Treena."

"Hey, Treena, you like to go a bit faster? I've got to be at my appointment in fifteen minutes."

"Treena, you think we'll make it in ten? Look at all this traffic, man."

"Treena, can't you step on it, girl?"

The pink phone rings and I take the call. It's Amy.

"Kathy, it's me."

"Hi, Babe," I say into the phone, and lower my voice to a whisper. "You were great last night. I wish I'd been able to stick around for longer but you know how it is."

"I certainly do." She sounds pissed off. "Where are you, Kathy?"

"Just on my way to Putney. Why?"

"I want you to come over here."

"Sure." The thought of another night like last night is alluring. "I should be done driving by about ten. That OK? I could bring some take-out with me."

"No. I want you to come over now. As soon as you can." There's a wobble in her voice. Is she crying?

"Amy, what's wrong?"

"Nothing. Just get over here." And she hangs up.

"Are you listening to me, Treena?" My passenger is knocking on the screen in a fractious sort of way. Two little mirrors glaring at me. "I asked you to take a right. You missed the turning."

"Oh. Sorry," I say without conviction. "I guess I'd better turn round."

"Never mind. Just pull over and drop me here."

I do as he suggests. He pays—no tip.

"Why do you keep calling me Treena?" I ask as he gets out.

Twin mirrors turn and stare at me. "What the hell are you talking about, lady?"

Amy has lit a bonfire in the back garden and the flames are leaping high. She's got a load of bits of crate and cardboard and what looks like sawn-up old chairs, which she's slinging on piece by piece. She's wearing her red silk pajamas—I wouldn't have thought these were ideal bonfire-building attire—and wellies. I stand and watch her for a while, trying to keep out of the plumes of smoke.

"Rehearsal for Guy Fawkes Night, is it?" I ask.

It's raining very slightly, and the raindrops are making the fire fizz and smoke all the more. Amy is mostly busy but every now and then she turns to look at me. I wish I could see her face clearly in the darkness.

"How did your mother's hospital appointment go today?" Her voice is thin and high.

"Oh, fine. We had to wait for an hour before she got to see the specialist, but you know what hospitals are like . . ."

She turns back to the fire and I see her shoulders shaking. I want to go over and kiss her but I don't dare. Last night her mouth tasted of sweet things—a sugary mingling of Butterkist popcorn, minstrels and smoothies.

"Amy, what's going on?"

"Can't you guess?" comes that fragile voice.

I can only think this must have something to do with the incident with Willa. I thought I did the right thing by that bloody woman . . . Is she really so bitter about me turning her down and so in love with Amy that she's told some nasty little lie to try to break us up? Would she *do* that?

"Willa's said something to you, hasn't she?"

She says nothing. Hurls another chair leg into the fire.

My face is hot from the flames. I don't suppose you're actually allowed to have bonfires in Islington. I turn and gaze up at the neighbors' houses—a couple of curtains are twitching. "Amy, whatever Willa has said to you, it isn't true. I didn't blab about what happened last night because I wanted to spare her the embarrassment. I guess I'm going to have to tell you the whole story. Come on—let's go inside."

I've moved closer to her while I'm saying this, and I lay a hand on her shoulder but she wriggles free. Close up, I can see that the streaks across her face are not just dirt—she is crying.

"Don't you go blaming Willa for what you've done. She's my

friend." The tightness in her voice makes me think of one time when Jonny was trying to play his guitar drunk and he kept tuning one of the strings higher and higher—so high that you could actually *see* the strain in it, a delicate taut thinness becoming clearly visible in the final seconds before it snapped.

"Well, what am I supposed to have done? She made a pass at me, Amy. She's in love with you and she couldn't have you so she threw herself at me—"

"Shut up." She is so close to the fire that I'm worried the leg of her pajamas is going to catch alight. "I don't want to hear any more of your lies, Kathy. I've had it with you."

"What?" Now I'm really confused. What could Willa possibly *know*? I'm becoming aware of high-pitched giggles and whispers from just behind the fence on the left perimeter of the garden. The next door neighbors' children must have snuck outside when they saw the bonfire and now they're eavesdropping. "Let's talk about this inside, Amy."

"The only way a relationship can work is when there is a foundation of openness and honesty." I can't stand the preachy note in her voice, and now I feel my own anger rising. There's another giggle from behind the fence.

"You're a one to talk about openness and honesty—you've been sleeping with Cheryl behind my back, haven't you."

She stiffens. "Why would I want to do a thing like that?"

This feels better. I have her on the defensive. I'm starting to see a way to maneuver through . . . "I don't know, *honey*. Maybe when you can have caviar every day, you find yourself craving the occasional Fray Bentos pie . . ."

"What are you talking about? I've never eaten a Fray Bentos pie in my life."

Trust her to come over all literal on me. "It's a *me-ta-phor*, Amy. I am the caviar and Cheryl is the Fray Bentos pie."

I see her recoil. She wanders across the lawn and sits down at Willa's picnic table. I follow cautiously, trying to dispel an unwanted mental image of Amy and Cheryl giving each other 69.

"Well, what do you expect?" she snaps. "I've been waiting and waiting for you, Kathy. Who can blame me for looking for a bit of comfort? God knows, I get precious little emotional support from you."

"We're not talking about emotional support. We're talking about you and that big ugly dyke getting your rocks off together."

"Fuck off, Kathy. Just fuck off." She buries her face in her hands and sobs. Slowly, carefully, I sit down beside her and put my arm around her. The scuffling and giggling behind the fence finally stops as the kids get bored and go back inside. Show's over.

"It's the desk, isn't it? You're burning the desk."

She nods, emerging from her hands. Her face is swollen and blotchy but there is the hint of a smile as she sees she has succeeded in hurting me.

"I'm very angry with you, Kathy." But her voice isn't angry anymore. She looks oddly happy. Perhaps she has moved beyond anger.

"Why?"

"You've been making out you live with your mother when really she's been dead for fifteen years . . . All this time I've accepted that I can't visit your flat because your mother will find out about us. I've been putting up with the fact that I only see you twice a week at most, I've been kissing you goodbye when you have to go and take her to the hospital or the church or to see your fucking Auntie Betty—"

Of course. Last night I told Willa I was upset because of my mother's memorial service . . . "Oh, honey—"

She gives a hard little laugh. "How do you think it makes me feel to discover you're so desperate to keep me out of your life that you've reincarnated your own mother as a ready-made excuse to keep me at a distance?"

"I don't want it to be over between us, Amy. What can I do to make it better?"

She's smiling now—a sunshine in rain smile. "It doesn't matter what you want, Kathy. It doesn't matter what *I* want. The fact is there's no way of going forward from this. There've been too many lies."

I don't know how to respond. We sit together in silence for a long time, watching the flames shrink down into glowing red embers while I play with strands of her hair.

Later, as I'm leaving—walking through the hall to the front door—I catch a glimpse of something out of the corner of my eye. Someone at the top of the stairs moving quickly out of view.

At Joel's place, the tape is untouched.

I wash a couple of paracetamol down with a swig of Craig's Laphroaig and shove the bottle back in the glove compartment. Then I start the engine and drive over to the Crocodile. It's 9:10 P.M. and I haven't eaten since those croissants Amy brought me this morning. Jesus, what a long time ago that seems.

"Sausage, egg and chips, please, Kev, and a Diet Coke."

They're all staring at me and whispering to each other. Steve Ambley is nudging the bald geezer next to him. Orhan Ataman seems to be doing a crossword but in fact he's writing something on his newspaper—pushing it across to Rog Hackenham, who looks up at me and grins.

"All right, Kathryn?" says Frank Wilson.

"Wotcha, Frank." I sit down alone at my usual table with my back to them all, staring out of the window at the passing traffic, vehicular and human. Couples are wandering by with their arms around each other. A group of Essex girls with ankle chains, short skirts and high heels are screeching and laughing as one of them trips on her stiletto and blunders into the gutter. They're so young, so nubile and gorgeous. And here's me—not been to the gym for days, aware of a new slackness in my body—about to tuck into a plate of molten grease.

Pulling the red phone from my jacket pocket, I try Winnie again. Still no answer. Big Kev comes over with my dinner.

"Has Winnie been in, Kev?"

"Nope."

"When did you last see her?"

Kev scratches his head. He has one pace and he thinks as

slowly as he moves. I notice a nick on his chin where he must have cut himself shaving. I stare at it so hard that I go cross-eyed.

"Ain't seen her in days, Kathryn." Then he notices my worried face, bless him, and tries to be sweet. "Maybe she's gone on holiday with the family."

"Maybe. Bring my ketchup over, will you, Kev?"

"Yeah, right." He takes a bottle off Orhan Ataman's table, plonks it down and lumbers away.

I squeeze a pool of ketchup onto the side of my plate, dip a couple of chips in it and use my fork to break my fried egg yolk. Ooozing yellow goo . . . Repulsed, I push the plate away. My appetite has vanished.

I drive till 2 A.M. That's as long as I can cope with. I'm barely aware of who's in the back or where I'm going. I just go. My headache won't clear up and I take another couple of paracetamol around midnight with a burning mouthful of Laphroaig. When passengers try to talk to me I pretend not to hear. I switch on the radio to drown them out but I have no idea which station I'm listening to.

Back at my flat the bulb in the living room blows and I can hardly see to pick my way through the rubbish, only just about making it to my bedroom without doing myself an injury.

I'm too tired to sleep. Feels like I'm tossing and turning for hours but whenever I look at my alarm clock no time at all has passed. Then I realize the clock has stopped. The battery must be dead.

Twinkle is sitting in the back of the cab laughing at me. I ask him to stop but he won't. There's someone next to him but I can't see who it is—too much darkness. I'm driving fast along the side of the river and the traffic is heavy. I want to stop but I can't—there's nowhere to pull over. I'm sweating and my hands are shaking so I have to grip the wheel hard to keep them steady. The cab isn't behaving as it should and Twinkle is still laughing. I yell at him to shut the fuck up but he isn't having any of it. And still I can't see who is sitting beside him. Then we drive onto a better-lit strip of road and the streetlights flick their vivid orange light through the cab. A flicker of light then darkness. Flick and out. Flick and out. I glance into my rearview mirror and see a flicker of face—then nothing. I'm wondering if it's that loon who tried to set fire to my cab but when the light flicks through again I realize it's a woman. It's my mother.

I call out, "Mum!" but she says nothing. Twinkle is still laughing.

Her eyes don't show that they know me. They're devoid of any expression.

Her mouth opens—clank, like a drawbridge coming down.

And out spews—

The color.

I'm awake—stumbling through the living room, sobbing and retching. My eyes are wide open but all I can see is the color, stretching out beyond the limits of my vision, shrouding everything. I'm groping for the light switch but when I reach it and flick it nothing happens. I blunder through the debris, desperate for a glass of water, for *something*—trip and fall headlong, bash my head against the wooden leg of the armchair. I lie there on the floor for a few minutes, waiting for the color to fade, waiting for the pain in my head to abate, before I can gather the strength to get up.

By the time I move, the color is gone and I'm beginning to see through the darkness. I find my way to the kitchen where I switch the light on and drink glass after glass of tap water till my stomach feels like a heavy bucket filled to its brim. The dream has never been like this before. And I haven't dreamed about my mother since she died.

Jesus, I'm in a state. I need a massage. The kitchen clock says it's 4:27. I can't call Stef at this hour.

Can I?

The yellow phone is sitting on the kitchen surface.

❁   ❁   ❁

The phone is answered after three rings.

"Hello?"

"Stef? Stef, it's me. K. Listen, I'm sorry about Sunday. I—"

"K . . . K, it's not Stef. It's Jimmy."

"Oh, Jimmy . . . I'm sorry to have disturbed you. I need to speak to Stef if he's there."

A pause. Awkward and weighty.

"Jimmy? Is he there? I don't like asking you to wake him up but—"

"K, he's not here. He's been arrested."

22

"I want to see Stefan Muchowski."

The duty sergeant has a thin face and a girlish mouth with full lips. He pouts at me. "Stefan Muchowski?" A quick glance at a piece of paper on his clipboard. "We don't have anyone here by that name."

"Sorry. I mean Steven Moore. I want to see Steven Moore."

He raises one eyebrow and stares at me. Runs his pencil down the clipboard. "Ah, yes. We do have a Steven Moore."

"So can I see him, please?"

"Who are you exactly?"

"I'm his girlfriend."

He gives me an absolutely filthy look and wanders away from the hatch through which we've been speaking—moving past filing cabinets, desks and computer screens, to talk to a woman with a sharp bob and big shoulder pads who's looking through a file.

I'm left standing there for what feels like a really long time, with nothing to do but gaze around the room. High coved ceiling, polished woodblock floor. Benches running along the walls, on which sit several waifs and strays. There's a teenage girl with makeup smeared all down her face, mopping her cheeks with a tissue. A friend is whispering to her and patting her shoulder. Across the room a heavyset Asian man sits with his arms folded, still and straight-backed, his face revealing nothing. A thin, pale couple in their forties are at the far end, perching silent and tense, hand in hand.

The duty sergeant returns, looking all prissy.

"Well? Can I see him?"

"One moment please, miss." He leans forward over the hatch to speak to the Asian man. "Mr. Yatrik? The Urdu interpreter? Would you come through, please." He indicates a door in the wall next to the hatch, and the man half nods and gets to his feet.

He seems about to disappear again, but then turns back to me. "Miss . . ."

"Cheet. Ms."

"*Ms.* Cheet. Look, I'm sorry but I can't do anything for you at the moment. Why don't you go home for a bit and come back after eight o'clock when Sergeant Cryer's here? He'll be able to help."

"But I need to see him! What's he doing here? What has he been charged with?"

Another upward shift of those mobile eyebrows. "Ms. Cheet. You can either take a seat here or you can go home and come back later. It's up to you."

"Did Craig Summer bring him in?" I blurt it out without thinking.

He gives me an odd look. Suspicious. "I'm sorry, Ms. Cheet. I have no idea who you're talking about."

I put my life at risk telling you any of this shit.

I bite my lower lip hard, breaking the skin and tasting blood.

Another man in uniform. If you can call him a man. It's Terry, behind the desk at Craig Summer's apartment building in Chelsea Harbour. It's 6 A.M. and he has his breakfast hiding behind his computer monitor. I can smell the Marmite on his toast.

He looks nervous when I walk into the lobby, and who can blame him. I must have that look of a woman on the edge—wild eyes with big dark circles around them, shaggy unbrushed hair, clothes all messed up and mismatched. And if I look even half as angry and violent as I feel, I must be a frightening sight indeed.

I want to barge straight into Craig's apartment and punch him with closed fist, right in the stomach. And then I want to kick him in his lousy balls as hard as I can. And while he's doubled over, unable to breathe, I want to grab him by the collar and make him tell me why he has broken his promise and arrested Stef. He told me that Stef was "nobody," that he had "no interest" in him. But less than twenty-four hours after he made that promise, Stef is in custody and I'm not even allowed to see him.

"Oh. It's you." Terry's mouth is quivering slightly at the corners. His zits are worse. He looks like he's going to cry.

"Yes, Terry, it's me." I'm not taking any crap from this shit-for-brains.

"How's the diabetes?"

Jesus, he's giggling. The little runt is laughing at me!

"Do you know if Craig Summer's at home?"

"No. I mean yes. I mean—yes, I *know* that he's not here." He's stopped giggling now but the smile still plays around his acne-ridden mouth.

"Are you sure?"

"Sure I'm sure. He moved out yesterday."

"He *what*?"

"He moved out. Put all his stuff in a van."

"You're lying!" I lunge at him, trying to grab him by the collar, but he steps back quickly and evades my grasp.

"Don't take it out on me if your boyfriend's gone back to his wife," he snaps, all snarky. "It's true, you know . . . She introduced herself to me—ever so friendly. She drove him away in the van. Lovely woman, that Marianne. Beautiful blonde hair, like a princess."

I can't listen to any more of this. I need air—need to breathe.

Run. Smack into the glass door. Fucking blonde princess.

I'm calling Craig's mobile as I'm driving away. Leaving a message on his answering service.

"Craig, you lying fucker, you promised you wouldn't arrest Stef. You fucking *promised* me. I want you to sort this out and get him off. I don't know how but there must be a way. You owe me that much."

And you're still married, you bastard, to Marianne the blonde princess . . .

At North Cross Road, the Scotch tape is gone.

He's back!

The relief is so powerful and all-consuming that it makes my legs turn to jelly as I'm getting out onto the pavement. I can hardly hold the key steady to lock the cab. But eventually I'm there at the front door, ringing the bell over and over and yelling his name through the letter box.

Feet on the stairs, hurrying down. A bolt being drawn back on the inside. The door opens just a crack. He has the chain on. It's dark inside but I see his big puppy eyes peering through at me.

"Joel!"

The chain is taken off and the door opens fully.

An older Joel stands there. A fifty-year-old Joel with a buttoned-up cardigan and gray bits in his hair.

"You must be Kathryn."

"Oh. I'm sorry, Mr. Marsh. I thought . . ."

"I know." He tries to smile.

"He's not back then."

"No. Do you want to come in? My wife is just making some tea."

"Thanks, but . . . no. I have to be getting on."

He looks kind. A nice man. A decent man.

"The police are looking for him," says Mr. Marsh. "To begin with they didn't seem interested, but I think that now I have made them understand something is very wrong." His voice is shaking.

"Yes."

"They've taken his address book."

"Right."

"Well . . ." He shuffles about awkwardly.

The note I left for Joel is peeping out from under the doormat where it must have been kicked accidentally.

I drop in at the Crocodile, hoping that Winnie may have crawled out from whatever rock she's been hiding under, but she's not there and Kev still hasn't seen her. I'm wondering whether she's avoiding me after our night mission to Turnpike Lane. I sit for over an hour, fretting and drinking so much coffee that my heart starts fluttering and palpitating. Then I go back to the cab and call Craig again on the red phone.

"Please leave messages here for Craig Summer."

"Craig, it's me again. Where *are* you? Listen, this is about Joel. You told me I should wait twenty-four hours. Well, I've waited. And he's still missing. His parents have called the police. They'll want to talk to me, won't they, and I need you to tell me what to do. I think I should tell them about Henry . . . You have to help me, Craig. Joel's full name is Joel Marsh. He's seventeen and black. He lives in the flat over the greengrocer's at 57 North Cross Road, East Dulwich. He's about five feet eleven, and fit. He has a shaved head and piercings: three in the left ear, one in the lower lip, one in the right eyebrow, and a nose stud. When I last saw him he was wearing a black Armani suit."

I check the pink phone for messages, hoping that Amy may have changed her mind but knowing that she won't have. As I replace the phone in the glove compartment there's a sharp pang in my chest that may just be down to the coffee . . . I move on to check the other phones. Nothing on any of them except the yellow one:

"K, it's Stef. You've got to help me. I've been arrested. I'm in the cop shop on Larimer Street. Can't talk now but it's about the Rioja thing. I need a lawyer. Can you get me one?—a good one. Get here as soon as you can . . . I'm frightened."

The pouty sergeant has gone now and a thick-necked bruiser has taken his place. I suppose he must be Sergeant Cryer.

"Can I help?" When he speaks his face softens and becomes more kind.

"I'd like to see Stef—Steven Moore, please."

"And you are . . ."

"Kathryn Cheet. Steven's girlfriend. I came in at half past five and was told to come back after eight. Well now it's"—I glance at my watch—"nine forty-three."

The sergeant heaves a sigh. "You can't see him right now, Miss Cheet. He's being interviewed."

"I *have* to see him. He asked me to get him a lawyer."

He's confused now. He looks at his paperwork and tucks his pencil behind his ear. "Well, you needn't worry yourself on that score, Miss Cheet, because his lawyer's in with him now."

"*What?*"

He spreads out his big hands in a gesture which is a sort of general disclaimer. "It would seem that Mr. Moore has made his own arrangements. Perhaps you'd like to take a seat."

I glance around the room at the people sitting on the benches. A tired-looking woman with straggly hair and a track suit is breast-feeding a baby. A guy of about sixteen or seventeen with bleached-blond hair is gazing up at the clock and looking sorry for himself. An old bloke in a mac is asleep near the door.

Ten o'clock passes while I sit on the bench, and so does eleven o'clock. Uniforms come and go, talking to each other and laughing. I stare at their heavily laden belts—the radios, handcuffs, truncheons. Police kit. I stare at the women's sensible shoes. After a while the bleached-blond boy is taken through. The bint with the baby breast-feeds intermittently. The old soak in the mac sleeps on.

At 11:14 the door through to the back opens and a thin, middle-aged man in a pinstriped suit with wild gray hair and a hawk nose appears, flanked by two uniforms. Sergeant Cryer calls out to me from the desk:

"Miss Cheet? You might want a word with that gentleman. It's Mr. Prosser, your man's lawyer."

Mr. Prosser and I are drinking double espressos in a coffee bar at Liverpool Street Station.

"I don't get it. If they haven't actually charged him with anything, why's he banged up in there?"

"They don't have to charge him yet. But they will, don't you worry about that. For now, they're trying to frighten him into saying something he shouldn't?" Mr. Prosser smiles at me. He looks relaxed, easy.

"Are you saying it's not really this Rioja business they're interested in? That it's something else?"

"It seems that way, but you tell *me*, Kathryn. What else *is* there?" Mr. Prosser is a clever man. You can see how clever he is in the brightness of his pale gray eyes and in the lines around them.

"I don't know, Mr. Prosser. Probably nothing."

"Probably?"

"There's nothing that I know of."

"But as you rightly surmise, Kathryn, they would appear to be interested in something our Steven hasn't told them yet. They have enough evidence to charge him in relation to his role in this Spanish table wine fiasco but they haven't done so."

I take a gulp of my industrial-tasting espresso and Mr. Prosser drains his cup. His hands are old and gnarled, betraying his real age as more advanced than I would have expected. He gets to his feet and glances at his watch.

"I have to call in at the office now but I'll be back later. I think they might let you see him soon. I should warn you—his appearance may alarm you. He's had a bit of a time of it, our Steven."

"What, you mean . . ."

"No, no." He chuckles. "Nothing untoward. He's just a very frightened boy." He hands me his business card. It has the name of the firm: Bing, Bing and Claythorpe, and his name, Gareth Prosser. "Oh yes, and I have a message for you, Kathryn."

"A message? From Stef?"

"From the gentleman who hired me to handle this case. He asked me to give you this." He produces a folded piece of paper from his pocket and passes it across. "I apologize if I haven't got it quite right. He dictated it to me over the phone."

Then he stoops to pick up his briefcase, gives me a sharp nod and heads out of the coffee shop, leaving me to read the note:

Dear Kathryn,

I didn't actually promise you anything, but for the record, I had nothing to do with this. Nevertheless I've hired Gareth Prosser to help Stef as far as he can be helped. I've done this as a gesture of goodwill toward you, and not because I am in any way responsible. I am also looking into the situation with your friend Joel. I will report back to you on that matter.

　　Best wishes,

　　Craig

"Best wishes" indeed. "I will report back to you on that matter." What a prick.

Mr. Prosser was wrong. They don't let me see Stef. I'm stuck on the bench yet again. At 1:30 P.M. they drag in a couple of pissed football yobs, effing and blinding and shouting their innocence. At 2:00 a small, sad-looking man in a blue yachting blazer is led through, cuffed. The woman with the baby is finally dealt with, thank fuck. I've had enough of watching that sprog latching on to her tits like a little suction plunger. At 2:30 Sergeant Cryer takes pity on me and brings me a mug of tea.

　　"I hope he's worth it, love."

　　My companions on the bench come and go but the sleeping tramp and I sit on. At 2:57, two guys arrive—late thirties or early forties. All suited up. One flashes ID at Sergeant Cryer and the sergeant goes straight away to let them through. He glances over at me as they go in and gives me a smile. This makes me nervous. A few minutes later Mr. Prosser gets back, red-faced with hurrying and short of breath. I start to get up when I see him and he half nods but then flaps a hand at me as though to tell me he doesn't have time to chat. Then he's through the door too. Now I *am* worried.

　　I go down to the cab to take two paracetamol with the last of Twinkle's Laphroaig. On the way back to the police station I buy some chewing gum so nobody will smell the whiskey on my breath.

　　By 4:30, I've bought and read *The Guardian*, *The Independent*, the *Mirror* and *Private Eye*. I've also bought a bottle of Glenfiddich which I've stowed in the cab. Sergeant Cryer can't or won't tell me what's going on. At five he goes off duty and is replaced by a long-faced sloping-shouldered sergeant with a Welsh accent who reminds me of one of my teachers from school. I hear some-one call out his name. Sergeant Clearwater.

"Ms. Cheet. Kathryn . . ."

I wake up with a jolt. I'm still there on the cold, hard bench. My neck is stiff, the muscles twinging. There is a hand on my shoulder. It's Mr. Prosser, accompanied by long-faced Sergeant Clearwater.

"What . . . How long have I . . ."

"Kathryn, you can see Steven now," says Mr. Prosser. "But I think you and I should have a brief word first. Are you all right? Do you need to freshen up?"

"No, I'm fine." I run a hand over my aching head, try to swallow though my mouth is dry and bitter-tasting. "What time is it, please?"

"Twenty to seven," says Sergeant Clearwater.

"Jesus . . ."

"Let's step outside for a minute," says Mr. Prosser.

It's dark and the wind is strong and sharp. City types are scurrying to Liverpool Street Station, or sidling into the doorways of bland franchise wine bars and pubs. Pitcher and Piano. Slug and Lettuce. All-Bar One. Ordering their spritzers, their gin and tonics, their bottles of Corona or rarefied Belgian blond beers. I need some more paracetamol.

Mr. Prosser is talking to me but I'm finding it difficult to tune in to what he's saying. The world is buzzing around me like radio interference. The firefly lights of the cars and buses, the clouds of exhaust, the *Big Issue* salesmen and the dusty builders from the site up the road—they're drowning him out. I'm nodding as he's talking to me but what I'm thinking is that I'm cold and I need to sleep; proper sleep, in my own bed, alone. Some people are huddled nearby smoking and stamping their feet for warmth. They're talking about Crete—one of them's about to go there, while another's been before. They sound happy, normal. I'd like to walk over

and ask for one of their cigarettes. It's not that I want to smoke—
it's just that I'd like to be one of them instead of being me.

"So all in all the Rioja scam is little more than a side issue," Mr.
Prosser is saying. "And the negotiation is finally over." He looks
pleased with himself. "Do you want to see him now, Kathryn? Or
would you rather sleep on this?"

"What? Sleep on what?"

"Well, my dear, on the question of whether you will go with
him. It would require you to start a new life, take on an entirely
new identity."

Stef looks mangy. Like a puny sick cat with the mange. His hair is
greasy, his jaw spotty, he needs a shave. It's not ink he smells of today—it's something more potent, toxic. Sweat begins to stink
when it dries on clothing. Seems like fear must have that same
property—there's a stench of dried fear on Stef.

He's smiling though, as he crumples the Coke can in front of
him. There's manic light in his red-rimmed eyes when he sees me
following Mr. Prosser into the room.

"K! I thought you'd never get here!"

"I've been here all day."

I sit down on the opposite side of the table from him. My chair
makes a scraping noise as I draw it up. There's a uniform in the far
corner, sitting very straight on a chair, making like he's not here.
The walls are painted a murky pink, a bit like my old bedroom
back at my dad's house. A tape machine is on the desk, switched
off. There are two empty chairs where the suits must have been
sitting. The striplight on the ceiling is flickering, making my headache worse.

I'm not sure if I'm allowed to touch him but I don't want
to anyway. He has his hands on the table. He's been chewing
his knuckles as well as his finger nails and the skin is raw and
ripped.

Mr. Prosser sits down beside him. This positioning—the two of
them on one side of the table and me on the other—makes me
feel as though I am Stef's interrogator.

"They're finding a safe house for me," says Stef. "They reckon they'll have it set up later tonight." He smiles, and it's an odd side-long smile—one I haven't seen on his face before. "Kind of exciting, isn't it."

"It's not my idea of excitement, Stef."

"No. Right." He looks chastened, realizing he's said the wrong thing. But that little side comment of his has shown me something about what's going on in his mangy head. We sit looking at each other, each trying to gauge how to handle this.

"Steven is a very important witness," says Mr. Prosser, breaking the silence. "All the charges against him have been dropped provided he's willing to give evidence."

"What evidence?" I snap at Stef. "What do you know that's so important?"

"It's about that money we were holding." Behind his dried fear and exhaustion, he actually sounds proud of himself.

"I thought you didn't know anything about it."

"Yeah, well . . ." He gnaws again at the bitten-down nails on his left hand.

Mr. Prosser clears his throat loudly. "If I might just interrupt . . . Kathryn, Steven has spoken in some detail and with a commendable frankness to the police today. I would suggest that now is not the time for the two of you to discuss this matter at length. There should be a safe house ready for Steven later tonight . . ."

"I see." I'm thinking about Joel getting into that Mercedes on the Strand. I'm thinking about the man in the back. I return my attention to Stef. "So you just acted ignorant to fob me off . . ."

"K—" His head droops. He can't look at me.

"You pissy little wanker!"

"Kathryn, perhaps—" Mr. Prosser begins, but I glare at him and he shuts up.

"Thank you, Mr. Prosser, for all your help. Could I have a few minutes with Stef, please?"

Prosser gives a questioning look at Stef, who nods sharply before letting his head droop again. There's something in this exchange which makes me realize Mr. Prosser has remained in the room until now on Stef's request—because Stef can't face me.

"All right, Kathryn." He gets to his feet. "I'll be outside if you need me." This comment seems to be addressed to both of us.

Stef looks more nervous as the door closes on us. "Thanks for sorting me out with Mr. Prosser," he says, trying to sound upbeat. "He's cool."

This stops me short, but I decide to play along. "No problem."

"I'll pay you back later. When this is all over."

"Whatever."

He's reaching across the table for my hands but I shrink away from him.

"So, what did you have to tell them to buy your freedom, Stef? Who did you have to sell?"

He shifts uncomfortably on his chair. "I had no choice, K—I couldn't go to prison . . ."

"Well, perhaps you should have thought of that before you embarked on your career as a master criminal." And now I see, in the way he's avoiding my gaze, that it's not just fat cats in Mercedes he's sold. "What's going to happen to Jimmy and Eddie?"

"K, listen to me. This is a whole new start, yeah? I can get out of all this shit. Live somewhere new—maybe somewhere pretty. I'll go back to college or something. Clean up my act. You could come with me, K. Haven't you ever wondered what it would be like to wipe your slate completely clean? To change your identity—become another person?"

And I suppose, in a way, that Stef *has* become another person. The wreck across the table is not the Stef I have known and loved. "What about Jimmy and Eddie, Stef? What about your friends?"

He sighs and his thin body hunches even further over the table. Then he turns his big eyes up at me—doleful, pathetic. "I want you to *be* with me, K. I want you to come to the safe house with me tonight; move on with me into my new life. We could get hitched or something."

Even the expressionless policeman in the corner seems to raise his eyebrows slightly when Stef speaks those stupid words. Though maybe I just imagined it.

"Christ, you are unbelievable." I'm thinking about all those nights when I lay in his arms, all the time he ran his magic hands over my body.

"Well? K?"

There is desperation in his eyes. He's almost feverish with neediness.

"What about Jimmy and Eddie?" I say it again but I know the answer. He has given up his two best friends to save his own miserable neck. He would sell anything and everything if he had to. He'd sell *me* if he could. I'm remembering the first time I met Stef—when I saved him from those meatheads who were after him and he repaid me by trying to scarper out of my cab without paying his fare . . .

"I didn't have any choice." He turns his palms upward. A shrug, a gesture of humility.

"You always have a choice, Stef." I get to my feet. Once again the world around me is becoming hazy, the radio static is returning.

"K, don't leave me." Stef's voice is almost lost in the hissing and crackling in my head. "*Please* don't leave me like this. I love you, K. I want you to be with me . . . Come back here, K . . . Don't turn your back on me, you bitch!"

"Save it for someone who cares, Stef."

I can still hear him shouting as I walk back down the corridor, past a silent Mr. Prosser and out of this hellhole. I am gone. I am so gone.

23

"PLEASE leave messages here for Craig Summer."

"This is Kathryn. Stef's done a deal but I suppose you know that by now. I guess he wasn't so useless after all, eh? But listen, I'm assuming this deal involves Henry Fisher and that makes me scared about Joel. Craig, would you call me as soon as you get this? Please. I'm leaving my red phone on so you can get me at any time . . . Oh, and do give my love to Marianne."

Why did I say that last bit! Jesus, what's the matter with me? I wish I could unsay it.

I'm driving through Hackney, heading east, and something is bashing around inside my head, beating to be let out. I'm swallowing some more paracetamol with a mouthful of Glenfiddich to help it down. I have a dim suspicion that the headache is related to the fact that I haven't eaten all day, and I contemplate stopping off at a kabob shop. But when I slow up in front of one, the sight of that huge wodge of glistening gray flesh revolving on its spit makes my stomach lurch and I pull sharply back into the traffic, almost knocking some poor old git off his bike.

When I stop at lights, snarled up in a long line of cars, a plump Asian woman with a small kid of indeterminate gender balanced on one hip knocks on my window. I shake my head at her. My light is not on. She indicates the child—it's crying. It looks vaguely ill. Her lips form the single word, "Please." The lights change to green and I move off, leaving the woman standing in the road, gazing after me, kid on hip now screaming. I should have taken her, it's shitty of me not to have done. But tonight I must look after myself. To hell with the punters, however needy they are.

I have to see my friend. I am driving to Ilford, to Winnie's house.

Sandra carries the tea in on a tray. She's put some bourbon biscuits on a plate. She has her blonde hair in two plaits and she's trying not to trip on the bottom of her long white cotton nightie as she comes barefoot into the lounge.

"Cheers, love," says Paul. He's sitting on the couch smoking. His white T-shirt is dirty and he needs a shave. He looks as tired as I feel. Tommy is curled up on the cushion next to him, asleep, sucking his thumb. Lindy is already in bed. The nine o'clock news is playing itself out silently on the wide-screen TV in the corner.

I take a bourbon even though I don't like them. Sandra sets the tray down on the coffee table, sits down on a dining chair and lifts the edge of the nets so she can gaze out of the window. What she finds so interesting about the council estate outside I have no idea. Maybe she fancies some kid in the house over the road.

I force myself to look at Paul. "Pleurisy?"

"That's right. They're draining her lung. She's got this tube stuck in her and there's this big glass bottle on the floor." He looks as though he might cry. I don't think I could handle it if he cried.

"But she *is* going to be all right, isn't she?"

He nods. "So they say. It's hard, though, Kathryn, seeing her all helpless, stuck in that ward full of half-dead old biddies . . ."

"I'll go in and see her tomorrow." Guilt is needling me. I've barely given a moment's thought to Winnie in ages—or rather, I've only thought about her in relation to me and my problems: whether she's being a good friend or not, whether she's pissing me off. Jesus, it's only a few nights ago that she was helping me drag an unconscious Jonny out of my cab and up to the seventh floor. She was coughing and wheezing for all she was worth and I barely registered it. Maybe it's my fault that she's in the hospital now. Hospitals . . . mazophobia . . .

"I'm surprised you haven't been in to see her already." His eyes narrow ever so slightly as he says this.

"How was I supposed to know she was in there, Paul? Telepathy?"

"Yeah, well." He sniffs and reaches down for his mug of tea. "I've got three kids here and they're all missing their mother. Hasn't given me much time for phoning all and sundry."

"Sorry, Paul—of course you've had more important things to think about. It must be very hard for you all." I hate him—his limpness, his reluctance to communicate with me. I hate his moral high ground and his dirty white T-shirt. And he hates me too, I see that clearly now.

"Just don't you be going in there loading her down with your personal problems." His voice has become fierce. "She needs to concentrate all her energy on getting better."

He thinks he can see right through me, the shit, but he's wrong. I care about her. I *do*. I can't look at him anymore. I take a sip of my tea—it's sugared. I can't stand sweet tea. I try to make myself look warm and smiley as I turn to Sandra.

"Lovely cup of tea, Sandra."

She is leaning on the window sill, playing absently with her plaits.

Back on the road my mind is turning every which way and I don't know where to put myself. If it wasn't so bloody late I'd go and see Winnie. Gives me the shivers to think of her all alone and frightened in the hospital. And poor little lost Sandra looking after her brother and sister while her father sits around feeling sorry for himself. I can still see her staring out through those nets as though she's hoping to see her mother's big shiny cab coming round that corner at any minute. And then I'm thinking about Amy's streaky face in the light of the bonfire and Jonny with his fresh bruises and old scars and red-eyed Stef gnawing at his knuckles and Joel in the back of the Mercedes.

Shit—my cab bumps through a pothole and I jolt back to the

here and now, realizing I have no idea where I am or where I'm going. I've been driving on automatic pilot with no consciousness of the outside world. I have the strangest sense that I'm not in London at all but somewhere else—somewhere utterly alien . . .

And then I spot Plumstead bus depot and I'm back on the map.

Heading down the South Circular, my head is still throbbing and my stomach is churning. I'm switching on the radio, not much caring which station it's tuned into, and I'm singing "Say a Little Prayer" with Aretha.

And there's a trilling which I initially think is only inside my head, or else it's coming from the radio.

But it's my red phone. "Katerina?"

"What."

"It's about Joel."

24

PECKHAM Rye in the dark. The grass purple, the trees whispering in the sharp wind like nasty old women. The squelch of dead leaves and mud underfoot. This park is not fenced in and locked up as many would be after sunset. It's open and vulnerable, the domain of late-night dog walkers, joggers and pissed people staggering home to Peckham and Nunhead from the pubs and restaurants of East Dulwich. Cars are flashing by ridiculously fast on all sides of the park. Hope the speed cameras get them. There was a circus here last week and the Rye was full of music and kids. I saw it when I drove past with a fare in the back and it made me think of my trip to the circus with Richard and Dotty, though this wasn't the same one. Now all that's left of it are several freaky yellow circles on the grass near the car park, and a couple of balloons stuck in a tree.

I know this park well. The flat where I used to live before I moved to Balham is just off the main road on the east side, two minutes' walk from where I'm standing now. The openness of the Rye has always been a problem. Every now and then you'd go out to get your paper in the morning and see tape strung between the trees, notice the police cars and vans in the car park. It's not that the Rye is especially rough. It's just that it's an easy place to drive into at night when you need to dump something.

As I make my way slowly down the path, following the line of orange streetlamps, I see torchlights dancing across the grass, highlighting the white tape snaking between the trees. People are moving around in the darkness within. I hear the clicking and fuzzing of police radios, the murmur of deep, officious voices. The flash and whirr of cameras. I count eight police cars, three vans and an ambulance in the car park. A group of uniforms are talking near a van with its rear doors open.

There are spectators lingering on the fringes of the park. A young couple, an old woman, several dog walkers. They're hanging about to get a glimpse of something lurid but keeping a respectable distance so nobody could accuse them of voyeurism. A few yards away from me, under the spreading limbs of an oak, a black guy with an Alsatian is talking to a copper. The copper is taking notes. The guy's voice is loud, shrill. He sounds as though he is excited about his role in this—relishing the attention he's getting. Without even trying to listen, I catch some of what he's saying:

"I knew something was wrong when I heard the tires squeal and I saw the speed it drove off . . . You just don't drive at a speed like that in a park, do you? I mean there could be kids around . . . And it was funny how he didn't have his lights on, not till he hit the road . . . All too fast. Couldn't even be sure what sort of car it was, let alone the registration number . . . No, I couldn't see who was in the car. I mean it was dark, wasn't it . . ."

I'm cold. Cold in my stomach. Cold in my legs. Nothing else. I'm listening to the booming bass from a car that's cruising slowly down Nunhead Lane. I'm noticing the friendly lights from the Clockhouse pub over on the west side of the park, the Dulwich side. I'm wishing I was in there now, drinking a pint, eating crisps, being among people, instead of standing here in the park on my own. My head is hurting. This has nothing to do with me. None of this has anything to do with me.

I must have lifted the white tape and stepped under it—I'm dimly aware of having done so—because now the copper talking to the man with the Alsatian is calling, "Hey, you!"—and two guys in waterproofs are moving briskly toward me, their plastic trouser legs brushing against each other, scraping and squeaking like windscreen wipers as they walk. One of them takes my right arm, and they're starting to tell me that I have to get on the other side of the tape but then I hear a familiar voice:

"Kathryn! Hey, it's OK, she's with me. Kathryn." Twinkle, running out of the purple darkness toward me and the plastic men. His face milky white through the gloom. He looks thinner somehow. The plastic man lets go my arm and Twinkle takes it, gently. He steers me back toward the tape, away from the two men.

"Are you all right?" His eyes are scanning my face, looking for—what?

"Where is he, Craig?"

"Look . . ." He's flustered, nervous. He keeps glancing back at the cluster of people under the trees. "You're not supposed to be here. OK? Christ, *I'm* not supposed to be here, let alone you."

"What do you want from me—everlasting gratitude?"

He notices the aggression in my voice and lets go of my arm. "I'm not going to fight with you, Kathryn. Not here."

There's a sudden commotion from somewhere within the group of plastic people and uniforms. Two luminous yellow waistcoats are trudging this way, down toward the car park. They're carrying a stretcher.

"Wait here. Don't move," says Craig, and he sprints off over the grass. I watch him speak to one of the ambulance men. They set the stretcher down, stand talking to him. There is a bag on the stretcher. A black body bag like you see in films. After a moment one of the yellow waistcoats bends down and I hear the groan of the zip being opened a little way. Craig is turning. I can't make out the expression on the white face. Then he beckons me over.

Joel in a body bag. My lovely Joel who wanted to dance and wasn't good enough. My Joel who couldn't fuck for toffee—but who gave the best cuddle in the world. Joel who used to hold me close and sleep with his head against my shoulder. His gorgeous little boy's head. Joel who made the worst tea ever and who served up minikievs and oven chips day after day. Always the same thing. I used to call him Shelley, back in those early days in the gym when he glared at me like a panther and I couldn't work out whether he was a girl or a boy. He called me Kat. Joel's face when he was sleeping—the peace of it—he was at his most beautiful when asleep.

He's not sleeping now.

His eyes are shut, thank God. His skin looks green. His mouth is slightly open, the tongue lolling in front of the bottom set of teeth. There's a lot of gunk on his face—dried gunk—puke, saliva, whatever it is. Traces of what looks like blood. It's been running down his neck, too, staining the collar of his new white shirt. There's nasty gray snot all over his nose and upper lip. But the worst thing is the stillness. That, and the stench.

Twinkle is by my side, steadying me as my legs buckle. For a couple of seconds I loll against his chest and I smell cheap men's deodorant, pungent like fly spray, and the faint whiff of sweat. Then I'm back on my feet, pulling away from him. I hear the zip being closed with a backward groan, and when I turn around the yellow waistcoats are picking up the stretcher again, moving off toward the ambulance in the car park.

"It's him, then?" Twinkle's voice.

"Yes."

"Are you all right?"

"No."

He looks fidgety, as though torn between standing with me and running off. Eventually he says, "Wait here," and goes striding back to the uniforms.

This is only the second time I've seen a dead body. My dad wouldn't let me see Mum. He thought it would upset me too much. What really did upset me was being denied the chance to sit beside her and look at her face one last time. Though in retrospect I'm sure she wouldn't have looked the way I remembered her. I did see Maeve after they'd disentangled her from the pink shower curtain in which she was found and "made her look nice." She was all done up in her best blouse with that weird fake smile and the shiny shrink-wrapped look. I stormed out of the funeral home in disgust. Well, nobody can say Joel has been tarted up to look like someone else. Nobody has "made him look nice." I stand shivering as I watch the yellow waistcoats load him into the ambu-lance—casually, like you'd load your shopping into the car at Sainsbury's. I watch them slam the doors on him.

"Come on." Twinkle is back at my side, putting an arm around my shoulders. "You need a drink."

Green faces, dribbling blood, torn white sheets . . . Fuck, I'd for-gotten that it's Halloween. I so wanted to be in here, among nor-mal people, having a normal night. But now I wish I'd gotten straight back into my cab. Got on the road where I can breathe. All these people with their bad makeup playing at ghouls and ghosties and corpses. And I've just come straight from the real thing.

We've got a corner table. I've left Twinkle the seat that faces out into the room and have chosen instead to face the wall. I don't want to have to look at the costumes.

The geezer on the next table is mouthing off while his sidekick nods and laughs.

". . . He took her for dinner at Bel Air House the other day, and you know what happened? His credit card got refused. The waiter was being OK about it, and Jim was giving him another card, but she stood up, bold *as*, and shouted 'Well, I guess I'll have to sleep with the waiter, won't I!' . . . Can you *imagine*?"

Twinkle is bobbing around at the bar trying to get served, but the place is heaving. And in the meantime all I can hear is this twat's opinions on the various women in his life. He's a smarmy git in chinos and a leather jacket, and he thinks he's so smart. I can feel my hands contracting into fists under the table.

". . . I mean, you *know* me, Giles. I've always liked her. She's got that black humor, you know what I mean? That dark side . . ."

A grandfather clock stands next to our table and two more clocks are hanging above me. Each of them has a pendulum, and they're all swinging out of sync with each other. One shows 10:52, one 10:49 and one 10:47. There's something about this inexacti-tude that infuriates me—makes me want to pull them down and smash them up. Inside of me, bits are moving slightly out of kilter with other bits.

Tick. Tick. Tick.

"There you go." Craig's voice cuts through my stupor. He sets down a pint of lager and a Scotch. I'm about to ask which is mine when he returns to the bar and collects a pint of Guinness for himself.

"Trying to get me pissed, are you?"

"Leave it out, Kathryn. How are you feeling?"

"How d'you *think*?"

He accidentally jogs the little round table as he pulls up his chair, and spills some of our beer. I watch him pull out a white cotton handkerchief and mop up the mess.

"Bet Marianne washes your hankies. Bet she irons them too."

He gives me a filthy look and thrusts the handkerchief back in his trouser pocket. I take a gulp of lager. It's Stella. My favorite.

Turning my head to look out at the street, I catch sight of a couple of police cars, driving past. "I suppose those guys are on their way home to their wives and kids . . ." Then realization hits. "Oh, shit! Joel's parents. They don't know yet."

"We've got it covered."

I feel his hand—his fingers touching my hand, reaching out to me, and I flinch away as though burnt. When I look up, I notice a slight bruising on his cheek and realize it's where I slapped him.

"You mean someone's gone to tell them?"

"Yes."

"Will they . . . Will they clean him up before they let his parents . . ."

"Don't worry about that." He looks away and I realize he really has bent the rules by calling me tonight. I suppose I should thank him but the words stick in my throat. I reach for the whiskey and swallow it down in one gulp. Feel it zinging its way down my gullet. "What do you think happened to him? Was he . . ." But I don't have the heart to continue.

"We don't know for certain yet."

"Don't fob me off. You must have some idea."

"Well . . . I did talk to the guys back in the park." He hesitates. "This is only a theory, Kathryn."

I nod, urge him on.

He sips his Guinness and it leaves a mustache of white foam on his upper lip. "I would say Joel overdosed while he was with a punter. The punter panicked and drove here to dump the body."

"But Joel doesn't do drugs!"

"Are you sure about that?" He looks irritatingly knowing. On the next table the smarmy git's voice rises still louder:

"Well, I've had it with her, Giles. When you get down to it she's just another clingy woman . . ."

I try to ignore the geezer. "What if he was murdered? Is that possible? Could Henry have killed him?"

Craig shakes his head. "Think about it, Kathryn. Joel's body is dumped in a city park at eight in the evening, in full view of a bunch of dog walkers and anyone who happens to be driving past. Does that sound to you like something a real pro would do?"

I shrug.

"Of course it's not. They'd wait till the dead hours—four or five in the morning. They'd drive him a long way from here. Well out of London, I'd say. And they'd make him . . . unidentifiable."

The guys on the next table burst into raucous laughter and somewhere in my head I see blood. I gag, swallow heavily and reach for my lager.

Twinkle's looking sweaty and embarrassed. "Sorry, Kathryn, I didn't mean to—Look, the point is that's *not* what happened to Joel. OK?"

I nod, blinded by tears.

"My guess is he's with some guy in a car and he takes something to make the job easier . . . But it goes wrong. Very wrong. Joel ODs and the guy freaks out, doesn't know what to do. Maybe the guy drives around for a while with Joel ill in the back. Perhaps he doesn't want to be the one to bring Joel into a hospital—married man or whatever, I don't know. But while he's driving and panicking, Joel is dying."

A gag turns into a huge sob and I'm crying noisily into my lager. The smarmy git with the loud voice turns in alarm and sees me. Gives his friend a look that says: *Another bloody clingy woman.*

Twinkle is still speaking intently. "And when our man realizes he has a corpse in the back, he drives to Peckham Rye and dumps it."

I hear the thud of something heavy and lifeless hitting grassy ground. The slam of the car door and the screech of tires. I close my eyes for a moment to blot Craig out. And I see Joel in his Armani suit, all sassy and hopeful, giving me a twirl.

"Do you really think that's what happened?" I ask, blinking my tears away.

He pulls out the handkerchief again. Offers it to me. "Well, we'll have to wait to see what the postmortem shows, but . . . yeah, I think that's what happened." He takes his cigarettes out of his jacket pocket, lights one up, watching me carefully. "Boys like Joel—they don't live long."

"Like butterflies." I'm talking into my lager. I take the handkerchief and blow my nose loudly.

"Look, I know this is bad timing, but . . ."

Oh Christ, what now?

He's picked up a crisp packet from the ashtray between us and is folding it up into smaller and smaller squares, then into a triangle—tucking it tightly into itself. "I have to talk to you."

"I don't want to hear this." I move to stand up but he grabs my wrist tightly and I sink back down on my chair.

"I love you, Kathryn."

"You're full of shit, Craig." I'm thinking about what Amy said to me, about how there was no way forward for us after all the lies, no matter what either of us wanted. "And you're still married, aren't you?"

"Not for much longer." He finally lets go of my wrist.

"Oh, for Christ's sake . . ." I pick up my pint glass and gulp down as much as I can in one go. There's not much left when I set it down on the table again.

"My marriage is over. It was dead long before I met you and it's even deader now. Marianne and I are separated."

"Yeah, *sure*."

I must be looking at him as though I want to slap him again.

He's edgy and nervous, reaching up to touch his bruised cheek. But then he seems to pull himself together. "Why don't you stop playing the victim, Kathryn. You haven't been straight with me either. How many lovers were you stringing along while we were seeing each other, eh? You fuck Stefan Muchowski? You fuck that kid on the common?"

"You're a cunt, Craig."

"And you're the same kind of cunt."

"I've had enough of this." I'm on my feet now, reaching for my jacket from the back of my chair but he's still ranting at me.

"That first day in Saffron Walden we were *real* with each other, Kathryn. I've never been so real."

"Oh yeah? Well here's a little reality check for you, Craig—I faked it every time we did it."

The smarmy git and his sidekick are staring, open-gobbed. Twinkle's mouth hangs open too. I've caught him out just as he was about to say something clever.

"Bye, Twinkle." I wish I could feel pleasure in this moment. I'd like to stand and gloat—maybe say something that would stab him harder. Have a crack at the guys on the next table too. But my tears are coming back and so I run for the door.

I'm driving and crying and driving and crying. Crawling through Camberwell, buzzing around the Elephant, sliding through Southwark, crossing Blackfriars Bridge where the river runs smooth and dark, and dodging into the City. Crying all the way. I should have gone to see Joel's parents, to try to give them some comfort—to get some comfort for myself. But I feel too much of a fraud for that.

I reach for the Glenfiddich and take a couple of mouthfuls. Only the booze seems to help still the thing that's fluttering and bashing around in my head . . .

Dropping the bottle I catch sight of something in the rearview mirror. My insides leap and I almost scream—Joel is sitting in the backseat, his head rolling and jolting as the cab hits a speed bump, his nostrils streaming blood and snot. As I slam on the brakes his head lolls forward and I glimpse the eyes that were closed back there in the park. The eyes, once so beautiful, are still and empty and dead. I twist the wheel and pull into the mouth of an alleyway to recover myself. It was nothing, of course—just a crack in the slippery surface of reality, a delusion built from shadows and fears and waking dreams. Jesus, I'm losing it.

When my heart has stopped racing and my breathing is under control, I start up the engine again and head for the place I want to be more than anywhere else in the world right now—the only place that's real for me. Richard's house in Crouch End.

All the lights are out. I push the button on the doorbell once only, and very briefly—not wanting to wake Dotty, who sleeps in the bedroom immediately above the front door. I wait impatiently for thirty seconds or so, then ring once more. When Richard doesn't come to the door after a full minute I get desperate and ring the bell over and over again. Still nothing. Where the fuck *is* he? He must surely have woken up by now.

I'm panicking—bashing on the door with my fists and bending down to scream through the letter box, "Richard, it's *me*. Open the door . . . Open the *fucking door. Lemme in!*"

The lights are going on upstairs. There's a wail and the sounds of sobbing from Dotty's room. Feet on the stairs, running down. I hear a bolt being drawn back. The chain is let off. As the door opens I'm bathed in light.

"Kitty . . ." He's wearing his dressing gown and rubbing at his head. His hair is sticking up in tufts. His face is angry, but in a split second the anger is replaced by concern. "Jesus, Kitty, you look terrible. What's happened?"

"Cup of tea. I want a cup of tea."

I have to push past him to get into the house. Dotty is crying loudly upstairs as I head for the kitchen.

"Hadn't you better go to her?" I'm blundering over to the kettle, pouring in water from one of the filter jugs and flicking the switch on.

"No, it's OK." And as he says it, Dotty falls silent.

"Wow. Neat trick." I'm taking a mug off the mug tree. "Do you want a cup too?"

"Kitty, what's going on?"

"I can make you a hot chocolate if you'd rather. I know caffeine keeps you awake." I'm taking down a second mug.

"Kitty, stop it!"

Stung, I wheel around, and find myself staring at a hollowed-out pumpkin with a crooked smile sitting on the kitchen table.

He wanders over to the table, all slouchy and tired—sits down on a chair and pulls one out for me. "Come and sit next to me for a minute."

"All right." Slightly hesitant, I cross the room; bend to kiss the top of his head before sitting down. "Your head . . . smells of bed." It's something I often say to him. One of our cute couply lines. I feel better for saying it.

He smiles but the smile is as crooked as the grin on the pumpkin head and it slips quickly away into tiredness. "Do you know what time it is, Kitty?"

"Nope. No idea."

"It's nearly half past twelve."

"Oh."

"Yes, that's right—'oh.' What do you think you're doing, coming here so late? . . . Have you been drinking?"

A hollow laugh escapes me. "No. Course I haven't." Richard's gaze moves down over my body, taking in my new flabbiness, my scruffy unwashed appearance—and back up to my face. I'm wobbling on the edge of hysteria. "Well, maybe I've had one or two. Richard—"

"What?"

I try to muster my energy. "Look, I'm sorry I've come here so late. And I'm sorry I woke Dotty up. It's just—"

"Just *what*? Kitty, if you could see yourself . . ."

"I know. I know I look a mess." I reach out to take his hand but it isn't there. Both his hands are shoved deep into the pockets of his dressing gown. I clear my throat, try to assemble my thoughts into some sort of workable order. "Richard, I've seen things today—things that . . ." Joel's dead face looms in my mind with its trails of blood and snot. I can still smell the rich mud and dead leaves in the park; the hot, sweet smell of something rotting.

"Kitty, what are you talking about? What *things*?"

I shake my head, trying to dispel the images, to keep my focus on Richard's face—his worried brow, his kind mouth. "It doesn't matter. The point is that I've understood something—I know what I *want* now . . ."

He's rubbing his eyes and blinking, saying nothing.

"I want to settle down and have a husband and a family. I want to marry you, Richard—to share everything with you. I want to be a mother to Dotty."

"Oh, Kitty . . ." There's something weird going on with him. He seems unable to continue.

Another voice. A voice I haven't heard before:

"Dotty already *has* a mother."

Jemima has big lips. Her eyes, nose and bones are so soft that I feel I could grab her face and mold it like Play-Doh. She has long, thick auburn hair and pale skin. Very feminine. Very fucking Pre-Raphaelite. She's wearing a sky blue cotton robe that comes almost down to her smooth white knees. Her arms are folded tightly across her chest and she's looking at me with contempt, like I'm some sort of baby snatcher.

"What's she doing here?" My voice is small.

Richard is looking at the floor.

"Tell her, Richard," says Jemima, haughty and smug.

"Tell me what?" But I already know what . . .

"Kitty, it hasn't been easy." Richard is all limp.

"You told me you weren't going to take her back. You told me it was *me* you wanted." I lean forward and grab him by the shoulders. "Make her go away, Richard. *Please* make her go away."

"I'm not going anywhere," says Jemima. I ignore her—keep my focus on Richard, my hands gripping his shoulders. There is something dead in his eyes.

"You can't trust her," I say. "She left you. She abandoned Dotty.

How can you let her worm her way back into your lives after what she's done to you! She'll fuck you over. She'll do it again!"

"Get out of here." Jemima stomps across the room, her feet slapping on the quarry tiles. I clock the beautifully varnished toenails, pretty pink, as she grabs my arm, tries to yank me to my feet.

"Take your hands off me." I growl out the words. She's tugging at me, putting everything she has into trying to drag me off my chair. I can feel her throw her whole weight into it. I'm staying put, grabbing the edge of the table with one hand. Richard won't look at me.

"Richard." My voice is shaking. I'm not sure if it's anger or sadness that's making it shake. "I can only see one way forward, and it's you . . ."

Jemima yanks hard, almost pulling my arm out of its socket, and I yelp in pain. There is a strong whiff of sex from her neck. *Your head . . . Smells of bed . . .*

And now it's like a crack has opened up and split my reality. One second I'm anchored to my chair—the next I'm standing in the middle of the room and Jemima is slumped on the floor by the cooker. Frightened eyes looking up at me through a mess of auburn hair and pink nails. Her robe has fallen open, revealing a smear of white flesh and a snatch covered in red fur. She's touching at blood on her forehead.

Richard has covered his face with his hands.

I can hear my voice in the distance, like it's someone else's. "*You fuck with me and I'll kill you . . .*" I'm holding my hand out in front of me, palm up, spreading my fingers wide. My knuckles throb.

"Mummy!"

She's running into the room in her nightdress. The one with the strawberry pattern; the one I bought her from Marks & Spencer—her feet patter-pattering on the tiled floor. She's running straight past her father, past me, not noticing either of us.

"Baby, it's all right. Mummy's OK." Jemima enfolds her daughter in her arms, pulls her close, whispers into her ear, "Hush now, Dotty. It's OK." She's smiling over Dotty's shoulder. Smiling at me. There is blood on the strawberry nightdress.

25

BREATHING is difficult but the whiskey makes it easier. I have one hand on the steering wheel, one hand wrapped around the Glenfiddich bottle. The stars are bright and sparkling above me and the roads are clear. Don't know where the fuck I'm going. Narrow lanes. Big posh houses. Traffic lights—who fucking needs them . . . the traffic on this road melts away before me in any case. What's that huge expanse of deep green darkness over there? Hampstead. It's Hampstead fucking Heath.

Got to decide where I'm going. Got to head for somewhere. Can't just drive aimlessly or I'll end up going round in circles. Spinning.

Horrible old Camden. Stench of hot dogs that won't go away. Wankers wanting a cab, crowding the filthy pavements clutching their kabobs. Light's not on, you bunch of cunts. I'm not your fucking slave. Saw Jonny for the first time down here, didn't I? Blown along by the wind like one of those stick figures you draw, only with a big flapping coat. Asked me to drive him to the Elephant . . . No idea who I was. Never told him I knew him from before.

King's Cross . . . St. Pancras—fucking red wedding cake. Euston Road—you see, I *do* know where I am. I *do* . . . Empty office blocks. No one around down here. Only the night people like me, and we don't count . . . Gower Street . . .

Jesus, where's this, then? I'm going round and fucking round.

Russell Square, innit. British Museum. Bunch of fucking sar-cophagi. Can't be doing with all that. Where the hell am I going? Not home, that's for sure. Home—what a joke! Got to find a place where I can breathe. Fresh air. *Proper* fresh.

Centre Point. Surely they weren't *serious* when they built this penis-palace . . . and into Soho. Nightmare—people spilling out of bars onto the roads. Walking right in front of you like they don't give a shit. Lines of dodgy mini-cabs, white stretch limos and those gimmicky Chinese cyclos . . . Air so thick and stinking you could take a razor to it . . . Soho—hairy armpit of London.

I seem to be going west. Hyde Park, Bayswater Road. What is there that's west? Where can I head to? Out and out and out. Devon . . . Cornwall . . . Wales . . .

Wales.

North Wales—the mountains, the fresh clean air. Get myself a cottage, maybe a few sheep. Winnie could come visit. Breathe some quality pollution-free oxygen into her lungs. We could hang out, the two of us. Bake Welsh cakes. Why not, eh? Wales—why the hell not? Go the A40—M40—M6—up and up and up.

Shit. Where am I? I'm supposed to be on the Westway now. I've taken a wrong turning . . . But I don't *take* wrong turnings. It's not what I do . . . Wide open roads, white Georgian houses and trees. Bloody west London, it's all the fucking same. Turn left. Got to keep left. Yes, that's . . . no, it's not. It's bloody *not*. More of the white houses, more of the trees. Another left should sort me out. Don't you fucking toot your horn at me, you BMW cunt! Maybe a right . . . Oh, Christ. More white houses, more trees. Goes on for-ever. It's all fuzzy. All radio interference. Trying to see a road sign . . . can't make one out. Reaching for my A-Z somewhere down in the . . . hand closing on a loose piece of paper. What . . .

Dear Kathryn,

Forgive my intrusion but I thought you should know that I'm holding a memorial service for your mother . . .

Crumple the letter. Throw it on the floor. Can't bear to have that man's voice in my head . . . A trilling . . . Loud trilling . . . the red phone! What the . . . Jonny? Grope about for it. Press OK to take the call . . .

"Kathryn, where are you?"

"Craig?"

"I'm worried about you, Kathryn. Where are you?"

"How the fuck should I know!"

"Are you in the cab? Are you *driving*, Kathryn?"

"Butt out, Twinkle."

"Look, why don't you just pull up somewhere and park for a bit . . . I can come and get you."

"I don't *want* you to come and get me. I don't *want* you in my life!"

"All right, all right. Just take it easy, OK? Take it nice and easy . . ."

"Stop talking to me like I'm some moron."

"Sorry, Kathryn. I'm sorry. Now, are you on a road where you can stop? Would you do me a favor and just *pull over* . . ."

"I don't owe you any favors, Craig."

"Yes, I know, I—Look . . . You sound like you've had a lot to drink. You could hurt someone . . ."

"I don't care."

"Kathryn, you've had a nasty shock and you're not yourself."

I have to swallow hard. Something's rising inside me. Something that's been hiding inside me for a long time.

"What part of London are you in? You can tell me *that*, at least."

"West. White houses. Trees. White houses . . ." This is getting crazy. Straight lines, corners, more straight lines, and none of it connecting up to anything. I'm sure I've been down this road before. I *know* I saw that car a few minutes ago . . . I'm starting to feel like a rat in a maze. A *maze* . . . Jesus, the steering wheel is slippery with my sweat.

"I can't breathe, Craig. I can't . . . breathe!"

"Can you see a road sign, Kathryn? A pub, a restaurant, *any-thing* . . ."

"Dun . . . Dunsany . . . something."

"That's good. You can park now. It's OK."

It's not OK. It's rising and rising. Fogging around me like it fogged around my mother.

"Katerina? Say something to me."

A cab—a big black one—coming right at me . . . Horn blaring in my head. Wrenching the wheel and I'm missing the cab but there's something else . . . the color. The fucking color with no name.

It's everywhere.

PART V

~

STARFISH

26

I don't feel like me anymore.

"What are you on about?" Winnie sounds worried. There's no need for her to be worried.

"I mean that I'm different from how I was before—" The pay phone boop-boops at me and I scrabble around in my dressing-gown pocket for another twenty-pence piece with my right hand, shoulder gripping the receiver to my chin. The maneuver is a bad one. Something seems to catch under my broken ribs and there's a searing jab from the place where the chest drain tube is sewn into my skin. I wobble and cling to the crutch that's propped under my left armpit. It's all I can do to keep hold of the glass bottle I'm clutching in my left hand—the bottle that is attached to the chest drain tube. Finally, struggling to stay upright, I shove the coin into the slot.

"What sort of different—good different or bad different? Kathryn, you still there?"

"Ah, *shit* . . . Yeah, sorry, Win, I'm here."

"You all right?"

"Sure." I wipe the sweat from my forehead.

Doctor Jennings is walking down the dank gray corridor with a young black male nurse, their shoes squeaking on the resin floor tiles. She sees me at the pay phone and frowns, gives me that, "what are you doing out of bed" look. But then, unexpectedly, she smiles and walks on. Horrific Julie, the square-faced middle-aged woman from the bed next to mine, is wandering to the toilet in her drab purple robe, and I turn my back to her, face the wall, half read the poster about breast-checking. "Sorry, Win—what did you say?"

"I was asking you what sort of different—good or bad?"

"I don't know. I don't feel frightened anymore. I didn't know that I felt frightened before . . . but I did. Does that make sense?"

"Mm." She seems to be chewing this over.

It doesn't make sense—not even to me.

"Thing is, Kath, you've looked Death in the eye, haven't you. You've stared him out and you're still here. That's why you feel different. 'S logic, innit. There's this book I've read—now, who was it by . . ."

"Anyway, Win, how are *you*?"

"Me? Oh, I'm much better, thanks, now that they've got the tube out. Hey, Kath, you've got to see the funny side, eh?—Both of us in hospital having our chests drained at the same time!"

"Hilarious." I've been lucky: Pneumothorax—that's punctured lung to you and me, mild concussion from a lump on my head the size of a golfball, couple of broken ribs, spot of whiplash, badly bruised left knee, face that looks like an aubergine . . . It's a painful fucking cocktail and yet I know I've been lucky.

"I've *had* it with smoking," she's saying.

"Yeah, right." What a picture we must be. Me struggling about in my nightwear; hanging on to the pay phone and cramming more and more coins in the slot while a nurse at her end wheels a courtesy phone to her bedside. The two of us exchanging awkward but affectionate greetings; enfeebled like a couple of old biddies with our shuffling slippered feet, our thin crackling voices.

"No, I have. *Really* . . . Paul said you came round," she continues. "Thanks for that, Kathryn."

"Shut up. Least I could do. I'd have been in to see you if I wasn't unavoidably detained . . . But, Win, there's a chance I'll be getting out in a few days. I'll come over and see you. Bring you some grapes."

"Actually, Kath, I'm coming out tomorrow, so *I'll* be over to see *you*."

I only give a little chuckle but it damn near kills me. "Looking after me, as always. Well, get one of your wisdoms ready, girl. I bloody well need a bit of wisdom, I can tell you."

There's a pause. I hear Winnie sigh. This phone receiver smells putrid. The smell of sick people's breath. My money is ticking down and down . . .

"What're you going to do?" she says, finally.

Boop-boop-boop—I'm struggling to shove my final twenty pee in. The phone spits it out the bottom. As I bend down to pick it up, dab a bit of saliva on it, and slot it back in again, the shifting of the tube and the stabbing of my ribs is excruciating, and I yelp aloud. The saliva trick works, though, and the phone accepts the coin. It's a trick my mother taught me.

"What're you going to do?" Winnie persists.

"How should I know? I can't think beyond the next few days. I'm just living for the moment when this fucking chest drain comes out!"

An old lady staggering by with a walking frame turns to shoot me an evil look. I'd give her the finger if I had one free.

"Have any of *them* been in?" she asks.

"Them? What, you mean . . . Nah, course not. They've all gone. All bloody six of them. Except Jonny, maybe . . . No, the only person I've seen is Kev."

"What, you mean *Big* Kev? From the Crocodile?" She can't hide her amazement.

"Yep. The very same. I called him up and he went round my flat for me. Brought me some of my things. You know, Win, I've realized something very important about my life over the last couple of days."

"What's that?"

"I don't have one."

I'm tottering very slowly back down the corridor to the ward. I'm carrying the bottle with my right hand. My left side—the side with the bad knee—is propped up by the crutch. Having to lean so heavily to the left is not good for my chest—the broken ribs are digging and stabbing, making me catch my breath; the area around the tube is raw and painful. But I'm determined to keep moving about. Can't stand being stuck in that bed all the time. The pain in my head is not so bad as yesterday—just a dull ache and the occasional odd fluttering sensation, as though something is taking off and landing again inside my skull.

It's all I can do to just get back to my bed, and on the way I have to pause for a break and loll back against the wall to get my breath under control. To think of myself on the treadmill or the stepper machine . . . I catch sight of my shadow looming up on the opposite wall and it fills me with horror, the way it hunches and stoops. I look like I'm in Halloween costume.

Today I'm getting to know this corridor very well. The crack in the floor tile just next to the fire extinguisher, the damp patch on the ceiling near that striplight, the opening that leads to the lifts . . . I must have walked up and down here eight or nine times now. Sometimes with a purpose—phoning Winnie, going to the loo—sometimes just to practice getting on my feet again. It's funny how differently you see things when you're moving slowly and concentrating on every step, every detail, one by one. The world changes . . . details come forward out of the background. Everything becomes more intricate, more real . . . less like a maze.

I'm nearing the nurses' station. People in uniforms are buzzing back and forth. Even the little rushes of air they leave in their wake would be strong enough to blow me right over. The two phones on the desk are taking turns ringing and the tall nurse called Frances with the short hair is answering them alternately. I hear her bland voice, saying over and over: "Duke of Edinburgh Ward. Can you hold the line, please?"

I'm turning to the left now, limping back into the long rectangular room that's lined on both sides with beds, including mine. Third on the right, that's me. Horrific Julie in the neighboring bed is sitting up, all perky, chatting with a visitor—a thin man with white hair who looks like my father from the back. It's the first time I've seen Julie look human: her heavy, square face is losing its corners, rounding up. She runs a hand through the lank hair, pushes it behind her ear and grins. Then she glances up and notices me, raises her other hand to point. Her mouth forms the words, "There she is."

When the white-haired visitor turns his head to look, the fluttering in my head becomes a frenzied flapping.

"Whoops—she's going . . ." Nurse Yvonne's voice.

Thousands of colored dots dance before my eyes. The blood is rushing into my head like a river bursting its dam.

"Let's get you into bed, shall we?" Nurse Frances is propping me up, removing the crutch and laying it down next to the bed. Nurse Yvonne is taking the bottle from my sweaty hand and pulling back the covers.

"You're lucky we were here," Nurse Yvonne is saying. "That was a well-timed bit of fainting there, Ms. Cheet."

Yet more good luck . . .

"Now, you're to stay in bed for a while and get some rest, Kathryn," says Nurse Frances. "You've been overdoing it, haven't you?"

My head is still woozy. Between the two of them they've somehow eased me down onto the bed and lifted my legs under the covers, making me lean forward to put pillows behind me. I'm all floppy and useless like a rag doll. My bottle is down on the floor.

"Is she all right?" comes my father's voice—the first words I've heard him speak in fifteen years.

Somewhere in the background, Julie is saying, "I'm in for my thyroid. Took them three years to diagnose me properly. *Three years* of relentless suffering."

I'm too breathless and exhausted to speak. When the nurses turn to walk away I want to shout out, to plead with them not to leave me alone with my father. He's just standing there, staring at me with his usual dispassionate headmasterly expression.

"How did you know I was here?" I force out the words between shallow, jagged breaths, and reach for the glass of water on my locker.

He moves quickly, far faster than I'm able to, grabs the water glass and hands it to me. Our fingers brush together as he does so and I recoil from his cold skin.

He stands awkwardly about as I sip my water, eventually saying, "Shall I draw the curtain around?" His voice is gentler than I remember.

I'm about to tell him no, hating the idea of being enclosed in a small space with him—but then Horrific Julie pipes up again with more scintillating information about her thyroid operation, and so I give him a half nod.

The green curtain shushes closed around us, and I panic at the thought of being cocooned with him. But as he turns back to me, gestures at the orange plastic chair by the bed to check it's OK for him to sit there, I glimpse an equivalent panic in him—a slight twitch at one corner of his thin-lipped mouth, a tremor in his hands as he pulls up the chair and sits down.

He's staring nervously at the bottle, and at the tube leading into my pajama shirt. His timidity makes me bold. I'm beginning to recover from my dizzy spell. "You look old, father dear. Old and tired."

He looks down, plays with one of the buttons on his mac. "What happened, Kathryn? Tell me about it."

"I drove my cab into the back of a builder's lorry. Not one of my best ideas but at least it was stationary at the time." I notice how shiny his black leather shoes are. I guess he still gets out his polish and brush and cleans them every night. He used to do mine and Mum's while he was at it; leave them parked in a little row on a sheet of newspaper next to the boiler.

A flicker of impatience in those cold, dark eyes.

"But they've told you that, of course." I try a sarcastic smile.

"They said you'd been drinking."

"Oh, *fuck you*, Dad!"

He flinches, lifts a trembling hand and holds it over his eyes for a moment, rubs at his forehead. I can feel a smile building, warming my bruised face. The number of times I've imagined telling him to go fuck himself. I've never actually done it before.

Once he's regained his composure he tries again. "What were you doing, Kathryn? It's not like you to be drunk driving."

"How would you know what I'm like?" But I'm overcome with tiredness and I can't be bothered to keep fighting. I let my head loll heavily back against the pillow. "You're right, of course. It's *not* like me to be drunk driving. If you must know, Dad, I was kind of . . . out of control that night. If you must know, I think I wanted to die."

As I say the words, a shiver goes right through me and I close my eyes . . . They tell me I must have turned the wheel and swerved to avoid the scaffolding sticking off the back of the lorry. They tell me the left side of the cab took the worst of it—the door crumpled in on me as though it was made of tinfoil. They say I was lucky to go face down on the steering wheel—I would have gone straight through the windscreen and lacerated my face if I didn't have my seatbelt on. I could have come out of this looking like Jonny, or worse . . . But I can't actually remember any of this. All I can see in my head is a flash of orange light from the cab I narrowly missed, and then nothing. Only the nameless color, all around me. "You see, Dad, I'm the same as Mum. It's been hiding inside me for a long time like it hid in her—waiting to come out."

With an effort, I drag my eyes open again and shift my head so I can see him. His face is deathly pale. There are dark shadows in the hollows of his cheeks and under his eyes. I'm expecting him to say something, to attempt some kind of response, but then I realize he can't speak. He's struggling to keep from crying. I'm uncomfortable with the silence that's opened up between us and I try to lighten up.

"Did you know, Dad, when they get you out of a crash scene they strap you to a spinal board covered in *Velcro*. Great stuff, Velcro! And then they put this spongy head box around your head to protect your neck in case it's broken . . ." God, it's horrible being stuck inside that head box, unable to move, the world muffled around you, all claustrophobic. You're staring up at the ceiling and faces keep bobbing in and out of view, asking you your name over and over again, and smiling these bright fake smiles . . . "I'll lose my driving license of course. Three-year ban, I expect. And I've blown it with the Public Carriage Office—they'll never let me have my badge back. The cab was written off. They're pretty robust, Fairways, but they don't mate well with lorries. Poor old Maeve—she'll be somersaulting in her grave."

"What will you do?" His voice is small.

"I have no idea." So is mine. "Pour me some more water, will you?"

He refills the glass from the jug on top of the locker. I manage to avoid touching his fingers again when he hands it to me. I take a mouthful of water and he settles down on the chair. He puts his hands in his lap, knitting his fingers together.

"I saw you," he says, looking shyly at me. "At the memorial service. I saw you running away. I didn't spot you till you'd got right down to the bottom of the hill. My eyes aren't so good these days, but I knew it was you . . . There was a man in a sports car who went tearing off after you. I heard him call out your name . . . Why did you run away?"

"I didn't want to be there. The man you saw . . . He tricked me into it."

"Oh." He looks disappointed. "I thought perhaps—"

"No." I take another sip of water and set the glass down. I have a strong need to be alone. "Would you go, please? I need to rest."

He seems not to have heard me, ploughs on regardless. "Kathryn, I know I've made a mess of things with you. I just couldn't cope after . . . You reminded me so much of *her* . . ."

"I don't want to hear this, Dad."

"I was glad when you went off to live with Maeve. I couldn't cope with you. I couldn't cope with anything anymore. It was such a relief when they offered me early retirement . . ."

"Do me a favor, will you, Dad. I'm on a fucking chest drain . . ."

"Maeve was very good to me. I bet you didn't know she used to come round and help me clean the house, did you? She'd stop for a cup of tea and tell me all about how you were getting on—"

"*Dad.*" Everything jars and judders inside me and I'm wincing and gasping.

He looks so old. He's become one of those frail, shrunken men you see drifting to and from bus stops with their single Tesco's carrier bag full of meals for one, their thin sad faces and huge ears.

"I'm sorry," he says. "I didn't mean to upset you and tire you out. But when that man phoned me and told me you were here—"

"What man?"

"I was so worried about you, Kathryn. I know I can't ever make it up to you, but I was hoping—I *am* hoping—that we might find a way to be friends—that maybe you'd come and stay with me and Patricia for a while when you get out of hospital. Give you a chance to recover, to get back on your feet."

"Hey, whoa!" There's an avalanche going on in my head. Facts and memories are slipping and sliding and I'm not sure what to try to hold on to. I lunge randomly: "Who the hell is *Patricia*?"

He's blushing! My father is actually *blushing* like a *kid*.

"She's my . . . my lady friend."

"Your *what*?"

"We've been courting for just over a year. I met her at my bereavement counseling group."

Him—going to counseling . . .

He pulls himself more upright on his chair. He actually seems to grow about three inches in front of my eyes. I need more codeine and I need it now.

"I had to do *something* to help myself. I spent almost fourteen years hiding from the world. *Fourteen years.* Yes, I should have paid more attention to Marie. *Yes*, I should have been a better father to you. But you can't change the past, can you?"

It's so weird to hear him speak her name.

"I just can't imagine you sitting in the sodding library or church hall or wherever, pouring your heart out to a bunch of strangers."

"I know. Odd, isn't it." He gives a sort of nervous giggle but then his face becomes serious again. "Kathryn, I loved your mother more than I've ever . . . But now . . . now I've met Patricia. She's . . . nice."

"*Nice?*" A sharp twinge from my ribs.

He's blushing again. It's sickening. "Yes. Nice. She's a lovely woman. The memorial service was her idea."

Could it be possible that Dad has changed? I couldn't see it at first, but now that he's talking about Patricia—now I'm beginning to see it. The mac is the same, the shiny shoes, the cartridge pen in his shirt pocket and the way he knits his fingers together—but he seems to have acquired a life. He has a woman called Patricia—with *ideas*.

"And was it her idea for you to come visit me?"

"No. No, that was down to me. I'd have been here days ago, but we were away on holiday in Paris. We only got back this morning. That's when I got the message."

My father and some woman on top of the Eiffel Tower, wandering by the Seine, visiting the Louvre, eating escargots . . . coming home to—"What message? Who told you I was here?"

"It was on the answering machine. Someone called Jamie."

"Jamie? I don't know anyone called Jamie."

He looks baffled. "I assumed it was the man I saw chasing after you. The man in the sports car."

"Dad, are you sure he didn't say his name was Craig?"

"Yes, I'm positive. Jamie Lawrence. That was his name."

The last of my energy is ebbing away. Now I really must rest. My eyelids are heavy. "Dad, I have to sleep."

He gets slowly to his feet, starts buttoning his mac. But he's somehow distracted. "Will you think about what I said, Kathryn? About coming to stay with us?"

"Give me a break, Dad. I can't cope with this now."

The sad look is back. But what does he expect—that he can come in here and say he's sorry and magic away the last fifteen years, just like that?

"Well, can I at least come and see you again?"

"I don't know." I can't keep my eyes open. There's a distant clatter of the dinner trolley being dragged around.

My eyes are closed but I hear his voice. "Shall I phone the ward tomorrow, then? When you've had a chance to think about it?"

The curtain is shushed open and there's a sudden foul smell as a pointy-faced youth with a white apron pushes the trolley up, checks the chart on the end of the bed and consults a list. "Kathryn Cheet . . . vegetarian, isn't it?"

"No." Irritation is rattling me awake. "I'm not a vegetarian. I want *meat*."

"Well, it says here you're a vegetarian," he drones.

"I'll phone you, then," says Dad.

"If you like."

27

DURING my final few days in the hospital, I find myself thinking more and more about Jonny. For all I know, he may have
tried many times to call me on the red phone, but the red
phone no longer exists. I was so angry with him about the gambling and his cavalier attitude to the three thousand pounds, but
my anger should really have been directed at myself. He didn't ask
me for the money. I took it upon myself to give it to him, and
handing him that cash was like putting petrol into a car. Lying here
in my hospital bed, I've come to acknowledge that I always re-
garded my relationship with Jonny as essentially masochistic on
my part. I was punishing myself for being a lousy person by letting
him abuse me. Now I see there was a sadistic side to it too.

It's all over with the others but Jonny is unfinished business.
When I'm at last unhooked from my tube, patched up and re-
assembled—when I'm leaving the hospital in the back of a mini-
cab—a *mini-cab*!—I'm telling the driver to take me to Elephant
and Castle.

I'm fluttery and nervous waiting for him to come to the door. I
don't really know what I want to say to him. But as it becomes
clear that he's not in, the nervousness turns to leaden disappointment. I'm about to turn and go tottering back to the lift when the
door of the adjacent flat suddenly opens and a middle-aged
woman with a towel around her hair and a cigarette hanging out of
her mouth sticks her head out.

"Oh Christ, you must be Mrs. Jennet," she says without removing the cig. And before I have a chance to deny this she carries on talking—rapidly. "I'm ever so sorry but I forgot you were coming and now I'm in the middle of dyeing my hair. Would you mind very much if I just gave you the keys and left you to show yourself around? After all, I only said I'd take people round as a favor to Mr. Triggs. He's *my* landlord too, you see. Decent enough bloke as far as landlords go but they're another breed really, aren't they? I mean, what sort of a person makes his living from letting out old council flats, eh?" She pauses for long enough to take in my face—still a mass of purple bruises and swellings, sweaty with the exertion of getting up here. She clocks the crutch under my left arm, the visible stiffness in my body. Her face looks concerned but this quickly evolves into suspicion. "Here's the keys," she says, sticking out a bare arm and dangling Jonny's doorkeys in henna-stained fingers. "Come and knock when you're done and if I don't answer straight away it's because I've got my head under the tap."

The flat doesn't smell much of Jonny anymore—the familiar heady mixture of whiskey, dope, fried bacon and unwashed clothes is gone. You can still smell the cigarettes and the mustiness of the old carpet, but even these odors are fading. Most of the windows are open and a breeze is blowing through the lounge. The heating's off, and my breath clouds the air in front of me.

I've never seen this place in full daylight before. Jonny used to keep the curtains closed out of laziness and the desire to hide himself away. I'm gazing at the damp brown patches on the walls, the stains and cigarette burns on the carpet—more noticeable now than when Jonny's stuff was here. The guitar is gone, of course. It used to stand in that corner over there. And all the old newspapers and take-out boxes have been collected up and thrown away. The coffee table has been wiped clean but you can still make out the ghosts of some of the more ingrained and persistent rings and spillages on its wooden surface.

I am hobbling, light-headed, through the living room, trailing one finger along the sticky back of the old couch. For weeks my wanderings have been confined to hospital corridors and on my release today I was supposed to be going straight home to bed. My dizziness is lending a sense of unreality to this scene. I could easily be dreaming it all.

That's where I lay on the night when Jonny finally hit me—right there on the carpet. I lay there and I thought about a time on the beach when I was a kid, bending to look at something in a rock pool. A starfish, washed up after a storm.

Parched and faint, I go to the kitchen for a glass of water. Wow—it's so clean! I bet it wasn't Jonny who cleaned this place up. Maybe the landlord paid the woman next door to do it. I imagine her henna-tipped fingers poking about in corners with Hoover and cloth . . . Wait—what's that? There's a piece of folded paper propped up on the shelf next to the bread bin. It has my name written on the front.

Dear Katy,

I've acted like a wanker and I'm sorry. I know you don't care whether I go to Berlin or to hell—but anyway it's Berlin. I'm going to help Stuart run his bar. I'm going to start again.

I will always love you, Katy. I hope you can be happy.

Jonny

There's another piece of paper on the shelf too. An old gas bill with song lyrics written on the back.

You are sailing
While I am trailing
Through the water

Weeping willow sees you sail
I look on behind the veil
Of leaves.
As you leave.

28

I'M up a stepladder, rollering mango paint onto my living room walls when the doorbell buzzes. Whoever it is, fuck 'em.

I love the crackling feeling you get when you run the roller back and forth in the paint tray. I love the pure intense color that rolls onto my walls. This is the first time I've had a go at this decorating lark, and I reckon I'm a natural.

Shit—there goes the buzzer again. Forget it—I'm just not going to scramble down this ladder with my ribs and my knee in the state they're in for the sake of a Sunday morning Jehovah or Betterware salesman. God knows it's tricky enough managing the decorating, without having to pander to some uninvited bod outside. Nurse Frances would have me chained up if she could see what I'm doing. I'm proud of myself, though. Only two weeks since I got out of hospital and now look at me. And I've done it all by myself.

Fucking thing is buzzing over and over again. Who the hell would be that persistent? I lean to the right, trying to peer out of the window, but I can't get the angle I need. OK, you bastards, you've got me—I'm coming down the ladder.

Taking it slowly. Left foot down a rung, then right foot joins it. Left foot down a rung, then right foot. *"All right, all right! Stop your buzzing, I'm up a fucking ladder!"*

My bare foot lands on the upturned lid of the paint tin. That makes me *so angry* . . . I wipe it on a piece of newspaper, and it's only when I'm scrunching the paper up that I notice Amy's face smiling at me from her "Muff Matters" column, smeared in mango. It's the publicity photo that makes her look like she's got a bit of a moonface and no neck. Hello, Amy. How's life? Do you think about me? Do you miss me?

I chuck the balled-up newspaper in the rubbish bag, slide open the sash window and stick my head out into dank November air, but still I can't get the angle. The caller must be standing right up close to the door. The buzzer is droning on, alternating between long and short blasts. I shout, "Shut up and show yourself!"

It's him.

"Craig." My voice is flat. It's not a greeting, more a sort of statement.

He's shuffling about on my step, proffering a bunch of droopy pink carnations. He's wearing a black roll-neck sweater, a leather jacket and dark green trousers, and he has a new haircut. The outfit makes him look French. Suave.

I reach out, take the carnations, stand staring at them. I'm painfully aware of the overripe bruising on my face, the old baggy T-shirt and paint-stained trackie bottoms.

"Sorry. They were all that was left at the stall," he says. It's weird hearing his voice again.

"You took your time coming over."

He looks like he's about to respond but then changes his mind and says something else. "Is that paint on your face?"

"Yes. I'm decorating."

"Can I come in?"

"All right. But stick these in the garbage can, would you?" I shove the flowers back at him. "I hate carnations."

"Wow," he says, looking around at my living room. "Cab-light orange . . ."

"It's mango!"

He walks toward me, picking his way carefully across the plastic dust sheets and newspaper. "Got any coffee?"

"Sure."

In the kitchen, pouring water into the percolator, I hear his voice close behind me.

"I've left Marianne."

I jerk round to look at him and my ribs spear me. He has taken Stef's Spanish flamenco doll down from the shelf where I keep it, and is lifting its skirts, raising his eyebrows at its white bikini briefs.

"No more lies, Craig."

"No more lies." There is an openness, even an innocence in his face when he looks up at me. I can suddenly imagine how he must have looked at sixteen. "My name is Jamie. Jamie Lawrence."

"I know."

"Craig Summer was the name they gave me for the job. What a waste of time all that was." But he's smiling.

"Why didn't you come and visit me in the hospital, Twinkle?"

"I didn't think you'd want to see me."

Suddenly there's a weird sound. Frenzied flapping. It's coming from the living room.

"Christ, it's a pigeon!"

It must have flown in while we were making the coffee. The window is still open but the stupid thing is throwing itself over and over at the closed one next to it, almost knocking itself out against the glass. It looks enormous in my small room.

"Make it go away." I'm backing off, my arms wrapped tightly around my injured chest.

"Right." Twinkle clears his throat and does his best to stick his chest out. He's struggling to be manly. "Do you have an old towel?"

"Yes." I slip past him to the bathroom—grope about in my airing cupboard, bringing out a pink hand towel that dates back to my years living with Maeve. Returning to the living room, I see the pigeon swooping—narrowly missing my stepladder, and finally landing with a clatter in the paint tray.

"Oh, fuck!"

"Shush." He shoots me an irritated glare. "Calm down, you're scaring it. Give me the towel."

Shakily I hand it over and retreat to the kitchen doorway, chewing on one of my nails. It tastes of paint.

He's stalking slowly across the room, brandishing the towel like a matador's cape. "All right." His voice is low and soft. "OK, little pigeon."

"Little!" The word comes out shrill and loud, and the pigeon flaps suddenly back into the air and dives once more at the window, splattering droplets of paint all over the woodwork and smearing the glass with its mango feet.

Twinkle darts me a look and I put my hands over my mouth to stop myself shouting again. The bird settles on the windowsill and drops a shit. It starts making strangled-old-lady cooing sounds.

"You're a daft thing, aren't you," he soothes. He's moving closer, towel outstretched. "I'm not going to hurt you, stupid. I just want to help you. That's all I'm going to do." He's holding out the towel, bringing it around the pigeon to coax it to fly the other way—out of the open window.

It's silent in the room. I can hear Twinkle breathing.

After a moment, the bird flutters—and flies.